Trees Cry For Rain

by Dr. Jeri Fink

Trees cry for rain.
And mountains for wind.
So my eyes cry for you.

-an old Sephardic (Ladino) folk song

Trees Cry for Rain
Copyright 2011 Jeri Fink
All Rights Reserved
First PRinting April 2011

ISBN 978-0-9829769-2-0

Written by Dr Jeri Fink

Cover by Windward Design

Published by Dailey Swan Publishing, Inc

Dailey Swan Publishing, Inc
2644 Appain Way #101
Pinole Ca 94564
www.daileyswan publishing.com

Acknowledgments

How can I thank everyone who supported me during the four years it took to write this book?

Meryl, Stacey, and Unkka – you were with me, every step of the way.

The input of my "readers" was critical to the final book: Ricky Fink, Russell Fink, Fern Friedman, Herbert Michelson, Craig Oldfather, Donna Paltrowitz, and Meryl Waters – without you, I'd still be fitting the pieces together. Extra kudos goes to Donna and Fern, who kept me writing through the worst storms. As you would both say, "it *is* what it is."

My friends cheered me on throughout this project, willingly listening to 500-year old stories as if they were today's news. Thank you: Nancy Allegretti, Jason Braiman, Joyce and Joel Feldman, Mary Ann and Pat Hannon, Janet and Richard Kam, Jill and Jerry Lash, Marge Mendel, Barbara and Carl Saks, and John Violas. Listen carefully and you'll hear your voices in these pages.

Hugs to my family – this is your legacy as well: Harvey Fink, Laura Fink, Ricky Fink, Russell Fink, Herbert Michelson, Greg Rossi, Stacey Rossi, Meryl Waters, and Tony Waters. Extra hugs for Herbert Michelson, who shared family stories, as well as his unique approach to spiritual and secular Judaism. Perhaps Johnny and Nicky Rossi, Ari and Leiba Fink, and Samantha and Jason Michelson, will one day give this book to *their* children.

Loved ones who passed over before this book was written, live within these pages: Judy Becker, Persis Burlingame, Dora Eisenstein, Edna Fink, Rose and Benjamin Michelson, and Ruth Roth.

I could not possibly mention all the writers, books, articles, websites, and researchers that informed my travel through time. However, Gloria Mound, Executive Director of *Casa Shalom* in Israel (The Institute for Marrano-Anusim Studies), stands out as a hero dedicated to helping Jews around the world. We *all* owe her our appreciation.

Special thanks go to Casey Swanson for listening to my character's voices, and making sure they will be heard.

To Ricky
Here we are, soul mates - still dreaming and holding hands . . .

and

for Russell
who makes sure it happens!

Gilgul gives people the chance to make things right.

Since the beginning of human thought, mystics have believed in the transmigration or reincarnation of souls. The Early Kabbalists (Jewish Mystics) first wrote about it in the 12th century. They maintained that every soul is destined to return to its heavenly source. If a soul hasn't worked things out on Earth, it can assume a new body to correct a wrong or to repair damage from a previous life. They called it *gilgul neshamot* – the cycling of souls.

Prologue: Taymullah

The heavy man in cargo pants trembles with rage.

He stands on the Upper Library Terrace, at the end of the Great Lawn, watching. His head throbs. Blood fills his fiery eyes. He shivers in the late afternoon sun.

Suddenly, he hears an old couple singing an oddly familiar song. It's in a different language, and for a moment, the song brings back an ancient anger. He stands rigid on his carpet of cobblestones, searching for them.

The heavy man sees the old couple. He hears them. But he can't touch them.

Furious, he rubs his Glock, his fingers itching to squeeze the trigger. He knows it's too soon. For now, he has to wait.

Angry with his impatience, he scans the Great Lawn, hunting for the three women. When he finds them, God has told him what to do.

He's ready.

One: Rozas and Shira

Rozas

I see it clearly. Purple flowers shudder in the wind. Trees cry for rain. The sky fills with thin clouds that shape-shift as they pass overhead. A bird cloud suddenly transforms into a handsome trovador; a child cloud drifts into a crouching man. Suddenly there's a dull thud; a large cow with dark, soulful eyes faces me. I've seen this creature before; she's visited my dreams many times. She wears a broken iron key on a leather thong around her neck. I reach out to touch the key and the metal burns my fingers, the sky turns black, and the clouds scatter in terror.

I scream, but no sound is heard.

I linger with the memory of last night's sleep. It's a dream that peppers my life, triggered by bits I sense, but can't always identify, like a gust of wind that swoops down from the hills. It's strange and comforting, all at the same time.

Now I know the source.

The meat.

It began yesterday with the cold slab of beef that trembled beneath my fingers. Once it had been a living, breathing animal that roamed the hills surrounding town, contentedly grazing on sun-heated grass, drinking sweet water, and staying close to the herd. Maybe its hide was black; maybe it was white . . . or both? Questions danced through my mind . . . when it went to slaughter did it beg for life or face death with stoic acceptance? Did the lumbering animal bow to the inevitable when the knife slit its throat in one, single motion or was it overcome with the injustice of its blood staining the ground?

How did the human butcher kill so easily?

I shake my head. I can't stop myself from conjuring pictures and questions that send me careening into surreal places. I shudder - was the dream and my thoughts an omen or just another day? I don't share this with my husband, Lucas. Maybe he'd laugh when I told him

I sensed danger, a secret revealed, words that wrenched me from home like the poor animal whose flesh I was about to cook. The old question returns, like a dream molded into words.

How does it feel to be roasted . . . burned by fire while others watch?
I shiver.

They're crazy thoughts - a way to deny the meat. Yet images of fire and burning are far too real. Would I have these thoughts if I had been born a Christian? Why couldn't I pray to a carved crucifix?

I am a simple woman with a husband, three daughters, and a hunk of precious meat to cook.

I was born a *Converso* – a secret Jew. I pray in church, I wear a cross around my neck, and profess my loyalty to Our Lord and Savior, Jesus Christ. When no one is looking, deep beneath the streets of my home, I secretly follow the Laws of Moses – a crime punishable by death in Spain.

It's 1492, and the Holy Office of the Inquisition is hungry for Converso blood.

Sighing, I examine my big black cooking pot. The beef will make a delicious stew, cooking for twelve hours over the fire. The creature, although dead, will meet an honorable end in our bellies. I know it's dangerous - but who's watching? We're always so careful. There are no spies at my family dinner table.

I glance at the purple flowers placed neatly in a pot of water. I always keep purple around me. It's the color of my life. Purple gives me strength. Odd, how colors can affect one. I recall the first time I found Lucas spying on me in the patch of purple flowers outside of town.

Again! My head wanders to different places and times, like old leaves drifting downstream.

I have to think about the meat.

I wonder if I should feel guilty replacing purple flowers with a slab of meat. Instead, my mouth waters. I should be wiser. I think about the stew that will emerge - the rich scents filling the house, the thick gravy bubbling overnight. Pushing away flowers and soulful cattle, I prepare the meat. I make sure no one sees me trim the fat with my thumbnail and break a treacherous rule. I have already soaked and salted the meat several times until it's completely drained of blood. No one was around to watch or report. I glance over my shoulder. No one is around to see me chop garlic and onions and send them sputtering into hot oil on the bottom of the black pot. I add cabbage, chickpeas, and finally, the beef, covering it with sweet water.

Everything I've done to prepare the meat can cost me my life.

I smile at yet another secret - my Jewish feast. Time will ready the meat.

One day later, a skip in time, the beef stew sits in front of us. Instead of filling our bellies, the meat indicts us from bowls on the table. We listen to menacing voices rise from the street. Accusations echo like unseen fingers pointing at our meat. I tremble. Occasionally, faint cries shatter the air.

Was the meat worth it?

Someone bangs on my door.

A deep, paralyzing fear invades me, numbing my hands and feet, making my heart race, blurring the images in my mind into bloody streaks. We stare at one another – my husband and three daughters.

We know what it means.

We have been betrayed.

Lucas takes a deep breath and stands away from the table. He's a big man, with long thin legs and the round belly of middle age. The girls huddle around me, their eyes wide with terror. The meat is ash in my stomach, swelling until it feels like stones splitting me from within.

Lucas squares his shoulders.

"Don't say anything," he commands in a whisper.

"Don't answer it," I hiss. My arms feel like raw meat, cold and bloodless.

Lucas smiles sadly, his beard shimmering in the dim light. "I have to. We have nowhere to go."

"They'll kill us," the words rip through my throat like the knife that sliced the meat in our bowls.

9

Slowly, Lucas shakes his head; his dark, green-flecked eyes fill with grief.

"You're my husband," I beg. "You *have* to listen."

There's a tiny pause; time jolts to a halt. I hold my breath. Zara, my youngest and most insightful – the one that seems in touch with old spirits - senses that something ominous is approaching. Nine years of life still hasn't taught her how to contain fear. She cries, soft wails renting the air. I pull her close, rubbing her back, whispering soothing words I don't feel, and pressing her head into my breast to stifle the sound.

"Nooooo," I plead, matching the cries of my child.

Lucas gently touches my shoulder, runs his thick, stubby fingers up my neck, and kisses my daughter's head. "There's no choice," he whispers, more to himself than any of us. He backs away from the table, his legs heavy, moving as if in a swamp. Suddenly he pauses and in a moment that lasts a lifetime, Lucas memorizes the sight of us together. It will be the last time. Our eyes lock above the heads of our three children, desperate to save them.

He chokes back a sob, tears glisten in his eyes. He's a great man about to be brought to his knees. I know it's already too late. I can only clutch Zara and wait for the scene to play out. I struggle to conjure a soothing image in my mind but all I see is wrenching pain.

No!

Time has to reverse - the meat must disappear, and yesterday returned. In my heart I know that like the stewed beef congealing in our bowls, there's no going back.

The banging is more insistent. Lucas leaves us behind. I can't see him, but I hear his footsteps and the agonizing intake of his breath as he slowly opens the heavy door.

"Run!" A young voice roars. "They're coming for you. Run *now*."

Rafael shoves my husband from the door, quickly slamming it behind him. He rushes to our table, his swarthy young face sweaty, and the nostrils in his aquiline nose flaring like an Arabian stallion charging the hills.

"Rafael," I cry.

"Listen," he bellows. *"They're coming."* He pauses, giving us a moment to absorb his words. Lucas stands next to him, his head bowed in defeat.

"They're coming," Rafael repeats, his words stumbling over one another. "Right now. You only have a few minutes - you have to run. Before it's too late."

Rafael is not one of us — he's not family or even part of our community. He's a *limpieza de sangre* or pureblood. He stands tall and slim, black hair framing high cheekbones, piercing dark eyes, and thin lips. Yet for some unknown reason, he's connected with us, thrown his youth and strength into our midst. His songs and stories fill our lives — music to soothe the fear. He sings to us of cavaliers, love, and a time and place we can never touch.

"No time," he grabs my shoulder. "There's no time. You have to run now."

I meet Lucas's eyes. We know the truth without speaking.
Save the children.
Please God, save the children.

"Our time is over," Lucas says softly, recovering from the horror of what looms before us. "If we wait here, if we give ourselves to them, they'll forget the children. They'll take us and come back tomorrow for the girls. But if you take them, Rafael, lead them to safety . . ." His unfinished sentence hangs in the air.

Rafael's eyes widen, trying to grasp the words. His hair shimmers in the light, his six-foot frame bends slightly, as if struggling against a relentless wind.

"Yes," I agree, "it's our only chance."

Rafael doesn't know what to say. He turns to Marianna, our oldest daughter, and the strongest of the three. She's the practical one, determined to think in logical steps that flow jaggedly across time.

Unexpectedly, an image of Rafael and Marianna dances through my mind. I take control. "Quickly," I stand up. "You'll go through the tunnel, turn left at the fork, and escape to the road. You can join the others who are leaving town. Lucas and I will be your decoy."

There's dead silence.

11

Lucas leans over and grabs my hand. "This is how it'll work," I continue breathlessly. "Marianna will tell everyone that she's Rafael's wife, and Catalina is the nursemaid of their young daughter. Zara, you won't tell anyone your age. You look young enough that people will believe Catalina," I look at my middle daughter, "No one will guess the truth."

Catalina stares at me. Her eyes are large and fawn-like. She's always been fragile, born too small and growing into a thin, sickly child. Will Catalina be able to survive this? I see the same question in her eyes.

"Mama," she whispers, "I'm not strong enough."

Lucas' eyes harden. "Of course you are," he says firmly. It's the words he doesn't speak that count.

It has to be done or none of us will survive.

He runs from the room, searching for something.

"My Catalina," I say gently, touching her check. "You'll be strong enough."

We both know the truth.

"Help me," I demand, locking Zara's hand inside Catalina's long fingers. Rafael, Marianna, and I use all our strength to move the heavy table. We splash stew and wine in all directions, as it edges across the floor. Beneath the table is an old, worn rug. I roll up the rug to reveal the trapdoor in the floor. Marianna helps me lift the door, exposing steps that lead into a dark, gloomy tunnel.

The voices are outside the door. Someone pounds with his fist.

"They're here," Rafael whispers.

"Move quickly," I hiss.

"Wait," Lucas reappears with a worn leather pouch. "This is all the money that I have, but it should be enough." He thrusts the pouch into Rafael's hands. "Take it and save my children."

Rafael stares at him. There are no words. Lucas has entrusted the lives of his children to this young man.

I fumble in my pocket and pull out a key that has been broken into four pieces. Each piece is strung onto a sturdy leather thong. I've been ready, carrying these iron pieces in my pocket every day. I tie one around each daughter's neck.

12

This is the heart of our home.

I speak softly. "The four pieces apart are useless. Put them together and you have the key to our home and our family. Someday you can reclaim what's rightfully yours."

"No . . ." Marianna cries but her voice is drowned out by the pounding on the door.

"Rafael," I say, tears choking my words. "You have the fourth piece . . . the circle that binds them together." I tie the circle, the top of the key, around Rafael's neck. "You're the one that protects my daughters . . . and my family's future. You saved Catalina. Now you'll save all of them."

Rafael freezes.

There is a bubble in time; a moment when everything is forgotten but our links to one another.

"Go," Lucas says, shattering the moment, his eyes wild with fear.

"Grab each other's hands," I say to my three daughters. "I want you to make one promise for me before you leave." The pounding on the door is louder. Catalina tries to speak, but I quiet her with my eyes.

I devour the sight of my children - their beautiful faces, unaware of their future. I wish I could hold and protect them from the flood of pain that they'll face without me. I cry for the games we'll never play and the songs we'll never sing. I mourn for the husbands I'll never meet and the grandchildren I'll never hold.

Be strong, Catalina, I pray silently. You can do it.

"Mama," Zara says in a tiny voice, tears streaming down her face. "Aren't you coming with us?"

"No, my love," I say softly. "This is a trip you have to take by yourselves. Rafael will be with you."

"Then," she plants her feet firmly on the floor, "I'll stay with you."

"Quiet," Marianna says sharply. "We do what we're told."

Zara's lips tremble.

"Be strong," I repeat, closing our circle. "You can't cry – you have to be brave."

13

Zara's shoulders shake, but the tears stop.

The girls look at one another uneasily. Rafael is not part of their circle, but inextricably linked to them. He lays his hand gently on Marianna's shoulder.

"Promise me," I speak my last words to them. How precious they are . . . "Promise me that you'll stay together, connected through time, and meet once again beyond the horror of today . . ."

The pounding on the door sounds like claps of thunder as the three girls whisper their promises.

Rafael's lips move, forming words without sounds.

"Go," Lucas orders.

Marianna grabs a candle and disappears into the tunnel, followed by Catalina, Zara, and Rafael.

"Godspeed," I whisper as tears drench my face.

Lucas and I close the trapdoor, roll the rug over it, and drag the table back into place. He takes a purple flower from the pot, tucks it into my hair, and kisses me in our last moment together. We walk to the door, hand-in-hand, knowing that our lives are over.

Lucas opens the heavy door to soldiers wearing shiny, metal helmets, large red crosses on their chests, and horrific weapons slung from their waists. Their eyes burn with evil determination; their lips twist into smiles. They roar words at us that I don't hear – condemnations that have no meaning. They poke at our bodies and pull at our clothes. I ignore their fiery touch - the only thing that's important in this tiny sliver of time is my children. They *must* be safe. They *must* survive. Lucas and I have offered our lives, like a dowry to God.

Please God. Take us and save the children.

The soldiers howl with pleasure as they confuse my desperation with fear. Lucas and I are mice, and the cat-soldiers toy with their prey. The fun lasts long enough to give Rafael and the girls time to go deeper into the tunnel, further away from the soldiers' claws. Suddenly, a soldier senses my resolve. His satanic eyes pause, a question rising in the dark. Does he see the tiny shift in my eyes, suggesting hope? I won't ever know.

The soldiers seize me and Lucas, spinning us around, twisting our arms until we shriek with pain. They tie my wrists together and spit in my face, sending thick wads of spittle down my cheek. They tie Lucas' wrists together and knee him in the groin. He doubles over in pain.

The soldiers laugh, proud of their game.

They drag Lucas from the house. He can barely stand upright. Our eyes meet.

I love you.

Then they drag me into the street behind Lucas. The soldiers don't look back.

The cobblestones echo with their boots. Our neighbors peek out from behind their doors and windows. They don't dare say anything or try to rescue us. We all know that the soldiers will take great joy in dragging them alongside us, or simply killing them on the spot. They will weep, but remain silent.

There's no forgiveness here, under a full moon, wrapped in the icy embrace of the soldiers.

Please God, save my children.

The flower falls from my hair, left to die on the cobblestones in front of my empty home.

Shira

Shira closed her eyes and listened to the breeze stir the leafy canopy of the London Plane trees. Their pale speckled bark contrasted with the Manhattan skyscrapers that hugged the park. She heard the harsh sound of traffic - engines idling, buses sighing, trucks groaning, and an occasional chopper or airplane above.

She raised her face to the sun and patted a worn leather pouch in her pocket. Shira always brought the pouch with her when she worked at Bryant Park. It was her good luck charm. Here, in the Outdoor Reading Room, she could transport *anywhere*.

Shira turned her attention to the silver laptop on the table in front of her. She had just written the opening pages to her latest book, a romantic mystery that merged b-movies, ghosts, and trash TV. The publishers loved her; her drivel was a solid seller on supermarket and airport shelves, easy reads that went smoothly from a few bucks to the recycle bin. Her readers were people who didn't like to read - they munched on words like their morning multigrain cereal - quickly, with little taste or attention, spending a few moments in a written world that fed them tidbits of useless information. No one would have believed that Shira was once obsessed with literature and history, feasting on *Canterbury Tales* and *Beowulf*, devouring medieval literature and ancient battles along with hazelnut latte. Her critics called her an unforgivable mix of primetime horror and *Wal-Mart* romance, while her fans giggled and bought more books.

It was a good gig.

The book on her laptop would become yet another title in her personal list, providing new royalties *and* adding to her growing index fund. Writing trash novels didn't make her rich, but it kept her in a decent West Side Manhattan apartment without a roommate, dressed in designer jeans, and supplied with *pad thai* and *po pia* from her favorite Thai restaurant on 66th Street. She didn't have to drag herself to an office each morning and tolerate chat that made her skin crawl. Nor did she have to flatter a narcissistic boss while surreptitiously planning a hierarchical rise through corporate ranks. Shira was in control of her life and her time, unlike most people in the city.

It was all deliciously surreal. She could lose herself in words and the frenetic city streets; write tacky stories that accrued money not quality; and compose a quiet life that sounded more exciting on paper than in the minutes that trudged by each day. Loneliness shared her space like an old, familiar friend. She avoided people jarring her space, turned away men who demanded company and sex, left single bars and online meets, and denied the search for that illusive soul mate. Years ago, she concluded that people were simply impractical. They took too much time and effort to nurture relationships that invariably led to aching conflicts, endless negotiations, and exchange of secrets mired in delusion. She had more fun watching people then relating to them. Similarly, it was easier to write a trash novel filled with hot words, sweaty descriptions, and no depth than to plunge into literary illusions that tempted longevity and that over-rated moniker, *art*.

Art didn't make money. Shira had no interest in wearing the shredded jeans, dirty tee shirts, and disheveled hair of a struggling artist. Shira didn't even call herself an *author*. She was a wordsmith playing with lazy, overeager readers who loved the feel of paper between their fingers and throbbing words before their eyes.

Shira giggled and pushed her black, curly hair behind her ears. Her pale skin framed dark, smoldering eyes flecked with green and a nose sprinkled with light, orange freckles. Shira wasn't exactly ugly but her face put off people, set with a faintly blank, frog-like expression that didn't invite company. Her eyes were distant and unfocused, moving back and forth as if searching for something never found. People loved the tacky, shallow books but not the detached writer.

Shira had perched herself in the Outdoor Reading Room, her favorite spot in Bryant Park. Located in midtown Manhattan, between 5th and 6th Avenue, 40th and 42nd Streets, summer in Bryant Park was unlike any other place in the city.

She sat on a small, green plastic chair in front of a tiny matching round table. The ground was slate; her table placed against the concrete, waist-high French Classical railing that lined the promenade.

17

If she looked across the Great Lawn she saw the slatted screen that was flattened every Monday to host the annual Summer Film Festival, New York's version of a drive-in movie. After sunset, people settled on the lawn, munching sushi, Panini, and Mississippi mud bars, to watch free summer films. Shira loved those nights when she could be part of the group and alone at the same time.

She glanced at the bronze face of William Earl Dodge, a 19th century businessman and philanthropist, with a warbling pigeon on his head. Shira laughed out loud.

Although considered the sunny side of the street, the Outdoor Reading Room was always bathed in shade. Originally, the space had been created as an "Open Air Library" to give depression-era unemployed workers a place to go where they didn't need money, a valid address, or a library card to enjoy free reading. Resurrected in 2003, the Outdoor Reading Room was dedicated to the same purpose. Alongside the Great Lawn, adjacent to the rear terrace of the iconic New York City Public Library, and beneath the dramatic slope of the travertine-and-glass W.R. Grace Building, the Outdoor Reading Room made her feel like she was nuzzled in a timeless green corner, conveniently equipped with Wi-Fi.

Shira loved the history and personality of Bryant Park. The park had been originally designated as public property in 1686. It had a long, uneven story that piqued her imagination. Now nestled like a canyon in mountains of skyscrapers, Bryant was shadowed by some of the most dignified buildings in the city. It had been the 19th century site for New York's first World's Fair where the famous iron and glass *Crystal Palace* stood, symbolizing cutting-edge architecture of the time. In 1884, the park, once known as Reservoir Square, was renamed for William Cullen Bryant. Shira loved Bryant, the famous poet and newspaper editor, whose 1911 bronze memorial was the centerpiece of the Library Upper Terrace.

Shira grinned and recalled a few lines from *The Poet* by Bryant, as if they had been written for her.

While the warm current tingles through thy veins
Set forth the burning words in fluent strains.

Happily, Shira shifted into her *fluent strains,* pounding out next month's rent. Perhaps she'd get a new pair of jeans, with a hand-painted design or a special order of the expensive *nua pahd prik,* steak Thai-style. Maybe this book would make her the extra money needed to pay for a trip to Spain, where she would walk the delightful *Las Ramblas* in Barcelona or explore the cobbled alleys of the *Juderia* in Girona?

Grinning, Shira began her story.

Emma opened her eyes sleepily. She was bathed in luxury, from the silky, ice-blue sheets to the fluffy down pillows. The room was thick with the shimmering gilt, icy crystal, and purple glass flowers of a jet-setter. She stirred, and the sheets caressed her naked body with the same tenderness that Mason Portsmith had shown her only a few minutes earlier.

Ah, Mason Portsmith. She loved him until her heart nearly burst. She loved the soft, dark curly hair on his chest; the amorphous brown glow in his eyes; the smile that was charmingly crooked, as if he had been caught sneaking an extra chocolate chip cookie from the jar. She loved his voice that was smooth and cajoling; that could convince her of everything and nothing; that could wrap her in an unbearably sweet verbal embrace. Most of all, she loved his soul, tightly concealed beneath layers of dark, golden tanned skin, outrageously expensive thongs, and clothes she saw modeled in the top fashion 'zines. She knew he was real, just like her . . . but in his world he had to hide it. Having a heart, much less a soul was a burden among the fantastically rich. All they wanted to do was play, party, and flaunt their horrible wealth. His dark hair and machismo smile were as much a part of his business as her weekly paychecks.

Inside, Mason was very different from the others who moved people and money like toys; fat cats playing with poor mice. How could Mason Portsmith show his true self in their midst and reveal that he really cared about the others who struggled to eat, battled to work, and muddled through lives of quiet desperation? The real Mason stood beside trees crying for rain, and a sky filled with shape-shifting clouds.

She glanced at his face, sleeping next to her. Mason had tossed aside the sheets, exposing his nakedness. He was one of those men who had natural 'roids - his biceps rippled perfectly on his arms, his washboard rib cage looked more like a Greek statue than flesh and blood. His legs were perfectly muscled, years of tennis, personal trainers, and workout rooms in the Long Island mansion where he grew up, made sure that his body was flawless.

Mason Portsmith's body, she thought, is like a limpieza de sangre - pure-blooded work of art.

She first met Mason Portsmith in the media. She had watched him for years, fluidly moving through his world – on television clips, in gossip columns and business magazines with his father, and in photos of gala events for the rich and powerful. Never, in all her imagination as a standard issue suburban teenager, and later a freelancer for a popular entertainment magazine, could she ever envision that she would be in his bed, Mason's proclaimed "love of his life."

Life was really strange.

Her eyes began to close when she heard a noise from behind the bedroom door.

Mason awoke immediately.

She heard the noise again . . . it sounded like someone moving outside the room, walking quietly on the hardwood floors . . .

Mason shot to a sitting position.

"What is it?" Emma whispered.

"Sssh," Mason shook his head, listening intently.

"What's wrong?"

"Shut up," he turned to her. In the dim light his face was twisted into a wolf's snarl.

"You're scaring me."

Mason ignored her. He reached to the black granite night table that served as a bedpost.

She watched him silently, frightened by the sudden change in the man who had just made such tender love. As if in slow motion, he opened a small drawer. He pulled out a "baby" Glock-26, the smallest model on the market.

The noise outside their door was louder, like a big man fumbling through the house. She heard a faint voice but the words were unfamiliar - a curse in a language that she couldn't identify.

Emma had never been so frightened in her life.

"What are you doing?" She hissed.

Mason ignored her.

He leaped from the bed, his flaccid penis bouncing off his muscular thighs.

"Please," she begged, *as he raised the gun in front of him, his eyes fixed on the bedroom door.*

"I love you," Mason said, *without turning around. "Everything will be fine."*

She wondered about his strange choice of words and oddly calm tone, but was too scared to think deeper. "Please don't leave me," Emma begged.

Mason was already half-way across the room.

The noise outside the room grew louder, the voice roaring on the other side of the door. It was another language - a foreign invader . . .

Thoughts of terrorists and suicide bombers raced through her mind so quickly that she had no time to stop and consider. Mason was rich and famous. Someone was after him. Was she going to die, naked in bed, the victim of a political attack or a disgruntled employee? She could see the headlines now:

PORTSMITH HEIR AND LOVER MURDERED BY UNKNOWN ASSAILANT

She saw her mother, tears running down her face, sobbing hysterically . . .

Mason was at the door, his gun pointed ahead of him. He was firm and determined. Confident. Perhaps too confident?

Her blood turned to ice.

He's done this before.

The thought bombarded her senses. Mason Portsmith has held a gun in his hand and crept to his bedroom door . . . ?

Impossible.

She yanked the sheets up to her chin and waited, heart pounding, and cold sweat swathing her body.

The voice outside shouted a war cry . . .

"I love you," Mason said *above the noise, as he put his left hand on the doorknob. "Everything will be okay."*

Suddenly, a purple glass flower on the night table dropped to the floor. It shattered into hundreds of tiny pieces. Emma snapped.

"No!" She cried.

It was too late.

Mason flung open the bedroom door, pointed the Glock, and pulled the trigger.

Shira laughed out loud. The stuff should sell.

21

Rozas

My family have been Conversos - Secret Jews - since they escaped the 1391 massacre of Jews in Seville. Their choice was simple – accept baptism or die. Some people called them *anusim* – Jews forced to convert. Others cursed them as *Marranos,* the word for swine.

Our lives are complicated. We live as Catholics, and our hearts belong to Judaism. It's a crime punishable by death – burned at the stake. Yet we persist. As a community, we meet to follow the Laws of Moses, deep beneath the ancient streets of our town. The tunnels are dark and damp; we travel through them led by flickering lamps that toss strange, dreamlike shadows against the walls. It's like drifting silently into another world; a secret place that thrives dangerously beneath the busy homes and stores of our neighbors. Even my closest friends, who sit devoutly next to me in the large, cavernous church where I pray to another God, have no idea. They think we're all *Christianos,* worshipping His Lord Jesus Christ, beneath the gold and crystal of the church, under the watchful eyes of the priests . . . and each other.

The world believes we have left the faith of our fathers to embrace Jesus. We pray, celebrate holidays, disdain the Jewish Sabbath, wear crosses around our necks, and send one family member in each generation to a convent or monastery to "prove" our faith.

It's a dance we perform, a crazy disguise that rips us from within. We're never who we appear to be, we carry secrets that can mean death. In these days of *reconquista* in Spain, where infidels and heretics are identified by their refusal to comply to every tenet of Christianity, Jews are seen as the enemy of the soul, the companion of Satan, and the killers of Christ. Ironically, when we become Conversos we betray the faith we adopted to secure survival. While the Jews are periodically massacred throughout Spain in bloodbaths of religious frenzy, we *Conversos* fear a different evil, discovery and death by fire through the Holy Inquisition. Torquemada leads the charge - the horrific priest who holds the ear of Queen Isabella, and transforms our lives into a daily terror that we might be discovered praying to our God.

No one knew how my family lived our lives as two souls - Christian and Jewish - in constant fear of being reported, exposed by our neighbors, friends, or enemies.

Mama never liked to talk about the dangers to her family; instead she would concentrate on not dirtying her skirts as we slid through the tunnels to join our underground community. Papa would stride happily in his fine leather boots, quietly mumbling prayers. To the world, we were the Tapiador family, *Novo Christianos*, faithful churchgoers, and successful merchants. Papa traded in olives and oil, brought in from the countryside, cured in big, fragrant vats, and sold to the servants from the wealthiest homes in our community. He believed that no one knew about the tunnels; God would protect us from the Holy Inquisition, and life would continue, as planned, forever. Mama followed carefully with her brood - I was the youngest of four boys and two girls, all married, and all eagerly pampering me.

What did I know? What did I think when they gave me the easiest chores, the best tidbits, and sent me to play in the patch of wildflowers just outside of town? Like Papa, I believed that God watched over me, and life would continue, as planned, forever. I felt I was charmed, surrounded by doting family, and immersed in a mysterious life that was more romantic than treacherous.

Now, as the soldiers march us across the cobblestones, I realize how fragile our lives have been. We wanted to believe we were safe. We wanted to believe in a *forever*. Instead, we were like trees crying for rain, living in the illusion that we controlled our destiny.

I see Lucas ahead of me, his back bent. I know he's in pain, but won't show the soldiers.

Please God, save the children.

I turn to see if there's anyone behind me. A soldier slaps my face, my head snaps. It gives me a few precious seconds to see that no one is following.

Perhaps Rafael has made it into the tunnel with no one seeing? Perhaps my children are safe?

I thank God. It's been a good life until this moment, although sometimes I never knew what I had. I was often spoiled and blind, lost in fantasies . . .

The soldier booms a command. I lower my head and move faster.

At the end of the street is the entrance to the Inquisition dungeons. I shiver. I'm nearing the most dreaded place in Spain, where *Christianos* use the name of their God to inflict pain and evil.

I try to control myself. I struggle to contain the fear. My body denies my mind; my blood turns to ice and my knees buckle.

The soldiers yank me upright, cursing. I see Lucas descending in front of me.

God give me strength.

They drag me toward the dark, stone entrance.

My mind crumbles in terror. My feet scrape the cobblestones as we approach the entrance. Only five words break through the fear.

Please God, save the children.

I descend deep into the bowels of the Earth. Darkness and stench surround me; cold, damp stone forms the deadly corridors of dungeons. I hear the sounds of human misery – cries, moans, and demented voices of people already broken. The soldiers pause; one opens the heavy door that will be my home for the rest of my life. Another soldier rips off my clothes, laughing loudly. He shoves a coarse shift into my arms.

"That's what you wear now, Marrano," he taunts me. "Clothes suited for a Christ-killer."

They shove me inside and lock the bars.

I'm engulfed in complete dark. It holds me in a tightly wrapped pouch. I wait, trying to understand what has happened. I cry; I wail; I beg for God to hear me. The dark is unrelenting. Finally, I sleep, exhausted. My dreams are wild and incoherent. When I wake, fragments float through my head – pieces that I can put together into a whole.

It's still dark and I quickly discover that here, time passes without meaning. I'm trapped . . . moving from coldness inside to hot terror that lingers, like a wild predator, outside. I know the road, although this is the first – and last – time I will ever travel it.

My tiny stone cell is lined with thick rusted bars. Beyond the bars I catch light that momentarily casts eerie shadows before returning to total black. Occasionally harsh voices cut through the void, colored with an undercurrent of misery. Sometimes disembodied screams echo through the dungeons . . .

If there's Hell, I'm in it now. I know I'm not dead – my heart pounds, there's an icy numbness to my skin, and a pulsating revulsion in my soul. This is evil created by human artistry.

Lucas is gone. I haven't seen or heard him since the soldiers separated us at the entrance. He's down here with me, but I don't know where or for how long. Quickly, I lose track of time – how many minutes and hours pass, how many days are yet to come? My cell is so small I can barely stand, instead I crouch on the stone floor with my back against the damp wall or curl up, fetal-like, to sleep. My bed is a stack of old straw, piled loosely in the end farthest from the bars.

If I stretch out on the straw my skin itches from mites and dried human feces. Other living things share my prison - things I *feel* rather than see. Bugs march across me like multi-legged soldiers; the vermin find my most private places even when I tightly wrap the coarse shift around my body. Rats explore my legs, sinking their sharp teeth into my ankles, drawing blood. I try to bat them away but the rodents are relentless.

A nauseating stench permeates everything – the cell, my shift, and my knotted, dirty hair. Everything reeks of decay, urine, feces, sweat, and blood. My eyes tear and my stomach recoils. When the guard comes to drop off a bowl of thin soup and slabs of stale bread, I can hardly eat. If I force myself, I crunch on drowned insects.

I hold on to my sanity by conjuring images in my mind. There's Rafael and my daughters, racing through the streets, totally free. Perhaps Rafael and Marianna are falling in love? See – they're sitting in a beautiful park, nestled in a canyon filled with trees and purple flowers. Children are playing everywhere. Catalina is dreaming of beautiful designs, her long, slender fingers drawing pretty creatures in radiant colors. Where is Zara? Why isn't she with them? My heart races so I shut the questions from my mind, following a different set of images. Marianna comforts her baby beneath a part of the iron key that hangs securely on her neck. Rafael is tall, and strong, and very graceful. Perhaps one day they will return home?

And Lucas?

Shira

Shira paused.

Where were the words coming from? For a brief moment she was confused, as if strangers had invaded her mental space. She shook her head angrily. Now she was even thinking like a horror movie character.

She glanced at the clouds, distracting herself from Mason's attack. The tiny French Classical kiosks were busy with the crowds - tourists, people leaving work early, others browsing, enjoying the midsummer sun and the cool breeze. *'Wichcraft* was serving its usual sandwiches, *Sanpellegrino limonata,* and ice cream. Dressed in summer business casual, office workers carried large plastic cups filled with iced *mochaccino* from PAX, bottles of yellow, pink, and blue *Vitamin Water,* or brown *Snapple.* Some picked at early dinners served in Styrofoam containers - there was colorful sushi, tasty *pressata,* and chopped salads sprinkled with chick peas, artichokes and goat cheese. Many were gearing up for Happy Hour at the B.P. Café, *ThursdaysAt5* live music-in-the-park, or a simple respite in one of the city's prettiest canyons.

If Shira had her choice, she would be nibbling on a Napoleon from *Ferrari's,* a container of *Dublin Mudslide* from Ben & Jerry's, or a skewer of shish-kebob from one of the street vendors.

A thin, ebony-skinned man in a dirty, sleeveless baseball jersey walked along the promenade, pushing a shopping cart full of soda cans. He stopped at each trash bin, picking out empty soda cans and tossing them into his stash. No one took notice of his glazed eyes or the shopping cart that he parked each night on a street corner.

That was New York.

Shira smiled. Bryant Park was like a window in time, moving in its own jagged frames. It was the perfect place to write, to follow Emma and Mason's bizarre romance, and when needed, look into faces to provide description and dialogue. What did the intruder look like? How did Emma's fear play on her face? Mason's arrogance?

She scanned the faces in the park. There was a dark-skinned man with a fashionably ragged red t-shirt printed with *Nweke's Art,* selling beaded bracelets and earrings on a pegboard, near the steps on 42nd Street. An old couple sat on the Upper Library Terrace, beneath a green and white umbrella stamped with *Bryant Park,* and next to a concrete pot of purple flowers. They held hands and watched the world before them, their silver hair shimmering in the summer sun, sharing the terrace with concrete garlands, urns, and ram's heads.

For a moment their eyes met.

The old couple smiled and Shira quickly turned away, embarrassed. Maybe she could find a Mason Portsmith look-alike at the park – a man dressed in expensive clothes with a lithe body and hazel eyes that broadcasted insight, caring, and power? Shira smiled.

In my dreams.

Literally. In her thirty-two years, she had always known that the people and plots conjured in her writer's mind were far more fascinating than reality.

That's what kept her running. Shira sighed and returned to her laptop.

The Glock reverberated throughout the room. Emma never knew a gunshot could sound so loud. She instinctively covered her ears.

"Got him," Mason shouted victoriously.

There was an eerie silence.

"We're safe," Mason grinned, as if this had been a video game. "I did him."

Emma struggled to find her voice. "You shot *him?"*

Mason held the Glock loosely in his right hand.

It's a smoking gun, she thought.

He nodded. "The guy's dead."

"Call the police . . ." she hissed. Emma reached for her cell phone on the granite table.

"You don't want to do that," Mason said, moving toward her.

She paused. Their eyes locked in the dim light. Emma couldn't help it. Her gaze drifted down his body until she saw his huge erection.

His penis was big and deliciously hard.

Emma's eyes widened.

28

Mason Portsmith laughed. *"Don't worry. That always happens. I don't usually have someone around to see it."*

"You killed . . . someone?"

"Yeah," Mason grinned boyishly, giving his penis an affectionate pat. *"All by myself."*

Emma watched in shock as he circled the bed and put the Glock back in the night table. He slipped beneath the sheets and grabbed her breast.

"I'm hot," he mumbled erotically.

Emma froze. *"There's a dead . . . body outside the door,"* she choked on her words.

"Not for long," he slipped her nipple into his mouth.

Emma pulled away from him, yanked the nightshirt from the floor next to the bed, and threw it on.

"What's wrong?" Mason looked surprised.

"There's a dead body outside the door," Emma gasped.

"Trust me," Mason sighed, *"it* will *go away."*

Emma had never been shocked like she was at that moment. Mason Portsmith had just killed a man. The body was outside their bedroom door and he . . . wanted to make love?

"You're crazy," she cried, her voice shrill and unfamiliar.

She grabbed her cell phone and ran to the door. Maybe she was the next name on this killer's list?

"Don't do it," Mason advised, following her. *"It's not a pretty sight."*

Emma flung open the door.

Run, a voice in her head screamed. *Before it's too late.*

"I love you," Mason shouted. *"I love you more than all the beautiful people, the yachts, the parties . . . more than my life."*

Run, the voice in her head commanded. *Now, when you still have the chance. Before he snares you into his web, tying you with invisible threads that can't be broken. Before he kills* you. *Run!*

Emma looked down. She froze in horror.

Shira took her fingers off the keyboard. She had a seething picture in her mind, riddled with humor and speculation.

Every one of her eighteen romantic mysteries had the same

general plot. Only the characters and context changed. Once, her editor had commented on it.

"Don't get me wrong, Shira," the editor said, brushing back her dyed blond hair. "You're the best writer we have. But don't you think it's strange that your characters are always running away from something into a world of illusion? Doesn't that say anything about you, living alone, in your thirties . . .?"

Shira glared at the editor. "Let's stick to books," she said sharply. "I don't need any amateur shrinks."

The editor shrugged and never said another word about Shira's personal life. Her books sold well - that was more important.

Shira stared out at the Great Lawn. Back in the 30's, Bryant Park had become one of the most awful parks in the city. Robert Moses had rescued it during the depression, but in the '70s and '80s it was overrun with muggers and druggies. It wasn't until recently that Bryant Park had been refurbished, transformed into a haven for midtown workers, a refuge for chess players, a home to the city's famous outdoor summer film festival, a site of the infamous *Fashion Week,* a colorful winter holiday market, and a host of daily summer events.

Shira glanced at her watch. Sure enough, as the digital numbers crept toward five, more people invaded her space, supplied with food, laptops, newspapers, and books until the park was *crowded.* Shira sighed. She didn't love the crowds but it gave her a new source of information to plow into her books.

Shira played her private game. See the banker over there in the *Brooks Brothers* suit? With perfectly-trimmed brown hair, plastic smile, and narrow eyes, he could be Mason Portsmith's brother. The woman in the yellow sundress and sandals, with a long ponytail of blonde hair could be Emma's alter ego. The man in the stylishly frayed blue jeans, sky blue shirt, and striped tie could be a strange invader from the future. Even Nweke the artist could be someone from another romance.

She glanced at the Upper Library Terrace.

What about the dark, chubby guy with his hand in his cargo pants pocket, standing stiffly on the cobblestones, watching everyone?

Or the old couple with the silver hair, by the concrete pot of flowers?

Shira couldn't help it. She laughed out loud.

"What's so funny?" A man said, sitting down in a chair next to her and smiling crookedly. His pale brown eyes sparkled in the summer sun.

Shira watched as he balanced a tuna fish sandwich with lettuce and tomato on thick, whole wheat bread. He was forty-something, dressed in dark khaki pants, a pale blue button-down shirt, and a silver tie. She hated the combination.

Someone needs to dress this guy.

"My name is Jake," he said. "What's so funny and what's your name?" He asked again, not waiting for an answer before taking a bite from his sandwich.

"Do you know," Shira stared at him with her dark, smoldering eyes, "that in 2002 Bryant Park was given the title of having the best bathroom in America?"

He stopped chewing. "Good talking to you," he said quickly, swallowing his mouthful of tuna fish. He gathered his dinner and headed off.

Jake the tuna fish-man, Shira thought. A few feet away, the tuna fish-man engaged a pretty twenty-something in conversation.

Shira nodded, pleased. One of her greatest skills was keeping people out of her life. She posed new questions. What did Emma see? Who was the real Mason Portsmith?

Would readers buy the story?

Across the Great Lawn, Bryant Park was alive. A man and his son tossed a Frisbee, a group of people played cards. Shira glanced up at the red-and-white umbrellas that marked the Outdoor Reading Room. Each one was printed with *The Reading Room Bryant Park*. She scanned the bookshelves scattered through the area - newspapers, books for children, and "Bryant Park Favorites" that ranged from John Connolly's *The Unquiet* to Norman Mailer's *Harlot's Ghost*. For one startling moment, everything looked *different*.

Shira shook her head, trying to scatter the thought. Years ago, after she graduated from NYU, a friend convinced her to apply for a job in corporate Manhattan. She went through all the motions, charmed the people from human resources, and found herself face-to-face with an editor-in-chief at an antiquated bricks-and-mortar textbook publisher. The editor-in-chief questioned her mercilessly, leaving Shira drained at the end of the interview. She left the building and raced straight for ice cream at the café across the street.

Chocolate chip always soothed her traumas.

Shira didn't get the job and knew, instinctively, that she wasn't designed to work the corporate crowd. The next day she sent off her first proposal to write a romantic mystery.

A few hundred feet from her, two suits with loosened satin ties were comfortably settled around their own tiny green table. They watched young women stroll by, smiling with pleasure. Shira watched *them*, taking mental notes. It was as if they were in a theater, scrutinizing people instead of actors, commenting on breasts instead of lines. Shira shifted her gaze past the suits to another man. He was studying the suits. Shira smiled. It was New York after all.

She glanced at the opposite side of the Great Lawn, on the promenade near the small carousel. It was framed by leafy *Solomon's Seal* plants that grew wildly, without abandon. She watched a small group of young people dressed in casual, funky-looking clothing. The guys wore jeans; one girl wore a sundress, the other wore a light, sheer shirt with rolled-up sleeves. They all had a counter-culture look, as if they worked corporate but lingered on the edge of suits. In the middle of the group was a fragile-looking, olive-skinned girl, with large, fawn-like eyes, twenty-something, wearing cropped jeans and a flowing pink shirt. Shira watched as the girl laughed, her thin, graceful neck stretched to the fullest; her thick, long curly hair tucked behind her ears. Even at this distance, Shira could see that the girl was breathlessly beautiful, with the kind of face and body that fit an ad for organic food or green responsibility. Perhaps that was why she seemed vaguely familiar – a character stepping out of her fiction?

She's sick.

The words popped, unbidden, into Shira's head. She looked at the olive-skinned girl more carefully. She was very thin and moved purposefully, as if her body was delicate and she needed to save energy. Interesting.

Was she Emma?

Shira shook her head. No, Emma wasn't nature-girl. Nor was Emma sickly or fragile. But it was fun to consider the possibilities. Emma was a histrionic, not a health food princess.

Shira watched the play between the olive-skinned girl and her friends. Clearly, the olive-skinned girl was the heart of the group; when she laughed, everyone laughed. When she spoke, everyone listened like they were there to protect the olive-skinned girl, ready to catch her in a fall, prepared to shield her from attack. Shira wondered what it would be like surrounded by people who cared - not breathe through characters created by fantasy. How would it feel not to be plagued by the constant need to run – run from an unseen enemy, run from a friend, run from the sameness and, most of all, run from time?

Shira knew instinctively that she was different and at the same time, similar to the olive-skinned girl. It was her job to run. Run away from things she couldn't define – that gave her an otherworldly sense, as if she were connected to times and places she couldn't see. She preferred the safe world of her stories and characters, pages that defined her life. Shira sighed. She patted the leather pouch in her pocket for reassurance.

Shira returned to the laptop because that was what she was meant to do.

Rozas

Time loses meaning in the darkness of the dungeon. Day and night blend together. Seconds, minutes, and hours hold no substance. Instead, memories embrace me. I drift backwards in time, reliving moments from my youth.

I had been promised to Pedro de Montoro when I was only a few years old. He was eight years my senior and I remember staring at him, through five-year old eyes, wondering how the dark, handsome man would treat me when I became his wife. The Montero family had wanted Pedro to marry one of my sisters, but they had already been taken. It was decided that when I turned fourteen, I would marry him and bear many sons. My future was secure, my family was together, and one day I would join Pedro and lead the *Conversos* community.

It all changed in 1474, my thirteenth year.

Mama had sent me out to bring home a basket of wildflowers that grew in a patch just beyond the edge of town. The flowers were in full bloom, and mama loved to have them around the house. I took a large basket and walked to the meadow, basking in the warm spring sun, the sky filled with shape-shifting clouds, and the delicious fragrance of flowers and green spring grasses. I was completely alone! How well I remember that moment. I was young and strong, filled with hope that within the year, I would be an adult. A wife! Until that day, I was still a child. Laughing, I tossed my basket on the ground and threw myself into the purple wildflowers, rolling over and over until their fragrance permeated my skin and clothes. I stared up at the sky. There was a cloud that suddenly shape-shifted into a *trovodor*, singing a ballad that I heard in the breeze. The birds chatted happily and the flowers, dancing in the sun, sounded like they were whispering in my ears.

I lay still and stared into the warm blue sky, tracing the paths of the clouds. The *trovodor* moved on as another cloud transformed itself into a crouching boy. Mesmerized, I watched the display above me, clutching flowers to my newly-developed breasts, breathing in the thrill of my heart beating, my fingers tingling, and the quiet, faithful rhythm of the sun, the sky, and the world that held only promise.

Until the shadow crept over me.

"Rozas," he said.

I squinted against the sun.

"Rozas," he repeated.

I sat up so quickly that flowers flew in every direction.

"What are you doing here?" I asked sharply. I scrambled to my feet. "Did you follow me? Are you trying to make fun of me?"

I looked into the large, intense eyes of a boy only a few months older than me. He had just taken his secret *bar mitzvah* that we celebrated with the other *Converso* families. The *bar mitzvah* marked a boy's passage into manhood, under the Laws of Moses.

His name was Lucas, and none of the children liked him. He reminded me of a toad - with a glistening, misshapen body, oily skin, and strange, orange freckles that crept up his nose like tiny warts. His curly, unruly hair framed an odd-shaped face, propped by a painfully short neck and a belly that promised to grow along with his age. Long, scrawny legs, slightly bent at the knee, balanced his body like a toad ready to leap. He didn't speak to anyone; instead, he hid in his books, and behind the arrogance of his older brother. It was said that he survived the massacre of Conversos in Córdoba, a year earlier. His mother, two sisters, and infant brother were slaughtered. Only Lucas, his father and older brother, escaped. They were grim, unsmiling people that had become part of our community. His father, once a prominent merchant, became a *ropero*, clothes peddler, and could barely support what remained of the family. Many times I saw Papa slip them olives, oil, and slabs of bread that mama baked. He did it quietly, believing no one would notice.

Everyone knew the *ropero* and his family.

So unlike my Pedro. I'm so lucky to be saved for him and not this ugly boy.

"Rozas," Lucas repeated.

"What do you want, toad?" I asked gruffly.

"I just saw you and . . ."

"And?"

He lowered his ugly, orange-freckled face.

"Can't you talk?"

"No."

"Why?"

"Because . . ." he rubbed his hands together frantically.

"Because why?" I had no patience for this ugly boy; he had ruined my moment.

Lucas struggled to speak. His lips tightened and his face shifted into an amphibious green.

"You can't talk?"

Lucas turned his strange eyes to me. They were too large for his face, dark and flecked with green. His eyes burrowed inside me, fat and unwanted.

"Leave me alone!" I shouted.

Lucas' eyes widened and then he turned and fled, like a toad jumping through the thick spring grass.

I wrinkled my nose.

What a strange, ugly boy.

I laughed.

Not like my Pedro.

A loud noise shatters the images.

Someone is approaching my cell. Are they coming for me? How long have I been here? Frantically, I try to count the days. Without night and day, I have no way to keep track.

A light glows behind the rusty iron bars. The metal clangs as the guards enter my cell. One guard grabs my arm roughly, wrenching me to my feet. I stumble and he drags me like a useless side of raw beef. He pulls me outside the bars, and another guard joins him. There's not enough room to walk three abreast in the dark stone corridor. Instead, one soldier drags me while another follows, poking me with a pointed weapon. In front of us is a stocky monk in brown robes, his face partially concealed by a hood. He mumbles Latin words as we go through the dark tunnel, his voice bouncing against the stone in a singsong chant.

I'm pushed into a tiny room where I fall, my knees scraping the stone floor. The light is so bright! I can't see anything for a few seconds; my eyes are acclimated to the darkness of my cell. The guards wrench me from the floor and force me to sit in a narrow, hard chair, tying me securely by my arms and legs.

Finally, my eyes adjust. Four men sit behind a large table, all dressed in identical brown robes, wearing large silver crosses. They watch me as if I'm an evil curiosity, frowns covering the flickering of smiles. At the head of the table is a priest named Tomás, a man I know well. His heavy face is shrouded in thick layers of fat, his beady eyes squint in pleasure.

The guards test the ropes that bind me to the chair and back away.

Tomás is our town's Chief Inquisitor.

Tomás nods pleasantly. "I trust," he says in a voice that is hauntingly gentle, "you're enjoying the accommodations."

I remain silent.

"Good," he replies, as if I had been staying in an elegant room. "We have a few questions for you. If you answer them, you'll save your soul and perhaps your life. If not . . ." He shakes his head. "Let's begin."

"Where's Lucas?" I demand.

"I ask the questions," Tomás responds his voice tinged with impatience.

"I want to know where Lucas is."

Tomás nods. One of the guards grabs my throat and began to squeeze. "That's your answer," Tomás smiles evenly.

I can't breathe. I gasp for air, my lungs burn, as the guard squeezes tighter. Is this my death? Right here, right now?

Five words remain, pounding through my mind.

Please God, save my children.

Suddenly the guard releases my throat. I gasp, sucking in air.

"Now we understand one another," Tomás speaks pleasantly in his gentle voice. He could be talking about the taste of sugar cakes or the smell of fresh-picked flowers.

I nod, unable to speak.

"Good," his lips twist into a demonic smile. "Let's start with *my* questions. Once again, if you cooperate, if you answer *everything*, things will go much better for you."

I take a deep breath, imagining the guard's fingers on my throat.

"There was meat in your cooking pot," Tomás says. "It wasn't the first time that you cooked like that. Witnesses have seen you cutting the fat off beef. Did you throw away the fat?"

Who saw me?

Who told Tomás?

It was the meat - the cold, bloodless flesh in my stew. Now I was the animal, a living, breathing creature waiting for the butcher's kill.

"No answer, eh?" Tomás smiles. "Did you cook the meat for twelve hours - to eat on *Saturday* afternoon? After dressing in *clean* clothes?" Tomás chuckles. He waits, pleased with my silence. "You don't want to talk, do you? We have ways, you know. Eventually you'll tell us everything. Everything *and more*."

I summon my courage. "I have nothing to say," I whisper.

"Yes," Tomás shakes his head thoughtfully. "Of course you have nothing to say. You people never do . . . Satan is very brave. We can't let Satan take your soul, can we?" He examines his fingers. "No," he adds haphazardly, "we surely can't let that happen."

He folds his hands together as if in prayer.

"You will tell me." He lowers his voice. "Where are your children, Jew?"

"Never," I hiss.

Tomás eyes darken, his cheeks flush in anger. "I always win, Rozas, you know that."

I do know that. But I'll remain steadfast for as long as I can.

"This is your first interrogation," he sighs, "your first chance to denounce Satan. It will get worse. Talk, and the interrogations are over."

I answer with silence.

Tomás tilts his head and the guards untie me, their hands lingering on my breasts. Then they take me back to my cell.

Once again, in the darkness, I drift back into the past.

Mama had sent me to pick more flowers. I sensed that someone was following me. I knew it had to be the ugly boy, Lucas.

"Leave me alone, toad," I cried, not turning around.

"Can we talk?" Lucas begged.

"I have nothing to say to the son of a *ropero*," I snapped over my shoulder.

Lucas was silent, but stayed close. I could feel him, rather than see him, his dark, green-flecked eyes following every movement.

I was determined not to let him ruin my day. I circled through the grasses until I found a fresh patch of flowers. I almost forgot him as I picked each flower and lay it gently in my basket. Soon my basket was overflowing and I couldn't wait to get home and show Mama. Suddenly, I *felt* Lucas creep closer. I turned around, furious. He was only a few feet away.

"Why are you following me, toad?" I yelled.

Lucas jumped back several steps. He shifted his eyes to the ground.

"Why?" I insisted.

He could barely speak. "I h...h...heard there were *banditos* around. I didn't want to see you get hurt."

I shook my head angrily. "There are no *banditos*," I screamed, "only ugly toads."

Lucas' face drained of color. His eyes dimmed, as if dark clouds had drifted across them. I shook my head. I was sorry for hurting the ugly boy, but I didn't dare admit it. "If you don't stop following me," I added, "I'll tell Pedro de Montero, who is to be my husband."

"I'm sorry *senorita*," Lucas said formally. "Please forgive me . . . but please don't come out here again, all alone. Maybe Pedro will watch over you. It's far too dangerous for such a . . . beautiful girl."

Lucas turned and leaped through the grasses until I could no longer see him.

I grabbed my basket of flowers and returned home, oddly sad that I had hurt the ugly boy. I had this feeling that he was still watching me, unseen.

Perhaps his ropero father will find him a suitable wife.
Make the ugly boy happy?

39

Many times, in the years after, I thought about Lucas watching me pick the wildflowers, with his large, green-flecked eyes, and the ugly orange freckles that sprouted like wheat grains across his face. Sometimes when you believe that everything is set, that *forever* is well in hand with a clear path to follow - a path that will lead you into a well-defined life - there's a sharp turn in the road and you're plunged into a direction you never imagined.

Perhaps the new direction was always meant to be?

I arrived home, to the sounds of my mother wailing, angry words from my father, and my two sisters, with babies at their breasts, scurrying around trying to quiet the chaos.

"What's wrong?" I demanded, dropping my basket on the clean-swept floor.

"Rozas doesn't know," Mama sobbed.

"What should I know?" My blood turned cold.

"Rozas doesn't know," Mama cried louder.

"Quiet, woman!" Papa roared.

My heart pounded crazily.

"He's run," Mama screamed, as if someone had beaten her. "*He's run.*"

"Who's run?" I asked quietly, the words scraping my suddenly dry throat.

Papa pulled me close to him, in a way he hadn't done since I was a child. He held me tightly and kissed my head. "I'm so sorry, child."

"Sorry about what?"

Mama's wails rang louder, sending icy shivers through my body.

"Quiet, woman!" Papa demanded again.

Mama couldn't stop. My sisters tried to quiet her, but instead, their babies began to scream until the house was full of sharp, awful cries, shaking with grief.

"My baby, my baby," Mama cried in awful, heaving gulps, as if she were choking on chunks of secret meat.

Papa pulled me from Mama, my sisters, and the babies, through the heavy wooden door that led to the street. "We must talk," he said stiffly, leading me through the twisting street, to the wildflowers. People leaned out their windows and stared at us, on the street men moved aside as if we had the sickness, children stopped playing and watched us, their eyes big, their games silenced.

What's happening?

Papa and I sat on a rock in the middle of the wildflowers. He paused for a moment, taking gulps of air like drink.

I was drenched in fear, my hands were wet, my body leaped between fiery hot and icy cold, a lump stuck in my throat.

I couldn't speak.

"You and your mama love these flowers," Papa said slowly.

I nodded.

"I have to tell you something," Papa struggled, rubbing his hands frantically. "It will make you very sad, my child. I love you as my youngest, my sweetest child and I hate to bring such pain to you. We've all been deceived . . . all of us, in our tiny community . . . have been deceived. He's turned his back on the Laws of Moses and   ran . . ."

"Who?" I demanded.

Papa shook his head. He touched my cheek with his stubby, calloused fingers and glanced away. I waited for him. When he spoke again, his voice was thick with anger. He looked into my eyes. "Pedro de Montero has run away to become soldier," he whispered.

"What?" I couldn't fully understand the words. Pedro was to become my husband in a year; we were betrothed to marry, live together, bear children, stay near Mama and Papa, and my family and his family . . . *forever.*

"He's gone," Papa said.

"He can't be," I laughed, making a thin, ugly sound. "He's my betrothed."

Papa shook his head. "Pedro is gone."

I thought of the tall, handsome man who I always knew would be my husband, the father of my children . . .

Gone?

I noticed a movement in the grass, and then two green-flecked eyes. Watching.

I fainted.

Shira

The words flowed quickly and easily, as if someone else was telling the story. Shira was merely a scribe.

There was a dead body outside the bedroom door.

Emma was frozen, mesmerized by the pool of blood forming beneath the body. She could actually see the bullet holes, like bloody spots on the chest.

"The bullet went right through his chest and exited from his back," the M.E. on television explained. "It was a clean kill."

Clean kill.

Emma had only seen a few dead bodies in her life - her grandparents and of course, those on the big and little screens. She always avoided "viewings" - peering into a coffin at someone's funeral was too macabre for her tastes. This body was different. Mason had killed him . . . before he could kill them. Although Mason was untroubled, waiting for her to return to bed, Emma was in shock. Who was the man? Why did he want to kill them? Why was Mason so blasé about the whole thing?

The questions soothed her panic; slowly, rational thought took over. She peered at the body. Something was wrong. It took her a few minutes to process what she saw.

He was a large man, with a thick barrel chest, clipped beard, and mustache. The skin was pocked and ruddy, as if he was accustomed to living outside in all elements. The eyes were open, intense and unseeing at the same time. He hadn't died with the fear of death.

Emma cautiously surveyed the larger scene. Next to him was an antique rifle, clearly an old-fashioned musket that had dropped to the floor. His other hand gripped a long, heavy wood staff that ended in a sharp, shiny blade, and on the bottom, in a decorative curling wood point.

It was a war axe.

His clothes were different as well. He wore high leather boots beneath a long, heavy coat slung with ornate daggers, ammunition, and a heavy leather pouch. He had an odd-looking hat with no brim and an oblong top that looked more like a uniform than protection. She had never seen anyone who looked like the man . . . except in movies.

"He's a Cossack," Mason said from behind.

Emma jumped at the sound of his voice.

"They've come after me before," Mason explained lightly, "that's why I recognize him. Although this guy is a bit different . . ."

Emma was speechless.

"I know!" Mason snapped his fingers. "He's a Ukrainian Cossack, that's why he's different." Mason studied the body. "This guy looks like he came straight from Kishinev, Mogila . . . The Deluge."

"The Deluge?" Emma echoed his words.

"Yeah," Mason said. "These guys were brutal, ruthless . . . they drowned, slaughtered, dismembered, skinned alive, buried alive, tortured, murdered babies at the breast. . ."

"What are you talking about?" Emma shrieked, swinging around to meet his eyes.

Mason's face was filled with intrigue.

"They killed tens of thousands of innocent Jews in the 17th century." He continued. "Men, women, children . . . they didn't care."

"This can't be real."

"Touch his blood," Mason sighed. "The first time I didn't think it was real, either."

Belligerently, Emma bent down and dipped her fingers in the quickly widening pool of blood. She stared at her hand, vaguely expecting someone to shout "cut" and a make-up person to appear with a rag. Then the Cossack would rise, shake off stiffness, and disappear into the dressing rooms.

Her fingers were covered in human blood.

Shira took a deep breath. Poor Emma. She was about to become a victim of the rich, famous, *and* bizarre. Life was tough. Smiling thoughtfully, Shira scanned the park.

The Great Lawn was full, the carousel was busy, and B.P. Café was filling up with bottled beer drinkers. The olive-skinned girl was still laughing with her friends. The old couple with the silver hair was still watching. The dark man in the cargo pants was still fumbling with something in his pocket. Nweke was selling a beaded bracelet. The two suits were commenting on women's breasts. Jake the tuna fish-man was jotting down a woman's telephone number. His prey was a plastic smile dressed in tight clothing and heavy makeup that belied her age. Good for you, Shira thought. They would probably be in bed within the week, after a slow, erotic dinner in a restaurant that served sushi and boasted a live pianist on Thursdays and Fridays.

That was food for another book.

People were drifting toward the west end of the park, past the giant movie screen that opened into white vertical slats. *ThursdaysAt5*. Shira watched as more people headed in that direction. Crowds were always interesting in New York. They could be friendly, hostile, or aggressively curious. They could last for hours mesmerized by a fire or other disaster, or form and disperse within minutes. They could watch a boy from the 'hood scam tourists with cards or shells, or gather, like dust bunnies, around a captivating street performer.

New York crowds loved both music and disasters.

Who knows what I'll find in this crowd, she thought. Maybe the Cossack will be standing there, waiting for me. Shira laughed. It was New York City, the 21st century, and the second millennium. Anything could happen.

She wanted to follow the music, but Emma and Mason were not ready to let her go.

Shira returned to her laptop.

"Can you hear me," Mason demanded. His voice was tinged with anger. "He's real, but you don't have to worry. He won't be there in the morning."

Emma waved her hand in front of him. "Clearly, he's real. Clearly, he's dead. And clearly, you killed him."

Mason shrugged.

"We have to call the police. We'll tell the truth . . . self defense. He had weapons, he was a . . ."

"Ukrainian Cossack," Mason sighed. "Like I told you, he was a brutal murderer. He hated the Jews."

"You're not even Jewish. I am. Not you."

Mason shrugged.

Her voice was high-pitched, near panic. "You said he was four hundred years old."

"No, I didn't say he was four hundred years old. I said he was from the 17th century."

"You're crazy, totally insane. You don't know what you're saying or doing, and there's a dead man right here . . ."

Mason grabbed her arm. "You're panicking, Emma. Stay calm."

"Stay calm?"

Mason gritted his teeth. A tiny muscle twitched in his jaw.

Suddenly, it was painfully clear.

"This has happened before?"

Mason nodded. "Many times."

"You've killed many people?"

"Yes."

"You're a serial murderer. I just slept with a serial murderer. . ." she leaped away from him, but his grip on her arm prevented her from getting very far. She turned and slapped him, spreading the Cossack's blood across his cheek.

"Are you going to leave me?" Mason whispered. "Like the others?"

"The others?"

Mason nodded slowly. "The others."

"What do you mean?"

"The other women. No one believes me. They think I'm some super rich guy with the Russian mob behind me. They come to whack me, I beat them to the punch, and by morning everything is gone, clean and neat, like it never happened. A movie saga."

"What should they believe?"

Mason ran his fingers through his golden hair.

"The truth."

"The truth? Isn't the truth lying right here at our feet?"

"Come with me - I'll show you."

Mason led Emma down the hallway and through a door that led to the famous Portsmith library. The room was huge, darkly paneled, with thousands of volumes organized in floor-to-ceiling shelves. On one wall was a large glass case, specially sealed to protect rare old books prized by the Portsmith family.

Mason walked to a set of shelves on the far side of the room, next to the glass case. He pulled out a book wedged between The Zohar *and* Kabbalah for Beginners. *Mason flipped through the pages, and then brought it back to Emma.*

He held the book open to a page with a large drawing.

 Ukrainian Cossack, circa 1649.

It looked exactly like the man Mason shot.

"I don't understand," Emma's voice trembled.

"I don't either," Mason admitted. "All I know is that they come for me, I shoot and kill them, and the next morning they're gone. Like a dream. Some kind of timeless payback."

"It's not a dream or a game," Emma whispered. "I saw it."

A cold shiver ran down her spine.

Mason was silent.

"Why you?" Emma asked finally.

"I don't know," Mason admitted. "Maybe it's some kind of divine penitence. I've never been able to figure it out."

"You know what all this looks like," Emma said, her voice rising in hysterics.

"Yeah," Mason frowned. "I know."

"Gilgul," Emma said softly. "Old souls returning to repair the damage they created in previous lives."

It was the craziest thought she ever had.

Shira leaned back, satisfied. She liked the sound of *gilgul. Emma and Mason* would not let her go.

They spent hours in the library, talking and asking questions without any answers.

"Will you stay with me?" The rich and famous Mason Portsmith begged.

Emma didn't know what to do. She decided to give him the night and when the morning came, prove the body was still there. She would call the police and . . .

She had no plan past that point.

When the sun filtered through the library curtains, Mason said it was time. The bodies were always gone in the morning.

Emma followed him as he led her back to the bedroom.

What will I say? *She thought.* Will I tell him that he's crazy, that I never believed his story? Will I tell him that all I did was humor him, make sure he didn't turn the gun on me?

A mixture of fatigue, confusion, and raw fear swarmed in her mind.

Suddenly, Mason stopped.

They were in front of the bedroom. There was nothing . . . not even a stain from the pool of blood that had gathered beneath the Cossack.

Everything was gone.

Emma gasped.

"Do you believe me now?" Mason said.

"Got it!" Shira grinned.

Mason and Emma were exactly where she wanted them to be. Trapped.

Rozas

The second interrogation begins the same way.

The soldiers drag me through the stone corridor, led by a priest in brown, flowing robes. They tie me to the same chair. I face the four priests, with Tomás sitting in the middle. I'm weaker. My shoulders sag and it seems incredibly difficult to hold my head upright.

"Do you work on Sunday?" Tomás demands. "Do you ignore the Lord's Prayer in church? Do you use a fresh tablecloth for Friday night dinner?"

Again, I say nothing.

"Speak," Tomás roars, "or you'll face the consequences."

Trembling, I remain silent.

Tomás' eyes flash with anger. "You have been accused of very serious crimes. You must confess."

"I'm not guilty," I whisper.

"Do you eat meat during Lent? Do you fast on the High Holiday? Do you wear clean clothes on Saturday?"

I will not speak.

"Where are your children, Jew?"

I meet his eyes, staring into the beady, squinting darkness. "You won't ever find them."

Tomás rises from his seat, the fat jiggling beneath his robes. "You have been accused of being a heretic - a ritual murderer, apostate, and grasping power for your own evil needs. We found poison in your home, plans to betray us, and proof of participating in activities designed by Satan, the devil incarnate. You have betrayed the love and trust of our Lord Jesus Christ. We want to know the names of your accomplices, all the people who have joined you in these crimes, and the location of your children."

"Show me proof," I say weakly.

"Proof?" Tomás laughs, his face moving closer, inches away from me. I can smell his rancid breath, and feel droplets of his spittle spray on my cheeks as he speaks. "A witness has attested to your heresy."

"Who is he?"

"*You* will never know. The witness is a God-fearing Christian. He will be protected from Satan and rewarded by Jesus Christ our savior."

I shake my head. "I'm not guilty of anything," I hiss.

"You'll confess," he said confidently. "Let me show you *why*."

Tomás backs away as the guards release me. They grab me beneath my armpits and wrench me to my feet. Tomás nods and they drag me down a different tunnel. There are no cells, but as we approach our destination I hear blood-curdling wails. I shiver. The guards laugh.

"Eh, she's already scared," one guard bares his rotted teeth.

"It's a good thing," the other spats, "she'll break faster." He laughs, a shrill, demonic sound that reverberates against the stone walls.

They bring me to a large, cavernous room filled with many guards and monks in brown robes. The room is brightly-lit, whitewashed, and lined with fabric. I have heard of these rooms – the fabric is used to stifle the sound of screams. A large crucifix hangs limply on the wall, partially covered with a sheer material to "protect" Christ from the horrors committed in his name. Everywhere I look there are strange, primitive instruments that I don't recognize. As we enter the chamber, I see that all eyes focus upward. I follow their gazes and discover, with horror, *my future.*

A naked, emaciated man is tied by his wrists, over his head, to a thick rope. The Holy Inquisition *verdugos* or torturers are dressed in long, dark robes with hoods that completely conceal their faces. They slowly raise him off the floor, using a pulley mechanism. The man grunts as the rope carries him up high above the floor.

Tomás licks his lips. "Do you like what you see?" He blissfully whispers in my ear, spittle dripping down his chin. "Watch carefully."

I struggle to turn away, but a guard grabs my head and forces me to look. The man dangles near the ceiling; I can hear his joints creaking from the weight of his own body. I *feel* the wrenching pain in his shoulders, his chest muscles stretching to support him. Beneath him, a monk mutters some prayers. It sounds more like a curse than an incantation. Suddenly the *verdugos* or torturers release the rope, dropping him into a free fall until his feet dangle only just above the ground. The rope pulls his shoulders out of their sockets.

I have never heard a man scream like that – his shrieks are horrific, his eyes rolling white in agony, his mind shocked into unconsciousness.

"What we do," Tomás speaks, as if teaching me some interesting fact, "is drop the man until the rope catches him, thus breaking his body. His muscles tear, his shoulders break, and he experiences a pain like no other. I assume," he adds jovially, "you've figured *that* out."

Tears sting my eyes as the guards toss a pail of cold water over the prisoner's head, bringing him back to consciousness.

"We're very careful," Tomás added, "to make sure that there's no blood. We can't have our people *bleed*, can we? The Holy Church isn't permitted to draw blood." He laughs, peering happily into my face.

Slowly, they raise the man back up to the ceiling.

"Don't worry," Tomás smiles sweetly, "it doesn't take much time."

The man breaks after the third drop. He babbles incoherently, saying anything they want. I hear names, places, confessions . . .

Tomás nods with approval. "She's seen enough." The guards don't have to drag me away. Tears burn my eyes and cheeks. A sickening ache permeates my soul.

Did they do this to Lucas?

Am I next?

"Wait," Tomás says to the guards, as if reading my thoughts. "Yes, this is going to happen to you," he licks his lips and savors his words. "Unless, of course, you answer the questions, give me names, and confess to all of your crimes. And . . . tell me where your children are."

In the background I heard the prisoner's wails cutting through my soul.

Please God, save my children.

"I'm not guilty of anything," I whisper, my voice trembling.

Tomás is not disappointed. "We'll see. All the more fun for me." He looks at the guards. "Take her back to her cell and give her more time to think."

They drag me back to my cell, shoving me into the vermin-infested hay, infused with dried human feces. Rodents nibble at my skin. I refuse to eat the bug-infested soup. People in town used to talk about the third interrogation in whispers, afraid if they spoke loudly it would be brought down on them. Everyone was so frightened. Now, I'm the one they speak about. I know Tomás will come again. Soon.

I close my eyes and dream, traveling back to Lucas, and better times.

Life changed after Pedro de Montero ran away. *Everything* was different. People shunned me, as if I had the sickness. Although it wasn't my fault, I was still the spurned woman - the poor creature who would spend my years, alone, without family, to fend for myself. When Mama calmed down, she looked at me differently . . . I had failed her, in a way I couldn't quite define. Papa was kinder, but distant. I knew he worried about what was to be done with me. Who would want a woman abandoned by the most elegant man in our community? No one of any status would dare to request my hand in marriage. Perhaps I had an evil eye looking down on me? Perhaps I had *scared* Pedro away? Before Pedro left, I was seen as beautiful and desirable; now I was as ugly as Lucas, a cast-off, rejected by all. When I walked through the streets people whispered behind my back, children laughed and taunted me, and older people shook their heads in dismay.

There was only one man who wanted me.

"I will not marry the son of the *ropero*," I screamed at Papa, two months after Pedro had run away. "He looks like a toad . . . he's poor and worthless . . ."

"There's no one else," Papa yelled back.

I had moved from the very top to the very bottom of my world. "No! I'd rather die."

Papa shook his head. "Go out to your purple flowers," he stomped his feet. "Do what you want. In the end, you will do what *I* want, and marry the *ropero's* son."

I rushed from the house, tears streaming from my eyes. My life was ruined with no hope for the future. I fled, dragging my skirts through the streets, sending up clouds of dust, until I was beyond town, running, running . . .

I stopped suddenly.

I was in the flowers.

I fell to my knees, pleading with God to change my fate. I begged Him to do anything but make me marry the *ropero's* son. I cried to the shape-shifting clouds, screaming, and then cursing my fate. When I could cry no more; when my voice was so hoarse I could hardly speak, I collapsed into the flowers, burying my face in their perfume.

I didn't know how long I was there before I noticed a shadow over me. I rolled over, only to see the ugly face of Lucas.

"Leave me alone!" I cried. "Why did you follow me when I said never to . . ?"

"I was afraid," he said softly, "of the *banditos*."

"Let them take me!" I wailed. "It's better than my life now."

The large eyes filled with hurt.

"Better than marrying me?" Lucas whispered.

"Yes! I want my Pedro, not a toad."

Lucas sat in the flowers next to me. He was silent.

"I want my Pedro, not a toad." I said again, although not as fiercely.

He remained silent.

"Why won't you talk to me?"

He shifted his eyes to the sky. "What do you want me to say?"

"Something. Anything. Promise I don't have to marry you."

He took a deep breath. "I can't make that promise. Our fathers have already negotiated a betrothal."

"Change it . . . stop it. Anything."

Lucas selected a large purple flower and plucked it from its stem. He brought it to his nose, sniffed it, and then sent it sailing through the air.

"I don't want to marry you."

He took a deep breath. "Is it worse than being a spinster, with no one to care for you?"

"I'd rather be a spinster."

Lucas nodded.

We stared at the sky.

"I want to tell you something before I return to my father and tell him I can't marry you."

"What?"

"Do you know why I really follow you?"

"The *banditos*?"

Lucas mopped his forehead with the back of your hand. "I love you. I've loved you from the moment I saw you, even when I believed I could never have you."

I laughed cruelly. "What can someone like you know about love?"

Lucas eyes were fiery as he wrenched me in a visual embrace. It took my breath away.

How can a toad feel passion?

"Maybe someday you'll understand, Rozas. You wanted Pedro, but he didn't want you. There was only emptiness inside him . . . he ran away to find adventure. Pedro had no idea that the adventure lies within," Lucas pounded his chest, "not on a horse in the royal army."

I had no words.

Lucas stood up. "I'll give you what you want, Rozas, I'll tell my father that I won't marry you."

He held his head high and marched away from me on his long, scrawny legs.

"What about the *banditos*?" I cried.

"They can have you," he said over his shoulder.

Father was furious when I returned home. "What is this about you refusing to marry the *ropero's* son?" He demanded. "Do you dare to disobey me?"

Shira

Shira heard the amplified sounds of a guitar being tuned. She couldn't see the musician on the other side of the slatted film festival screen, but knew, from past concerts, that the performer was setting up on the terrace in front of the Josephine Shaw Lowell Memorial Fountain. The memorial was a classical pink granite fountain installed in 1913 and best known for the city's first major monument named for a woman. Lowell was a progressive reform leader, who created the New York Consumer League in 1890, and later, The Charity Organization Society.

Shira loved the memorial, imagining what life must have been like for a social worker in late 19th century New York.

Shira strained her eyes, trying to get a glimpse of the *ThursdaysAt5* performer. There were too many trees and people to see anything. Instead, Emma and Mason called to her.

The second time it happened, Emma and Mason had just made love. It was the same scenario, like a movie rerun.

She glanced at his face. Mason had tossed aside the sheets, exposing his nakedness. His biceps rippled perfectly on his arms; his washboard rib cage looked more like a Greek statue than flesh and blood. His legs were perfectly muscled; years of tennis, personal trainers, and workout rooms in the Long Island mansion where he grew up, made sure that his body was flawless.

Mason Portsmith's body, she thought, is like a limpieza de sangre - *pure-blooded work of art.*

It had been two months since The Cossack.

Her eyes began to close when suddenly she heard a strange noise from beyond the bedroom door.

Mason awoke immediately.

She heard the noise again . . . it sounded like someone moving outside the room, walking quietly down the hardwood floors . . .

Mason shot to a sitting position. He pulled on his tee shirt and shorts. Emma dressed quickly, her heart pounding.

"What is it?" Emma whispered.

54

"Sssh," Mason shook his head, listening intently.

"A Cossack?" She tried to put some laughter in her voice. Instead, it came out high pitched and thin.

In the past two months Emma had convinced herself that the Cossack was a dream, a shared consciousness with Mason. Maybe it had been caused by the expensive wine they drank that night for dinner or . . .

"Shut up," he turned to her. In the dim light his face was wrenched into a snarl. "You're scaring me."

Mason ignored her. He reached to the black granite night table that served as a bedpost.

She watched him silently, frightened by the sudden change in the man who had just made such tender love. As if in slow motion, he opened a small drawer. He pulled out the baby Glock-26, the smallest model on the market. His hands were trembling.

The noise outside their door was louder, like a big man fumbling through the house. She heard a faint voice but the words were unfamiliar - a different language, or curse that she couldn't identify.

Emma was terrified.

"What are you doing?" She hissed.

"You know the routine."

"We dreamed that. It wasn't real."

"Well dream again baby, because it's happening all over again."

"Another Cossack?" She hissed.

Mason paused. "They're never exactly the same."

"Please," she begged, as he raised the Glock-26 in front of him, his eyes fixed on the bedroom door.

"I love you," Mason said, without turning around. "Everything will be fine."

Something inside her wondered about his strange choice of words and calm tone of voice, but she was too scared to think deeper. "Please don't leave me," Emma begged.

Mason was already half way across the room.

The noise outside the room grew louder, the voice roaring on the other side of the door. It was another language; a foreign invader . . .

She leaped from beneath the covers, yanked the nightshirt from the floor next to the bed, and threw it on. Emma crept up behind him.

"Get back," Mason warned.

"If this is the real thing," Emma whispered, "I'm staying with you."

Mason shook his head, but didn't stop her. Slowly they crept toward the door. The angry screams were louder. Mason put his left hand on the doorknob and released the gun lock.

"Are you ready?" he whispered.

Emma nodded.

Mason flung open the door to a small, stocky man wearing a tunic emblazoned with a huge Red Cross and mail-style fabric covering his head, neck, arms, and legs. The man yelled something that sounded Germanic, raised a thick, heavy sword and aimed for Mason's heart.

Mason shot him dead.

The two of them stared at the man as he fell to the floor, his sword dropping beside him. A pool of blood formed beneath his head.

"I got him in the head," Mason explained. "One shot to the forehead . . ."

Emma shuddered.

They were silent as he went through the death throes, his legs and arms twitching in a demonic dance.

Emma could hardly breathe. "Who is he?"

Mason shrugged.

"Will he be gone . . . by tomorrow morning, like The Cossack?"

"Yeah," Mason sighed, "they always are."

Mason backed away from the body. "Let's figure out who he . . . was."

Emma delicately stepped over the body, avoiding the widening pool of blood. She was numb, all feeling drained from within.

Mason led her to the Portsmith library and the same shelf where he had found the picture of The Cossack.

"Wait," he said.

He examined the spines.

Emma was silent.

"Here," Mason said, pulling a book from the shelf. He went through the pages until he found what he had been searching for . . . a picture that looked just like the dead man. He showed it to Emma.

It was the same man, the same dress, the same heavy sword.

<u>The People's Crusade, May 2, 1096 (First Crusade).</u>
One thousand Jews massacred in the Rhine Valley city of Mainz after Pope Urban II promised that God would reward them for killing infidels.

"But you're not even Jewish," Emma wailed.
Mason just shrugged.
The next morning, The Crusader, his sword, and the pool of blood beneath his head was gone.

Shira shrugged. The next slaughterer to come alive beneath Shira's fingers appeared a few pages later.

"What's going to happen to us?" Emma asked a few days after the Roman Centurion disappeared. He was dressed in a cape, heavy metal helmet, a dagger on his hip, and a spear in his hand. One book told his story: he was a soldier of the Roman Emperor Trajan who was responsible for slaughtering 50,000 Alexandria Jews in Egypt, between the years 115-117. Mason had shot him in the chest, piercing the leather armor with two bullets and drawing a lot of blood.

"I don't know," Mason admitted. "I don't know why they come and I don't know why they go. It just happens.*"*

Emma was silent. She was somewhat adjusted to Mason's bizarre lifestyle. She wondered if she would ever completely get used to watching him kill a man in cold blood, step over the body, and plunge into the library to figure out where the invader came from. How could she live the rest of her life like that? Yet Emma was deeply in love with Mason, entranced with his touch on her skin, his tongue on her breasts . . .

Shira's fingers ached. Still, Emma and Mason killed three more intruders before she got bored with the bloodshed. The crowd behind the film festival screen was growing as the clock edged closer to the 5 p.m. concert. Shira struggled to switch from her story to the reality of what was happening in the moment, but Emma and Mason refused to let go.

57

The next one was a Polish rebel who participated in slaughtering almost all the Jews in the town of Kazimierz on June 20, 1768. He was followed by an Austrian peasant from the fourteenth century Black Death Massacres where Jews were blamed for the death of Christians, accused of poisoning wells and other water sources. Then there was the Russian peasant from 1881 who joined the pogroms in the Jewish Pale of Settlement. By the time the 7th century Visigoth surfaced boasting about outlawing the Jewish religion and making all the Jews slaves, Emma had lost her fear.

She began to think of herself and the future. The dead men from the past always disappeared, leaving Mason in their wake. There had to be a solution, some explanation, some way to stop the assaults. What was going to happen to her, Mason, and the two of them as a couple? Most importantly, why?

Shira typed the final *Why?* She was tired. She hoped that Emma and Mason were doing all the right literary things.

She saved the manuscript twice on her computer and once on the flash drive, careful to separate the two before she closed down and tucked the laptop into her backpack. She snapped the straps, put the flash drive next to the leather pouch in her pocket, and stood up, ready to investigate *ThursdaysAt5*.

Shira forgot about the dark man in the cargo pants and the old couple sitting beneath the green and white umbrella next to the pot of purple flowers on the Upper Library Terrace. She glanced at Nweke the artist and Jake the tuna fish-man, without really seeing them. She pushed away the questions about *why* Emma and Mason's life was playing out that way in her book. She left her green metal chair and table in the Outdoor Reading Room in a pleasant, existential fog, fully expecting to be entertained by the present.

Suddenly, she froze. A thin, gaunt man approached her from the east side of the Great Lawn. She blinked her eyes. He was dressed in . . . costume?

It was late afternoon on the Great Lawn in Bryant Park. The air was cooling and a gentle breeze blew across the grass.

It was New York City.

With skyscrapers, cars, and computers.

The man looked like he had just stepped out of 15ᵗʰ century Spain, wearing a shiny, evil-looking metal helmet, a large red cross on his chest, and primitive weapons slung from his waist. His eyes burned with evil determination; his lips twisted into a horrific smile.

Was he an actor who didn't have time to change costume?

Shira shook her head, trying to make the apparition disappear. He looked like someone from her book - someone Emma and Mason would see - an attacker from the past, destined to be shot.

Shira's laptop was tucked away in her backpack; the flash drive in her pocket next to the leather pouch.

I'm not writing this.

Why am I seeing him?

The man came closer, raising his spear.

She grasped the leather pouch in her pocket.

He's not really here.

He was only a few hundred yards away. Frantically, Shira searched for other people. No one seemed to notice him.

He's in my mind.

Heart pounding, Shira took a deep breath and closed her eyes.

He'll be gone when I open my eyes.

Like my book.

Dead.

But when she opened her eyes, he was still there.

Suddenly, he changed. His shiny, evil-looking metal helmet became a baseball cap; the large Red Cross on his chest became a t-shirt with skull and crossbones. The primitive weapons slung from his waist transformed into a microfiber backpack and a cell phone holster. His eyes still burned with evil determination, his lips twisted into a horrific smile.

The 15ᵗʰ century soldier was gone . . . just like in her book.

Shira nervously laughed out loud. Sometimes her books felt more real than the life around her.

As if I was seeing those warriors from the past.

Shira looked around her. No one had noticed. She took a deep breath. The music drifted over, muted sounds of a singer with a guitar, words she could hear but not understand. The crowd was growing around the fountain terrace so she continued making her way across the lawn.

Once again, she froze.

A priest in a black shirt with the traditional white clerical collar stood in front of Shira.

He's enjoying the sun.

Before her eyes, his simple black pants and shirt transformed itself into ornate ecumenical garb with a draped cowl topped with fur, and long, shimmering robes.

Another actor?

Shira gasped. She shook her head and rubbed her eyes, but the vision remained. He had a fat face, beady eyes, and twisted smile.

Another Mason stalker?

Shira closed her eyes and took a deep breath. She forced her heart to slow and reviewed in her mind, what she was really seeing.

Maybe I need a break from Emma and Mason?

Shira stroked the flash drive next to the leather pouch in her pocket. Crazier things have happened, she said to herself softly.

He'll be gone when I open my eyes.

Taking a deep breath, she opened her eyes and stared directly at the priest.

"Enjoy the music," he smiled as he passed her, wearing a black shirt, black pants, and a traditional white clerical collar.

Rozas

The guards shatter my memories.

They have come for the third interrogation. I don't know how many days have passed since I last saw Tomás and the emaciated prisoner dangling from the ropes, his body torn apart. I sit, numb with fear.

Their laughter jars me as I struggle not to tremble. I silently repeat my prayer.

Please God, save the children.

I know what to expect. In the third interrogation they ask the same questions. When I refuse to answer, they will torture me. There's no hope. Ultimately, I will die. Now I hunger more for death than I ever hungered for meat.

The guards drag me from my cell. This time, Tomás is with them. He wrinkles his nose at my stench.

"She stinks," one of the guards says, and they laugh gleefully, like cats toying with their prey.

The man in the brown robe chuckles gently, the sounds muffled beneath his hood.

"We've asked you questions," Tomás said, "and you've refused to answer. For the sake of your soul, we have to do what's necessary to get you to confess."

I think of the man dangling from the ceiling.

"Yes," Tomás says gently, "you're remembering what you saw. That's a good thing. You can stop everything now and confess."

I know what's coming and have convinced myself that I'm ready. Nothing will make me confess to crimes I didn't commit; incriminating the innocent people I love.

"Stubborn," Tomás mumbles, "just as I thought. These apostates always *are*. They're made willful by the hand of Satan."

Tomás is pleased by my refusal. I look into his eyes and see that he savors the torment, feeds upon it like an animal devouring his kill. Tomás is inhuman – a living evil who thrives on agony, sustaining himself through the pain of others.

61

My legs collapse and the guards hold me up, grabbing me beneath my arms and fondling my breasts in the same movement. I bristle; the guards laugh and squeeze my nipples until I cry out in pain. Tomás pays no mind. They drag me behind the Inquisitor through a tunnel lined with cells just like mine. I know I shouldn't look in the cells but Tomás invites me by shining light into each we pass. I can't stop myself - in the brief glow I see many people like me - men and women crouched beneath low stone ceilings, laying on vermin-infested straw, their eyes glazed. One cell holds a child – a boy with a haunted face fringed with straight black hair covered in filth. His big, dark eyes glow with a knowledge far beyond his years. His limbs are twisted and broken - he can hardly move. What evil can a child commit? I want to take him in my arms and comfort him, replace the parents he's undoubtedly lost. I can't – I stumble past as he plunges back into darkness.

I think of my daughters. So beautiful. So young.

Please God, save my children.

Perhaps Lucas is here too? I search each cell but see no sign of him. In my mind, Lucas is holding me; his strong arms give me strength. He whispers in my ear to be brave. How can he be doing that if he's not already dead? Or is it just my imagination, conjuring images so I can feel him with me?

The guards bring me to the large, cavernous room. Tomás smells my fear like a feline predator. "You'll tell us all the names, confess the crimes, and admit to everything *we* want."

I'll say nothing, I vow silently. I won't endanger the people I love. I won't confess to crimes I didn't commit or give them what they want. I'll remain strong.

Tomás' lips twist eagerly in anticipation. "Eh," he says sweetly. "You're probably thinking that you'll remain strong and silent." He laughs, sharp, cutting sounds. The guards and men in brown robes laugh along with him.

"*No one* resists me," he hisses.

One of the guards comes up behind me and rips off my shift. I wail for my nakedness as the men's eyes greedily consume me. They don't push me to the floor, touch me, or try to rape me. Instead, they drool over a greater pleasure, eager to see me tortured, slobbering over their power. I close my eyes and pray that death takes me quickly. I vow that whatever they do, I'll hold onto my spirit, cling to the soul that celebrates Lucas, my children, Rafael, purple flowers, and the life I once lived.

The memory of the broken, emaciated man dangling from the rope tells a very different story.

They lay me spread-eagled, across boards, on a rack, tying my hands and ankles to ropes attached to wheels. The Holy Inquisition *verdugos* or torturers, dressed in long, dark robes with hoods that completely conceal their faces, stand at each wheel, eagerly waiting to begin. I want to hide my nudity but it's not possible. I momentarily find relief – I'm not dangling from the rope in the ceiling. It passes quickly as the torturers turn the wheel and my body is stretched tight, to its maximum limits.

There's no pain.

Tomás leans over me, drool escaping between his fat lips. "You give me no choice," he says softly. "Will you answer the questions – confess the crimes – tell me where your children are?"

There is only one thing I can do. I'll regret it later, but now it gives me strength, a small vestige of dignity. I take a deep breath and with all my power, spit in his face.

Tomás' fat cheeks burn red with anger as he wipes the spittle from his cheek. Without thinking, he smashes his fist into my nose, breaking it, causing blood to gush.

"No, Tomás," a monk in a brown robe cries. "No blood."

Tomás backs off as the guards wipe my face and stop the bleeding. It seems to take forever. Tomás leers at me. "You'll be sorry for *that*," he hisses. He nods to the *verdugos*.

My body, already pulled tight in four directions, is stretched further. I can *hear* the tendons crack and my joints split. I am burning with excruciating pain; tears blur my vision as Tomás leans over me.

"Would you like to spit again?" He taunts.

I can't speak.

63

One more turn of the wheel.

Pain spreads like a fire throughout me – I am being pulled apart, severed into pieces of my own flesh. I scream as if I'm in a fiery pit, everything breaking and splitting in my body. All thought rushes from my mind; I'm drowning in the pulsing agony of my flesh.

"More," Tomás cries.

I crash into unconsciousness.

Icy water shocks me back to Tomás. They've thrown it onto my face and I sputter, trying to catch my breath.

"More," Tomás cries, "for the grace of God."

I make horrifying animal sounds. Now I'm the beef, butchered for human pleasure.

"Talk!" Tomás demands.

Blessedly, I lose consciousness again.

It doesn't last long – a guard tosses icy water over my head to bring me back.

"Talk!" Tomás roars at me.

He touches my right shoulder and nods to one of the guards. My right arm is pulled from its socket. It's as if a dozen hot irons sear my skin; I scream my agony, enhancing Tomás' pleasure.

Nothing is left. I will do anything to get them to stop.

"Talk," Tomás says gently.

I talk.

I say whatever he wants, rattle off names that he requests and names that he doesn't request, confess to any crime he chooses.

"Where are your children, Jew?" Tomás asks greedily.

"Gone," I cry. "Where you can't touch them."

"Where?" Tomás demands.

Tomás has broken both my body and my spirit. So quickly. So easily. But I will not tell him where my children have gone.

Please God, save my children.

My silence will make it possible.

The scribe, standing next to Tomás, writes everything I say.

When my throat is sore from my words, Tomás releases the tension on the ropes. My right arm dangles uselessly from my shoulder.

"Where are your children, Jew?" Tomás asks again.

"I don't know," I gasp.

"Where!" Tomás roars.

"I don't know," I say beneath the searing pain. My voice is barely a whisper.

There are no words left.

Tomás knows it.

The Inquisitor nods pleasantly. "We'll make sure that she's told us everything," he says to the monk in a brown robe. "My dear," he whispers, "you're coming back. We'll find your precious little ones, don't you worry."

In my mind's eye I see it clearly. *Trees cry for rain. Purple flowers shudder in the wind. The sky fills with thin clouds that shape-shift as they pass overhead. A bird cloud suddenly transforms into a handsome trovador; a child cloud drifts into a crouching man. Suddenly there's a dull thud; a large cow with dark, soulful eyes faces me. I've seen this creature before; she's visited my dreams many times. She wears a broken iron key on a leather thong around her neck. I reach out to touch the key and the metal burns my fingers, the sky turns black, and the clouds scatter in terror.*

I scream, but no sound is heard.

"Get her up."

I press my back against the damp stone wall, trying to hide. I have to get out of here. I have to!

"Get her up," Tomás repeats, his nose wrinkling in disgust.

Hands wrench me away from the wall. Although my right arm hangs uselessly, permanently pulled out of my shoulder socket, when the guards touch it I scream in agony, a burning pain coursing through my body.

"Not spitting at me, eh?" Tomás grins, licking his fat lips.

I stare at him, terrified by his next move.

His fat fingers shiver with anticipation. "We're taking you back," he says pleasantly, "to make sure you haven't left anything out."

"Noooooooo," I wail, "I've told you everything. There's nothing left."

"Maybe," Tomás agrees, "but we have to make sure you don't know where your children have gone."

The guards drag me from my cell. The cold, rodent-infested space and filthy straw is my only sanctuary.

"Please," I beg, no longer embarrassed to show my raw fear of the tunnel and the cavernous torture room. "I'll do anything you want – say anything you need."

"God's will," Tomás says flippantly.

I plunge into a black despair. There's no hope. No breath without pain. I'm immersed in evil that controls me; I want to be heroic but terror and weakness pervade, drowning my soul.

Tomás leads the way now, along with the monk in a brown robe. The guards drag me behind, through the tunnel. Again, I search the cells, this time hoping to see Lucas.

"Oh," Tomás says over his shoulder, "your husband died today."

Lucas? Dead?

My legs buckle and I collapse. The guards pull me up by my armpits. This time I feel no physical pain.

"Lies," I scream hoarsely. "You're lying."

Tomás pauses and slowly turns to me. He pushes his fat, malevolent face into mine. "*A man of God does not lie,*" he hisses. "You'll be sorry you said that – I'll make sure that things go worse for you today." He grunts like an injured pig, swings around, and continues down the tunnel.

Lucas is gone. He's dead at the hands of these animals.

Dead.

Grief washes over me in waves like water at the river, attacking, receding, and attacking again.

Lucas. Memories seize me. My father's anger.

What is this about you refusing to marry the ropero's son?

The wedding, where I cried for Pedro de Montero and agonized over the reality that I was marrying the ugly boy.

The moment I knew that Lucas, not Pedro, was my soul mate.

Tomás laughs. "Unlike you, he never told us anything. Not a blessed thing."

Lucas.

Images of our life together flood my mind: Lucas a young man in love; Lucas my lover, his large hands incredibly gentle against my skin; Lucas, the father of my beloved children.

Dead?

I struggle to bring the pieces together – to find reason in the insanity. Is there ever any reason, ever any justice? Does life give only to unmercifully take away? Images, real and recalled, flood me, as the guards drag me toward another torture; the dark cells with human eyes light momentarily as we pass; Lucas holding me one last moment before opening the doors to the men with metal helmets, red crosses on their chests, and horrific weapons slung from their waists; Rafael and the girls disappearing through the trapdoor.

Lucas dead?

Softly, barely perceptible, a voice whispers from within.

I'm fine. No more pain my love.

I look around and see only Tomás, the monk in a brown robe, and the guards.

You will join me soon. Be brave.

No more rats, I say silently, no more vermin, torture, and pain. No more Tomás.

They can't hurt you anymore, my love.

You're beyond them.

Tomás roars with laughter, never turning to look at me. "By now," he says, "she's hearing voices from her dead husband in Hell. Maybe he's telling her how hot it is."

The guards join in the fun, slapping me across the back. A hand creeps beneath my shift and grabs my breast. "Ugh," the man mutters, "it's just a scrawny Jew's tit."

I feel nothing.

"Lucas," I whisper, but there's only silence.

I pass out.

My face is drenched in icy water.

Where am I? Lucas . . . dead? I lurch back into consciousness. I open my eyes and I'm in the large, cavernous room filled with guards and men in brown robes. I'm bound to a ladder that's tilted downward with my head lower than my feet. My head is held fast by a metal band and someone has stuffed twigs in my nose so I have to breathe through my mouth.

Tomás leans over me, the rolls of fat on his face distorted until he looks more swine than human.

"She's back," he says matter-of-factly.

The man in the brown robe at the edge of my vision nods silently.

"Are we ready?" Tomás asks the *verdugo*, dressed in a dark robe with a hood that completely conceals his face. The *verdugo* moves behind me. I can't see his response. "Good," Tomás wipes sweat from his brow. He stares at me for several minutes. "Do you have anything else to tell us," he asks sweetly. Tomás' teeth are brown and rotted. Several of them are broken, leaving thin, fang-like remnants - the teeth of a predator. His breath is putrid, engulfing me in a cloud of decay. I try to turn away but my entire body is immobilized. I can only speak.

"No," I whimper. "I've told you everything."

"I believe you have," Tomás concedes, "except where your children have gone. Perhaps you don't know, and that's why you're not talking. Perhaps they're at Satan's feet right now . . . waiting for you? But, my dear, I have to make sure. You see, *no one* can resist me."

His smile burns through my soul.

Please God, save the children.

"Perhaps, Jew, you are praying to Satan as I speak?"

"No," I cry. "I'm not praying to Satan. No more torture. You don't have to. There's nothing left." My voice trembles. I'll do anything to stop the pain.

"This is for your own good — so you can cleanse your soul and the souls of your children."

He stands back and the *verdugo*, his face draped, pries open my mouth. I fight him but it's useless. He puts a cloth over my mouth and starts pouring water.

I struggle to swallow the water, but it comes too quickly, making me sputter and gasp for air. The guard doesn't stop and I'm drowning, unable to breathe, unable to swallow water, my body swelling inside as I fight for air.

"Do you have anything more to tell us?" Tomás asks, his voice barely audible, muffled in the suffocating water. "Where are your children, Jew?"

I can't speak, I can't breathe, and my lungs feel as if they're going to burst. I panic, knowing I'm minutes away from death.

Tomás nods.

They stop the water. Gagging, I realize that with each swallow of water, each gasp for breath, I've drawn the cloth deep into my throat, saturating it until it's wet and swollen. I can't breathe because the cloth is stuck – I gag and sputter, but can't cough it out. My life is quickly slipping from my body.

Tomás' face dims, I plunge into twilight, my fingers and toes grow numb . . .

Is it time to join Lucas?

Without warning, an unspeakable pain sears through my body – a red-hot iron burning everything within. They're pulling the cloth from my throat, taking my flesh as it rips me apart inside. Suddenly I can breathe but the air feels like shards of glass in my throat, the wound an open gash . . .

"So," Tomás grins. "Do you have anything else to tell us?"

I can't speak.

"Convicted," Tomás says gleefully. "Heresy," he adds. "You will be burned at the stake so your sins can be wiped out."

Crossing Over

I die on a beautiful day, beneath a cloudless blue sky, with a warm breeze blowing from fields of wild flowers. My death is the highlight of a public celebration called an *auto de fé* or act of faith. I once attended them as a viewer, drawn by social demand and the ever-present need to hide our secret lives. I was horrified by the festivities; sickened by my neighbors. As a *Converso* there was no choice but to remain silent. Our small, hidden Jewish community was forced underground while wearing the stiff garments of Catholicism and claiming allegiance to the Church. We sported the veneer of New Christians, denying the reality to ourselves and the world. We were, in soul, *Judaizers* – believers in the Laws of Moses. Our parents, grandparents, great grandparents had all converted to Christianity to save their lives – it was a choice between baptism and death. Many Jews who refused to convert were slaughtered. The Jews who chose baptism became *Cristianos Nuevos* - New Christians. Many embraced the church and became fully practicing Catholics. The *Conversos*, like us, worshipped publicly as Christians and secretly as Jews. We practiced our faith in hidden rooms, underground tunnels, and secret meeting places when no one was looking. We had tunnels that connected our homes, sharing hidden books, *Judaica,* and communal prayer spaces in concealed rooms. We were very careful to keep our secrets. Outside, above our hidden rooms, we attended church and followed all the papal laws. We protected our families by making us "look" more Catholic – every generation usually had someone in the clergy. There were *Converso* priests, nuns, monks – it's been said that some of the most powerful church leaders maintained *Converso* secrets. My cousin became a Dominican Brother; one of Lucas' first cousins spent her life as a nun living in a cloistered convent. Even they managed to secretly uphold the Laws of Moses! It was an edgy, duplicitous existence. Our children weren't told the truth until we felt they were old enough to keep the secret, joining our treacherous lives. Sometimes, they were angry; other times they were sad; but they were *always* afraid.

I often wondered how secrets, passed down through the generations, affected us. Were we stronger? Were we weaker? Were we better off than our brethren, the Jews who were sealed into the *Judería* – Jewish quarter in the city – and periodic victims of attacks, massacres, and crushing prejudice from the *Old Christians*?

I never had an answer.

I simply went along with the traditions, hiding sacred books, lighting candles in windowless rooms, saying prayers when no one was listening, and passing the beauty and burden of our history and faith onto my children.

We remained safe, living a Christian life outside the *Judería*.

Until the Inquisition.

Our sins have come back to haunt me.

The medieval inquisition was a scattered movement that began around 1184. The goal was to remove anyone who challenged the church – like the Cathars in France and Italy. Fifty years later, the pope took over with a series of papal bulls and Inquisitors, usually from among the Dominicans, and kept detailed records of imprisonments, interrogations, tortures, and executions of heretics. A heretic was anyone who challenged the church, investigated new ideas, practiced non-Catholic religions, and did not follow the rules set down by the church.

The Spanish Inquisition led to the second Jewish Diaspora. Queen Isabella and King Ferdinand decided, in the late 15th century, that Spain needed to be reunited under the Catholic Church and rid of all heretics. Under the control of Tomás de Torquemada, the first Grand Inquisitor of Spain, and confessor to Queen Isabella, more than two dozen Holy Offices of the Inquisition were established. Torquemada's goal was to rid Spain of all Jews, Conversos, and Moslems. Ironically, Torquemada's grandmother was a *Converso*. It didn't matter that for nearly one thousand years, the Christians, Muslims, and Jews lived together peacefully. We shared one another's cultures; our diversity made us stronger.

Torquemada became Grand Inquisitor in 1483 and began his holy reign of terror. He had insatiable hunger for Jewish and *Converso* blood. King Ferdinand, a mixture of Old Christian and *Converso* blood, didn't go along with Torquemada's plans. Queen Isabella and Torquemada plotted to convince Ferdinand that there was evil in his kingdom. Eventually, Torquemada demonstrated that every *Converso* seized by the inquisition lost his worldly goods, confiscated by the church and state. The more *Conversos* convicted, the more money flowed into the royal treasury. Expel the Jews, and even more money would flow into their coffers.

It had been expensive to rid Spain of the other heretics, the Moors (Muslims), and Ferdinand needed money. Ferdinand and Isabella were eager to raise money to back a new explorer, Christopher Columbus, and remain competitive in the European race to establish new trade routes and colonies.

Ironically, Christopher Columbus also came from a *Converso* family that fled to the Italian city-states to escape the 1391 massacre of Jews in Catalonia. Columbus spoke and wrote in Castilian, the language of Catalonia Jews, not Italian, and his original family name, Colon, linked him to the Jews.

After living side-by-side for nearly 1000 years, there were no *pure* Christians in Spain. It's said that if you cut open any Spaniard, you'll find Jewish blood somewhere inside.

We all knew about Torquemada and his "Holy Offices." As *Conversos,* we were terrified that we would be the next to be marched off to the dungeons. Lucas and I had been prepared, ready with a plan to save the children. We held on to our beautiful home, our money, and our comfortable lifestyle even after the *Alhambra Decree* or *Edict of Expulsion* was issued when the Moors were conquered in Granada. Signing the decree at the *Alhambra,* on March 31, 1492, the Jews had four months to convert or leave Spain forever. The goal was the total Christianization of Spain. The consequences were clear:

It is well known that in our dominion, there are certain bad Christians that became 'Judaized' and committed apostasy against our Holy Catholic Faith, much of it the cause of interactions between Jews and Christians . . . Therefore, the

Council of eminent men and cavaliers of our reign and of other persons of knowledge and conscience of our Supreme Council, and after much deliberation, it is agreed and resolved that all Jews and Jewesses be ordered to leave our kingdoms and that they not be allowed to ever return. We further order in this edict that all Jews and Jewesses of whatever age that reside in our domain and territories leave with their sons and daughters, servants and relatives large or small, of all ages, by the end of July this year, and that they dare not return to our lands and that they do not take a step across, such that if any Jew who does not accept this edict is found in our kingdom and domains or returns will be sentenced to death and confiscation of all their belongings.

. . . Signed, I, the King, I the Queen, and Juan de Coloma, Secretary of the King and Queen who has written it by order of our Majesties.

We had been watching the Jews slowly pack up and leave when the Inquisition arrived at our front door.

Rafael, although he was neither Jewish or *Converso*, gave us the opportunity to put our plan into action.

It's ironic that a *limpieza de sangre* – a pure-blooded Old Christian like Rafael, would be the one chosen to save my family.

Now I sit here and think about the Inquisition, the expulsion, my family and Rafael. I wait for my death. Their destiny will unfold without me. Today, my death is welcome.

The walls of my dark, dank cell cradle me in the last moments of my life.

Shema Yisrael Adonai Elohaenu Adonai Echad
Hear O Israel The Lord is God, The Lord is One.

I whisper the words into the stone.

The Inquisitors publish guidelines so neighbors can identify Jewish heretics. It's their Christian duty to "turn them in" and bear witness. Many New Christians – some in families that converted over a century earlier – are swept up with secret Jews like me. Witnesses are always anonymous – if your neighbor is jealous, if a business competitor wants the upper hand, he or she can get you thrown into the Holy Office with only a few words.

73

Who was my witness – the person who betrayed me? I'll never know. I can only think about the accusations used to convict me . . . the definition of a Converso:

Anyone who wears clean or fancy clothes on Saturdays.

Anyone who uses clean linens on their beds or tables on Saturdays.

Anyone who doesn't work on Saturdays.

Anyone who cleans meat and removes the fat.

Anyone who removes the sciatic vein from a leg of mutton.

Anyone who does not eat pork, hare, rabbit, strangled birds, conger-eel, cuttle-fish, eel, or other scale-less fish.

Anyone who soaks meat in water to remove the blood.

Anyone who goes barefoot on the Great Fast Day.

Anyone who eats unleavened bread and begins their meal with celery, lettuce or other bitter herbs during Holy Week.

Anyone who celebrates the Festival of Lights.

Anyone who lights candles earlier than usual on Friday.

Anyone who keeps Sabbath in honor of the Law of Moses.

Perhaps God is punishing me for living my life in secret? If so, I accept that punishment. If so, I accept my death. But . . .

Please God, save the children.

I know that one of my sins was the meat - the cold, slimy beef that led me to my day of death. My *Shabbat* – Sabbath – feast had turned into my death warrant.

Not only the meat! I cried into the darkness. There was something else.

A witness.

Someone had betrayed us to the Inquisition.

I thought back on my life, and how I hid my Jewish soul deep within the dark tunnels and secret rooms of my home – constantly afraid that prying neighbors, jealous business people, angry friends, or disloyal servants would see through our deception. It was a necessary double life. Did I tear my children's souls in two, split from within, forced to move through life as runaways with heavy secrets and double identities? Will the fear of discovery live within them, passed from parent to child, like coiled snakes, ready to pounce? Will our betrayer follow them?

Did Lucas and I have any choice? Did our parents and their parents have any choice?

My grandparents *tried* to refuse conversion. They were brought to the baptismal font along with others from the Jewish Quarter. They had six children, and vowed to honor the Law of Moses. The priest demanded conversion. They refused.

They killed their oldest son first.

My grandparents watched his small head, hacked from his body, roll across the plaza.

I can hear their wails in *my soul* – feel their agony as their second son was wrenched from their arms. They did not believe that *anyone* could slaughter a second, innocent child.

They were wrong.

My grandparents, through their tears, accepted baptism. They and their remaining four children became Christians as the blood and decapitated heads of their two sons swirled at their feet. They became *anusim* – forced Christian converts.

Their third son would have been the next to die. His name was Miguel, and he was my father.

Was there any choice? I asked that question many times during my life. I asked that question when my daughters were born, wondering what kind of burden I was laying on their shoulders. While Lucas never wavered, I often wondered *why?* Why was it so wrong to believe?

Shema Yisrael Adonai Elohaenu Adonai Echad

Hear O Israel The Lord is God, The Lord is One.

I ask *why*, in my vermin-infested cell, waiting for my death. Was it my punishment for being *Converso* instead of openly practicing my faith? Was it our destiny for being God's Chosen People? I think of Lucas dead, relieved of secrecy, of concealing his soul from those around him. I think of Lucas resisting Tomás and his torture –

something I was far too weak to accomplish. I think of my beef, simmering for twelve hours for our Saturday Sabbath meal. And I think of my betrayer.

They were all pieces that led to this moment.

A rat skitters over my legs and I hardly notice it. Soon it won't touch me again.

Most of all, I think of my children, praying they're safe, far from the clutches of the Holy Office. I wonder about the duplicity of their legacy – forced to run away, torn between opposing forces, committed to a history that secretly connects them to a thousand years of family, living, loving, and dying here in Spain. What terrors do they carry within – will the battle of keeping the secret, and the fear of *not* keeping the secret, wrench their souls? Have we *Conversos* doomed our children to an eternal split, a fury that forces them to look like the rest on the outside and carry, forever, the truth on the inside? It's my fate. It was Lucas's fate. Will it be their fate, too?

I take a deep breath.

Today, the day of my death, is a beginning as well.

I hear the guards before I see them. They arrive at my cell, their faces smeared with smiles of disgust. They wrench me from my sanctuary on the filthy straw. They don't touch me because all sexuality is gone. My right arm dangles uselessly, my body is emaciated, my skin is grimy, and my hair twisted into filthy knots.

They dress me in a *san benito*. It's a yellow tunic that hangs to my knees, made from rough flaxen cloth and painted with pictures of me burning in flames, surrounded by devils and dragons fanning the fire. They put a *coroza* on my head, a high, conical hat, ending in a sharp point, and painted with similar flames and devils. I'm barefoot.

The guards drag me through the dark tunnels. Suddenly we emerge into light. I blink my eyes, barely able to see. I can't remember when I last felt the sun. I pause and raise my face to the sky. My mind fills with images of purple flowers.

The procession forms around me.

76

There are many other prisoners. I see the boy with the haunted face, fringed with straight black hair. His eyes are still big and dark, filled with knowledge beyond his years. He can't move his emaciated legs; the soldiers drag him like a sack of grain.

Today will be a long day. We're led by guards on either side, and surrounded by barefoot Dominican monks holding the banner of the Inquisition - a green cross of knotted wood flanked by an olive branch and sword that represent forgiveness and reconciliation. I shudder at the irony.

Leading the procession is Tomás, radiant in his finest ecumenical gown with a draped cowl topped with fur, and long shimmering robes. Behind us are the local magistrates, soldiers hauling wood for the fires, men carrying ax lances, hooded, chanting friars, and drummers pounding the slow beat of death on their kettle drums.

The prisoners' hands are tied behind their backs.

They bring me further into the light. The sun's warmth is on my skin, purple flowers sway in my mind, and a sweet breeze blows through my hair. Right now, I'm alive.

The procession slowly snakes through the narrow streets of my beloved town. There are crowds everywhere, yelling, jeering, shaking their fists. They scream *Marranos,* or filthy swine, spit, and throw rotten food at us.

What have I done so wrong?

Shema Yisrael Adonai Elohaenu Adonai Echad

The guards hear me whispering the words. One kicks me in the back. I stagger under the sharp pain.

"Silence *Marrano,*" he catches me by my good arm. "Or we'll have to gag you."

I'm soundless.

Shema Yisrael Adonai Elohaenu Adonai Echad

I fill my soul with memories of the town where I grew up, married Lucas, and raised my children. There's Aben's store and Pombo's home. There's where my children played with Isabella and Juanita. Up the steps and to the right is the Judería, Jewish Quarter, where *Conversos* rarely entered. It was always too dangerous to risk being identified with openly practicing Jews.

The lifeblood of my home rages through me.

Why do they scream at me, curse me, and hate me *today* when yesterday they were my friends and neighbors?

What have I done so wrong?

Once again, my heart aches with thoughts of my children. Are they safe with Rafael? Is Marianna playing the good mother, Catalina playing the good nursemaid, and Zara the little girl? Where are they running *to*, and will they treasure the key, broken into four pieces, until they can come home?

Will they be able to continue the precious seed of our family?

Where will they go to be safe?

Is there anywhere that's safe for a Converso or a Jew?

The questions are more painful than the procession; they pound unmercifully at my soul; what is fair and what is evil? If I'm destined to die, are my children destined to live? Please, God, show me some answers. Give me some hope.

Please God, save my children.

Suddenly we burst into the plaza where the tribunal will take place.

It's filled with excited, laughing crowds of people. Food and drink flow freely. There are seats set up for the wealthy people, who wear elegant dresses and velvet jackets. Young children are everywhere; they play with each other and cavort for the adults. The plaza is immersed in music; trumpets and coronets welcome people as if it was a tournament or grand royal ceremony. Special wooden platforms have been built, reserved for noblemen, court officials, and their families. There's a shaded stage erected for Tomás and his entourage – the church's way to demonstrate their ethereal link to God and righteousness.

Close by is a stone scaffold with large, rough stakes.

That's where I'll die.

Entertainment, laughter, food, and drink are ubiquitous. My beloved town, my beloved people, are ready to celebrate my death.

What have I done so wrong?

I enter the plaza with the other prisoners, and the boy, our shoulders slumped and heads down.

The crowds roar as Tomás dramatically takes his position. He lets the people continue their shouts, curses, and threats for several minutes. The royal soldiers mingle among the people, ready to maintain control.

Tomás meets my eyes. A small smile flickers across his lips. He raises his arms for silence.

He begins his long sermon beneath the blazing Spanish sun, staring at our pitiful, broken bodies. "You are all baptized Catholics whose souls have been defiled by Satan in the evil practice of Judaism." He pauses; sweat drips down the rolls of fat that frame his face, staining his magnificent ecumenical garb. "Beg forgiveness," he roars at us. "If you go to death after you beg forgiveness, carrying a crucifix, your soul will go to heaven. If not, your soul will go to Hell with all the Jews of the world. What say you?"

There is dead silence in the plaza.

No one begs forgiveness.

The prisoners are condemned. The boy is one of *us*; no one seems to notice his age. The notary reads their crimes and confessions. Each prisoner has one last chance for full admission of guilt and consequent repentance. If they repent, the prisoner is strangled before being burned at the stake.

No one speaks; the prisoners' eyes fill with an inner fire.

It's my turn to face Tomás.

The notary reads out my list of crimes.

The prisoner engaged in Jewish rituals.

The prisoner ate unleavened bread and kosher meat.

The prisoner removed leg tendons and fat from meat.

The prisoner attended secret services in the house of Jews.

The prisoner disbelieved the concept of Christian Paradise.

The prisoner scoffed at the Host as the body and blood of Christ.

The prisoner profaned the sacred rites of true Christians.

The prisoner wore clean clothes on Saturday and used clean tablecloths on Friday.

The prisoner cooked meat overnight for a Jewish Sabbath meal on Saturday.
The prisoner demonstrated all of the hateful habits of Jews – polluting our Christian land.

Tomás bellows his conviction. "You are a baptized Catholic whose soul has been defiled by Satan in the evil practice of Judaism."

He pauses, sweat drips down the rolls of fat that frame his face, staining his magnificent ecumenical garb.

"Beg forgiveness," he roars. "If you go to death after begging forgiveness and carrying a crucifix, you will be forgiven. Our Lord, Jesus Christ, is merciful. Your soul will go to heaven after you're burned. If not, your soul will go to Hell with all the Jews of the world. What say you?"

I stare at him in stony silence.

The crowd waits breathlessly for my response.

"*Shema Yisrael Adonai Elohaenu Adonai Echad,*" I scream as loud as I can.

Tomás turns bright red. The fat ripples across his face like water when a stone shatters its surface.

"*Marrano! Marrano!*" The crowd chants.

"Relaxed!" Tomás roars, rage filling his eyes. "I hereby relax this prisoner to the royal guard."

I know the term well. The Office of the Holy Inquisition will not be responsible for shedding blood. Instead, they "relax" a convicted heretic into the hands of the king's soldiers who tie them to the stake and light the pyre, responsible for the execution by fire.

I want so much to be brave! I want to hold my head up and feel no fear. Instead, my tears deceive me. They race down my face, streaking my gray, dusty skin in the hot sun. My legs turn to water; I'll collapse if the guards, standing on either side, don't hold me upright. My heart pounds in terror and I'm awash with the raw fear of death.

Say the Shema.

The voice comes from inside me.

Say the Shema.

It's Lucas. Somehow, he's here with me.

It won't be long, my love. We'll be together.

"The children," I cry out loud.

Tomás chuckles at my words.

We'll be together very soon.

The guards lead me to the scaffold where three other prisoners and the boy have been tied to stakes.

They tie me to the fifth stake. There is a sixth stake. I stare at it. There are only

five of us . . .

The crowd roars and the trumpeter's clarion alerts the people that it's time for the execution. Soldiers pile dry branches and tinder around my feet and ankles.

I stare at the sixth stake and then turn to meet Tomás' eyes. The Holy Inquisitor grins.

The stake is for Lucas. Although he is dead, Tomás' has arranged to have him burned in effigy.

Tomás has shattered my resolve.

Have faith, Lucas whispers.

I cry out the *Shema,* stumbling over the words in my terror.

Shema Yisrael Adonai Elohaenu Adonai Echad

When the pyres for all five prisoners are ready, a soldier with a torch approaches. With one, swift movement he lights the first, going quickly down the line. He does not even hesitate when he reaches the boy.

I'm the last.

Before Lucas' effigy.

I hear the screams of my fellow prisoners, and the cries of the boy, as I watch the soldier touch the torch to the tinder at my feet. In seconds, flames rise around me.

The crowds gasp in delightful terror; many women weep, others rejoice, and some fall to their knees in prayer, pity, fear, and thanksgiving.

Tomás' eyes are the last worldly things I see. They glint with evil hunger; devouring the flames.

The fire is on my skin – the pain is beyond anything I have ever experienced. I'm cocooned in agony, the flames licking at my skin, burning deeper into my soul.

Almost there.

Lucas cries above the pain of the fire.

For one tiny moment, a vision breaks through the anguish.

I see Marianna, Catalina, Zara, and Rafael.

They're together.

"I know where they are," I shout my last words to Tomás . "*God has saved my children.*"

Tomás' eyes fill with rage.

I smile with what's left of my lips.

I'm coming, Lucas.

The Old Couple

They sit beneath a green and white umbrella on the Upper Library Terrace in Bryant Park. It's a beautiful summer day. Their silver hair shimmers in the late afternoon sun. The old man reaches out to a concrete pot of purple flowers. He plucks a single flower and hands it to her. She smiles girlishly and pins the flower in her hair.

The Great Lawn sprawls before them. The old couple sees and hears everything. But they can only watch *gilgul* unfold.

They sing softly to one another.

Where is the key that was in the drawer?
Onde sta la yave ke stava in kashon?

My forefathers brought it with great pain
From their house in Spain.

Mis nonus la trusheron kon grande dolor
De su kaza de Espanya.

We told our children this is the heart of our home.

Taymullah

The dark man in the cargo pants listens to the song of the old couple.

He rubs the Glock. Back and forth, hardening with rage.

I want to kill them.

He shakes his head.

That's not my job.

Not God's will.

He waits.

Salaam aleikum, mister.

He grips his Glock tightly and searches for the source of the greeting. There are people everywhere and he shudders. The old couple holds hands and watches him.

Are they closing in on me?

He looks down at the pavement.

A Middle Eastern child stares at him. The boy's face is haunted, fringed with straight black hair. His eyes are big and dark, glowing with knowledge far beyond his years. Scrawny arms and legs stick out from a stained white tee shirt and plain brown shorts. There's a scar on the side of his face, as if he had been burned. The boy moves awkwardly, his limbs stiff and somewhat twisted.

Salaam aleikum, mister, the boy says again.

The dark man in the cargo pants forces a smile.

Salaam aleikum, the boy giggles and scampers back to his mother on the Upper Terrace. She wears a cream-colored *hijab,* and pushes a stroller with a baby.

Leave the man alone, she says to the boy in English. She makes sure it's loud enough for him to hear.

He loosens his grip on the Glock. His eyes dart back to the Great Lawn. He sees one of the infidels in the Outdoor Reading Room.

He smiles.

Only two more.

Time embraces him.

It won't be very long now.

He's waited all his life for this moment. He knows that now; knows that every action taken throughout his life was in preparation for today. He searches his earliest memories - life in a Palestinian refugee camp, the struggle to leave, his parents dragging him to New York, ignoring his cries to remain home.

It's God's will his mother told him.

He believed her.

He believed her through the taunts at the American school; the ridicule over his accent; the fear of being a Muslim. He believed her through all the bombs, the international terrorism, the icy words of fundamentalist leaders. He believed her through 9/11.

He believed her because he *knew*, like any martyr, that he was born with a single purpose to fulfill; an act that would bring him to the feet of God in eternal reward.

Two: Marianna and Ria

Marianna

We're plunged into darkness. Mama and Papa shut the trapdoor over our heads. I have never been so terrified in my life. I want to crumble to the stone floor and cry out my grief.

There's no time.

In a few short moments I've been transformed from a child into an adult; it's up to me to make sure Mama's wishes come true.

I don't think I can do it.

I close my eyes and pray that it's yesterday; all of this has never happened and we're back in the house, with Mama singing songs and doing chores, laughing over Zara's antics. What kind of world would do this to *us*? We've been good to our neighbors, given food to the poor, attended church every Sunday.

Who turned us in?

Rafael touches my shoulder, shattering my thoughts.

"I don't know the way," he whispers.

I'm the only one who knows the tunnel. Rafael will protect us, but I have to show him how to move through the tunnel. Catalina is sickly and Zara is just a child.

It's up to me.

I take a deep breath, raise the candle, and look forward. I ignore the sobs from behind me – Catalina's soft cries and Zara's harsh, angry wails.

"Silence!" I demand, turning to my sisters. My voice is hard. "They'll hear you."

Catalina and Zara are quiet.

I meet Rafael's eyes in the dim light cast from the candle. We lock in a timeless embrace. Rafael's face is haunted. My sisters and I had no choice to enter this tunnel and escape into a new and dangerous life. It was simple – die or run. Mama and Papa forced us to run – sacrificing themselves so we can survive. Rafael, so strong and handsome, has left everything he's known – his family, his life, his identity as a *limpieza de sangre* – for us. He carries the top circle of the iron key to the heart of our home, his fate entwined with ours. Like braids, carefully twisted around each other, we're inseparable.

"Let's go," I move forward into the tunnel.

I've been in this dark, twisting hideaway many times with Mama and Papa. Every holiday, every celebration of our true *selves* began in this secret tunnel. We would follow the walls, trying not to think of the bats and vermin that live underground. The air is cold and damp, filled with the musty odor of age and secrets. There's a fork not far ahead.

"Go right," Papa directed years ago, "and you'll find our hidden communal room where we store our sacred books, garments, and precious Jewish treasures. Go left and it means you're being pursued – it leads to a door outside, away from the streets in town. You'll find safety and time, if you need to escape."

Escape?

I thought he was silly and dramatic. We would never need an escape – we were the perfect *Conversos*, attending church every Sunday, seen working every Saturday, and never far from a crucifix or rosary. We had a cousin who was a priest and papers that attested to our family's four generations as *Cristianos Nuevos* – New Christians - Jews who had embraced the faith of Jesus Christ. We would live forever in Spain; no one would know our secrets.

I caught my breath, lost in the memory.

That's all over now.

We're on the run. *Forever* is over, an idea shattered in time, our future scattered in the purple flowers Mama loved. For the first time, we will turn left in the tunnel.

Perhaps Papa knew that some day it would come to this?

Peering through the flickering light, I realize that when we emerge outside we'll no longer be *Conversos,* but Jews, fleeing Spain forever, under the *Edict of Expulsion.*

"The Jews will take care of you," Mama had whispered.

The only Jews I knew were the *Conversos* who shared the underground communal prayer room and Blanca, the baker's wife who sometimes brought bread to our home. We stayed away from the *Judería*, where the Jews lived, afraid that neighbors or servants might see us and report to the Inquisitors. We were so careful.

What went wrong?

As we move further down the tunnel, I strain to hear sounds from my home. Where's Mama's soothing voice – Papa's protective words? There's silence. I can't even hear the banging on the front door, the soldiers' voices, cries . . .

I shake my head. Now I'm the mama and the papa – Catalina and Zara are my responsibility. Oddly, strange words bubble to my lips.

"Say this," Mama told me many years ago, "when you're afraid. God will help you."

Now they emerge like a whisper in the candlelight.

Shema Yisrael Adonai Elohaenu Adonai Echad

The words give me strength, although I'm not exactly sure what they mean. "We're going to make it," I say softly to myself. "We have to."

I think of the days of my childhood, with Mama and Papa always there. I think of my sisters and my friends and my relatives. I think of all the people and places I will never see again.

How did this happen?

It must have been the meat. Mama loved her meat, the fat cut away, salted, soaked, and put in a pot with onions, garlic, chickpeas, cabbage, and sweet water. It was her secret *Shabbat feast*. She loved to cook it, and tell us stories about the soulful animals whose flesh gave us life. She would speak of purple flowers and strong bodies; families that held together over thousands of years; and about how we all protected, within us, the heart of our family and home.

I would tire quickly from the stories and words. Sometimes, my mind would wander to other things and people. I thought I never listened.

Now, I remember each word, her eyes shining, and her face proud. I remember her staring at us with a mother's love, something I never recognized until this moment. I would do anything to sit and listen to her stories now! To change time and go back to yesterday, when everything seemed so safe and our lives ensconced in our home and town.

What did we do so wrong?

Horrendous grief wells up inside me. Where were Mama and Papa going? What was *their* future?

They have no future.

Mama and Papa will face the Holy Office, be interrogated, and then tortured.

Tortured.

I recall the stories I heard about the devastating torture tools of the Inquisition – the *strappado* where they drop you from the ceiling; the water boarding where they pour water down your throat until you choke; *el potro*, the rack, thumbscrews to crush fingers and toes . . . there are so many ways. I think about the prisoners as they were dragged to their *auto de fé* – flogged, burned, branded, tongues cut off, limbs hanging uselessly . . .

My body fills with nausea, my legs weaken, my heart pounds wildly.

That is Mama and Papa's future.

Hot, angry tears pour from my eyes and I stumble in the faint light.

Could something have been done differently?

Crazed thoughts spring through my mind – can I do something, can I change something, can I free Mama and Papa? I stop. Maybe we should return, maybe we should make things right, maybe . . .

"What's wrong?" Catalina asks.

"Why are we stopping?" Zara whispers.

Rafael understands. He circles my sisters and reaches for me. He pulls me into his arms. "There'll be time later to think," he whispers in my ear. "You have to move forward now. You have to save your sisters. Only you know the way."

His voice trembles. For a moment, I swoon in his arms. The darkness crashes in on me. I close my eyes and I'm in a different place, where none of this is happening. Purple flowers fill my vision . . .

89

"Stop," Rafael shakes me. "You have to be strong."

I open my eyes and his face is inches from mine.

Rafael is right. I must be strong.

He senses the shift and releases me. "Forward," he says softly. He moves away, taking his place behind Catalina and Zara.

I take a deep breath. I find a clear voice and face my sisters. "Everything is fine," I say, and raise the candle higher. "We're almost there."

I tuck the thoughts away and move forward.

I focus on the dark tunnel and the flickering light from the candle. I can almost hear the voices of people who went before us, soft words spoken only in secret, robes whooshing through the darkness, spirits guiding us from their perch in the past. Are they leading us to safety?

"Are we there?" Catalina whispers. "I'm so tired."

"Do you want to lean on me?"

"Can I?"

"Yes," I take her arm.

Catalina is so fragile. She was born sickly and never had much strength. Zara and I would play while Catalina watched. Her long, slim fingers created beautiful drawings that we all loved. Will Catalina survive our journey? I think of the time she was so sick. We believed she would die. Then Rafael came, with his *vihuela* and magical voice . . .

Don't think, just keep moving.

Everything I knew, everything I lived, is yesterday. The past is dead for us now. Our future is unknown. Time weaves a spell in my head; I grow dizzy with images of clouds, purple flowers, and bowls of beef stew. Instinctively, Rafael reaches out and steadies my shoulder.

"Be brave," he whispers hollowly.

I continue, the minutes stretch endlessly. Suddenly, I reach out in the darkness and touch cold, stone wall. We're at the fork.

Right to our old life; left to our future.

I pause. Everyone waits silently.

Nothing will ever be the same.

I turn to Catalina, Zara, and Rafael. "We're headed for the unknown," I whisper, "it will be very dangerous."

"There's no choice," Rafael adds, "it's the only way to move forward."

"I want Mama," Zara cries.

"Mama," I say quietly, the words catching in my throat. "Mama and Papa have given their lives for us . . . so we can survive. If we love them, we'll follow their last wishes."

"They're not dead yet!" Zara says angrily.

"No," I touch her cheek, "they're not dead . . . yet."

Soon. Conversos don't survive the Holy Inquisition.

I take a deep breath. "We have each other — we're all in this together."

"We're all in this together," Rafael echoes me.

"Let's go," Catalina adds.

Zara is silent.

I grab the part of the key that hangs around my neck. I take a deep breath. The most important decision of my life, up to this point, is upon me.

I take the left fork that leads out of the only home I have ever known.

The tunnel ends at a flight of dark, worn steps.

"We're here," I whisper.

It feels as if my voice echoes in time, capturing ancient footsteps that led to now forgotten destinations. Sounds fill my ears — a soft, whoosh from the robes of people who came before me, moving to fulfill their destinies.

I shiver.

"Let me check it out," Rafael breaks my thoughts. He pushes ahead of us. He takes the candle from me and slowly climbs the steps. We plunge into darkness. My heart pounds crazily.

What if the Inquisitors are waiting for us at the end of the tunnel?

What if I've led us into a trap that ends in prison and torture?

I grab Catalina's and Zara's hands, squeezing tightly. The only way the inquisitors would know is through Mama and Papa. They would never reveal our secret.

I shake my head, trying to dislodge the questions. Every step we take is a risk; we face only danger, not safety.

I'll never feel safe again.

Rafael struggles with the door on the top of the steps. I hold my breath. I can hear him breathing hard – I don't know the last time the door has been touched. We've always headed in the other direction.

A breeze of fresh air washes across my face. The door is open.

"It's okay," Rafael calls down to us.

Catalina, Zara, and I clamber up the steps. Rafael waits for us. It's a beautiful night; there's a full moon that casts a glow over the countryside. A dirt trail winds away from the door. It hasn't been used for a long time – the trail is filled with weeds and stones.

"I know this trail," Rafael says. "I used to play here when I was little. It weaves through the trees into the forest, up a hill, and ends on the main road out of town. They'll be a lot of Jews on the main road, headed for Portugal or the ships. They don't have much time to leave Spain before the soldiers will kill those who haven't been baptized."

I stare at the trail. "Papa had this all planned?"

Rafael nods. "He was a great man."

I notice he uses the word *was*. I don't say anything.

"I want to go back," Zara whimpers.

We ignore her.

"I think we should spend the night here," I suggest.

"No," Rafael says. "Let's keep on going. The full moon will give us enough light. We'll make it to the main road and then mingle with the exiles. Hopefully, no one will notice."

"I'm so tired," Catalina mumbles aloud.

Catalina. Is she strong enough to make this trip?

We push forward, Rafael now in the lead. Catalina and Zara follow him; I take the rear. The trail is slow but the full moon lights our way. The fresh air boosts my spirits – maybe we can pull this off? Maybe we can reach a safe place where there aren't Inquisitors?

Maybe.

The dirt is rough and uneven beneath our feet. We walk watchfully, careful not to trip. It takes an hour before we approach the trees. The air is very cold; I shiver in my thin summer clothes. The sun, that makes the day so hot, is gone, leaving a chill in the air. I'm strong, I can handle the cold. Catalina? How will she make it through the frigid air, dark trees, and unknown? I shiver again, but not from the cold. Am I seeing the future? My throat thickens with tears. How can everything have changed so quickly? I began the day as a child and end it as an orphan, exiled from my parents and home.

What went wrong?

We enter the forest and the air gets colder. All of us are shivering now. I touch Catalina's hands. Her fingers feel like ice.

"We can do it!" I hiss.

No one responds.

The trees grow thicker as we follow Rafael. I search for the moon, but its light barely penetrates the forest canopy. Rafael holds the candle as we stumble over rocks, dead branches, and other forest stuff. The sounds send chills down my spine – night birds cooing, strange animals scurrying, leaves and branches toppled by invisible creatures. I've heard stories all my life about the *banditos* that roam the forests and attack innocent people – sometimes beating and killing them. I recall Mama's story about how she fell in love with Papa. He followed her, in secret, outside of town, to the patch of purple flowers to protect her from *banditos*. The same *banditos* that may haunt the forest tonight, lurking behind trees, lying in wait . . .

I tremble, but this time it's not from the cold. There's a bitter taste in my mouth – a raw fear of the forest that shrouds us like a heavy woolen cloak.

What next, Mama?

"I'm scared," Zara sobs.

I stop and bend down in front of her. It's so dark, I can barely see her face; she's so little. I hug her gently. "It'll be ok," I whisper in her ear. "Be brave."

"Don't stop," Rafael demands sharply. "It's not safe."

Banditos.

93

I shake my head, stand up, and nudge Zara forward.

I don't know how long we're in the forest. Zara is silent. Catalina's breathing is raspy; she struggles without complaint. Rafael is determined to keep us going until we reach the road. Gradually, light begins to seep through the trees.

"We're almost there," Rafael says. "We'll rest at the edge of the road."

The sun is peeking through the clouds, lighting up the forest, when we finally reach the last hill. Zara stumbles from fatigue; Catalina wheezes; I fight to hold my questions and fear in control.

"Please stop," I beg Rafael.

"No," he says. "It's not safe."

Rafael forces us to continue, dragging us up the hill. We struggle to reach the top. Catalina is weaker, her breathing more ragged and her face pale. She looks so beautiful and fragile in the fingers of early morning light

"Are you ok?" I ask her.

She nods. It's too difficult for her to speak.

"Rafael," I cry, "we *have* to stop."

He points to three boulders, surrounded by trees, at the bottom of the hill. "It's on the edge of the road," he explains. "We'll see them before they see us."

"Who?"

"Whoever is traveling on the road."

It takes a few more minutes to reach the boulders, but it feels like hours. We collapse next to the rocks, quickly overtaken by sleep. I see one thing before my eyes close – Rafael stands guard over us.

When will he sleep?

Ria

Ria took a deep breath and exhaled slowly. It was their Thursday ritual. She left work at 4:32, after starting an hour earlier in the morning. She emerged like a cliff dweller from 70 West, easing through the gray marble entrance and heading toward *PAX,* a few stores down, while ducking the rushing FedEx workers in their purple and black shirts. She ordered her favorite, a chicken *Vera Cruz pessata,* purple *Vitamin Water,* and the best soft chocolate chip cookie in the city. Thus armed, she carefully crossed 40th Street, scooting between white *FedEx* trucks and up the steps to Bryant Park. She made her way to the same table that she secured every Thursday for her friends. Ria paused in front of a small green and white carousel – Bryant Park landmark. She grinned, checking out the peaks, carvings, and old-fashioned pictures of shape-shifting clouds. The brown, gold, grey, and green horses circled by, a plaster reminder of her childhood in New Mexico. She smiled at the green frog, gray rabbit, and red-brown cat, rediscovering them each week. Then she moved on to the promenade that edged the Great Lawn, located the tiny green plastic table, and carefully arranged her food. She gathered chairs for her friends, sat, and waited. Within minutes, everyone would be there with their choices for dinner, settling down to talk, listen to the music drifting over the Great Lawn from *ThursdaysAt5,* and later, a bottle of beer from the delightfully crowded B.P. Café.

Once seated, Ria's large, fawn-like eyes took in everything, from the dark man in the cargo pants and the old couple sitting beneath a green and white umbrella next to a concrete pot of purple flowers on the Upper Library Terrace. She saw the woman with dark, smoldering eyes, alternately staring at her and pounding a laptop. She pieced them together in a visual pattern . . . a landscape of the moment, shimmering in the hot afternoon sun.

Ria stretched her long neck, enjoying the warmth on her olive skin, the reprieve from chilly air conditioning, and the comfort in her sore limbs. She knew that people saw her as beautiful; her willowy body and sensuous smile appealed to anyone who met her. Few understood her fragile side . . . the struggle to breathe, the constant assault of physical illness, and the awesome burden of viewing the world in shades of color, light, and time. She carried secrets that she sensed, but couldn't define - a history without facts, as she drifted aimlessly in the hidden film of her internal visual art. Only music brought her alive . . . words and sounds entwined in a rhythm that made her hearing stronger and her breathing easier.

Slowly, one-by-one, her friends arrived. It was odd that they all worked together, but left different times and picked up different food. All of them were individuals on the edge of the social flow, New York emigrants who found comfort in the ability to blend in on city streets.

Ria loved these New York friends. They were remote, like her; living in screens and code, rather than the light of day. They laughed at jokes that only techies found funny, and ate weird combinations of food and strange gourmet imports. Suddenly, Ria felt *eyes* on her - a sixth sense that was oddly similar to online intimacy. It was an emotional nudge, something not physically concrete, a connection that science had never been able to define. Ria loved those moments because it brought her away from the pain of the concrete here-and-now where her gracefully deceptive body could slip into a deliciously safe virtual coat.

"What are you looking at?" Ethan demanded, a *chicken fajita pressata,* fruit salad, and diet coke in his hands.

Ethan doesn't miss a thing.

"Nothing," Ria shrugged. "I'm just checking out the park."

Ethan eyed her suspiciously. Ria toyed with her necklace, an L-shaped pendant formed from an odd sliver of iron, slightly rusted and worn smooth by time. It wasn't particularly pretty, but everyone who knew Ria admired her "lucky" pendant as if it were a crucifix. It hung from a southwestern leather thong that her mother made after Ria purchased the pendant in a local flea market. Mama never understood why Ria was drawn to the chunk of iron.

"It's magical," Ria laughed, half-believing her explanation.

Ria laughed. "C'mon Ethan, don't be so jumpy."

"I worry," he mumbled as Madison arrived at the table. His cheeks burned red and he descended into silence. Madison balanced a colorful chopped green salad, sprinkled with chick peas, red cabbage, and packed in a clear container, a huge bottle of water, and an elegantly packaged bar of chocolate.

"Not again," Madison shook her head. They all knew that Ethan was an odd mix - a gay man obsessed with a woman, the self-declared guard of the lovely, fragile, olive- skinned Ria. "Can't you leave her alone?" Madison had grown up in Montana sky country, her social skills honed by cattle.

Madison's arrival gave Ria the opportunity to track down the eyes focused on her. Ria was always amazed how one could *feel* a stare, and had discovered, after many tries, that it was easy to find the culprit. It was no different now . . . the same woman, with dark, smoldering eyes at the edge of the Outdoor Reading Room, was staring. Ria had a sudden feeling of *déjà vu* - this happened before. The woman tried to look away, but Ria persisted, studying the stooped shoulders and dark, curly hair. Their eyes met over the Great Lawn that separated them.

Ria froze. She felt chills in the summer heat. There was something familiar about the smoldering eyes and the determined mouth that refused to smile . . . *more* than *déjà vu*.

But I've never seen her before.

Yet the woman triggered . . . something.

Was there danger on the north side of the park? Was the woman going to suddenly pull out a shiny silver revolver from beneath her laptop, aim carefully, and shoot everyone? Ria tried to shake the images from her mind. She was always so afraid of getting sick or hurt; carrying her fears like a shroud wherever she went. She never spoke about it, but somehow everyone *knew*. People like Ethan appointed themselves her protector, making her feel safe and vulnerable at the same time.

A shiver of apprehension trickled through her - maybe she was getting sick? Ria was a target for pervasive viruses, bacteria, wheezing, stomach problems, and daily assaults on her fragile health.

A doctor once told her, using an old medical school cliché, that she always got sick because she was born with *bad protoplasm*. She laughed at the time, but the term stayed with her. *Bad protoplasm* – someone that gets sick all the time. Did the woman with the smoldering eyes *sense* bad protoplasm?

She tried to take a deep breath, suddenly aware of the pain that was forming in her back, an ominous threat of impending asthma.

Ria shook her head. It was all painfully cliché – too many television medical mysteries and crime dramas. It didn't take long before the screen leached into daily life, confusing reality with bad screenplays.

What else do sick people do?

Ria shook her head angrily. She refused to think of herself as a chunk of bad protoplasm. She refused to think about the bottles of vitamins that peopled her life like bad accessories; the mineral potions that accompanied every meal; the grainy health food that left her palate dull and uninspired; and the fistful of meds she was forced to swallow each morning.

Ria shifted her thoughts to a phenomenon that she and her friends had discussed many times. Fortunately, her mind was more resilient than her body.

"Yo," Hawk shouted. He dumped his hamburger and fries on the table, sipping a chocolate thick shake. Hawk was painfully thin; he arrived in New York straight from Jefferson County, Colorado, a graduate of the post-Columbine High School massacre scene. He was younger than the others.

"Hawk," Madison and Ethan greeted him. Ria said nothing.

"I see you have your usual health food," Ethan mumbled, poking at the hamburger.

Hawk laughed.

Hawk had told them that studies proved the human mind was programmed to interpret visuals in a very simple way: *if it looks human it must be human.* In the jungles of prehistory, it was a concept critical to adaptation. Humans survived by understanding immediately that a tiger was a tiger and not human; a human appeared to be exactly what she was. It didn't get complicated until reality went virtual. The human mind interpreted the digitized bits of information on screens as human.

If it looks human it must be human.

The stories, people, crimes, and activities viewed on television screens, movie screens, and computer screens were programmed to be experienced as real. The crossover was swift and subconscious. Television friends mingled with real friends; virtual buddies replaced drinking buddies; the mind had great difficulty distinguishing between concrete and virtual reality, and the past, present, and future. Time emerged as a fluid concept; yesterday easily coexisted with today and tomorrow.

Bad protoplasm didn't exist in that environment.

"Stop thinking so hard," Jaime poked her arm. He had grown up in an obscure evangelical sect in Texas. As soon as he was able, Jaime fled to New York. Now he dumped his dinner on the table for all to share . . . a bag of soggy salt 'n vinegar potato chips, a styrofoam container filled with greasy chicken tenders, three chocolate sticks, and a two-liter bottle of *Dr. Pepper* that he swigged like beer.

Ria sighed. Virtual reality was a better home for people like her. In real life, she had been born weak. Sickness and disease were her companions. In virtual reality, she could run, dance, and play without hurting or getting hurt. She could be as strong as the others. She could live *forever*. There were very few obstacles on the screen.

Like the woman staring at me.

Ria summed it up scientifically in her mind's eye. There was this woman, with dark eyes and depressed stature staring at her from across the Great Lawn. She seemed vaguely familiar, but how many depressed people with dark eyes filled Ria's life? *Everyone* in New York was depressed, anxious, manic, or narcissistic . . . usually armed with a therapist and meds.

"What are you looking at?" Ethan demanded.

Ria backspaced to her friends. All of them came from different states where their hi-tech imaginations made them pariahs in the heartland. Together, as a web design team, they catered to a mass market in which none of them actually participated. They were runaways, escaping lives that were too concrete and exacting, scaling digital fences that straddled the virtual and the real. It was comfortable for them as long as they had each other, in the office and on the street. They fled social indictments as they shared exotic chocolate, rare sushi, Belgium Peach Beer, and lots of cheap junk food.

"Guess what," Madison whispered conspiratorially, as if she had heard Ria's thoughts. "I found a new chocolate."

Ethan sniffed, Hawk grinned, and Jaime shook his head.

"It's good stuff," Madison insisted.

It was ironic that this group found each other. Ria had grown up in a small town in the Mora Valley, between Taos and Santa Fé, in New Mexico. She was a *Hispano*, originally descended from Spaniards and Mexicans, living in a territory annexed by the United States. She was raised a devout Catholic, but always felt an outsider, as if something was different about her. One time she came home from school and told her *abuelo* that she believed she was a *Mestizo*, part Native American Indian, because she didn't fit in with the *Hispanos* at school. In those days it was popular to claim Indian roots; there was a romance about being born from the spirits.

"No!" The old man shouted his dark eyes fiery. "We're *Hispanos*," he grabbed her shoulders and held her stiffly in his old hands. "Never forget that."

"Let's face it," Hawk said slowly, "your fancy chocolate doesn't hold a chance against a handful of peanut *M&Ms*."

Madison frowned. "You're too young to have any taste."

The five of them – Ria, Ethan, Madison, Hawk and Jaime – made up the web design team for a company in 70 West, located in one of the buildings that hovered over Bryant Park.

"I," Ethan said stiffly, "am a chocolate gourmet. Most of Madison's finds are much better than *M&Ms*."

Hawk shook his head and smiled.

Ria grinned. She *loved* the gourmet chocolate in New York. She loved the clever marketing people that transformed dark chocolate into a health food. Most of all, she loved sharing chocolate finds with her friends.

"Look," Madison said, taking the elegantly packaged chocolate bar from the top of her salad container.

The five friends sat around the tiny green table and bent over to see. The chocolate was in a large, box-like brown wrapper. The top read *Cacao Reserve by Hershey's.* In a beige frame was a child-like drawing of an island, a red thatched hut on the water, palm trees, a sail boat, and white puffy clouds.

Ria read the name out loud, "São Tomé."

Something deep inside her stirred; the name touched a secreted nerve that made her heart beat faster.

"*A small island off the western coast of Africa,*" Madison read, "*São Tomé is also known as the Chocolate Island. This unique single origin chocolate made from São Tomé forastero cacao has a strong and well-balanced bitter and sweet chocolate profile. Underlying aromatic coffee tones and warm spice notes at the front of the palate call through the well-rounded long chocolate finish. Bold and satisfying, smooth and rich.*"

"It's *bad,*" Ria muttered.

"What?" Madison asked.

All eyes shifted to Ria. Instead of her usually cheerful face and smiling eyes, Ria's face was dark, smoldering like the woman on the north side of the park.

"How can chocolate be bad?" Ethan asked, grinning crookedly.

"Not the chocolate," Ria spoke slowly, "the place."

"What place?" Hawk demanded.

"São Tomé."

"I never heard of São Tomé," Hawk responded. "Have any of you?"

Everyone was silent, curious about Ria's reaction.

"What is São Tomé?" Madison asked.

They waited for Ria's response.

Ria mined her brain, scanned her mental files, searched for some clue to connect her discomfort with São Tomé and conscious data. There was nothing.

"I don't know," she said finally. "I just don't like it."

"Be cool," Madison laughed. "This chocolate cost me seven bucks." She unwrapped the bar and broke it into five pieces. Everyone took a piece.

"Mmmmmm," Ethan said, "dark and bitter."

"Strange," Madison added. "It's a bit sour."

"That's the cacao," Jaime noted. "It's 70%."

"There's a hint of coffee," Hawk laughed, reading the front of the package.

Ria turned her back to the team. She nibbled on her chocolate and it burned her tongue, sending her into a dizzying spiral. She grabbed her lucky pendant and blinked to regain her balance. She was staring into the eyes of a black woman lying on the Great Lawn, only a few hundred feet away.

Ria was mesmerized. Why was the black woman staring at her? She was in her mid to late twenties, cocoa-colored skin, fawn-like eyes, tall, willowy build, and body language that cried out to *stay away*.

An African version of myself.

This is turning out to be a very strange day, Ria thought.

"Do you like it?" Madison asked.

Ria shifted her gaze to an old couple, sitting beneath a green and white umbrella, next to a concrete pot of purple flowers, holding hands and *watching,* their silver hair shimmering in the summer sun. There was something about them that was comforting.

"Ria?" Ethan said. "Are you okay?"

She didn't hear him.

Marianna

Trees cry for rain. Purple flowers shudder in the wind. The sky fills with thin clouds that shape-shift as they pass overhead. A bird cloud suddenly transforms into a handsome trovador; a child cloud drifts into a crouching man. Suddenly there's a dull thud; a large cow with dark, soulful eyes faces me. I've seen this creature before; she's visited my dreams many times. She wears a broken iron key on a leather thong around her neck. I reach out to touch the key and the metal burns my fingers, the sky turns black, and the clouds scatter in terror.

I scream, but no sound is heard.

My eyes fly open, my heart pounds, and a clammy sweat covers my entire body. For a moment, I have no idea where we are. Then I see Catalina and Zara, sleeping against the rock; Rafael guards us, his eyes fixed on the road.

I struggle to stand up. Rafael turns to me, a finger over his lips. I follow his gaze – there are people coming down the road. I peer around the rock. It's the most remarkable sight I've ever seen.

Hundreds, maybe thousands of people pass before me.

Rich people, dressed in the fine clothes made from the costliest fabrics that only merchants and traders can afford, lead the way on large, spirited horses. They're followed by a sea of old, creaky carts with wooden wheels, piled high with household possessions. Straining donkeys pull the carts. Men cajole the donkeys, urging them to move forward. Some try to whip the animals to keep them in motion, but it's clear that these people have no stomach for hurting animals. They snap the whip over the donkey's head then coax him with their voices.

Small children and old people are wedged between piles of stuff in the carts, moving back and forth with the motion, steadying possessions so they don't topple when they go over the ruts and rocks in the dirt road. Everyone else walks – children, young men, mothers carrying babies, men and women hunched over with huge packs on their backs. Some struggle to maintain their balance, staggering along with the flow of humanity. Many men, dressed in black, are walking and reading prayers, their lips moving rapidly in Hebrew. Most speak

Ladino. Older children play games as they walk, leaping like cats around the adults, finding small rocks and dried branches to use as toys.

Suddenly a group of monks appear, shouting "repent, repent, it's your last chance to be saved by God." They wave thick, heavy crucifixes and plunge into the people on the road.

One man on foot, clearly the leader, turns to the people. "Sing," he cries, "sing unto the Lord for His everlasting grace! Show them that we're the proud and strong Children of Israel!"

The people burst into song – their voices rise in the early morning air in a sweet, haunting melody that is both familiar and strange. Young men and women dance, playing *timbrels* or small drums, tambourines, and clapping their hands. Children scamper to the rhythms. Even the animals pull harder. Everyone joins in the wildly infective music.

The voices of the monks are drowned out in the music and singing.

I watch in awe.

"The Jews," Rafael says with admiration. "They leave Spain proudly, and with joy."

"You've seen this before?"

"Yes," he admits, "this has been going on since a few weeks after the Alhambra Decree - *Edict of Expulsion* - was posted. The king and queen have stolen their homes, thrown them from their lands, taken their money, but have not been able to steal their spirits."

I watch the Jews and for the first time in my life, feel embarrassed that my family has hidden our identity for four generations. I remind myself that it had to be done – I would not be here if my great-grandparents hadn't accepted baptism and saved their children's lives.

"Don't think badly about your family," Rafael says, reading my thoughts. "They did what was necessary to survive. In many ways, it was harder to live as *Conversos* – torn between the secrets of the soul and the reality of daily life. What's most important is that they preserved your identity, under threat of death."

I think about his words. Our identity preserved? Mama and Papa will die in the dungeons of the Inquisition; our family is wrenched apart. Was it worth the price?

Mama and Papa – where are you now?

"You sound envious," my voice shakes, as I struggle to erase the questions.

Rafael shrugs. "My people have good hearts, but their spirits have been fouled by the Inquisition. Once, we all lived here together – the Jews, Christians, and Moslems. Now," he sighs, "they've ruined our harmony. We'll be weaker over time."

I stare at him in surprise. Rafael has never really said things like that before. His voice is far more serious than his songs or stories ever suggested. I want to ask him why he's given everything up for us. He answers before I have the chance to say anything.

"Like every Christian Spaniard," Rafael continues, "there's Jewish blood in me, too. It's the spirit and history of that blood that dominates me now."

"I don't understand."

"Nor do I," Rafael lies. Darkness fills his eyes. "Something has drawn me to . . . you and your family. Your Mama and Papa have entrusted me with the most valuable thing in their lives. I will honor that trust."

I stare at him quizzically.

Rafael shrugs. "We don't always do the most practical . . . or reasonable thing." He tapped his chest. "Sometimes, we follow our hearts and where they bring us. Sometimes we sacrifice ourselves for sins committed in our names."

Our eyes meet, frozen in time.

"You sinned?" I ask.

It's barely an instant. But I see it. A wave of pain contorts his face then quickly disappears, glazed over by the present.

Zara tugs at my arm. "What's that?" she asks sleepily, pointing at the people on the road.

"The Jews," I respond. "We'll be joining them soon."

Rafael says nothing.

Catalina stirs from sleep. The four of us wait for the Jews to pass.

"We don't want them to know we're *Conversos,*" I whisper.

We all agree.

The Jews are angry at *Conversos;* they see us as defectors, abandoning the faith, turning our backs on the Laws of Moses. Most believe in the sanctity of the soul and the importance of honoring our God. In that way, the Jews are not very different from the Christians. However, the Jews expect only their *own kind* to follow the law; the Christians demand and kill those who don't comply. *Conversos* live a dual faith; we pander to Christianity while secreting our Jewish souls. No wonder the openly practicing Jews, who have been beaten, massacred, and expelled from their homes, don't like us.

Papa once told me that Jews were called *the chosen people* not because they were given money, fine clothes, and great abilities. Rather, Jews were chosen to take on the burdens of humankind, to bear the very best, the very worst, and everything in-between; to face life with the strength of their faith and the determination of thousands of years of thought, law, and belief in the Jewish soul. Being "chosen" was a responsibility, not a luxury.

I think about Papa's words as I watch the Jews make their way down the road. Now we're like them, destined to leave Spain. Four generations of secrets end on a dusty road that leads away from home - the only place I've ever known.

It takes about an hour before we can no longer hear the Jews' music. The last stragglers have drifted down the road. We slip from behind the rocks and walk, moving slowly to keep pace with Catalina, who struggles with every step. Her breathing is raspy, and I know she's sick again. We have no medicine for her, no doctor to help us, not even a bowl of warm soup.

"Where are we going?" I ask Rafael.

"We have to choose," he replies softly. "We can go to the boats. They'll take us out of Spain to places like Naples, Greece, Morocco, and Turkey. We can head to the border, pay the tax, and enter Portugal. I heard that the Portuguese are welcoming the Jews."

"We have no food or clothing," I shrug.

"When we get to the next town," Rafael says, "we can use our money to buy a cart and a donkey so Catalina doesn't have to walk.

Everyone will assume we're just another family of Jewish exiles."

I glance at Catalina. "That sounds good."

"Or," he continues. "We can walk to the boats, find one to take us on, and use the money to buy passage. Either way, we can't bring any gold *with* us. The king has forbidden it."

"Let's go to Portugal."

Mama and Papa would want us there.

I lower my voice. "I don't think Catalina can survive a sea voyage."

Rafael nods. "We'll buy a cart as soon as we reach the next town. We can make our final decision when we're further down the road."

The hours pass slowly as we walk the dusty road. Suddenly Rafael stops. He tilts his head, listening.

"There," he points and heads down a trail that is barely a footstep wide. It's not long before we come face-to-face with a peasant, leading two donkeys and an empty, broken-down wood cart. Rafael waves at me to stand back with Catalina and Zara. He approaches the peasant and talks quickly, his hands waving. Rafael knows how to bargain. In a few minutes the peasant smiles, accepts the coins that Rafael places in his dirty palm, and walks off with one donkey and the old cart.

Rafael grins like a little boy. "Our donkey's name is Juan."

Juan is skinny with sad eyes and a sway back, but I love him instantly. He comes with a broken down cart, straw, a lot of dirt, a filthy, coarse blanket, and a basket with stale bread and cheese. The large wheels on the cart sputter and creak like an old man.

Rafael pulls me aside as Zara and Catalina pet Juan.

"I used your papa's money to buy Juan and the cart. The peasant knew we were desperate and charged a crazy price. He knew we would pay whatever he asked."

I nod.

"Here," Rafael hands me Papa's empty leather pouch. "It belongs to you. I have just enough coins to buy our way out of Spain."

I stare at the worn leather pouch that Rafael lays gently in my hand. It smells like Papa – a tiny piece of home. "Thank you," I whisper, and slip it into one of the hidden pockets in my dress. "Let's go."

107

Juan is old and tired, so we only let Catalina ride in the cart as he pulls it. The three of us walk. Zara takes a liking to the donkey, stroking his soft muzzle and talking to him as we return to the main road. The road grows very quiet as dark begins to settle over the land. We find a thick cluster of trees and hide behind them. Rafael builds a small fire for warmth, and I prepare a tiny dinner from the stale bread and cheese.

Catalina lies on the ground, covered by the coarse blanket. Her breathing is worse; she's getting sicker. Zara sits next to her, holding her hand and telling stories.

She'll be better tomorrow. She has to . . .

I hand everyone food, but Catalina shakes her head.

"You have to eat," I insist.

She nibbles on a bit of bread.

"More!"

"No," she whispers.

Rafael and I look at each other. "Stay here with Catalina," I say to Zara. "We're going to get more wood for the fire. We won't be far."

Zara nods, but doesn't reply. I can see the fear in her eyes as she huddles against Catalina.

Rafael and I walk far enough away so they can't hear us, but close enough to see them.

We stare at each other in the dimming light.

"She's getting worse," I say finally.

Rafael nods.

"What can we *do*?"

He shrugs. "No one will help exiled Jews," he explains. "They risk being discovered and sent to the Inquisition. Everyone is afraid."

"We need a doctor."

"We need a *Jewish* doctor," he corrects me. "But all the Jews are on the move; the *Juderías* are empty."

"What about a *Converso* doctor?"

Rafael laughs bitterly. "It's even more dangerous for them to help the Jews . . . if you can find them."

My heart pounds in fear. "What are we going to do?"

He has no answer.

After several minutes of silence, Rafael speaks in an unbearably gentle voice. "Let's think this through. It's a long, hard road to Portugal. King João has agreed to let six hundred families into the country – with a tax of one hundred *cruzados* per family and one-fourth of all the possessions they carry. He's said that he'll deliver ships to all those Jews who don't want to stay there – allowing them to go wherever they want. He's allowing them to stay in his country for eight months."

"Can we trust the king?"

Rafael shrugs. "If the Jews can't trust Ferdinand and Isabella, in lands they've lived in for almost 1000 years, who can they trust?"

I look at him thoughtfully. "You're not Jewish," I say.

"I know," Rafael mumbles. "You can enter as a Christian . . . my wife . . . if they believe you. I don't have any papers with me and . . ."

"I don't want to hide anymore," I say firmly. "I'm tired of being a *Converso* . . . I don't think that's what Mama and Papa ultimately wanted for us."

Rafael nods. "You can try the ships. They're closer, and Catalina will have to do less traveling."

"You think that's what we should do?"

"I'm not sure . . . I've heard stories."

"Stories?"

"I've heard that the ships are overcrowded, the captains are cruel, and the seas full of pirates. Women and children are raped and families wrenched apart. If the pirates capture you, they make slaves of all the healthy people, whores of the women, and throw the rest overboard."

I shudder.

"Some of the places are very good to the Jews. The people in Naples are very kind, the King of Turkey welcomes them, as does Ferrara, Romagna, Rome, and North Africa."

"If the ships reach their destination," I add.

Rafael rubs his forehead with his thumb and forefinger.

Mama. Papa. Where do we go?

"It's said," Rafael continues gently, "that there are *hundreds of thousands* of Jews trying to leave."

"Who wants hundreds of thousands of people who have lost all their possessions and money?"

Can Catalina make it?

Can any of us?

I cry out and Rafael catches me in his arms. His body is hard against mine; he holds me in a powerful embrace.

What is he doing?

Rafael has been like a brother to me and my sisters. This is different. Here, in the midst of so much danger, I feel safe. My heart races, but not out of fear. He kisses my neck and my body tingles with his touch.

I pull back from him. His face is only inches from mine. We stare into one another's eyes, lost in a visual embrace.

Rafael touches my cheek with his fingertips and kisses me on my lips.

What am I doing?

I kiss him back, forgetting for the moment that we're acting the role of exiled Jews, escaping the Inquisitors, and desperately searching for a way to stay alive.

I kiss him harder and my body stirs, flooded with warm, incredible sensations . . .

"Marianna!" Zara cries. "Help."

Rafael and I break apart.

"Zara," I whisper, touching his lips with my fingertips.

We run back to our campsite.

Zara's small face is filled with fear. "Cat . . . a . . . lina," she stutters. "She's *hot*."

I kneel down and feel Catalina's skin. "She has the fever," my voice shakes. "Cover her!"

We tuck Catalina tightly in the coarse, dirty blanket until she looks like a swaddled baby. Her eyes are half-closed and her body trembles.

Rafael and I look at each other. Zara crawls next to Catalina, and wraps her small body around my sister. I lie down next to Zara and Rafael stretches out on the other side of Catalina. His long arms circle all of us until we're in a tight huddle. Our bodies shield her against the cool night air.

For a moment, I catch Rafael's eyes in the flickering firelight. We speak without words.

There's nothing we can do now but wait.

Ria

Ria assembled the pieces in her mind. She was used to taking parts and forming them into a whole; it was part of web design to select elements and electronically fuse them into a page. Ria knew the dangers of overthinking a composition . . . too much conceptualizing could destroy the final effect.

She was fairly sure that wasn't happening now.

"Are you okay?" Ethan asked again.

Ria looked at her friends. They were *all* watching her with strange expressions.

"I'm okay," she smiled.

No one believed her.

Ria knew that there were pieces, like lines of code, which belonged together in some unknown order. She wasn't sure of the exact nature of the order; she simply knew it existed. Her background was Bryant Park, her design a summer day with a hot Castilian sun. The elements were placing themselves in the design, moving in a barely perceptible rhythm that would ultimately - perhaps timelessly - bind them together. She searched for the pieces playing out before her eyes. It was more of a process of elimination; selecting chunks of code that belonged in her composition. She touched her lucky necklace for confirmation. It was hot; it burned her fingers.

She was on to something.

"Why don't you like the chocolate?" Madison asked.

The chocolate.

"Are you allergic to the chocolate or something?" Hawk asked, smiling.

His voice sounded like it was very far away. Chocolate always reminded her of *Navidad* at home. Good food, family, lighting the nine candles, one each day, until December 25. She remembered playing *pon y saca* with her cousins, a gambling game that used a spinning top to determine whether you "put in or took out" from the pot. She recalled going to midnight mass and listening to the priest rail about the Christ Killers, or Jews, wondering what these evil murderers looked like, enthralled with the haunting prayers, incense, and shimmering beauty of the church.

Yet there was always something slightly wrong - a hidden line of code that surreptitiously influenced the entire program.

Like this chocolate.

"Try some more chocolate," Madison suggested.

"She hates it," Ethan mumbled.

"I'm not so crazy about it either," Jaime said.

The black woman on the Great Lawn sat up.

Ria shook her head and took another bite of chocolate.

It tasted of mold and hard-to-breathe humid air. It tasted of bad people, angry and unrelenting, hurting children . . .

Ria shook her head as her friends talked around her, wondering about her reaction to Madison's chocolate.

Chunks of data jumped out at her, as if highlighted by an invisible cursor. She went from the woman with the smoldering eyes, the dark man in cargo pants, and the old couple, beneath the green and white umbrella next to the concrete pot filled with purple flowers on the Upper Library Terrace.

Once again, her gaze settled on the black woman sitting on the Great Lawn. Once again, Ria felt that she was an African version of herself. They were all parts to a whole that eluded her; elements in a design yet to be completed. Ria wanted to call out - tell them that they're all connected, and it was a good thing - but it was New York, and people didn't behave that way.

It will happen.

Ethan said something and Ria ignored him. There was conversation around her, but she slipped away, drifting from her friends, dragged toward the crowd gathering for *ThursdaysAt5*.

Maybe it was like baking a *pan de semita* at Easter or leaving tiny pebbles on her *abuelo's* gravestone. She was different, somehow within her knowledge and outside of it. There *had* to be a secret program embedded in the code, a Trojan horse that silently directed the application.

Ria shook her head.

If it looks human, if it sounds human, it must be human.

Music drifted to Ria, the muted sounds of a singer with a guitar, words she could hear but not understand. The crowd was growing around the fountain terrace.

ThursdaysAt5.

"Let's go," she said.

The others looked confused.

"Now?" Madison asked. "We haven't finished . . ."

"Now." Ria said sharply.

The others knew not to argue. They gathered what was left from their dinner. Madison wiped the table clean.

Ria waited for them on the promenade that led to the fountain terrace. She glanced at the black woman on the Great Lawn. The woman was standing up, looking forward, to the fountain terrace.

She's headed that way.

Ethan followed Ria's gaze. "Do you know her?"

"No," Ria said softly, "but I will."

Ethan looked at her quizzically. "I don't understand. She looks like you in a

strange way . . ."

"I don't understand either."

Ria glanced at the woman in the Outdoor Reading Room. She was also headed toward the fountain terrace.

A word popped into Ria's mind.

Convergence.

Ria impulsively turned to look at the Upper Library Terrace. The dark man in cargo pants was still there, not moving. The old couple next to the pot filled with purple flowers was there, too. Watching.

"Convergence," Ria mumbled.

"What?" Ethan asked.

"Nothing," she said to him and the others. "Let's go listen to the music."

Ria took a deep breath. The wheezing was beginning, the dark

114

pain in her back gathering momentum.

Ria moved slowly and methodically, unconsciously simulating the pace of the other woman on the Great Lawn. Her friends followed, leaving a safe distance. Ria *knew* that something would happen on the fountain terrace. She played with her "lucky" necklace, convinced there was a force gathering the pieces in this design.

Out of nowhere, a memory byte emerged.

They laughed. The kids taunted her at school.
"You do such terrible things," one said to her.
Until that moment, when she was nine years old, she thought that everyone refused to eat pork and shellfish; would never use an egg with a blood-spot; and became queasy when meat was served with milk.
"Loco," they shouted at her.
She was mortified. She begged Father Miguel for forgiveness.
"It's nothing, mi hija," the priest said gently. "Just family traditions. You're not committing any sins."
Nonetheless, Ria prayed for months, begging Lord Jesus to forgive her family for their silly ways.

Ria paused. The woman with the backpack paused. A priest in black shirt and pants with the traditional white clerical collar, stared. The woman with the backpack looked frightened. Ria wondered why anyone would be afraid of a priest.

A few tense moments passed. Ria wasn't exactly sure what happened; it felt like a ripple in her vision, as if her eyes were watering from a strong wind. She rubbed her eyes and it was gone.

For a brief moment, the priest looked as if he was wearing ecumenical garb with a draped cowl topped with fur and long, shimmering robes.

The pain in Ria's chest worsened, she began to wheeze. Ria reached into her pocket for her rescue inhaler. Maybe it was the park, or the hot summer day?

Ria was having an asthma attack.

Marianna

I feel the morning before I open my eyes. The sun pierces my closed eyelids and strange colors dance before me. I sit up and look at Catalina. She seems better. Her fever is gone, but her eyes are glassy and weak. We lay her gently in the cart and cover her with the blanket and handfuls of straw. She smiles wanly.

"Zara," I say gently, "why don't you walk with us for a little while and then sit with Catalina in the cart." Rafael nods his approval. The wooden cart is old and rickety, the donkey Juan on his last legs. We're afraid the creature won't make it to Portugal, so we have to lighten his load. Zara is quiet, almost sulky. I know she's scared. She's too young to be separated from Mama. As hard as I try, I can't replace Mama. I'm afraid to look at Rafael.

What happened last night?

Am I in love?

The questions sound like lyrics from a ballad and I'm scared to think about them. My sisters are my responsibility; decisions must be made - I have to concentrate on the moment. Should we head for the ships or Portugal? Do we take a chance against the pirates, angry sea captains, greedy Portuguese soldiers, or unpredictable royalty? What will happen when the money runs out?

Rafael holds onto the donkey pulling the cart. "Stand next to me," he pleads. I lower my eyes and go to him, walking slowly as the donkey works, Catalina rests, and Zara follows.

"Don't be afraid to talk to me," Rafael says.

I don't respond.

"When we reach safety, we'll talk about . . . what happened."

I nod.

"Good. Look at me."

I look everywhere but at him.

Rafael gently catches my chin and forces our eyes to meet. "I won't ever hurt you, Marianna," he whispers. "I'll do everything in my power to take care of you . . . and Catalina and Zara. That's my word."

I look into his eyes and want to topple back in, lose myself completely. I want to forget that we're on a dirt road, with only the clothes on our backs, a shaky wood cart, Catalina shrouded in a dirty blanket . . .

His eyes reveal what he can't speak. Fear. Anger. Perhaps love?

"We can only do what we are able," Rafael says gruffly. "It's our best – but we can't do the impossible."

"What do you mean?"

Rafael takes a deep breath.

"You're talking about Catalina?"

"She's very weak. I don't know if she can make it."

Tears spring to my eyes.

Mama where are you?

I want to lash out at the world, accuse everyone of putting us on this road, with no place to go, no words to describe the fear, no Mama and Papa.

Why?

What did we do to hurt anyone?

"Catalina will make it," I say firmly, as if the words will cure her, and tomorrow she'll be walking next to us, strong, beautiful, olive-skinned, and determined to survive. I pat Papa's leather pouch in my secret pocket as if it can bring me strength.

Rafael is silent.

Two days later we come to a fork in the road. One fork leads to the ships. The other heads to the border.

"Which way?" Rafael asks.

Catalina is weaker, her eyes heavy-lidded, her breathing shallow. Zara's head is down, her feet are swollen and bloody. She doesn't complain.

"We have to go to Portugal. Catalina . . . is . . ." I take a deep breath.

Rafael nods. "I agree," he says softly. "There's no choice."

We pause and stare at the road.

"Time," Rafael mumbles.

We settle down for what will be our last night in Spain. Rafael lifts Catalina from the cart, laying her gently on a bed of purple wildflowers. Zara sits silently next to Catalina, her eyes dull. Rafael releases the donkey from the cart and tethers him to graze. I take out the last bits of our food. Our supper is the same stale bread and cheese. Everything tastes from the road – dusty and dry. No one speaks as we eat.

"We'll have to give up the rest of our money," Rafael says finally.

"No!" I cry. "They've taken everything from us. They can't take our money."

Rafael shakes his head. "They'll take a *coima* or entry tax to get into Portugal. It's 100 *cruzados* to pay for permanent residency for our "family." The royal highnesses won't allow any gold or silver to leave Spain," he frowns. "That will be their excuse for taking our money."

"We have to do something," Zara cries.

Rafael takes a deep breath. "Some people swallow the money," he begins, "but we'll need every coin I have left."

I shudder, touching Papa's leather pouch.

Zara whimpers.

"A lot of people can't do that. I've also heard of thieves finding people and cutting their stomachs open to get the gold."

"No!" Zara squeals, horrified.

I glare at Rafael. "We can sew some coins into the lining of our clothes."

"That's what most people do . . . but we don't have enough."

"There are hidden pockets in my dress," I persist, "Mama made them especially for something like this."

No one speaks.

I glance at Catalina. She's looks peaceful in her sleep; her face red from the fever that returns every night.

Rafael watches me carefully.

He's always watching me.

Ever since we kissed, it seems like he's afraid I might suddenly disappear. I smile to myself.

That feels good.

"We should rest," Rafael says softly, changing the subject. "It will be a long day at the border tomorrow."

"Yes."

We find our places on the ground, close but not touching. Zara curls up against Catalina like a kitten with her playmate. Rafael tries not to sleep, but too many nights on guard have left him exhausted. Against his will, his eyes close and his breathing becomes rhythmic.

I watch all of them, beneath the stars, wondering what will happen next.

Mama can you tell me?

There are no signs or words from her.

Please Mama?

The wind is still in the cool summer night; the road is empty.

Trees cry for rain. Purple flowers shudder in the wind. The sky fills with thin clouds that shape-shift as they pass overhead. A bird cloud suddenly transforms into a handsome trovador; a child cloud drifts into a crouching man. Suddenly there's a dull thud; Catalina. She wears a broken iron key on a leather thong around her neck. I reach out to touch the key and the metal burns my fingers, the sky turns black, and the clouds scatter in terror.

Catalina! I scream, but no sound is heard.

My eyes fly open. I was asleep. I was planning to stand guard all night . . . my eyes must have closed without me realizing what happened. Something strange, something that sends chills down my back, woke me up.

Were you talking to me Mama?

I want to believe that Mama and Papa were both trying to reach me. If they did reach me, does it mean they're dead? I shake my head angrily.

They're not dead.

Who is?

I glance at Rafael. He's sleeping soundly, his breath even. Zara is still cuddled up against Catalina, like a ball of kitten fur. Catalina's face is pale; the fever must be gone. Her beautiful, olive-skinned face is peaceful, framed by her luscious black hair. She's not struggling to breathe anymore . . .

The scream rises in my throat before I can stop.

Catalina.

Rafael lurches from his sleep, leaping to a standing position.

Catalina.

Hot, furious tears drench my face. I wrench Zara awake, and into my arms. She fights me in her sleep. I grip her tightly, as if she can miraculously change time.

Catalina.

Catalina is dead.

Ria

It was hard to breathe. Although Ria had lived with asthma all her life, she never got used to the struggle to breathe, the ache in her back, and the sharply conscious rise and fall of her chest . . .

She sucked on her rescue inhaler, waiting for the drug to work.

This was turning into a very strange day.

Ever since she arrived in New York, so far away from Moro Valley, life had been strange and exciting. She didn't fit in with the fast-moving New Yorkers, dressed in skinny clothes and outlandish shoes, rushing through the streets with a purpose she couldn't fathom. Yet it was more comfortable than New Mexico where life was slower, people drifting through their days, connected to their dry, but breathtakingly beautiful world while she lingered on the perimeter.

Her identity was *Hispano,* her fate intertwined with the Church and its wondrous ritual. The gentle, reflective nature of New Mexico made Ria nervous. As an artist and techie, she naturally drifted into her virtual worlds until her family seemed like an anachronism, too religious, too quick to believe that everything was under the control of Jesus Christ. Their chosen mission was to go through life peacefully awaiting their God-given reward in heaven.

Ria fled with her asthma and her dreams, to the place where she believed that life flourished, even if one were sick.

New York was strange, exciting, and terrifying. But she didn't stand out like in New Mexico, and once she met Ethan, Jaime, Madison, and Hawk she was comfortable with her new family.

Until

Marianna

The truth is ugly. Raw. Like the stones that cut into our feet on the road to Portugal.

No one cares about a dead Converso girl.

Zara and I clean Catalina's body, washing away the dust from the road. We straighten her clothing, brush her beautiful black hair, and close her large, fawn-like eyes for the last time. I'm numb with pain - I've failed Mama, Papa, and Catalina.

I let Catalina die.

Zara clings to Catalina's body as if she agrees with me.

I am responsible.

Zara doesn't want to touch me. Rafael digs a shallow grave on the side of the road. We have passed many graves like the one now for Catalina. Who lies in them? Young girls like Catalina? Old people robbed of the opportunity to die in peace? Mamas and papas fleeing the expulsion and inquisition? So many die along the road . . . and many more will pass before they reach their final destination. I shudder, the tears well inside me. Angrily, I force them back into that raw, anguished part of me that has grown old and tired in such a short time.

Help me Mama. Please.

I hug Zara. She's stiff and unresponsive.

There's no help coming. It's all up to me.

We continue washing Catalina's body.

When Rafael is finished digging the shallow grave, we gently lay out Catalina. I toss a few purple wildflowers over her body. I turn to Rafael.

"You saved her life."

"Only to let it go," he chokes.

"Mama and papa *know*. You did your best. They'll be eternally grateful."

Rafael can't speak. His shoulders tremble and he bows his head. I wait.

"It's my fault," he says so softly I barely hear the words.

I shake my head. "It's God's way."

"No," he shouts, eyes blazing. "This isn't the work of God. It's the work of man."

Rafael falls to his knees. He reaches into Catalina's grave, stroking her face. "I'm so sorry, so very sorry."

Zara and I wait, watching Rafael's grief in aching awe. Why does he care so much? He's *limpieza de sangre*. He can go home if he wants.

I shake the thoughts from my mind. Who am I to question Rafael's grief?

Eventually, Rafael rises. "It's time," he says woodenly.

None of us have the heart to cover her up.

Gently, I lean over Catalina's body and untie the leather thong, with her piece of the key.

"She doesn't need this any more," I choke on the words.

I'm so sorry Mama and Papa. I'm so sorry Catalina.

I clutch the iron piece in my fist.

The three of us stand silently around Catalina. We have no words, only tears.

"We should say something," Rafael mumbles.

"What words can tell the story of a young *Converso* girl, with an ancient Jewish soul, that died too soon?"

Zara doesn't speak.

"I don't know any Jewish prayers," Rafael apologizes.

I only know the *Shema*.

We stare at the Catalina.

What next?

As if to answer my question, a small group of Jews pass on the road. There are a few families, with wooden carts like ours, mamas, papas, children . . .

"Wait!" Rafael cries. He runs to the family. "Can you say a few prayers for a dead Jewish girl?"

The papa looks at him with distrust.

"Our sister," Rafael explains, "has died on the roadside. We just buried her. Our parents died – the inquisition found them - they were *Conversos*. We decided to follow our Jewish souls out of Spain. We don't know Hebrew . . ."

It was risky. Many of the Jewish families saw the *Conversos* as traitors to the Children of Israel.

One of the women, dressed in sun-bleached, dusty robes, holding a tiny baby, spoke up.

"Help him, Samuel. We can wait a few minutes to make sure a Jewish child rests in peace."

The others nod.

Samuel, a small, thin man with a heavy, dark beard and intense eyes, looks at us, struggling to make a choice. His gaze is unnerving; it prickles my skin. He's trying to make a difficult decision, battling to overcome his anger with *Conversos*. Our eyes meet momentarily. I hold his gaze.

Samuel nods tiredly. "*Converso* yes," he mumbles, "but you're children, *Jewish* children. It's not your fault."

"Please," Rafael begs him.

Samuel's face softens. "You're one of us now, child, God protect you."

Samuel walks over to the pile of dirt that covers Catalina.

"Is she here, your sister?" he points to the mound.

I nod. I can't speak.

He looks at Zara.

"We're brethren," Samuel says gently, pulling at his beard. "God will protect all of us. Please," he says to his group on the road. "We need a *minyan*."

I watch, confused.

Slowly, nine men emerge from the group and surround Samuel. Two are very old; two are young, the others are Samuel's age.

"This, child, is called a *minyan*. Death is a natural process, part of God's plan. We need a minyan – ten men over the age of 13 – to say the Mourner's *Kaddish*, or prayer for the dead. First, I'll put a small tear in your clothing on the right side of your chest. This represents mourning."

As he speaks, a little girl squeezes between the men. She has large, fawn-like eyes and olive skin.

"This is my daughter, Ysabel," Samuel explains.

I nod. Ysabel can't take her eyes off of Catalina. She reminds me of Catalina as a little girl, although Ysabel seems stronger – not sickly.

The three of us watch in silence as he tears the edges of our clothes.

"One of the greatest *mitzvahs* or good deeds a Jew can do is to say the Mourner's *Kaddish*. It's a good deed because the dead can't repay you for your kindness – there's no expectation of any earthly reward. It's also a good deed because you're elevating a soul – helping her move to a higher realm. Do you understand?"

I nod; my eyes fill with new tears.

Samuel turns to his *minyan*. "We have done this too many times on this treacherous road. Too many Jews have died."

The men mumble their agreement. They begin. The words haunt me, as if they were buried deep within my soul and now, with these ten strangers on the side of the road, have returned to consciousness.

Yit'gadal v'yit'kadash sh'mei raba
May His great Name grow exalted and sanctified

b'al'ma di v'ra khir'utei
in the world that He created as He willed.

v'yam'likh mal'khutei b'chayeikhon uv'yomeikhon
May He give reign to His kingship in your lifetimes and in your days,

uv'chayei d'khol beit yis'ra'eil
and in the lifetimes of the entire Family of Israel,

ba'agala uviz'man kariv v'im'ru:
swiftly and soon. Now say:

Amein. Y'hei sh'mei raba m'varakh l'alam ul'al'mei al'maya
Amen. May His great Name be blessed forever and ever.

The ancient Hebrew is bitter-sweet, my tongue moves along with it in a strange, but comforting atavistic rhythm. Catalina would have loved to feel the sound, know that it belonged to her.

Yit'barakh v'yish'tabach v'yit'pa'ar v'yit'romam v'yit'nasei
Blessed, praised, glorified, exalted, extolled,

v'yit'hadar v'yit'aleh v'yit'halal sh'mei d'kud'sha
mighty, upraised, and lauded be the Name of the Holy One.

Samuel turns to me. "If you can, say the words with us."
I nod.
Is it possible? Mama can I do it?
I try to follow.
B'rikh hu.
Blessed is He.

l'eila min kol bir'khata v'shirara
beyond any blessing and song,

toosh'b'chatah v'nechematah, da'ameeran b'al'mah, v'eemru:
praise and consolation that are uttered in the world. Now say:

Amein
Amen

Mama and Papa told us that we had Jewish souls. However we *appeared* on the surface, inside, where it really counted, we were always the Children of Israel. Shaky at first, my voice grows louder, stumbling over the sounds.

Y'hei sh'lama raba min sh'maya
May there be abundant peace from Heaven

v'chayim aleinu v'al kol yis'ra'eil v'rim'ru

and life upon us and upon all Israel. Now say:

Amein
Amen

Oseh shalom bim'romav hu ya'aseh shalom
He Who makes peace in His heights, may He make peace,

Aleinu v'al kol Yis'ra'eil v'im'ru
upon us and upon all Israel. Now say:

Amein
Amen

Slowly, we bury Catalina's body with dirt from the roadside. When she's completely covered, I find a rock and place it on the mound of dirt. It's the only marker Catalina will ever have.

No one speaks or moves. We stare at the pile of dirt that covers Catalina's grave. The trees cry for rain; the wildflowers shudder with grief; the sky fills with shape-shifting clouds.

After many minutes, the men in the *minyan* drift back to the road and their families.

Samuel is the last man. "God bless you for the remainder of your journey," he says gently. He returns to his family and they continue down the road.

Ysabel doesn't move, staring at the mound of dirt that covers Catalina. I will never understand why I did this. Catalina's voice whispered in my mind.

Give it to Ysabel.
It must be kept alive.
I stare at Catalina's piece of key. It feels warm.
Do it.
Catalina's voice demands it.

I look at Rafael and Zara. They're silent. I bend down and stare into Ysabel's eyes. Gently, I tie the leather thong around her neck. "Catalina wants you to have this," I whisper.

Ysabel touches the key and nods, as if she understands.

"This is the key to the heart of her home. You must treasure it."

"Catalina," Ysabel whispers and then turns, and runs back to her family. I watch them disappear down the road.

Rafael and Zara never say anything about the precious gift I just gave to a stranger.

We stand silently around Catalina's grave, long after Samuel and his group is out of sight. I'm filled with a pain I cannot describe; it paralyzes me as if the grief is more powerful than the world around me. The *minyan's* words dance in my head; tears drench my face.

How can I go on?

I think about dying; it would be so much easier to lie down next to Catalina, close my eyes and make all of this go away. Anger, bitterness, and grief swirl inside me, knocking me to my knees.

This is the end; there's nothing left.

I don't know how long we stand beside Catalina. Maybe it's minutes, maybe it's hours - I don't want to leave my sister and her fragile beauty behind us.

The sun is high in the sky when Rafael finally speaks. "We have to go."

"No," Zara wails, "we can't leave Catalina."

I look at Rafael.

"Catalina is in a better place now," he says gently. "We have to go."

"No," Zara screams, "I can't go. I can't ever go! I want Mama and Papa and Catalina. I want everything the way it was . . . let's go back, make believe this didn't happen, go home to . . ."

I fold her into my arms. She's so small. She trembles . . .

"Mama and Papa want us to move on. So does Catalina. We have to do it for them."

Zara looks at me, her eyes filled with pain.

She says nothing. Zara won't speak again until we cross the border.

Rafael packs up the cart, hitches up the donkey, and lifts Zara on top of the coarse blanket that last covered Catalina.

"Catalina will be with Mama and Papa," I whisper, "in Spain forever. We're headed for Portugal."

Zara just stares at the purple wildflowers crushed by Catalina's body during her last night.

We move onto the road. I take one last look at the rock that marks Catalina's grave. Soon, the rock will be gone and no one will know that she lies there. Years will pass, grass will grow, and Catalina will remain.

Travel is slow, agonizing. Each step forward on the road carries me further from

Catalina.

Catalina where are you?

Mama, Papa, where are you?

Are you with each other?

Has God brought you together in an afterlife, where you're strong, and happy, and able bodied?

I think of Samuel and his *minyan,* speaking words we never heard, yet linger, protected, inside.

May there be abundant peace from Heaven
and life upon us and upon all Israel.

Is it my Jewish soul? Have I rejoined my true people? What about the people I loved and left behind? What's happened to Mama and Papa? Where will Ysabel take Catalina's key?

I beg . . . plead for a sign. Nothing comes. Just the dry, crowded road to Portugal; the dusty, exhausted exiles, the burning agony of my grief, and the terror of what is to come. I glance at Rafael over the donkey's sagging back. Our eyes meet. He holds me in a visual embrace, making love across the space that separates us.

Something is happening between us.

He glances at Zara, asleep in the cart.

"We'll make it," he whispers, "I promise."

I force a small smile. Can Rafael . . . or anyone . . . promise me that?

A few hours later, we reach the Portuguese border. I have forced away all emotion, moving numbly like a mindless creature. Instead, my back aches with the burden, my shoulders throb with tension, and my feet hurt from the road. Zara refuses to speak and Rafael, red-eyed, watches us with concern.

"Do you want to wait before we cross the border?" He asks.

"No," I say without expression. "I want to be out of Spain as soon as possible – before anyone else I love, dies . . ."

Rafael lowers his eyes as if he understands. *Does he?* He's left his family behind, but he holds them strong and healthy in his mind. My family is in shatters, death hovers over all of us. Who will be next? Me? Zara? Rafael?

We turn the bend in the road and I freeze, horrified at the sight.

There are hundreds . . . thousands of people waiting in the ruthless sun. The line to cross the border is long and slow; the donkeys, hitched to overloaded wooden carts, bray loudly, objecting to their burdens. Angry adults yell at one another and the donkeys, occasionally swatting the animals out of frustration. Screaming children are everywhere, mothers unhappily trying to quiet them. Women wearing black robes of mourning move like shadows throughout the melee . . . many loved ones have died on the road. Some carts carry hens in shaky wooden coops, the only food left to the travelers. Malnourished dogs protect family possessions by pacing back and forth, patrolling the carts, growling, barring their teeth, barking at anyone who comes close. Scores of refugees are bent and broken, victims of thieves that prowl the road, pouncing on unsuspecting victims. The animals, angry and grief-stricken human cries, babies and children wailing, all combine in an earsplitting roar drenched in dry, burning heat. Nuns and monks wander throughout the chaos, holding up crosses, begging for Jesus, promoting salvation through last-minute conversion.

I have never seen anything like it in my life.

Suddenly I feel a hand on my back.

"We have to get on line," Rafael says. "It's going to be a long wait."

Zara and I follow him woodenly to the end of the line.

It takes the rest of the day to reach the front of the line. The border guards are tired and annoyed; they look at us like we're animal carcasses to be tossed aside. We remain silent as they go through our cart. There's nothing but some food, water, and blankets. For some reason, that angers the guards.

They grab us and search our bodies, rifling through our hair, peeking into our mouths, ears, and noses. They search our pockets, unload everything in the cart and toss our only food in the dirt. They pour out our water, and poke their thick, dirty fingers into every crevice of the cart.

Two guards pull me aside and wrench up my dress, searching for gold hidden in my undergarments. They laugh as they fondle my most private places. Tears fill my eyes as fingers are thrust inside me, filthy hands squeeze my nipples, and tongues suck my skin like the wild dogs on the lines.

Rafael does not see because his back is to me, the soldiers roughly exploring every part of his body.

I pray they're not hurting Zara.

I endure everything because there's no choice. If I scream, they'll plunge deeper into me. If I cry, it will heighten their pleasure and they'll search me longer with greater cruelty. If I beg, they'll laugh. I close my eyes and pretend not to feel their greedy fingers, their hands on my breasts, or the sickening humping on my buttocks.

I'll survive Mama. I'll make sure the family continues.

I watch Rafael negotiate the exit tax. He hands them all our remaining coins, the donkey, and the cart. The soldiers shake their heads. A sickening feeling gathers in my stomach as Rafael removes his part of the key, hanging on a leather thong around his neck.

"Mágica," he says.

The soldiers stare at the iron circle.

"Spirits," Rafael adds. "They will protect you and make you rich."

One soldier grabs the iron circle, grins, and ties it around his neck. He nods. We've made it over the border.

For the moment, we're safe.

131

Rafael takes our hands and leads us down the road. He finds a hollow between a stand of trees, and settles us in. There won't be food or water tonight.

Catalina is dead. Two pieces of the key are gone. Will we ever be whole again?

We sleep.

The Old Couple

The old couple sees everything, watching with an eternal patience. They hold hands and wait, knowing that *gilgul* approaches. They sing softly to one another, passing the time.

Where is the key that was in the drawer?
Onde sta la yave ke stava in kashon?

My forefathers brought it with great pain
From their house in Spain.

Mis nonus la trusheron kon grande dolor
De su kaza de Espanya.

We told our children this is the heart of our home.

Taymullah

The dark man in the cargo pants catches his breath. The boy with the haunted face fringed with straight black hair, scampers away from his mother and back to him. This time, the man isn't surprised.

"*Salaam aleikum*," the boy says. "My name is Majaahid." He smiles proudly.

He stares at the child, fingering the Glock in his pocket.

"*Salaam aleikum*," Taymullah says finally. His voice is unsteady; it comes out more like a command than a greeting.

"What's your name," the boy insists, frowning, unsure of the dark man's response.

The dark man doesn't answer.

Go away. I have God's business to complete.

"I told you my name," the boy says sharply. "Now it's your turn."

The dark man stares at the child.

The mother moves next to him, one hand on the baby stroller and one hand grabbing the boy's arm. "I told you to behave, Majaahid," she says sternly.

She's concerned. There's something about the dark, fat man in cargo pants that she doesn't trust.

The boy ignores his mother. Instead, he stares steadily at the dark man, knitting his brows in an oddly adult-like expression, his eyes glowing with knowledge far beyond his years.

He has old eyes.

The dark man tries to shake off the child's eyes. He glances at the London plane trees, watches a man finishing what looks like a tuna fish sandwich, sees a group of young office workers chatting loudly around a small green table on the southern promenade.

The old couple watches him, only a few feet away on the terrace, beneath a green and white umbrella and next to a concrete pot of purple flowers.

The child is determined to win this game.

"My name means fighter," the boy growls. "My baby brother," he points at the stroller, "is named Hamza. That means lion."

134

He nods. He will not meet the boy's eyes.

"I know a lot about names," the boy boasts. "If you tell me your name, I'll probably know what it means."

"Stop bothering the man," the mother says, lowering her eyes. She will not look directly into the dark man's eyes. "We have to go," she pulls Majaahid's arm.

"What's your name," Majaahid demands, refusing to leave.

The dark man is shaken.

Is he a sign from Allah?

A sign for what?

"Taymullah," the dark man grumbles.

Majaahid and Taymullah stare at each other.

"Don't do it," Majaahid says softly.

"Don't do *what?*"

"Be bad."

As if he knows. Perhaps this is Allah's voice?

For a moment, Taymullah, the dark, fat man in the cargo pants, is unsure.

What exactly is God telling me?

"Let's go," the mother says firmly. She senses danger.

"Yeah," Majaahid grumbles. "Bye, mister. But you should listen to me."

Taymullah nods.

"Your name means . . ." Majaahid says over his shoulder, his voice heavy with doubt. "Servant of God."

The dark man stares at the child.

Allah has spoken.

The dark man shudders.

He turns to look at the old couple watching him. Their eyes are ice. He glares at them. The old man wipes his brow; the old woman shakes her head.

No.

The dark man fills with a new hate.

Who are they to tell me?

Who is Majaahid to tell me?

135

He grabs the Glock, ready to wrench it from his pocket and shoot the old couple, Majaahid, the woman with the *hijab,* and the baby.

No.

It's not time.

In that moment he locates the second infidel; a fragile, olive-skinned girl with large fawn-like eyes dressed in a flowing pink shirt. She's with a group of young office workers, chatting loudly and godlessly, sitting around a small green table. On the southern promenade.

The second infidel.

Allah told him there would be three, and now he has found two.

One more.

Then, it's time.

Three: Marianna and Aliki

Marianna

Castelo de São Jorge is the first thing I see as we approach Lisboa. It stands high and powerful, protecting the city that grows on the surrounding hills. My heart soars – perhaps this is the end of the horrors, the beginning of a new life. Rafael smiles and even Zara's eyes glow with excitement. We're now free Jews in Portugal.

Rafael thinks I'm foolish. He does not believe in freedom, especially for Jews thrown out of their home of a thousand years. Although Rafael is a Christian, he has little faith in his brothers.

"Torquemada hates the Jews," Rafael reminds me of the infamous Inquisitor and author of the expulsion, "and he himself is part Jewish."

Foolishly, I have to believe.

Zara and I need hope, however flimsy, to keep us moving, away from our grief, away from the dungeons of the inquisition and Catalina's lonely, roadside grave.

Castelo de São Jorge appears like a mirage - a return to peace and safety. With hearts pounding, we follow the masses of exiles trudging up the steep road that leads to the castle. A gentle breeze from the harbor encourages us, helps us ignore the crush of bodies all going in the same direction. From this distance Lisboa sparkles in the sun, spreading like tree roots from the feet of the castle to the harbor on the Tagus River, her houses appearing peaceful and clean.

The distance is deceiving. As we enter the city we discover narrow, twisting streets shaded by balconies and overhangs. Laundry hangs everywhere, perhaps the cleanest thing in the teeming roads and alleys. Many of the heavy wooden doors that open to the streets are shielded by thick, foreboding iron gates. The higher we climb toward the castle, the more we're engulfed in a sea of people. It doesn't seem possible, but we see more people here than at the border or on the road - more people than I have ever seen in my life.

Slowly, we make our way into an open plaza. Rafael, Zara, and I freeze. It's a sight I will never forget. People are everywhere. Some are curled up on the street, dressed in dirty rags, faces coated in dust. Children cry, run, play, and steal bits of food. Families claim tiny pieces of street, living in tight groups, greedily guarding piles of frayed possessions and stashes of water and food. Carts filled with household possessions and thin, emaciated animals are pushed into any corner or gap that can be found. Every part of the plaza is occupied, spilling over into the alleys and crevices between buildings. Newcomers desperately search for their own small spots amid the chaos. The stench is overwhelming — refuse and excrement, dirty water, food carpeted in flies, and unwashed bodies pressed together in unrelenting heat.

It's the noise that has the sharpest impact - chanting voices echoed by crying adults, mothers with no milk in their breasts desperately trying to nurse wailing babies, old men and women pounding their chests, begging for help from God, young men feverishly demanding justice, and children playing timeless games barely aware of the bedlam surrounding them.

Zara wraps her arms around my waist, trembling. Rafael and I stare.

This is the legacy of the Spanish crown and church.

My stomach turns as I'm hit with the full impact of what's before us. The people have *nothing*. Ferdinand and Isabella stole their homes and dignity; Portugal took what little remained. There's no food or water, no shelter or comfort, no place to be clean in the manner that the Jews believe. We have been thrust into a living hell on earth.

"We can't stay here," Rafael whispers.

I tear my eyes away from the sight before us. "Where can we go?"

"These people will be sick . . . very soon. If we stay, we'll die with them."

"I don't understand," I speak softly, afraid that someone might hear.

"I've seen the black death," Rafael says so quietly I can hardly hear. "This is what it looks like."

A new fear assaults me. I shudder. "Where else can we go?"

Rafael shrugs, "I don't know, but we can't stay here."

"Why don't these people *leave?*" I hiss. "Protect themselves?"

"They're waiting."

"For what?"

"The ships," Rafael mumbles, "that King João II promised. The sanctuary and shelter they thought they paid for at the border. They're waiting for help that won't come."

My hands tremble, and I try to hide them behind my back.

"No hope," Rafael says softly.

"There's always hope," a small voice cries.

We look down, startled. Zara has spoken her first words since Catalina's death. Her eyes burn and her mouth is set in a rigid line.

"We *have* to make it," Zara continues. "For Mama, Papa, and Catalina. It has to be."

Zara gives us courage. We can't disappoint her. I turn to Rafael – a silent question.

"There's only one way," he agrees. "We have to get out of here."

"Where?"

"I don't know," Rafael sighs. "Just out of here."

We turn back down the road that brought us here. It's still choked with exiles, flowing into the Lisboa streets, believing that they will be safe. We push against the tide of bodies, struggling to go in the opposite direction. There are hundreds of them and only three of us, but we persevere. I can't let Zara down again.

It takes us twice as long to get back down the road to Lisboa than it took to get to the castle. When we reach the bottom of the hill there are fewer people; the crush of bodies has lightened. Rafael finds a circle of trees off the side of the road and we slip in. No one can see us. We huddle together, without food or water, and sleep, not knowing what tomorrow or the next day will bring.

The next morning I awake to the sound of many voices on the road. Zara and Rafael are still sleeping, so I crawl around them to the edge of the trees. I peer through the leaves, trying to understand exactly what I see.

There are more people. Hundreds of them just like the ones that were on the road yesterday. As I watch, they seem to flow endlessly, pouring onto the doomed road that leads to Lisboa in the shadows beneath *Castelo de São Jorge*.

Where will they go?

There was no room left yesterday. What will they do today?

I try to shake off the vision of the Jews living in the streets of Lisboa, but it's burned into my memory and will remain for the rest of my life. I think of Rafael's words.

I've seen the black death. This is what it looks like.

I hear Rafael stirring behind me. I don't move. I can hear him standing and stretching, then coming to me to peer out at the road.

I feel his warmth and physical presence before I see him.

"There are so many," I whisper, without turning around.

Rafael touches my shoulder. Gently, he turns me around to face him. We're very close, our faces almost touch. I look into his eyes. For the first time since Mama slammed the trapdoor above us, I see fear.

"I don't know . . ." he speaks softly.

I put my fingers on his lips. "We'll find a way."

He caresses my face with his fingertips. "I don't know where to go," he whispers.

"You've taken good care of us . . ."

Rafael drops his head. "Catalina . . ." he can't say anything more.

"It wasn't your fault!" I cry. "She was too sick . . ."

"I promised your mama and papa," his voice trembles. "I've let them down. I saved her once, only to kill her later . . . now . . . I don't know what to do next."

"You didn't kill Catalina," I cry. But I see it clearly in his eyes. Rafael doesn't believe me. "You've gotten us this far. You led us through the night, brought us across the border, and saved us from the Black Death . . ."

"It's not enough," his voice cracks. "Not enough."

"No!" I take his head in my hands, forcing him to look at me. "It *is* enough . . . and will be enough. We'll find a way."

140

Our eyes lock. I don't know how long we stand in those trees, staring at one another.

"Marianna . . ." he murmurs.

Suddenly we're in one another's arms. He holds me so tightly I can hardly breathe; I cling to his hard body, my own skin infused with warmth I've never experienced. He pulls back then lays his cheek on my breasts.

"We're through the worst." I lie. "We'll figure something out."

Rafael turns his head and hungrily kisses my breasts. His lips slide up my neck, and then to my lips with a hunger that startles me, making my heart pound and my arms grasp him tighter.

I should scream, cry out for him to stop, but instead I want him to continue, stir the tingling fire that fills my soul. I kiss him back, crying as he plunges his tongue into my mouth and I press his head, deeper inside me . . .

"Marianna? Rafael?" a small voice breaks our embrace. "What are you doing?" Zara's eyes are wide with fear. We break apart immediately.

"Nothing my love," my voice trembles. "We're trying to warm ourselves."

The sun is high in the morning sky and the summer heat already building. Zara's eyes are suspicious.

Mama forgive me. These are troubled times.

"Leave her alone!" Zara shouts bravely.

"I would never hurt her," Rafael says breathlessly. "I love you. I love your sister. I loved Catalina. I would never hurt any one of you."

Zara and I freeze at the sound of Catalina's name.

"Understand," Rafael begs. "Please understand."

I stare at him. Rafael has given up everything to take care of us. *Why?*

"We need water," Rafael mumbles, "and food. We need to find . . . a place."

Zara creeps close to me. "Did he hurt you?"

"No," I smile. "He was comforting me."

"You're breathing like . . . Catalina."

Rafael smiles grimly.

"I'm fine."

Zara nods, but she's not sure.

I love you. I love your sister. I loved Catalina.

Rafael watches us, his eyes boring into mine. I want to leap into his mind, hear what he's thinking, and understand exactly who he is. I want to be back in his arms, and taste the heat.

I love you. I love your sister. I loved Catalina.

His words ring in my mind. Is that why he gave up everything to save us?

Me?

For a moment, the horror of what surrounds us - the exiles on the road to Lisboa, the people doomed to suffer the Black Death, Catalina, Mama, and Papa, all fade into those words:

I love you. I love your sister. I loved Catalina.

I run Rafael's caresses through my mind - his lips, his hands, his tongue . . . I return to the moment we met. I was hiding behind crimson and gold bolts of fabrics in Papa's store. Papa was conducting business and I was spying. I knew how it all worked, but women were not allowed to be part of the transactions. Papa taught me how to think like a businessman, but never *act* like one. Yet another split in who I was and how I appeared to the world. There were a few men in the store talking loudly. Suddenly his eyes grabbed mine - my hiding place was violated. I wanted to run, escape, do anything but the eyes held me in a visual embrace. It was Rafael.

Now I play Rafael's words through my mind, like one of his songs on the *vihuela*. I play his caresses, recalling his lips, his words, and his warmth. Why? Why did Rafael abandon everything to save me . . . us? Why did he choose to become an exile among the Jews? There are no answers. I'm too afraid to ask . . . if I speak the words he might choose to leave. Then what would Zara and I do? Where would we go? I've lost too much to risk another loss; become too attached to Rafael to take the chance that he might leave. I vow to keep quiet; never say the words or ask the questions.

Perhaps there *is* a future for us . . . the three of us . . . but I don't know the world well enough to predict what it might be. I believed in Lisboa, and now that belief is shattered. I believed that the King of Portugal would be kind and save us, but will that prove to be as fragile as the lives we led in Spain? Nothing seems as it was anymore; human deception fills me until I want to escape, dig myself deep in the earth and lie next to Catalina. But the words, *I love you. I love your sister, I loved Catalina* changes everything.

Rafael watches me, as if he can read my thoughts. He smiles crookedly.

"We do need to go," he says again. "We need food and water . . ."

"Where?" Zara demands.

He shrugs. "The countryside? Maybe someone will help."

I look at Zara.

"I'll know when we find it," Rafael assures us.

I take Zara's hand. "Let's go," I grin, touching Rafael's hand. Our fingers intertwine. I don't know if Zara notices; she says nothing. We step from behind the trees, onto the road to Lisboa, walking in the opposite direction.

"Lisboa is that way," a young, bearded man shouts at us, pointing toward *Castelo de São Jorge.*

"Thank you my friend," Rafael calls back. "But we're not going there."

We walk, holding hands for almost an hour. Rafael stops suddenly, dropping our hands. "There," he points.

I see a narrow, dirt trail leading off the main road. It's been pounded nearly flat with use.

"Are you sure?"

Rafael nods. "That's where we need to go."

We leave the road to Lisboa and follow the dirt trail. It meanders through summer-browned grass, pastures, and rocky fields, until we can no longer hear the noise from the main road. Occasionally we pass bleached white houses with red roofs clustered together like a mama with her babies. There are olive trees, small farms, and distant, isolated farmhouses. Rafael discovers a tiny creek and we drink from it with our hands, quenching the awful thirst. Then we wash our faces

143

and clean the dust from our clothes as best we can.

I love you. I love your sister. I loved Catalina.

We continue down the dirt path, praying that Rafael has made the right choice.

We walk for a day and night, deep into the Portuguese countryside. We're silent as we go down the dirt path, afraid that someone might see us before we see them. Although we're now Jews, in a country that accepts us, we have learned to question everyone. Even with all our caution, we're surprised when we meet the old man.

It's at a turn in the dirt path, where we can't see too far ahead. Suddenly there's a man. He freezes. We stop dead. His face terrifies me. He's old, but fearsome, with deep wrinkles cut into his skin, tiny, brown eyes, and a nest of wild gray hair. He's tall and painfully thin; although I see the large muscles of a lifetime of hard labor.

Rafael, Zara, and I hold our breaths.

He speaks rapid Portuguese; the words sound angry, even threatening. I don't speak his language so the man seems even more dangerous. I stare at the old wood staff in his hand. Rafael listens intently as Zara clings to me.

The old peasant has to be better than the crowds and imminent Black Death in Lisboa. I grab Zara tightly as Rafael steps protectively in front of us. He squares his shoulders and faces the old man.

They speak different languages.

"I know some Portuguese," Rafael says to us. "Let me try."

Rafael struggles in broken Portuguese.

The peasant shakes his head and raises his staff. Zara buries her head in my skirts and trembles.

Rafael speaks slower.

The peasant lowers his staff and stares intently at Rafael. I hold my breath. Finally, he smiles and shakes his head.

"Follow quietly," Rafael says to us in Spanish. "Don't say anything."

"Where are we going?"

"I told him that you are my wife, and Zara is your sister. We'll work for him on his farm in exchange for shelter in the barn, food and water. It's not much, but it will keep us away from Lisboa. He wants us to meet his wife. He says she loves children. They will decide then if we can stay."

Rafael grins at Zara. "Maybe you're going to be the one to save us."

Zara stares back. She's still not sure whether she can trust Rafael after he kissed me.

I look at the peasant. His clothes are worn, patched in many places. He's very old. What can he possibly do to us? How can he help us? I'm not as confident as Rafael, but the day is growing older and we have no other choice. We haven't eaten for a very long time.

The peasant watches me examine him. Suddenly his dark eyes soften and he comes closer to pat Zara's head. I hold her to me, trying to protect her from his touch.

He shakes his head and hums what is clearly a child's rhyme. Zara smiles.

"His children are married and gone," Rafael explains. "He and his wife can use help on the farm."

"I don't know how to do farm work."

"I know. All of us will have to learn."

"Is this okay with you?" I ask Zara.

She nods. "I don't want to go back to the Lisboa streets . . . ever." She looks at the peasant. "I don't think he'll hurt us."

"*Gratíssima.*" I say one of the few Portuguese words that I know.

He smiles. He's missing many teeth, but when he smiles, the old peasant is less frightening.

"Gonçallo," he says, pointing to his chest.

I look at Rafael. "It's okay," he says, "the old man means no harm."

"Zara," I touch her shoulder. "Marianna," I point to myself.

Gonçallo nods. "Zara, Marianna." He looks at Rafael.

"Rafael," he completes the introductions.

For some reason, we laugh.

145

Gonçallo waves for us to follow him. He leads us through a meadow with long, brown grass, past a small olive grove, and into a tiny rocky clearing. There's a very old one-room whitewashed house with a bright red roof. Next to it is a tiny barn with room for a cow, a few chickens, and a donkey.

A woman appears in the doorway to the house. She's old, like Gonçallo, with age-spotted skin and deep wrinkles that cover her entire face. Similar to Gonçallo, she wears clothes that are not much better than rags, patched so many times it's difficult to see what's original and what's repaired. Her face is different, though. It's soft and grandmotherly . . . she looks at us with gentleness.

Gonçallo speaks to her in rapid-fire Portuguese; so fast that neither I nor Rafael can follow the conversation. He points to us several times, and she stares, her eyes widen with empathy. Finally, he points to Zara.

The woman looks at my little sister, me, and then Rafael.

"*Pobrecito*," she says in Spanish, bending to look at Zara. "I'm Aldonça," she adds. I'm surprised and pleased to hear my language. "I lived in Spain as a child," she explains, "and never forgot the tongue."

"Thank you," I whisper. Her speech is heavily accented and slow, but I can understand her.

"You are Jews?" Aldonça asks.

"Yes."

Aldonça nods thoughtfully. "They do terrible things to you, Ferdinand and Isabella. *Demonios*." She frowns. "You went to Lisboa? *Sí?*"

"Yes."

"Too many people," she shakes her head. "We hear many stories. Bad stories."

"I'm afraid," I plead with my eyes. "I'm afraid that . . . my sister . . . Zara, and my . . . husband will get sick. My other sister, Catalina . . ." I can't complete the sentence.

Aldonça purses her lips, as if she understands everything that has happened to us.

"We can't do much," she says. "We're poor people, peasants whose daughters have married and moved far away. We have very little, barely enough for ourselves. We sell the olives we collect from the grove, drink the milk from the cow and the eggs from the hens. . ." She pauses. "We don't have much, but we will share with you. Our donkey has died, so you can sleep in his empty space in the barn. The straw is clean, and the cow won't mind." She smiles.

Gonçallo grins. Rafael bows cavalierly. Zara and I thank her with our eyes. For the moment we are safe with the peasants, in the tiny barn, with the cow, alongside the little olive grove.

Perhaps God really does work in strange ways?

Aliki

Aliki watched the shape-shifting clouds, outlined by towering skyscrapers. She was stretched flat on the Great Lawn; she looked up at the tops of silver and blue-mirror buildings. Best of all she like the gold-crowned Bryant Hotel, hovering like old royalty among the upstarts. She took a deep breath and savored the sweet grass smell, as old as time and as new as today. Turning her head, she viewed the world at ground level; a green plastic chair laying on its side, a college kid with no shirt and khaki shorts asleep on the grass, two lovers locked in each others' arms. Aliki felt as if she were in the center of the universe - a bubble in time that merged yesterday, today, and tomorrow in one instant.

Suddenly her gaze froze on the face of a fragile-looking, olive-skinned girl with large, fawn-like eyes, cropped jeans, and a flowing pink shirt. Aliki caught her breath.

The girl looks like a white version of me.

Aliki sat up quickly.

The girl turned away, back to her group of people huddled around a small round green table. Aliki counted them. There were five people. Aliki tilted her head. In numerology, "5" was the symbol of the human microcosm. Others interpreted "5" as life energy in its material form.

Intriguing.

Aliki forced herself to turn away, take a fresh snapshot of Bryant Park. In front of her was the slated screen, now open, for the Summer Film Festival. Beyond it, she could hear a performer tuning the amplifiers on the fountain terrace. To her right, a breeze rustled the leaves on the London Plane trees and a woman with dark, smoldering eyes worked on her laptop. Aliki watched her for a minute, oddly drawn to the intense figure. Aliki twisted herself to see what was behind her, on the Upper Library Terrace beneath the Bryant Memorial. There was a dark, fat man in cargo pants standing on the cobblestones.

He looked tense . . . frightened.

Nearby, an old couple sat beneath a green and white umbrella

148

next to a concrete pot of purple flowers. Their eyes met. Aliki nodded slightly, as she had been given permission to return to the white version of herself, sitting around the green table.

The beautiful, olive-skinned girl was sharing something with her friends. Aliki squinted and realized that one of them had placed a brown bar of São Tomé chocolate in the middle of the table.

Aliki gasped. She knew instantly that this was more than coincidence. Most New Yorkers didn't know about São Tomé chocolate.

That's my job.

Aliki watched the scene play out.

The five people stared at the odd-looking woman carefully breaking up the bar. Reverently, one by one, she distributed the pieces. Aliki had a *sense* for chocolate; she was keenly aware of all the rituals that surrounded it. She approved of the delicate handling of gourmet chocolates and was outraged when it was mistreated in the form of sprinkles over a drippy ice cream cone or waxy coatings on cheap packaged cookies.

Most Americans abused their chocolate.

Aliki was very pleased to see people in Bryant Park eating São Tomé chocolate, although it was clear that not all of them appreciated its unique aroma. *Hershey's* didn't make the purest São Tomé chocolate; they were compelled, like so many American companies, to add vanilla and milk that distracted from the deep, musky flavor. Aliki preferred the more readily available *Neuhaus* or *Lake Champlain*, with its robust, organic, single-origin bars. The purists reached for the fresh nose and intense palate of *Pralus* or the sharp, fruity tang of *Nirvana* while many savored the hint of allspice, wood, and tropical plants in the vintage production of *Chocolatour*.

Admittedly, the Belgian *Godiva* was her favorite, with 75% Cacao and cocoa nibs added, *Nestle's Crunch* style, into the bar. Cocoa nibs were perfectly roasted, unsweetened cocoa beans separated from their husks and broken into small bits. They were the essence of chocolate . . . some connoisseurs referred to them as chocolate deconstructed to the taste of unique individual beans without the influence of conflicting flavor. Aliki agreed that they were the purest, most elemental form of chocolate and Godiva's blending of cocoa nibs and São Tomé single origin was an act of culinary brilliance, creating a marriage of flavor and texture that titillated the tongue.

Chocolate – specifically, São Tomé chocolate – was Aliki's life.

Aliki would have been a lovely young woman, in her late twenties, if it wasn't for the smoldering look in her bitter-chocolate colored eyes and the rigid body language reminiscent of the faint crunch in a bite of *i cru extra fondente* bar. Her thin lips never really smiled; sometimes they would curl into a childish smirk that she offered only on special occasions. She was tall and willowy, with a long neck, fawn-shaped eyes, closely cropped hair, and cocoa-colored skin that broadcast mixed racial ancestry. She had a peculiar habit of twisting a ring that she wore on her right hand. The ring looked like a cross with one bar cut off, made from iron, slightly rusted, and worn smooth by time. Her voice was musical, tinged with a compelling Portuguese accent that New Yorkers loved. Aliki used that voice to her advantage; her job was to sell São Tomé chocolate to the Americans, and she did it well.

Americans loved to romanticize Aliki's origins. Buyers whispered that she was a runaway from São Tomé – escaping the poverty, mixed heritage, and paralyzing history of her home. Aliki agreed on her better days. São Tomé was a beautiful island ravaged by politics, humans, and mosquitoes; tethered between worlds that nurtured atavistic conflicts with origins difficult to define. Torn between pride and anger; punished with pain and disease; rejected and exploited by the world; São Tomé fought to establish itself in a world that had little interest, or knowledge, of its existence.

Like me.

Aliki's thoughts returned to the pretty, olive-skinned girl in the center of the group – the one who clearly didn't like the chocolate. The woman nibbled at her share, blinked her eyes, and turned away from her friends. Pity. It was obvious that she couldn't appreciate the finest, most natural taste in the world. Chocolate was much *more* than the cheap candy bars that Americans gulped down each day, filled with atrocities like crunchy rice, almonds, and, Aliki shuddered, peanuts. Americans put chocolate in *everything* – floated it in syrup over their ice cream, buried it in heavy pastries they called molten cakes, covered it in sugary, bright colored candy shells, and wrapped it in trashy silver, red, and green foil and called them "kisses." They even had a holiday where giving chocolate was ritualized into a sexual offering packed in loud red-and-gold heart boxes. As with so much of American culture, the packaging was far more important than what lay inside. Aliki sighed. When it came to American chocolate, the experience was equivalent to gobbling a fast food hamburger bathed in cheap ketchup next to slivers of salty, soggy fries.

Aliki shook her head. *Americans.* They didn't know what they were missing.

Aliki was a *chocolatier*, representing the farmers and producers of the unique, mystical, São Tomé dark chocolate.

Aliki knew her chocolates well; she could quickly discern the difference between the finesse of Belgium and the art of Switzerland; the gourmands of France and the daring tastes of Italy. Europe, however, held no real interest. It was the dark intensity of Africa that galvanized her attention – the sharp, pure flavor of the jungle, exotic spices, and adapted organic cacao beans. She respected the pungent, smooth experience of Madagascar chocolate, enjoyed the wild intensity of the Tanzanian offering, and the sweet punch of West Africa. Although, she said repeatedly to her customers, none approached the cherished richness of São Tomé.

Like Aliki, São Tomé chocolate was a treasure lost in time.

A century ago, São Tomé had been the world's leading provider of chocolate. Its organic *Forastero* cacao beans, raised on the tiny island off the West Coast of Africa, were considered the finest on the planet. It was a pure bean-to-chocolate product - never hybridized. São Tomé and its sister island, Principe, originally Portuguese colonies, were the first to grow cocoa in Africa, introduced by slave ships returning from the Americas. The dark, smoky flavor dazzled the palate. A history of rabid politics and slavery had destroyed São Tomé's position in the world market; now most of the world's cacao came from other

151

countries within twenty degrees of the equator, like Brazil and Ecuador. It was mixed and hybridized; pumped with impurities that made her shudder.

Aliki sighed. The history of cacao beans read like her own; hundreds of years wedged so close to the present that sometimes it was difficult to discern what belonged to the 15th or 21st century. Time had a strange way of leaping the years, transmitted in odd, genetic memories that were built into the psyche. Aliki shook her head.

Suddenly, the olive-skinned girl met Aliki's eyes. There was an odd glimmer of recognition as if Aliki had known her *before*.

Before what?

Aliki had survived her history and home as a mystic, believing deeply in the elasticity of time and connections made in the spirit not the mind. It was like the chocolate. The Aztecs, Mayans, and Toltecs were the first people to recognize the intrinsic qualities of chocolate – over four thousand years ago. They made it into a sacred beverage – a hot, frothy, bitter drink associated with fertility and wisdom, called *Xocoatl* or *chocolatl*. The first man to bring chocolate into Europe was Christopher Columbus or Cristobal Colon, a man of *Converso* Jewish descent. The cacao beans made their way to Spain, Portugal, and eventually to São Tomé.

Conversos, Aliki thought. Perhaps all of us are descendents of the Jews. The thought didn't shock her – she had turned it over in her mind many times while growing up in Catholic São Tomé. It gave her a pleasant, atavistic pride, along with her cocoa-colored skin, on an island dominated by the ebony of African black. Aliki knew her history well. After 500 years she was still considered a *Novo Christãos*, New Christian.

The olive-skinned girl stared at Aliki, as if she wanted to say something.

Aliki stared back, unencumbered by American manners, curious about this strange connection. Did the olive skin mean that the woman was Hispanic? Aliki tried to conjure images of the woman living in a *barrio*, surrounded by Spanish voices and bodegas, her plate filled with molé.

It didn't work.

Interesting.

The Catholic Church disapproved of the chocolate brought into their midst in the early 16th century. They claimed it was contaminated by its heathen origins and would corrupt the Christians. Of course, they also felt that the good Spanish Christians were contaminated by the heathen, heretical Jews and Muslims. The church was able to get rid of the Jews and Muslims but they weren't as successful with chocolate.

Aliki locked eyes with the olive-skinned girl. They stared, neither willing to break the visual embrace. Something deep within Aliki seemed to awaken. It was crazy-new and old at the same time.

I have to meet her.

The performer on the fountain terrace stopped tuning his amplifiers. She could hear his voice drifting over the lawn. A crowd was moving in that direction. It was *ThursdaysAt5* and everyone was ready to listen. Except for the old couple beneath a green and white umbrella next to a concrete pot of purple flowers and the dark, fat man standing on the cobblestones, both on the Upper Library Terrace.

They were frozen.

In time.

She quickly looked back at the olive-skinned girl. The girl was looking at the crowd. Aliki was aware of new eyes watching her. She perused the Great Lawn until she found them.

Why is the old couple on the terrace watching me?

Aliki shook her head. It was a lovely, sunny summer afternoon but she sensed dark clouds behind the blue. Something *was* happening, making her excited and frightened at the same time.

Aliki popped a square of *Godiva São Tomé dark chocolate with cocoa nibs* into her mouth. She paused, reveling in the sharp, sweet tang of the chocolate and biting crunch of the nibs. Then she took a deep breath, and followed her instincts.

She scrambled to her feet.

The music was beginning.

Marianna

I wake up, screaming.

Sweat pours off me, Zara clutches me in terror, and Rafael strokes my arm. We lay next to each other in the straw that now smells from my fear. The cow shifts nervously in the stall next to us, the hens squawk, disturbed from their rest. I can sense the body of the old donkey that once lived in this stall; I can feel its death, on my hands, taste it in my mouth . . .

"Shhhhh," Rafael says softly. "You had a nightmare."

Zara is silent, her eyes wide with dread.

It's dark and quiet, lit by rays of random moonlight. I remind myself that Catalina is dead, mama and papa are gone, two pieces of the key are on a different journey, and that . . .

"Shhhhhh," Rafael tenderly touches my cheek with his fingertips. "It's the middle of the night. We're safe."

"I'm fine," I force my voice to be steady. "Just a bad dream."

Zara accepts my words, and in a few minutes she falls asleep, her arms wrapped tightly around my waist. Rafael watches me in the darkness. I can *feel* his eyes.

"Really, I'm okay."

Rafael moves closer, folds his arms around me. I love the heat in his body, the strength of him hard against me.

"No," I whisper. "Zara."

Zara stirs in her sleep.

Rafael backs off.

"Go to sleep," I whisper. "We need to be alert in the morning."

Rafael nods and moves away from me.

I want to cry to him, tell him to hold me, protect me from this strange world, help me forget what's happened. I remain silent.

Rafael doesn't sleep.

He leans against me and brushes his lips against my cheek.

I remember his words.

I love you. I love your sister. I loved Catalina.

This time, he doesn't have to say anything.

154

In a few minutes, Rafael falls asleep too, and I'm left to my thoughts, unable to sleep, unable to find comfort.

I open my eyes and the sun burns my vision, a black silhouette rising above me. I open my mouth to scream, when an old woman's voice in heavily accented Spanish, soothes me.

"Don't be afraid," Aldonça smiles. "You're safe with us."

She offers a basket with bread, cheese, and a few olives. "It's not much," she says apologetically, "but it's all we have."

I look at the old woman and know, instinctively, that we have nothing to fear.

The days pass, and Aldonça and Gonçallo begin to treat us like their own children. They give us food and comfort; we learn their Portuguese and Gonçallo learns our Spanish. But words aren't necessary to speak with these gentle people. Their eyes and smiles say everything that's needed.

Rafael and I wonder how we were so lucky to have found them.

We settle into the old donkey's stall and make a home from the straw and dried purple wildflowers Zara collects from the meadow. Aldonça and Gonçallo have little, but they share everything with us. They're captivated by Zara, and spend many hours teaching her Portuguese, how to pluck eggs from the hens, milk the cow, and duck the fierce rooster who hovers over his harem. Aldonça teaches us how to cook food over the tiny fire in her kitchen, and wash our clothes in the creek. The old lady nurtures us like Mama, quickly winning Zara's trust.

Aldonça and Zara spend much time walking, Zara's hand comfortably held by the old woman, talking, pointing, and discovering things in the countryside. Zara begins to heal, in the way that only children can. The color returns to her cheeks, the deadness drains from her eyes, and she starts to jump and skip like a little girl.

Rafael works hard helping Gonçallo, doing unfamiliar chores that he learns quickly. I help Aldonça in her tiny home, doing chores difficult for her old, gnarled hands. I pick olives and collect berries, clean the barn daily, and attend to the cow when Rafael and Gonçallo are busy. Aldonça generously shares their bread, cheese, and meager larder. I think we bring pleasure to the old couple; Zara's experiments with Portuguese make them laugh and Rafael's gentleness toward me makes them smile, in the special way of old folks. Our pain settles beneath the surface, and I wonder if we can dare hope for a future. How strange that time can cure, as if it was a medicine. We don't *forget*, instead we ease into our strange new life trying not to think of what was happening to the Jews in Lisboa or what would come next for us.

A peasant, returning from Lisboa, brings us the news from the city.

"Black Death has broken out," he says, drinking the water Aldonça has given him. "People are sick and dying everywhere. There is fear wherever one goes." He looks at me threateningly. "They blame it on the Jews."

That night, I can't sleep. The light from a full moon filters into the barn. I watch the shadows dance across the straw, asking silent questions that send chills through my body.

What would have happened if we didn't listen to Rafael? Would we be dead, like the others, in Lisboa?

The stories get worse. The king claims that only 600 Jewish families were supposed to enter Portugal. In the rush to flee Spain, no one kept count. The king claims that any Jew beyond that number belongs to him. They are his captives and slaves, and he can do whatever he wants with them.

What does that mean?

We don't see anyone for a long time. Occasionally, travelers stop for food and water, and tell us about the continuing horrors in Lisboa – people dying from the Black Death, vermin everywhere, rats as large as dogs, and the river of fear that flows unabated throughout the city. It's blamed on the Jews and many Portuguese youth wander the suffocating streets, choosing men to maul, women to rape, children to brutalize. The Jews band together but they have little strength and no weapons. All they possess are their Jewish souls.

The numbers are staggering. Some say 80,000 Jews fled Spain into Portugal. Others argue it's 150,000 people. No one knows and stories run rampant, reaching out as far as the quiet countryside where I, Zara, and Rafael wait.

I'm not sure what we wait *for*. Some say that times will get better. The exiles will become Portuguese citizens and live like they once did in Spain. Others claim that King João II sees the Jews as an asset; he will not be as quick to throw us out as Ferdinand and Isabella.

Some people panic and demand that King João II provide the ships that he promised to the Jews – ships that will transport them to Africa and Turkey. The king is furious - he devises a horrific plot. He provides a ship, and sends the first group of people on their way. When the ship reaches the high seas, where no one can see or hear their cries, the men are bound and forced to watch their women raped. After the sailors have their fill, the Jews are dumped on a deserted African beach. Exhausted, spiritually devastated, the children beg for food as the adults dig their own graves. They're near death when a group of Moors appears and seizes them. The local Jews pay exorbitant prices to buy the survivors out of slavery.

The story is leaked and spread throughout Portugal. King João II's plot is successful – not a single Jew asks for transport again.

I know it's a matter of time until something bad happens to us. Rafael and I whisper our concern in the barn at night, trying not to frighten Zara. It doesn't work. Zara is too perceptive, as if she has an inner eye that sees these things.

"What's happening?" Zara demands.

Rafael and I look at one another.

Aldonça and Gonçallo are silent.

She's so young. So vulnerable.

"There are stories," Rafael admits, "about the Portuguese king."

Zara nods solemnly.

Aldonça wipes her eyes.

"He's claiming that all the Jews belong to him."

"Belong to him?"

"Yes, Zara," I say gently. "That means he *owns* us."

"Not us," Rafael adds. "We paid our 100 cruzados for permanent residence. We're safe, but the others . . ."

157

"The others who survive the Black Death," I whisper.

Zara's eyes fill with anger. "You mean, like the Jewish slaves in Egypt?"

I'm surprised and pleased that she remembers the Passover story. After all, we're not very different from them.

"Yes," I say proudly. "Some people feel that we're exactly like the Jewish slaves from Egypt. Now we're trying to find our way . . ." I can't complete the story.

Zara quickly picks up on my words. She shakes her head thoughtfully. "Why do they want to hurt us?"

"We're Jews."

"So?"

I search for an answer. "People always want to hurt Jews," I say finally.

"Why?"

I shrug.

"Is that why we were *Conversos*?"

"Yes. But never again! I don't want to hide who we are, I want the world to know that we're Jews and proud to be the Children of Israel."

Rafael's eyes fill with admiration. "How do you . . . believe . . . so deeply when so much hurt has been thrown at you?"

I look at Zara. "We have Jewish souls," I say firmly, suddenly realizing that I believe it as well. "It might have been hidden in church, but it was always there. No one can ever take that away from us."

Zara squeezes my hand and says nothing.

Tension continues to build in Lisboa and like a bloody stain, it seeps into the Portuguese countryside. Aldonça and Gonçallo try to protect us from the stories, but the more Portuguese we speak, the better we understand tales carried by travelers from the city. Some come on horseback, dressed in fine clothes; others are on foot, carrying all their possessions on their backs. They're young and old, some fleeing, some searching for a better life, all believing that their survival means leaving the city.

The words and dangers are clear.

After eight months of welcoming the Jews, King João II decides that time is up. He proclaims that all of the Jewish exiles in Portugal have to be baptized or become his slaves. He wants to *keep* the Jews, but only as Christians.

Rafael and I spend many hours talking about Portugal and King João II. We wonder if he is any different than Ferdinand and Isabella; was the choice to come here better than to risk the ships? We have no answer, only more questions. Aldonça and Gonçallo have been so kind to us; they treat us like their own. They remind me of Mama and Papa, and bring a smile to Zara's sad eyes.

"You're safe, child," Aldonça comforts Zara after one traveler, reporting on the chaos in Lisboa, has left.

"I don't want to be a slave," Zara cries.

Aldonça tries to smile at Zara's protest, but all she manages is a frown. "Our king won't hurt you," she strokes Zara's hair.

"You're not *Converso* . . . or Jewish," Zara shouts.

"Zara!" I reprimand my sister.

Aldonça's eyes fill with hurt. "I'll protect you like my own."

"You can't," Zara mumbles.

Aldonça hangs her head. I hate to see the gentle old woman at such a loss.

"Aldonça and Gonçallo have been good to us," I remind her.

Zara shakes her head. "*I love* Aldonça and Gonçallo," Zara confesses, "but I know they can't protect us against their king - like Mama and Papa tried."

I see orange and red and blinding rage. Aldonça grabs my hands.

"The child is right," her voice is heavy and slow. "I will try, but if they come for you, I'm only an old woman against the king's soldiers. They will strike me down quickly."

We stare at each other silently.

"Don't worry," I comfort Zara weakly. "They won't find us here."

We all know I'm lying.

Later that day, in the darkness of the barn when Zara is sleeping restlessly, turning and twisting in the straw, Rafael and I talk about

159

going to the local church and getting baptized.

"It's not like you haven't done that before," Rafael argues, "as a *Converso* you were a secret Jew. That's all the king wants - to *believe* you're baptized. He doesn't care what's in your heart."

"That's the whole point," I hiss. "Where did it get us? We did it their way and now Mama, Papa, and Catalina are dead. I won't do it their way again."

Zara turns in her sleep.

"I have heard," Rafael adds, "that far in northeast Portugal there's a secret community of *Conversos*, living in the town of Belmonte. They live quietly, and no one knows. . ."

"No!" I cry too loudly.

Zara stirs, and Rafael and I hold our breaths. When we're sure she's sleeping, we resume our talk.

"I won't be *Converso* ever again. I will be true to myself and my God."

Rafael shrugs. "I respect your choice," he says slowly, "but I'm not sure I understand it."

"I'm not sure I understand it either," I speak softly. "It just *feels* right. It's the only way."

"Even if it means your life?"

There's a long silence between us.

"It meant Mama, Papa, and Catalina's life because they were *Conversos*. It doesn't matter whether I try to hide, or speak out in the open. Either way, they'll get us if they want."

At that moment, we do not know that I speak truth. Of course, it isn't really an prophecy . . . it's the heart of the Jewish story.

Rafael has nothing left to say. I desperately want him to take me in his arms, and comfort me. Instead, he turns away from me and closes his eyes. In a few minutes his breath comes in an easy rhythm . . . he's asleep.

I peer through the dark at Rafael and Zara, my heart beating furiously.

Am I making the right choice?

A few days later a new story arrives from Lisboa, carried by a young traveler headed for Spain. His skin is scarred with pox marks, and his greasy dark hair falls loosely over his face, making him look frightening and weak at the same time. He stares at my breasts as he speaks.

"I hear," he says, wiping Aldonça's cheese from his beard and licking his lips with a thick, red tongue, "that there's a small uninhabited island off the west coast of Africa, discovered and claimed by Portugal. It's called São Tomé."

Zara is suddenly very still. I watch her and listen to the traveler at the same time.

"It's said to be filled with giant lizards, snakes, and other venomous reptiles." He grimaces, but there's amusement in his eyes. "People have never lived on the island until recently because it carries a deadly fever that kills most who get it." He waves his hand in the air. "Only the strongest survive."

Zara fixes her eyes on his scarred face.

Enjoying the tension he creates, the traveler lowers his voice as if confiding a secret. "King João II decided he wanted to settle São Tomé - but didn't want the lives of any good, God-fearing Christians risked on the deadly island. He came up with a great idea," he drops his head and rubs his hands together. "He decided to exile the *degradados,* Portugal's worst criminals, who have been jailed or exiled, to colonize São Tomé. You know, *assassinos e ladrQ´es,* murderers and thieves . . ."

Zara catches her breath. She shivers. I grab her hand, and rub her back. Aldonça moves closer to us.

"Ah, yes," the traveler rubs his nose and spats on the ground. "*That* was not enough." He grins. "The King decided that since he owned the Jews, he will send them to São Tomé along with the convicts. He doesn't want his colony to be filled with Christ-killers, so he decreed that all Jewish children, between the ages of two to fourteen years old, will be shipped to the island along with the *degradados,* and raised as Christians."

The traveler slaps his knee and roars in laughter.

161

The traveler leaves new fear in our hearts. Something has changed. Each day more people stop at our hut. With so many people in Lisboa, the Black Death raging and panic rising, there's a constant flow outward, escaping the city. More people find us; they pause to sit, barter trinkets and wine for food and conversation, and share new stories of the havoc in the city. I grow nervous - our secret hiding place doesn't seem that secret or remote anymore.

We try hard to hide our fear - cover our disgust at the stories, but we don't always succeed.

An aging merchant pats his belly and stuffs his face with olives as he tells us about babies and children ripped from their parents' arms by merciless soldiers.

"Women throw themselves at the king's feet, begging to be allowed to go with their children," he adds, his smile filled with rotten teeth. "I have seen it with my own eyes. Old men tear their beards as the children are seized right in front of them. If anyone fights, the soldiers beat them down, often killing them. And the crying! *Meu Deus*, the wail of babies reaching for their mamas' breasts as soldiers wrench them away is horrible."

The merchant smirks. "Christ-killers," he mumbles. "They deserve it."

It was a horror greater than any of us could imagine. I remember the children living in the streets with their parents; I hear their wails and see their eyes frozen in terror. King João II is more heartless than Ferdinand and Isabella; as evil as the ruthless Torquemada.

The countryside turns dark; threats lurk behind every tree. Will the soldiers come for us? We huddle, terrified by the latest change in our world. Aldonça and Gonçallo try to comfort us, but we all know that they would be helpless against the soldiers. I wonder how many Christians are like them - willing to risk their lives to protect us?

There are good people out there.
You knew that, Mama.

We now fully comprehend the truth - King João II is our enemy

- not our savior. We fled Spain only to confront a new, perhaps worse danger. Mama, Papa, and Catalina are gone.

Who is next?

Sometimes, I think of my own death. I imagine a soldier finding me kneeling by a patch of purple flowers. He's elegant in his armor, his horse breathing fire, his eyes large and black beneath his helmet. He raises his sword and plunges it into my heart and I feel nothing as I watch my blood drain from me. . .

My nightmare ends, but the daily fear of waiting for real soldiers to find us grows like an open sore. I sniff the air for dust from galloping horses and press my ear against the ground for the rumble of their hooves. Aldonça and Gonçallo cling to Zara as if she were their own blood. I marvel at the strangeness of it all . . . danger in the gnarled olive trees, fear in the purple wildflowers swaying beneath a watery blue sky, shadows dancing in untamed hills.

Zara is very quiet, as if she has already accepted her fate. She doesn't talk as much, and rarely laughs. She's grown up too quickly. With all our fears, with all the stories, with all our preparations, we thought we were ready for anything.

It begins with a young, pleasant-faced traveler from Lisboa, on his way to better fortune. He sits on a rock outside of the hut and tells us he is seeking adventure - perhaps on the sea, perhaps on the land, just away from the stink of Lisboa. He sips water and smiles, warning us that he's heard soldiers in the countryside, searching for hidden Jews. Smiling, he goes on his way, never knowing how his prophetic words would ring repeatedly in my mind, grasping for ways I could have changed the inevitable.

It's the first time I realize that there are others, like us, hidden in the countryside.

As if we were in Spain, all over again.

I think of that night; it feels like it happened in a different life: the untouched bowls of beef stew sitting in front of us, fists banging on our door, Papa standing away from the table, his face pale and frightened. Mama crying,

They'll kill us.

Rafael racing through the door, his face covered in sweat, yelling desperately.

They're coming. You only have a few minutes to run.

Papa's voice resounding, powerful in his determination.

Our time is over. If we wait here, if we give ourselves to them, *they'll forget the children.*

Time racing and frozen in the same moment . . . Mama reaching into her pocket and handing us a key that's been broken into four pieces.

This is the heart of our home.

Her last words.

Promise me that you'll stay together, connected through time.

The trapdoor, the tunnel, Catalina . . .

"Marianna!"

Rafael shakes my shoulders.

"Marianna!"

My eyes refocus to the present.

"Marianna," Rafael's voice is filled with urgency, like the last night in Spain. "I hear them coming."

Aldonça, Gonçallo, and Zara stare at me.

"We have to hide you," Rafael's hands tighten on my skin. We have to protect Zara from the soldiers."

The dust rises and I hear the sound of horses' hooves, see the fear in Aldonça and Gonçallo's eyes, and finally understand Rafael's words.

"Hide!" Rafael cries.

Aldonça and Gonçallo move as if they're young people.

"Follow me," Aldonça orders.

Gonçallo grabs their only cow, a large creature with dark, soulful eyes. We race into the barn, but this time we go into the cow's stall. Aldonça furiously digs a hole in the pile of straw and points. Zara and I crawl in, and she covers us with fresh straw. Gonçallo moves the cow into the stall; there is barely room between us and the cow's hooves.

"Quiet," Aldonça warns.

I nod.

"Deus ajuda-nos," she adds. God help us.

Zara's head is buried in my arms. I am curled into a tight, rigid position. Between the straw and the cow's hooves, I can peer outside where Aldonça, Gonçallo, and Rafael pretend to do chores. My world heats to a blinding red, as if there is fire within that pumps my heart, pounds my mind, and sends sweat pouring from my skin. This is the second time I have been so terrified . . . the first was when I was shoved through the trapdoor in Spain.

Zara and I tremble like animals caught in a trap, their predator lurking only feet away. Gently, I cover Zara's mouth to make sure she doesn't cry out.

I pray.

Shema Yisrael Adonai Elohaenu Adonai Echad
Hear O Israel The Lord is God, The Lord is One.

The words are spoken silently; only my lips move.
Will God hear me?

Outside the stall, the soldiers approach, their horses' hooves roar like thunder in the middle of the day. They stop in front of the barn and examine Rafael, Aldonça, and Gonçallo.

There are five of them on heavy, stomping horses; each soldier wears a red Christian cross on his gray tunic, a fearsome helmet, and a razor-sharp sword on his hip. One soldier holds a little girl with wild, tangled red hair, barely five years old, draped across his saddle like a sack of old grain.

They speak; harsh male voices in difficult-to-understand Portuguese. They make brutal, uncompromising demands.

"Where is the Jewish child?"

"There is no child here," Gonçallo lowers his head. "It is only two poor old people and our helper, my cousin. We could not feed another mouth."

"We *know* there's a Jewish child. A traveler told us so."

"There are no travelers here. We are too poor . . ."

One of the soldiers spurs his horse close to Gonçallo and kicks the old man's head. Gonçallo's legs buckle and he tumbles to the ground.

The others laugh as Aldonça screams and runs to his side, gathering the old man in her arms.

The leader laughs and then roars at the peasants on the ground, "By decree of His Most Catholic Majesty, King João II, all Jews fourteen years and younger are to be removed from their homes and sent to the Holy See of Africa to receive baptism and redemption in the faith of Our Lord Christ Jesus."

I'm numb. Zara whimpers in my arms. There's no trapdoor waiting to lead us to safety.

"Don't let them take me," Zara begs.

"Never," I assure her, my voice trembling.

"Leave the old people alone," Rafael confronts the soldiers. "It's been a long time since any children lived here. We're all good Christians and wouldn't harbor a Jew pig that belongs to the king."

The five horsemen are silent.

"You're not Portuguese," the leader says finally.

Rafael bows his head. "I come from Spain to help my family in need."

"From Spain?" the soldier holding the child, laughs. He spats on the ground. "He must be a Jew."

Rafael shakes his head. "I'm *limpieza de sangre*. I have the papers to prove that I believe in the Lord Jesus Christ."

The soldiers hesitate.

"Não," the leader says thoughtfully. "If you are *limpieza de sangre* then you won't care if we search for the Jew child."

"No." Rafael snarls. "I will not have my family searched by you."

The leader nods and two of the soldiers leap off their horses and head for the hut.

Rafael stands in their path. "The old man said there are no children."

The soldiers laugh.

Aldonça and Gonçallo stare helplessly.

"You can't go there," Rafael blocks their path.

"Eh, a Jew ordering a king's soldier?"

"I'm not a Jew, I'm *limpieza de sangre* and . . ."

Rafael never finishes his words. The two jump him, push him on the ground, and beat him viciously with their fists.

Rafael struggles to fight them. They overpower him easily.

"Stop," Aldonça cries.

Stop! I cry silently from beneath the straw.

They ignore the old woman. The soldier holding the little girl edges his horse to Rafael. He makes his horse buck, with two hooves landing on Rafael's chest. There is a sickening *crack* and Rafael loses consciousness.

"*O curse do diabo em você!*" Aldonça cries. The curse of the devil on you.

"Quiet, old woman," the soldier on horseback snarls, "before we do the same to your vermin-ridden husband."

Aldonça lowers her head. "*Assassinos e ladrQ ´es,*" she mumbles. Killers and thieves.

Rafael does not move.

We wait. Aldonça and Gonçallo on the ground, old and helpless. Zara and I beneath the straw, hunted.

The soldiers kick Rafael a few more times, until he's a bloody pulp, and mercifully, still unconscious. My heart wrenches violently, tears fill my throat and I cover my mouth with my hand. Zara presses her body against me, holding tight, her fingernails drawing blood on my skin.

The two soldiers stand over Rafael's motionless body.

Is he dead?

They laugh, slapping their thighs. "Now," one of them barks, "where's the Jewish child?"

Aldonça and Gonçallo are silent.

"Jew lovers," one soldier mumbles. "We should kill all of you."

"Hey," the other soldier says, pointing to the hut. "The King only wants the kids."

"Yeah," the soldier on horseback agrees. "Let's move it."

Shaking their heads, the two soldiers enter the hut. They break everything in sight; I hear the few precious pieces of Aldonça's pottery smash to the earthen floor. Soon, they emerge.

"No Jewish swine there," one grumbles.

"The barn," the second points.

The red-headed child on the saddle stirs. She begins to cry. "Quiet," the soldier slaps her, "or I'll feed you to the pigs."

She lays still.

I hold my breath. I put my hand over Zara's mouth. We lay still beneath the straw like dead people.

The two soldiers enter the barn. They poke around the donkey's stall.

"Ah," one says, "this is where the Jew-lover sleeps."

The second soldier kicks a chicken, sending it screeching across the floor.

They both pause by the cow.

"Is there room for a Jew child to hide here?"

I pray.

Please God, don't let them see.

"Hmmmm," he says, "the straw breathes."

Before I can do anything, the soldier parts the straw.

Aliki

Aliki stopped abruptly, shuddering.

Something was wrong.

She took a deep breath and broke off another piece of *Godiva São Tomé dark chocolate with cocoa nibs*. She popped it into her mouth like a pill, expecting a cure.

Aliki wasn't disappointed.

Chocolate makes me think better.

The wind had shifted across the Great Lawn. She raised her head, closed her eyes, and felt the sun on her face. It wasn't sun like home - hot, blistering heat, but it felt good anyway. The sun, the chocolate, the heat . . . it should make that feeling go away, the sense that there was an intrusion in the cosmos.

It didn't change anything.

Aliki opened her eyes and surveyed the park. She didn't like the dark fat man in the cargo pants. He was dangerous . . . but to whom? He was speaking to a little Middle Eastern boy. The boy's mother, wearing a cream-colored *hijab*, watched carefully, her hands on a stroller holding a baby, her eyes on the dark man.

Aliki shifted her gaze to the olive-skinned girl. She and her friends were walking down the 40th Street promenade to the fountain terrace.

ThursdaysAt5.

The old couple sitting beneath the green and white umbrella next to the concrete pot of purple flowers on the Upper Library Terrace was staring at her. Aliki smiled. They didn't respond.

It felt as if the world had suddenly shifted into slow-motion, like a movie with jerky frames highlighting the action.

What action?

The old couple shifted their gaze to a woman crossing the Great Lawn from the 42nd Street promenade.

Aliki followed their eyes and realized it was the woman with dark, smoldering eyes that had been focused on a laptop. Aliki had been oddly drawn to the intense figure.

The woman stopped. She stared at a priest in a black shirt and black pants with the traditional white clerical collar. The priest was approaching her. She looked frightened. Aliki wondered why she was afraid of the priest.

Aliki watched and waited.

A few tense moments passed. Aliki wasn't exactly sure what happened; it felt like a ripple in her vision, as if her eyes were tearing from a strong wind. She rubbed her eyes and it was gone.

For a brief moment, the priest looked as if he was wearing ecumenical garb with a draped cowl topped with fur and long, shimmering robes.

Aliki looked back at the old couple. They smiled.

They saw exactly the same thing as me.

Aliki couldn't make any sense of it.

What am I watching?

Why are the old people seeing the same medieval-looking priest as me . . . and the woman with the smoldering eyes?

Aliki had no answer.

She soothed herself, filling her mind with pictures of home.

São Tomé was a tiny volcanic island off the northwestern coast of Gabon in Africa. Sitting in the Gulf of Guinea, near its sister island, Principe, the two islands formed the Democratic Republic of São Tomé and Principe. They were part of an extinct volcanic mountain range, now mostly under water.

Few people knew about São Tomé. In her mind, Aliki painted a picture of the lush equatorial jungle, thick, beautiful, blazing hot sun, unrelenting heat and humidity. She saw the mountains, and felt the dry, cool air on her face. She dove into the turquoise water, off of empty khaki-colored sand beaches, and relished in the rush of fresh and wet, a shrug at the unchanging heat of the island. She ran through the towns with houses and buildings painted in cheerful, peeling colors. She lost herself in her people, lean and dark, moving slowly from the heat, women balancing bundles on their heads, workers coming in from the cocoa plantations, the plaintive cries of the babies and children who made up almost half of the entire island population.

For a moment she paused before an old colonial Portuguese

home, with pale stone walls and red roof, surrounded by lush vegetation. Then she moved to the fierce *Boca de Inferno*, a ravine along the ocean that ended in a cave with a hole at the top. When the waves poured in, they were forced upward, bursting out onto black volcanic cliffs with a roar of water that felt like an inferno.

Aliki knew better.

The only Hell on São Tomé was man-made, created through five hundred years of human assault, bringing havoc to its once-ferocious, untouched beauty. Aliki loved her home but hated its history; she was a living reminder of some of the most incredible cruelty known to humankind.

Ironically, few people knew about her home and its awful history. While she lived it every day in her cocoa-colored skin, most celebrated their newly won political freedoms, lived life quietly, and waited to see if the present scourge of humankind would invade their shores . . . drilling for oil from the Gulf of Guinea.

Inevitably, Aliki arrived visually at the mud-clogged, poverty-stricken *Angolares Market*. These were the descendants of Angolan slaves who survived a shipwreck in 1540 and made it to the island. Then again, everyone on São Tomé was a descendant . . . there were no natives; the island had been uninhabited before the Portuguese navigators had decided it would be a good location to establish trade routes with mainland Africa. It wasn't until 1493 that Álvaro Caminha built the first successful settlement after receiving the island as a grant from the king.

Today, São Tomé was home to *Mestiços* or mixed-blood descendants of African slaves from Benin, Gabon, and Congo . . . some people called them *filhos da terra* or "sons of the land." There were *Forros* or the offspring of freed slaves when slavery was abolished. *Serviçais* were contract laborers from Angola, Mozambique, and Cape Verde, and *Tongas* were their children born on the island. The Portuguese and European minorities mixed into the African population, creating a lovely array of brown skin tones.

Even with all that diversity, Aliki was in a São Tomé group by herself.

Feeling part of her home and outside of it at the same time, Aliki grew with a sense of worlds that operated beyond her tiny island. As soon as she was old enough, she fled São Tomé to attend college, learn English, and taste, like her chocolate, the dark, bittersweet tang of humans beyond the Gulf of Guinea.

Now, at this moment on the Great Lawn, Aliki knew that everything in her life was suddenly coming together; like a monsoon, it would blow through her leaving much to be repaired. At the same time it was exhilarating - nothing would be the same but perhaps, inside, Aliki would finally understand her reality.

Like the olive-skinned girl who drew Aliki into her sphere.

Why?

Aliki shrugged. Her origin was jumbled, an old puzzle that never fit together. Her *avó* or grandma had told her that there was an *Angalores* in their family line. A great, beautiful black man rushed through her blood; a man who was wrenched from his African home, forced into slavery, and battled to survive the 1540 shipwreck in the Gulf of Guinea. He had made it to shore on São Tomé, along with a small group of freed fellow slaves from the doomed ship. São Tomé wasn't kind to the newcomers. They battled ravenous crocodiles, suffocating heat, and a strain of malaria that was still known to be among the worst on the planet. Many *Angalores* died; enough made it through the island's assault, some marrying the people who already lived on the island.

Aliki never knew the name of the man who first penetrated her family. Instead, the *Angalores* remained a proud, fierce tale of her diverse heritage; a fantasy of love, power, and endurance. He was the first one to change her family skin to cocoa-color, marrying a woman who had been born to parents raised from a tiny cluster of white children, survivors of kids shipped from Portugal to settle São Tomé in 1493. The story was vague and undefined; it fluttered in Aliki's mind like a piece of European lace, filled with graceful swirls that had more holes than substance. There was a tale about kidnapped children and evil captors who kept monsters as pets. There was another tale of escape in the jungle, led by a dark angel, to God's home on the

172

mountaintop. The stories had been embellished so many times they sounded more like fairy tales than family history. As a child, Aliki even dreamed of green critters and flesh-eating worms!

There were many faces like hers' in São Tomé. There were stories lost in the violence of slavery, exploitation, and evil perpetuated like the jungles that grew wildly out of control. No one noticed except for the few whites from Portugal and Europe, people desperate to assign origin so they could lay claim to purity.

Here, in New York, no one cared and everyone cared. New Yorkers tallied secrets like numbers on the *Dow Jones*; never sure where it was going, only confident that it would always change. It was the perfect jungle for an island woman like Aliki; pavement instead of dirt roads, hawkers instead of equatorial critters, and the constant tension between what she saw and what she knew. Facts were as flexible as the winds; New Yorkers *believed* that the *Angalores* in their pasts were etched, along with a long list of characters, on their souls. It was an island filled with mysteries.

Aliki loved to walk the streets, staring into faces, guessing at who they were or where they came from. Sometimes, at night, she would search the windows through town, watching silhouetted people in their homes, moving to their own private dances, speculating on their stories.

Everyone has a story.

On São Tomé everyone had a rich story, but few had mysteries. They could trace their history for hundreds of years, recalling pirates, slaves, slave traders, convicts, laborers, rebels, and plantation warlords as characters in their personal dramas.

Aliki *knew* there was more to her history than the *Angalores* and the white-skinned Europeans that she wore on her skin every day. She twisted the strange ring on her finger that looked like a cross without the bar, formed from iron that was slightly rusted and worn smooth by time. The ring itself had a story that had been lost many generations ago. Aliki had received it as a gift from her *Mama*.

We pass this down to our daughters; Mãe, *her mother, explained when she gave Aliki the ring on her twenty-first birthday.*

173

Why Mãe?

That's the way we've always done it in our family.

What does it mean?

Mãe shrugged. Some say it's the heart of our home.

Heart of our home?

Mãe frowned. I don't really understand. We've done it so long that the story has been lost, but the ring remains. My Mãe used to say that if it was ever lost, its magic would find its way back into the family, curled around the right fingers.

Aliki accepted the ring and its mystery in the same way she accepted the island, she was part of *it* and not the other way around.

The mystery lived on.

Now there was a mystery unfolding in the scene, right before her eyes. What did it mean? Where was it going? Aliki took a deep breath. She took a moment to assess the clues: the lovely, olive-skinned girl with the fawn eyes, who looked like Aliki, heading toward a crowd gathering on the fountain terrace. The old couple, sitting beneath a green and white umbrella next to a concrete pot of purple flowers, watching everything. The dark man on the cobblestones. The woman with the backpack, her eyes smoldering, transforming a white-collared priest into a medieval cleric in full ecumenical garb that only Aliki and the old couple could see.

We're sharing hallucinations.

Or visions.

Aliki closed her eyes, hoping to see the dense jungles of São Tomé, the roar of *Boca de Inferno*, and the turquoise water lapping khaki-sand beaches. Instead, medieval sailors dripping in blood danced in the jungle, their swords raised over the heads of children.

Her eyes snapped open.

Aliki shifted her position and stared directly into the manic eyes of the dark man in cargo pants.

A little girl with green eyes and wild, tangled red hair stepped in front of the man. She held up her arms, as if warning Aliki.

Aliki blinked.

Was it happening again?

174

Aliki took a deep breath and closed her eyes again. She felt a buzz in the air; a shift in the pressure; a sense that something was opening and closing at the same time.

When she opened her eyes, the little red-headed girl was gone.

The dark man in cargo pants met her eyes. He trembled with rage, blood filling his dark eyes, his fat body taut with hate. One hand was in a deep pocket with a large bulge, as if he was fingering something very precious.

Why didn't I see it before?

A chill ran down Aliki's back. She shivered, but it didn't change the sudden sense of foreboding. Aliki glanced at the old couple.

Help me.

Aliki shook her head.

Why do I need help?

The Great Lawn began to move in fast forward; faces flying, sounds blurred, voices coming in high-pitched chirps instead of discrete words. Clouds raced across the sky and she heard a loud boom, as if she were in a movie running out of control.

Gunshot.

Aliki's ears pounded and she instinctively dove into the grass, shielding her head, curling into a tight fetal position.

Three more gunshots.

Aliki screamed, although she fought the panic. She covered her eyes, her heart beat wildly, and she heard feet pounding around her, people screaming, bodies hitting the lawn. It was as if she were in a horror show, ducking a sniper attack, as people fell around her, their agonizing cries of fear filling the sky, turning everything red and orange and black.

I'm in the open . . . so vulnerable.

Aliki had never been so terrified in her life. She locked her body tighter, buried her head deeper, and waited for the bullet to penetrate her, take her life . . .

The screams around her grew louder - a battlefield in the middle of New York. Hot tears stained her cocoa-colored skin; her muscles were so tight they felt like stone, flooded with adrenalin, shrieking to run, not hide, and flee the barrage of bullets swirling above her head.

"Are you okay?"

Aliki wrapped her arms around her head, trying to shield her ears from the noise.

"Are you okay?"

There were no more gunshots. Aliki waited for a stampede of panicked survivors, the wails of the wounded, the smear of bloody deaths.

"Should I call someone to help you?"

Just the sounds of the Great Lawn on a late summer afternoon.

The silence was deafening. Cautiously, Aliki unlocked her muscles. She dared to peer out at the world around her. There was no panic, no stampede, no bloody bodies. She raised her head.

Nothing had changed.

Aliki gulped for air.

A dark-skinned man stared at her. He balanced a board of beaded bracelets and earrings, and wore a fashionably ragged red t-shirt that read *Nweke's Art*.

"Are you okay?" He asked again.

Confusion replaced fear.

Where were the gun shots?

What happened to the killing field?

Where were the dead and dying, the screams and the panic?

"I can get someone to help you," Nweke said gently. "I think you might have had a seizure or something."

Have I met you before?

"I'm fine," she said weakly.

"You seem better," he agreed. "But maybe you should have someone take a look."

"What happened? Aliki whispered.

"Nothing," the man said. "Was it the helicopter that just flew over the park? I heard people can have seizures triggered from strange sounds."

"I didn't have a seizure," Aliki said stiffly, as she stretched her legs. She wasn't completely sure, though.

176

"Well, it sure looked like a seizure. I'm not a doctor, but I know what I see."

Aliki took a deep breath.

"You're okay now," he added. "But I think you ought to go to the doctor to take a look."

Aliki's head was clearing. "Thank you. I think I'll take your advice." She crossed her legs, sat up tall, and looked around.

Nweke smiled confidently. "I'm glad you're listening. Do you want me to call a cop or an ambulance?"

Nothing had changed on the Great Lawn.

No one.

"I'm fine," Aliki whispered, knowing she wasn't. "I just got . . . dizzy. And tripped."

He frowned sympathetically. "Definitely a seizure." He offered his hand. "Can I help you up?"

Aliki shook her head. "No, thank you. I'll be fine. I think I'll stay here for a bit and then go to my doctor's office. It's a short walk from here . . ."

Nweke glanced at something over her head. "Anything you want," he mumbled. "But be very careful." He hesitated. "This is a very strange time."

Aliki held her breath. She knew he had more to say.

Nweke shrugged. "Good luck," he added quickly.

He picked up his board of bracelets and earrings and headed for the fountain terrace. Sales would be good there.

Aliki was shaken. She wanted to call to Nweke, ask him to stay, calm her down, and help her figure out what had just happened. She knew he sensed something, too. Instead, she watched his back.

What happened?

What did I just see?

Was it a prophecy or an omen?

She looked at the old couple sitting beneath a green and white umbrella next to the concrete pot of purple flowers. The old lady mouthed some words.

It's coming. Be ready.

177

What was coming? What should Aliki prepare for?

Aliki shook her head. Impulsively, she reached into her pocket to retrieve the rest of the *Godiva São Tomé dark chocolate with cocoa nibs*. She stuffed the remainder in her mouth, waiting for the crunchy, tangy swell of pure São Tomé chocolate to lure her senses and bring comfort.

It tasted like ashes.

Marianna

I will never forget his hands. His thick, short fingers are calloused from hard labor; faint red scars crisscross the palms, and tuffs of short, wiry hair curl like stains at the base of each finger. His hands stop time. Zara and I plunge into a world where there's no sound or movement, just fingers plucking at our souls. We cling to one another, praying the fingers will be satisfied and retreat like an army that's savaged its enemy and is ready to return home.

Rafael is unconscious; Aldonça and Gonçallo cower helplessly in the dust; we're on our own.

Mama please.

God please.

Help us.

There's no trapdoor or tunnel - nowhere for us to go.

The hands part the straw.

"I found me some Jews," the soldier growls triumphantly, a predator exposing his prey.

He tosses away the straw and reaches for Zara. I tighten my grip on her, an animal wail bursts from within. I kick him with all my strength.

The soldier laughs. "This is a feisty Jew bitch."

"Can't handle swine?" The second soldier taunts.

"No," I shriek and sink my teeth into the hands grabbing for Zara.

"Ow," he retreats, sucking his fingers in thick, fat lips.

Zara howls in terror, a sound I will never forget. The soldier drags me out by my hair, beneath the cow, and into the sunlight. I scratch and bite, so he rolls me onto my belly and the second one presses his knee into the small of my back. I flail wildly, like a bird caught beneath a cat's paw.

There is nothing I can do.

The first soldier returns to the barn and carries Zara in his arms. She's paralyzed with terror.

"You're headed for São Tomé, Jew girl," he announces. Zara, as if suddenly awakened, spits in his face. He slaps her across her cheek with his thick, ugly hand. I scream in rage, struggling harder against the boot that pins me to the ground. Zara whimpers with pain, but otherwise remains still. All I can do is taste the bitter Portuguese dust and see the remnants of his fingers on her skin.

The soldier climbs on his horse and slings Zara across his saddle like the other little girl. The soldier pinning me to the ground releases the pressure and stands upright. I attack him, clawing and kicking until he balls his hand into a fist and punches me in the nose, knocking me flat to the ground. I'm stunned; the world revolves in red, orange, and yellow as I hear, as if very far away, the sound of horses moving impatiently around me.

"Should we burn them?"

"They deserve it."

"Let them be. We already got the best. We want to deliver these Jew kids before it's dark."

I force away the colors and open my eyes. My breathing is ragged and blood pours down my face and the front of my dress. The soldiers spur their horses away from us.

I don't remember scrambling from the dirt or screaming at their backs. I just remember running, chasing the soldiers, mad with grief and rage. I hurl every curse I know, peppered with pleas from them and God, to let her go. I run at them long after they're out of sight and hearing. Finally, my breath fails me.

"Noooooooo!" I cry as the sky fills with shape-shifting clouds. "Nooooooo!" I cry to purple wildflowers shuddering in the wind. The trees cry for rain. Agony seizes me; pain beyond belief.

The world turns black.

I have little memory of what happened after the soldiers disappeared from my sight. The days pass in a blur. Rafael tells me that when he regained consciousness, he, Aldonça and Gonçallo, carried me back to the hut. I fought them, crying, screaming, and cursing. They are afraid my mind is broken, shattered with grief and tragedy; they worry that it will never come back. I'm delirious with pain, as if suffering the Black Death in Lisboa. It isn't a fever of the body, rather a sickness of the soul; a heartbreak so deep that my body begs for death. I want to be with Mama, Papa, and Catalina. I want to be with Zara, protecting her from the soldier on the horse and whatever fate she faces. I want to be *anywhere* than beneath Aldonça's ministering hands, Gonçallo's prayers to Jesus, and Rafael's unerring loyalty.

I want to be dead.

Am I brave enough to take my life?

Aldonça and Gonçallo care for me, force-feeding me bread, water, cheese, and wine. I think only of death, not them, not Rafael, swollen and scarred, by my side, holding my hand, cradling me through my tears, calming me through my fury.

I want to be dead but I know, in my heart, that it's my mission to *survive;* to make sure that my family's bloodline doesn't disappear, buried with the hundreds of thousands of Jews scattered and dying, once again searching in a cruel and relentless desert.

It's weeks before one day, I wake to a dark, sunny morning. The sky will never be as bright and the purple flowers will never be as beautiful. There's a hollow inside, a void in my soul, which will remain my entire life. I am thin and weak, I see the reflection of a stranger in Rafael's eyes. My Jewish soul has been torn and brutalized. My family is gone; I am the only survivor.

Rafael speaks gently about moving forward, his words stiff through still-swollen, split lips.

"Zara isn't dead," he whispers, "just in another place."

Another place?

"What place?" I ask bitterly. I see her in the devil's jungle, crawling with snakes and poisonous lizards, fiery monsters, and evil vermin struggling to find a few berries to eat.

I see her dead.

"Too young, too weak to survive being alone."

Rafael shakes his head stiffly.

"It should be me," I mumble.

Rafael is silent. We both know that they didn't *want* me; only the child. Zara will die, along with the other Jewish children. Is this the Jewish legacy? Is that why Mama and Papa lived as *Conversos*? Should

181

we have allowed them to baptize us . . . and be safe? There are no answers, only bitter questions that linger, unanswered, on my tongue.

Aldonça and Gonçallo are amazingly gentle – it's through them that hope begins to stir inside me.

Perhaps I can continue . . . return to Lisboa and search for news of Zara?
When I first say that to Aldonça, her old eyes fill with tears. Rafael turns his head. They know there is no hope. I refuse to believe there is nothing I can do.

If I have to live, I will search for Zara.

The hut and the old couple are part of my past.

It's time to go.

"I have to look for Zara," I whisper.

Rafael doesn't argue. He knows it's hopeless . . . the ship is probably well on its way to São Tomé . . . but he understands that I need to live out this final scenario, like the last chorus in a *trovador's* song.

Aldonça and Gonçallo are heartbroken to see us leave. Their eyes are red with tears and they beg us to stay.

"There's nothing in Lisboa for you," Aldonça speaks softly, "but more grief."

I nod. "You're probably right . . . but I have to go. I have to *know*."

Aldonça hangs her head.

Gonçallo smiles sadly. "You always have a home here," his voice is scratchy with grief. "May God protect you."

I wonder *which* God he's talking about. Is it the Christian God in whose name we suffer these horrors? Is it the Muslim God who dragged the Moors from Spain? Or is it the Jewish God, the father of His Chosen People, hated by the world?

I think of Mama and Papa, Catalina and Zara.

Faith is believing with all your heart, Mama once said. *Even if life tells you otherwise.* I shudder.

Is my faith being tested? The question is old and unanswerable; I push it from my thoughts. It's like the shape-shifting clouds, always there, always assuming different poses.

182

We leave Aldonça and Gonçallo, carrying a small basket of bread and olives - all they can spare. Rafael and I don't speak as we cross the grassy meadows and follow the dirt path back to the road to Lisboa.

The road is strangely quiet. We pause on the edge, looking for people. The expulsion date is history; the only Jews left in Spain are *Conversos* – still terrified that the Inquisitors will find them. The exiles had packed into Portugal, sailed dangerous waters to North Africa, Naples, Turkey, Morocco, and other places. We pray that life will now settle in; that we'll find, or at least hear, about Zara and the other children sent to São Tomé.

It takes a long time to walk to the Lisboa Harbor. We trek through the countryside, silent and alienated, praying for signs. Everything is different and everything is the same, as if only our eyes have changed, not the world around us.

Who cares about another poor Converso child?

Lisboa Harbor, on the edge of the Tagus River that flows directly into the Atlantic Ocean, is a very busy place. Graceful *caravelas* are securely anchored, their masts standing tall in the crisp sea air. These fast-moving ships use large, square sails that take explorers into dangerous, uncharted waters. Names like Bartolomeu Dias and Vasco da Gama are on everyone's lips. The port is filled with people – merchants, sailors, captains, pickpockets, prostitutes, and gaunt men searching for business.

We pace up and down the pier, asking everyone if they have heard about the children sent to São Tomé. They shake their heads and turn away.

After a few days we realize that there is an ongoing contingent of Jews – parents, uncles, siblings, asking the same questions. They walk the docks with shoulders rounded, backs bent, and eyes brimming with grief.

Please God, save Zara, save the children.

Rafael finds a tiny area where we can sleep – it's more a crumbling inn than a home – where drunken sailors and prostitutes linger. I don't care; I only want news of Zara.

As I wander the port, searching for information, I meet Esperanza and Francisco, Jewish parents who have lost their only daughter to São Tomé. Esperanza has green eyes and wild red hair, tangled and unkempt in her grief. She's a broken woman, who also roams the quays, her eyes blank, quietly crying the name of her child in a constant, mournful dirge. I shiver when I hear her wails. Slowly, we become friends, colleagues in anguish and the struggle to find the truth. Similarly, Francisco and Rafael become friends. Francisco teaches him the ways of the port; how to make a meager living while we search and wait and mourn.

None of us will ever know if the children are alive or dead.

We survive that way for nearly two years, until King João II dies. We celebrate that day in 1495! It's whispered that he was poisoned by one of the nobility. Well deserved. Not only did King João II turn on the Jews, but he believed that his nobles were conspiring against him. Years ago the king had personally stabbed his cousin and brother-in-law, the Duke of Visev, killing him in response to a rumor that he was involved in a conspiracy against João. Many of the king's kinfolk were executed, murdered, or exiled. Some believe that his only son, Afonso was murdered in retribution. Afonso, married to Princess Isabella, the daughter of Ferdinand and Isabella, died in a suspicious riding accident in 1491. That left King João II with no male heirs to the throne.

We celebrate his misfortunes and his death!

The new king, Manuel I is crowned, and we hold our breaths to see how he will deal with the Jews. In the beginning, it's like a miracle. King Manuel I frees the Jews that were made captives and slaves under King João II. There is still no word from São Tomé, but at least we're finally safe. Hope trickles back. Rafael and I talk about leaving the port, starting a new life in the city. In two years of grieving, we live together, but have never been sanctioned by God or ourselves in marriage. Perhaps it's time?

Rafael has built a good business selling merchandise to the people in the port. We need to choose a new direction. We say goodbye to Esperanza and Francisco, sensing that our paths are destined to cross again.

Rafael and I find a new room and rent it from an old Portuguese couple who remind us of Aldonça and Gonçallo. It's our first real home. I begin to tolerate my grief over Zara, and think about the future. Perhaps my *children* will continue the family line?

Rafael and I discuss this for many nights. We grow closer, like brother and sister, until one morning I wake up and he's holding me tightly in his arms. The feelings that I experienced on the road to Lisboa return with a shock. My body is weak and hot, all at once, and when Rafael kisses me, I melt into him. His mouth grows more demanding, and his hands touch my body everywhere. We slip out of our clothing and consummate our "marriage" - without the grace of anyone's God. It was as if Mama, Papa, Catalina, and Zara were there, giving us *their* blessings.

We believe *our* time has finally come.

Life moves on; the mystery of Zara and all the children sent to São Tomé is never solved. I delude myself into a sense of safety in Rafael's arms, believing that nothing worse can happen to me.

We all did.

Until King Manuel decides that he wants to marry Princess Isabella – the widow of his nephew, Prince Afonso, and the daughter of Ferdinand and Isabella. The royals in Spain refuse to allow their daughter to marry the king of a country who tolerates Jews. Manuel's choice is simple – the princess or the Jews.

Our royals play their power games, never caring who's affected. While we bow and curtsy to them, they play their sport with us, moving people around like game pieces designed for their entertainment. Our lives have meaning only to ourselves; the royals hold value only for themselves and act accordingly. Some believe that they will be punished in the afterlife, but most accept it as part of daily life. So it's no surprise, in December, when King Manuel signs a *Portuguese* Order of Expulsion.

All Jews who don't convert within ten months will be put to death and their properties confiscated. If the Jews chose to leave Portugal, the king will provide ships, and they can take all their belongings with them.

185

We've heard that story before. Rumors spread throughout Lisboa that Manuel is smarter than the other royals – he recognizes the talents and assets that Jews bring to his kingdom. Some believe that his plan is to baptize his Jews so he can marry Princess Isabella, and satisfy the demands of her parents, Ferdinand and Isabella. After suffering the abuse of Spanish royalty, forced to leave our homeland of nearly 1000 years because we refused to convert, most Jews stand their ground. We prepare to leave. The choice is

simple for the most faithful. Life in eternity is more important than the fleeting time we spend on earth; loyalty to the Laws of Moses will not be questioned or sacrificed.

Yet, I'm so tired. I've lost my family because of my faith. I've lost my home because of my faith. I feel pain I never believed could exist . . . deep within my soul, bloodied from constant attack. Why doesn't God take better care of me? Why doesn't God spread the pain, forcing all people to share? Is it so noble to cling to a faith blindly, submitting to such intense human punishment?

I don't share these thoughts with Rafael. He's given all to assure my survival as a Jew. He doesn't need to know my doubts. They're private questions with no answers; a grief in its own. But the questions persist. Are humans an invention of God, or God an invention of humans?

Manual doesn't care. He maintains one critical step ahead of his Jewish flock. In the spring, he announces that no one can leave Portugal by ship without the crown's approval. The rich get through by bribing court officials to authorize their departures. Realizing that his plan is not enough, Manuel forbids any ship captain to transport Jews without authorization from a royal judge or counselor. The penalty is death by hanging. Is Manual's God so much more powerful than mine?

Now we're trapped again.

Rafael and I lay together, arms entwined, in our tiny room, wondering what to do next. Our worlds have shifted yet again; death and loss lurk alongside us, a familiar third person in our bed. Everyone we love is dead or scattered, and yet the royals continue to torture us. Will there ever be an end?

186

"Perhaps we should get baptized," Rafael suggests, his voice hoarse from our lovemaking. He buries his head in my breasts, clinging tightly to me.

"No!" I shout, pulling away from him. "After all this, after the destruction of my family, I'm not going to be baptized."

He winces, startled by my ferocity. "It will be in name only. We can be *Conversos*."

"Where did *that* get me?" I rage. "If I have a drop of Jewish blood in me, I am a Jew. It's all or nothing."

Rafael draws me back into his arms. "Then I'm a Jew, too," he whispers, "but it will make our lives very dangerous."

It changed, yet again, that Passover.

I love Passover – it's a celebration of freedom. Rafael and I join Yitzhak, Elvira, and their three young children to celebrate the holiday in the Christian calendar, 1497 or, as we preferred, the Jewish calendar, 5257. Our friends from the port, Esperanza and Francisco, are at the table. They are childless – unable to conceive after the kidnapping of their daughter and the ships that took her to São Tomé. They are like many parents in Lisboa - damaged beyond recovery, staggering through life, scarred and broken.

Like us, Yitzhak and Elvira are Spanish exiles, but unlike us, they had enough money to purchase decent living quarters and continue to earn money in the merchant community. Their children were not stolen and shipped to São Tomé; their lives are still intact.

We celebrate Passover *outside,* not in secret, in full revelation of my Jewish soul. It's frightening and exhilarating at the same time. In the past, Mama, Papa, Catalina, Zara, and I went through the trapdoor beneath the table, into the tunnel. Papa would close the door above us as Mama held the candle to lead our way. It was dark and spooky, filled with the excitement of the holiday and our precious family secret. We would walk slowly through the tunnel until we reached the fork. Instead of turning left, as we did later to escape the Inquisitors, we turned right and continued until we reached the secret community room. There were six families who gathered regularly in the room tucked beneath

187

the monastery. Sometimes there were additional trusted visitors or travelers; occasionally even a Rabbi would find his way into our midst.

Passover was the highlight of our secret lives; always festive, bright with flickering candlelight, lamps, the savory odor of lovingly-prepared food, the story of Passover . . . of freedom, thanksgiving, and deliverance . . . retold as it had been for thousands of years. There was the knowledge that Jews all over the world were doing the same – saying the same words – chanting the same prayers – and singing the same songs. Although we couldn't see them, we were bound by our Jewish souls, connected in a way that went far beyond our secret underground room.

Papa led the Seder, standing and reading from the *Haggadah*, the book that told the story of the Jewish exodus from Egypt. Miguel, Lorenzo, and Juan, first born sons in their families, had fasted all day and they stared longingly at the food set on the table. Some called Passover the "Festival of the Lamb," others called it the "Feast of Unleavened Bread." It was a celebration of freedom, of the Jew's escape from slavery and their hurried departure from their oppressors in Egypt. Our food represented the Exodus – we used parsley for the *karpas* or vegetable dipped in vinegar to represent the tears shed by Jewish slaves; we used lettuce for the *maror* or bitter herbs that represented the enslavement of Jews in Egypt. We ate *haroset*, a brown, pebbly mixture of honey, wine, nuts, fruits, and spices to symbolize the mortar used by the Jewish slaves to build the Pharaoh's cities; and eggs boiled in red onion skins, saffron, and vinegar, for the free-will offering that celebrated deliverance. Most important, we ate the *matza*, cakes of unleavened bread that some called *pan de la afliccíon* – the bread of affliction. The *matza* recalled the Jews rushing so quickly from Egypt that there was no time to wait for their bread to rise.

As *Conversos*, it was very difficult to get *matza*. It had to be brought into the house secretly, smuggled from a bakery in the Judería. Usually they were plain, flat white cakes made from wheat and water, without salt or leavening. Sometimes, Mama would get special *matza* made by Blanca and flavored with white wine, honey, clove, and pepper. Mama hid everything very carefully – an outsider stranger discovering *matza* might report us to the Inquisition.

During the Seder, I would listen to the stories and prayers, closing my eyes and imagining what it must have been like so long ago. The warmth of the room, the melodious voices, the lights, and delicious smells often made me sleepy, filling my head with wildly romantic dreams of ancient times. Suddenly Papa would grab a wooden staff and re-enact the story of Passover, his voice booming, his hands waving in the air, his green-flecked eyes sparkling. I think I loved Papa the most at those times - he wore the face of past and present, spoke the words of hope. I listened happily, waiting for when we would all recite the four questions:

Ma nishtannaw hallaylaw haze mikkol halleilos?

She-b'chol ha-laylot anu ochlin chametz u-matza, ha-laila ha-zeh kulo matza.

She-b'chol ha-laylot anu ochlin she'ar yerakot, ha-laila ha-zeh maror.

She-b'chol ha-laylot ayn anu matbilin afilu paam echat, ha-laila ha-zeh shtay fe'amim.

She-b'chol ha-laylot anu ochlin bayn yoshvin u-vayn mesubin, ha-laila ha-zeh kulanu mesubin.

Why is this night different from all other nights? Why is it that on all other nights we eat both bread and matzo, but on this night only matzo?

Why is it that on all other nights we eat all kinds of vegetables, but on this night we must eat bitter herbs?

Why is it that on all other nights we might not dip one food into another even once, but on this night we dip different foods twice?

Why is it that on all other nights we may sit or recline while eating, but on this night we all eat in a reclining position?

The responses are clear, as sweet as the honey on our table.

Through the foods we taste tonight and the manner in which we eat them, we learn the meaning of freedom. To appreciate what it means to be free, we must be reminded of how it feels to be enslaved.

And so, we recall tonight the historic experience of our ancestors who had

189

been enslaved in the Egypt of the Pharaohs. By recounting their experiences, the freedom we cherish so dearly today becomes ever more meaningful and vital.

Now, five years later I am the only one left from my family, sitting at another family's table in Lisboa. What's happened to the other families . . . where are Miguel, Lorenzo, and Juan? I force back tears; struggle to thank God for being able to celebrate this Passover. I look at Esperanza and Francisco and wonder if there is any thankfulness in their hearts. Have their souls been stained by bitterness? The words stick in my throat.

Thank God?

Esperanza once shook her wild, tangled red hair, closed her glazed green eyes and cried to the sky.

Why should I thank God?

Rafael says that if I fall into the same pit of sorrow, I will never recover. I need to resist the memories, the anger, and the bitterness, or I will become cynical and hard. My soul will ache, like Esperanza and Francisco.

Yet the questions persist.

Why can't the world leave us alone?

If we are the chosen people, why doesn't God protect us?

The questions are as ancient as Passover, but I still beg for answers. Rafael was not born Jewish, and yet his soul is as Jewish as the most devout of us. Do we have to suffer in order to live life as Jews? Is that what the story is about - time, suffering, and moments of peace sprinkled between waves of hurt? I shake my head.

If I don't believe in this, what do I believe?

Tonight, the prayers began.

Baruch ata Adonai, Elohaynu melech ha-olam, she-he-che-yanu vekiyemanu, vehigianu la'zeman hazeh.

Praised be Thou, O Lord our God, King of the universe, Who gave us life, and sustained us, and enabled us to reach this season of joy.

I don't *feel* thankful. I feel empty and displaced. I miss my family and my home, I dream of my house and my town, purple flowers, *trovadores*, and the piece of iron key that hangs on a thong around my neck. I know it's wrong but the grief of being the only surviving child hovers over me like a dark ghost, a constant reminder that I have to keep going . . . somewhere.

Rafael sits next to me, capturing every prayer, song, and ritual. His eyes shine; oddly, Rafael has found his place with us, the Jewish exiles. I wonder if part of his soul is Jewish and it's taken over the rest, making him one of us. Or is it the love of a young man?

Yitzhak, the father of the house, lifts the Seder plate, filled with special foods that carry ancient meanings, demonstrating that we haven't been beaten, that the Children of Israel continue to persist against the horrors thrown at us.

Yitzhak freezes.

A fire ignites in Esperanza's eyes.

We all hear it.

There are screams from outside the door. My heart pounds as I stare at Yitzhak's hand. It's trembling, shaking the food on the Seder plate. The boiled egg, representing the circle of life, our *future*, rolls over the edge of the plate. I watched it fall to the ground, as if in slow motion, doing a dance in the air before it lands and shatters. I can't take my eyes off it.

Outside, it sounds like Spain, Inquisitors breaking into homes . . .

No one moves.

It couldn't happen in Portugal. Manuel is on our side now.

I think of Mama and Papa, Catalina and Zara. The cries grow louder, voices begging, horrible, agonizing sounds of . . .

The door is forced open.

Suddenly our room fills with soldiers, dressed like the ones that beat us and yanked Zara away. A gaunt priest waves a crucifix in the air.

One soldier, with a terrifying helmet, mail, and a sword swinging from his hip, stands face-to-face with Yitzhak.

"King Manuel I, his royal highness, has proclaimed that all Jewish children under the age of fourteen years old will be taken from parents who refuse baptism. They will be removed and placed in Christian households to be raised as good Christians."

Nothing is changed.

The Seder plate falls through Yitzhak's fingers and crashes to the floor next to the egg, shattering into sharp, tiny pieces.

Yitzhak's wife, Elvira, wraps her three children tightly in her arms.

Esperanza screams in rage and grief.

The soldier ignores her.

"What say ye," the soldier bellows? "Will you be baptized? Will you take the Lord God, Our Savior Jesus Christ, into your heart?"

The priest steps forward and waits.

Rafael leaps blindly at the solider. Francisco follows. Two soldiers stop them, pinning them down on the floor, holding swords to their throats. Now I scream.

"What say ye?" The soldier repeats.

Elvira's eyes fill with panic.

"We will not forsake the God of Israel, and the Laws of Moses," Yitzhak says slowly, his voice thick with agony.

I will never forget the inhuman cry that comes from Elvira – the sound of a wild animal in unimaginable pain.

The soldier nods. Three men shove Elvira away from her children. She screams and claws at the soldiers, trying to retrieve her children. She's a small woman, and it takes little strength to pin her against the wall . . . only one soldier's meaty hand. Elvira goes mad, her eyes wild, her voice garbled, her wails renting the air. Esperanza and I try to help her but suddenly there is yet another soldier, wrenching my arms, twisting them until I'm dizzy with pain, knocking Esperanza to the floor. . .

Immersed in our agony, the soldiers grab the children, holding a sword to Yitzhak's heart. He would die for his children rather than let them be baptized. In slow motion, I watch the sword penetrate Yitzhak's chest. Blood spurts like a fountain, staining everything a brilliant red.

Then they are gone.

Yitzhak lies bleeding on the floor as Rafael and I race after the soldiers, into the street. Like Lisboa, Jewish quarters throughout

192

Portugal reverberate with similar cries of mothers, fathers, babies and children on that first Passover night.

How do I describe the *sound* of parents' cries, their wails reaching into the heavens? Fathers curse and rage, pulling mercilessly at their beards; mothers keen; anguish fills the air like thick smoke permeating everyone's soul. Soldiers are everywhere, knocking over desperate parents, killing fathers too distraught to realize that their unarmed attacks are fruitless. Children's cries echo through the streets, bouncing off the walls in sounds . . . and pictures . . . permanently staining my memory. Parents hopelessly calling their childrens' names, while howls of mama and papa, in Spanish, Portuguese, Ladino, and Hebrew cut through the alleys like swords ripping through flesh.

Esperanza and Francisco stand, staring at the streets, stunned. *What more do they want?*

Every Jewish heart is breaking. Tears choke me - Mama and Papa's faces fill my mind's eye, Catalina's grave beckons, and Zara's cries cut through my head like swords, tearing me apart. Rafael holds me in his arms, like a cocoon, fighting to keep me safe. Tears course down his face as his eyes flash in a terrifying rage. I hang onto *him,* afraid that he might go after the soldiers and be killed.

I can't bear to lose Rafael, too.

Some parents kill or drown themselves and their children before the soldiers come, preferring death to baptism. A few compassionate Christians, reminiscent of Aldonça and Gonçallo, hide the children until the night is over. Others just turn their backs. Many smile, pleased with their king.

Nuns, priests, and monks accept the children, rejoicing in their seizure of souls that will receive burning drops of holy water. Manuel, in his castle, celebrates. By stealing their children, he has kept more Jews in Portugal.

Many break. Perhaps the worst thing you can do to a Jewish soul is to steal its children.

In the story of Passover, the Pharaoh announced that he would kill the firstborn male of every Jewish family. The Jews marked their

193

homes with the blood of the Paschal lamb and the Angel of Death passed over the children of Israel, preserving their lives.

There was no one to pass over the Jewish homes in Portugal that night.

Hope dies.

I see scenes of horror that will stay with me until my death. There's a young father who strangles his son in a final embrace; a mother who suffocates her baby and herself to protect their souls in eternity; inhuman wails of pain that rise, like black smoke, into the air. My people believe that baptism and the abandonment of the Laws of Moses is far worse than death. In death you lose your life; in baptism you lose your soul. What is stronger and more resilient than the Jewish soul? What is crueler and more powerful than the religious zealots who try to possess it? For the first time, I fully understand the beauty and burden of a Jewish soul.

I will never grasp why people are so cruel; far beyond the assault of any animal seeking its prey. Why must the Portuguese, like the Spanish, destroy us? Why must they own our souls? The children they steal that night and drag to the baptismal font shatters their parents. One can't rob Jews of anything more precious than their children. It's the most suffocating evil, inflicting pain far greater than any torture. They force a choice between life and our God. When you believe that life is fleeting and God is eternal, the decision, however excruciating, is clear. I now have a deeper understanding of what my grandparents and parents had done. They made a compromise with the devil - *look* Christian and remain Jewish in their hearts. It was perhaps the most difficult and harrowing decision of all - to live a broken life, immersed in deception, and fanned with the pervasive fear of discovery. Ferdinand and Isabella, João, and now, Manuel, have broken our backs but not our spirits.

Will we ever be safe?

King Manuel is not finished with his Jews. He decrees that all Jews who will not convert are expelled. Although originally we could leave from three ports, he tells us that now all Jews will have to come to Lisboa where there will be ships waiting to take us out of Portugal.

Ripples of hope spread through the people. Jews come from all parts of the country - Portuguese Jews as well as Spanish exiles, are ready to leave. They surrender their property, synagogues, study-

195

houses, and books. They come with little more than the clothes on their backs and their precious, stubborn Jewish souls. Many hope to be reunited with their children and leave Portugal forever.

Rafael and I join the others at *Os Estãos*. We make it there in a slow, funereal walk. *Os Estãos* is little more than large, crude shelters set up in a plaza for the Jews to wait for the boats. It's an amazing group of people; poor and rich, Spanish and Portuguese, tall and thin; families, lovers, individuals, old people, children, and babies. I spot Esperanza and Francisco in the crowd - her red hair makes her stand out. They walk with their shoulders rounded, defeated. I don't try to reach them; it will only remind her of São Tomé and her lost child.

The crowding is fierce and Rafael once again talks about the Black Death and how it can take down most of us.

"The ships will be here in time," I assure him. "They'll take us out of Portugal and we'll be free."

Rafael shakes his head. There are *twenty thousand* Jews corralled in *Os Estãos*, waiting for the promised ships, sheep poised for slaughter, carrying their last vestige of life.

"There aren't enough ships in Portugal to carry out all these people," Rafael whispers. "Manuel has other plans."

I refuse to believe him. "The king just wants to get rid of us."

Rafael takes my face in his hands, and plunges deep into my eyes. "That's not his plan," he says fiercely.

"How do you know?"

"How do you *not* know?"

I pull my face from his grip.

"What will we do?" Rafael refuses to let go.

"What do you mean?"

"You were a *Converso* all your life. Will you be one again?"

"No!"

Rafael shakes his head. "Are you willing to give your life for your secret?"

"For my God," I correct him.

"For your God . . ." he says slowly. "Think, Marianna. You're the

196

last in your family, the only hope that Mama, Papa, Catalina, and Zara will live on. If you don't give in to Manuel's demands . . ." his voice drifts off, the meaning clear.

"No!" I cry again, turning my back to him.

I can *feel* Rafael shaking his head.

I stare at my present world - *Os Estãos.*

There is a family, huddled together in the dirt - three generations of people. The old ones sit with bent backs and fiery eyes. The parents tremble as they cling to their four remaining children. The baby cries for the breast.

Others are not as fortunate. They surround me in massive waves of humanity, so close that I can barely move among them. The parents who lost their children at Passover walk hunched over, their faces sunken in grief.

Will Manuel return their babies?

Many have snapped. They wander through the crowds, calling their children's names. Some beg the soldiers to return them only to receive glares, shoves, and carefully-placed kicks; others stare blankly at the nuns, monks, and priests demanding baptism.

"The children will be returned to all Christian families," the clerics speak with conviction. "Join us with Jesus Christ, our holy Lord, and you, too will be saved for all eternity."

Their words sound like wine turned to vinegar; sour and without life.

No one believes in Christ as God; these are the Children of Israel. Most ignore the clerics, turning their backs on pinched-face nuns, red-cheeked monks, and priests with eyes filled with the futility of their own brand of righteousness.

I hate them all.

A Jew occasionally relents: a young man stumbles through the crowds, led by a monk, headed for the baptismal font. Some taunt him, spat, and curse him for relinquishing the treasure of his birth. Most just move on, wandering and terrified, waiting, not knowing what will happen next.

The strongest and most arrogant Jews demand boats, waving

fruitless petitions and legal documents that fall on the laughter of heavily armed soldiers.

"You won't be Jews for long," they threaten, drunk with power.

"How long can this last?" I ask Rafael.

"Until the king wins," he replies softly, cradling my hands in his.

"Go! You don't have to be here."

His eyes filled with anger. "I *do* have to be here, Marianna. This is my fate as well as yours. You and I are one, together, forever."

"Forever," I laugh bitterly.

"Forever," he repeats without a smile.

I wonder if I could follow Rafael into this horror; if my love is as strong and determined as his.

Rafael is silent. He reads my thoughts.

The days pass without mass conversions. Manuel gets angry. He wants his princess *and* his Jews. He orders that all food and water be removed from *Os Estãos*.

We are like Mama's beef, ready to be tossed into her cooking pot. The king's threats will not force us to turn our backs to our God. We refuse to comply. We will live by the Laws of Moses. It feels right and feels good. It is what we must do.

Manuel's anger grows, enraged over the Jews blocking him from winning his precious Spanish princess. He can't allow Jews . . . swine . . . to control him. The king consults his advisors and once again resorts to cruelty beyond the imagination - wrenching apart innocent families. We quickly learn, as Rafael said, that Manuel never had any intention of providing boats for our escape.

The Jews of Portugal are trapped and caged like animals.

There is nowhere to go, nowhere to hide in *Os Estãos*. Manuel decrees that all Jewish youth up to age twenty-five, be separated from their families and forced to become Christians.

How do I describe the revulsion of the people trapped inside *Os Estãos*? Should they cling to their God and eternity or their children and worldly survival? The screams rip through me, knives splitting living bone, as children of all ages are swept away from their families. Terror reigns as the youth are forced with fists, beatings, and swords, to the baptismal font. Some are dragged by their arms and legs; others by their hair and newly-grown beards. The youth are as determined as their parents - their pain makes them fight rather than give in to the king's demands. They're dragged to churches and holy water tossed on them; given Christian names and put in the custody of old Christians to be raised in the faith.

At first, the soldiers ignore us. Although young, we're a childless couple and not of any interest. That changes as the violence grows. Clerics crisscross *Os Estãos* telling everyone that their children are now baptized, full Christians in the name of Jesus Christ; if they convert, their children and youth will be returned. No one moves or speaks.

No one believes.

A soldier who looks exactly like the savage who stole Zara, pauses in front of us. He stares, trying to connect our faces. An evil fire fills his eyes.

"Next time," he whispers, licking his lips.

I will never forget his face. It's him.

I spit. He grabs me by the throat, his fingers pressing hard. I can barely breathe. I struggle with my arms, but the soldier is too strong. Rage rises in my throat, and I see Mama, Papa, Catalina, and Zara. There are loud voices around me. My ears start ringing.

Rafael manages to yank me from the soldiers' grip. The soldier wipes my spittle from his cheek, his eyes red with fury.

"Not now," he snarls. "Soon."

Rafael holds me tightly. He covers my mouth to prevent any response. I twist and squirm, but Rafael is too strong.

"It's *him*," I hiss between his fingers. "The soldier who took Zara."

Rafael nods.

I can't speak.

"What next?" I finally ask, my throat thick with rage.

"They're going to come for us," Rafael says gently, his lips pressed against my ear. "We can try to resist them, but we won't succeed."

"No!" I cry. "These people killed my parents and my sisters. I won't go willingly."

Rafael says nothing.

Manuel refuses to be defeated by the Jews at *Os Estãos*. He orders that no food or water be allowed inside *Os Estãos* for three days to use the *"anguish of hunger"* to control the Jews.

It doesn't work.

Manuel understands that "his Jews" would rather starve than relent. He refuses to lose this resource to his treasury. He decides to do to the parents, what has been done to the children.

Baptism by force.

Complete mayhem bursts upon *Os Estãos*. Screams and curses fill the air. Wildly courageous, a mother and father hide with six children under his prayer shawl, shout their faith in God and Moses, and one-by-one kill the children and themselves. Another couple hang themselves, and when others tried to take their bodies away for proper burial, the soldiers spear them. Some jump to their deaths; others into wells, all desperate to avoid the inevitable hand of Christianity.

In the middle of this massacre, the soldier who had taken Zara returns with a band of laughing, rotten-toothed buddies.

"Now it's your turn," he boasts. "We never should have let you live in the first place."

They pounce upon us.

His hands are on my throat; I close my eyes and see his thick, short fingers through the straw, calloused from hard labor, faint red scars crisscrossing the palms, and tuffs of short, wiry hair curling like stains at the base of each finger. I don't struggle, instead visions of Mama, Papa, Catalina, and Zara drift before my eyes. As his left hand cuts off my air, his right fingers grab and twist my breasts, then paw my most private parts.

I welcome death, God.

Like an old friend that's never been very far away.

"Take them both!" a soldier's voice cuts through the fog in my head.

I open my eyes.

Rafael is fighting to reach me, his arms flaying the air, his face clenched in fury. I watch like a spectator, removed from my body, as

200

he knocks one soldier to the ground. A war cry bubbles from the lips of the soldier with the thick hands, he releases me like a sack of grain, and I drop to the ground. Two soldiers appear from nowhere and grab Rafael's arms. The soldier with the thick hands beats Rafael in the face, roaring with pleasure. The others goad him, encouraging him to beat the Jew until he's dead.

The thought of Rafael dead startles me out of my reverie.

"No," I shriek, as the soldiers smash him in the belly and toss Rafael to the ground, unconscious.

"No!" I shriek, and flail wildly with my arms and legs.

Don't take Rafael.

The soldier licks his thick, greasy lips, as the others pin me to the ground.

Then everything goes black.

Trees cry for rain. Purple flowers shudder in the wind. The sky fills with thin clouds that shape-shift as they pass overhead. A bird cloud suddenly transforms into a handsome trovador; a child cloud drifts into a crouching man. Suddenly there's a dull thud; Catalina. She wears a broken iron key on a leather thong around her neck. I reach out to touch the key and the metal burns my fingers, the sky turns black, and the clouds scatter in terror.

I open my eyes. All I can see are black spots on a field of blurry light. I blink, trying to clear my vision. Shadows move in and out, like black clouds in a dance. I work harder, praying my sight returns.

Praying to whom?

Painfully, the shadows stop dancing, and images begin to filter through. I don't *know* what I'm seeing; it's gray and stone-colored, speckled with blood and water stains. I'm stretched out on stone - it's a very old floor. I try to sit up but my body burns everywhere, I raise my hands to my eyes and they're bloody, the skin ripped in a dozen different places. My arms and legs ache, and my neck is bruised and painful. I touch my clothes and they're torn and ragged, the skin beneath sore to my touch.

What have they done?

201

I don't want to remember; I will put a dark blot in my mind that will forever erase the moment. I scream, my voice cutting through my throat like shards of glass.

Rafael?

"I'm here."

His voice is soft, barely audible. I struggle again to sit up and realize that I'm surrounded by bodies, the men and women from *Os Estãos.* I ignore the shooting pains that dart down my back, the blood stains, and the anguish that resides deep within.

Take a deep breath.

Be strong.

Tears fill my eyes. I shake my head furiously and look around me. Some of the bodies are stretched silently on the stone floor; others are sitting, staring up, still others are hunched, sobbing, clinging to one another. I shake my head again, fighting to clear my thoughts.

What happened?

I follow the gaze of those staring up, struggling to keep my vision clear. There, above us, are huge, stained glass windows tossing colored light like splotches of dried blood. Between the windows is an enormous crucifix with a carved Jesus nailed to the wood, his face twisted in pain.

Was his pain for us now?

I thought about the days, a lifetime ago, where we attended church, carried rosaries, and prayed to Jesus along with our neighbors. We said the right words, sang the right chants, and danced the right steps. Where did it get us?

Here, beneath this crucifix.

I always was, and will be, a Jew.

I raise my bloody fist to the crucifix.

I'm a Jew.

I shout.

"Sssssh," a motherly woman gently touches my arm.

I stare at her face, wrinkled with grief.

"What happened?"

"King Manuel lost his patience," she says hoarsely. "They dragged us through the streets and brought us here."

She tilts her head to the bodies that surround us. They must have dragged me, unconscious. I don't remember much . . . now I see the others, clad in ripped clothing stained with blood. They are literally *piles* of people, like cuts of meat strewn on the floor.

Rafael?

I panic.

"I'm here," he says again.

I watch in horrid fascination as an unrecognizable man, torn ragged, with blood dripping down his forehead and across his cheeks, crawls to me.

Rafael.

I struggle to meet him, squirming through the bodies, shivering at the touch of so much fiery flesh. I stretch my hand around two women, who have stirred into a dazed consciousness. Rafael reaches me. Our fingers touch.

Strength surges through me. I glance at the crucifix.

You will not kill me.

I roll between more bodies and suddenly I'm in Rafael's arms. For a moment, everything becomes dark as we sob our relief, cradling one another.

"Come," Rafael's voice was dry and cracked.

We crawl to an opening in the seemingly endless mass of bodies.

"What happened?" The words were nearly impossible to form.

Rafael puts his finger gently on my lips.

"We were knocked out and dragged here," he says hoarsely.

"Through the streets?"

"Yes."

"That's why my clothes . . ."

Rafael nods.

"Are you okay?"

"Just beaten up," he smiles weakly. "You?"

Every muscle in my body is alive with pain. "I'm okay," I whisper, lying. "Where are we?"

"I tried to help . . ." he says, but his voice shakes and he can't finish his words.

Rafael raises his eyes and is silent.

I follow his gaze.

The stone walls are so high that it looks like the ceiling can touch heaven. There's more stained glass, crucifixes, and statues. There are paintings and candles, gold, and crystal everywhere.

It's a place that shouts beauty; filled with art and sense of spirit, as if God could make a visit . . .

"We're in a church," I say bitterly.

"Yes."

"They're baptizing us."

Rafael is silent. Now I hear the chanting of the clerics, the drone of the priests . . .

"Many are unconscious, others stunned. We've been dragged here and . . ."

Rafael kisses my hand. "They can baptize you, they can give you a Christian name, they can tell the Spanish royals that there are no Jews left in Portugal - but they can't touch your soul."

Almighty God, who by our baptism into the death and resurrection of thy son Jesus Christ dost turn these filthy Jew heathens from their old life of sin . . .

I want to scream with rage.

Grant that we, being reborn to new life in him, may live in righteousness and holiness of all our days . . .

Rafael grabs me and holds tightly.

Through the same thy Son Jesus Christ our Lord . . .

I try to squirm away, run - do anything to get out of this church, the bodies, the voice . . .

Who liveth and reigneth with thee and the Holy Spirit . . .

A collective wail rises from the bodies around us.

One God, now and forever.

I hit Rafael's chest with my fists, I cry out to no one, I feel like

I'm falling to the depths of despair.

With the power of our beloved King Manual, and the sacrifice of our Lord Jesus Christ, I enter these Jews into our Holy faith, baptizing them forever as Christians who live within the loving kindness of our church and the eternal protection of our Lord Jesus Christ.

Drops of water rain down upon us.

They splatter on our heads, burning our scalps, wrenching our souls.

In the name of thy Son Jesus Christ our Lord, who liveth and reigneth with thee, Almighty God, and the Holy Spirit, one God, now and forever.

Amen.

The Old Couple

The old couple sighs deeply. They look into each others' eyes, wishing that things can be different. But there's an inevitability about them and this moment - a pause in the numbing march of time – that they can't control. Their destiny is to watch, and wait. They sing softly to one another, their voices eerie, like silky webs lighter than air:

Where is the key that was in the drawer?
Onde sta la yave ke stava in kashon?

My forefathers brought it with great pain
From their house in Spain.

Mis nonus la trusheron kon grande dolor
De su kaza de Espanya.

We told our children this is the heart of our home.

Taymullah

One more.

Gilgul.

The concepts merge in the dark man's mind, careening in dizzying spirals until he has to fight to maintain his balance. He staggers slightly on the cobblestones, as the Great Lawn blurs and colors swirl around him.

One more infidel.

He cries aloud.

The old couple glares at him, but they don't move.

I'm almost there.

God, I'm almost there.

Four: Zara and Cole

Zara

The wind tears at my face as I cling to the rough, scratchy brown mane of the horse. I hold tight - the soldier doesn't care if I fall off. The red cross on his huge barrel chest is pressed up against my back like a stone wall, hard and unyielding. I try not to tremble, but he feels like fire searing my skin. I hear Marianna's screams in the distance; I have a forever picture of Rafael lying still in the dust and Aldonça and Gonçallo watching helplessly. I love them . . . I want to cry out to all of them but each time I try, the soldier slaps my head.

It hurts.

I don't want to hurt anymore.

I'll never see my sister again. Fear takes hold of me; I shake inside like a baby, my hands tremble and my palms are wet. I remember when the neighbor's baby, tiny Isabelle, cried through the night. She screamed, and trembled, and sweat covered her body. Mama told me she was very sick. The next day I woke up and Mama said that little Isabelle had died. I wondered how that all happened, why a baby had to die. Mama said that Isabelle was taken back by God; she was happy and safe. I didn't believe her. Isabelle was dead, like the beef we ate for dinner.

Dead.

I don't want to die!

I don't want to be like little Isabelle, even if God is waiting for me!

A scream sticks in my throat.

Will God be angry at me because I don't want to be with Him?

I wish that Mama or Papa were here to answer my questions. Or Marianna, Catalina, even Rafael. Rafael isn't a *Converso,* so I guess he can't answer as well as them. Yet his music and songs seem like they're from God, so maybe he could help me as well. . .

I shake my head.

No one can help me anymore.

Now, it's up to me. I have to live for Catalina and Mama and Papa. Maybe if I live long enough I'll see Marianna and Rafael again . . .

I won't let God take me.

Angry tears race down my face, but the wind dries them quickly. I'm only nine years old, but I know that it's a message to stop crying. What's going to happen to me? I want to scream like Marianna, I want to hurt this horrible soldier; I want to go back.

Mama's arms are around me. Her voice is gentle.

Be strong my little one.

No! I cry. No!

I will be with you.

No! You're not with me, Mama. You're with the Inquisitors in a dungeon.

The soldier hits my head. I feel dizzy, like I might fall off the horse. I hold on tighter, my heart pounding wildly.

Be strong my little one her voice rocks me. *You'll be fine.*

I shiver. I have to believe her. Mama never lied to me. The big soldier pressing up against my back doesn't care. The horse racing across the land doesn't care. It's like we're flying, high off the ground, moving so quickly . . .

I would have loved this feeling of being atop a big, powerful animal flying across the countryside if it wasn't for everything else.

Be strong my little one.

Maybe Mama *is* here, hovering in the air above the horse's head. Mama and Papa and Catalina?

Be strong.

I'm so alone! I don't want to be strong. I want to be back with Marianna and Rafael; Mama and Papa and Catalina. I want to hear Aldonça laugh when I play with the pretty purple flowers that grow in the meadow behind the barn, and see Gonçallo trying to appear stern when a smile lights his eyes. I want to giggle and not be scared.

I can hardly breathe.

Please Mama?

Be strong my little one.

209

I can't hear Marianna anymore. She's gone, just like Catalina. Her voice is lost in the wind, as if it was never there.

I don't know how much time passes before the soldier slows his horse. It seems like forever, but I know it's only been long enough to see Aldonça, Gonçallo, Marianna, and Rafael disappear in the dust. They can't see or hear me. I can't see or hear them. The soldier points to a stream, then leaps off his horse, the red cross on his chest gleaming in the sun.

"Don't move," he warns me.

He leads the horse, with me on its back, to the stream. The other soldiers are there, guiding their horses to drink. As the animals noisily slurp the water, I notice the red-headed little girl. She's upright now, but so very tiny. She's no older than five. Her green eyes are wide with fear, her lips tremble, and her thick, curly red hair is tangled and messy.

"Hi," I whisper.

She looks at me but doesn't speak.

"I'm Zara," I say softly so the soldiers can't hear. "What's your name?"

The little girl blinks her eyes but says nothing.

"I'm scared too," I say bravely.

A faint smile plays across her lips.

"Can you speak?"

The little girl stares at me.

"Let's go," the soldier says, heaving himself back on the horse. Once again, he presses against my back. He kicks the horse and we're off, racing through the countryside.

It's nearly dark by the time we stop again. The soldier leads his horse into a large courtyard. There are two stone-and-wood warehouses with heavy wooden doors. Monks, nuns, priests, and soldiers mill around hundreds of children, from infants to older than me. Some of them look very angry, others are sad, their cheeks stained with tears. A few have blank faces as if they feel nothing. The soldiers roughly drop me and the little girl to the ground. A monk, dressed in heavy brown robes, drags us over to a large group of children.

210

"The girls go here," he points to one building on his left, "and the boys to the right."

The little girl from the horse grabs my hand.

"What's your name?" I ask gently.

She looks at me silently, terror in her eyes.

"If you don't tell me your name, I'll have to give you one."

She shakes her head and throws her arms around me, hugging tightly.

"OK," I tell her, feeling her small body shake in my arms. "You must have a name. I'll call you Tama, or the innocent one."

The little girl smiles bravely.

A short, gentle-faced monk pushes us forward.

"Stay with me, Tama. I'll take care of you."

Tama and I are not the only children clinging together. I see sisters and friends, neighbors and strangers, holding to one another for support. Some of the girls have tiny babies in their arms. Why would the soldiers steal babies? The girls try to feed the infants, but they cry for their mama's breasts, filling the air with their wails.

It's a horrible place - a cold, dark, filthy warehouse bursting with children who should be home with their mamas and papas. Monks and nuns mill through the crowd, handing out pieces of bread and offering water. Some children eat hungrily, others just stare, too frightened to eat or drink. Many of the older girls pray, but if they're caught, the monks or nuns slap their faces, leaving marks on their cheeks.

"By mercy of our Lord Jesus Christ, you will obey the one true faith," they cry.

Suddenly I hear strange words chanted over our heads.

The nuns and monks are crossing themselves. Several priests circle around us, sprinkling water on our heads.

"No," a girl, somewhat older than me, cries. Her light brown hair flies in all directions, her eyes are wild. "They're baptizing us." She shouts, praying loudly in Hebrew.

Shema Yisrael Adonai Elohaenu Adonai Echad.
Hear O Israel The Lord is God, The Lord is One."

211

Everyone starts to scream.

A priest leaps across some very tiny children, and grabs the girl by the hair. "The language of Lucifer," he roars, and beats her with his fist, screaming Portuguese words I don't understand. Her nose bleeds, dripping everywhere as she lowers her head, and wails pitifully beneath the blows.

"You're now a Christian," the priest roars. "All of you have received the Beneficence of Conversion and Redemption in The Catholic Faith of Our Lord Christ Jesus. If I hear any of you speaking the words of the devil, you will be beaten. If we catch you carrying any of the artifacts of the devil, you will be beaten. We must protect your souls!"

We're all silent. Tama holds on to me tightly.

"If you persist," the priest roars, "you'll be thrown into water when we reach the sea or thrown to the lizards when we reach São Tomé! You'll spend eternity in the fires of Hell."

Tama and I tremble - the priest's voice is so strong and his hands are covered in blood from the beating. We believe what he says.

What have I done to deserve the fires of Hell?

I hug Tama. "We'll be okay," I lie. "I promise."

It's a promise I don't know if I can keep.

I gently lead Tama to a bare spot against the wall. We sit and huddle against one another, shivering with cold and fear.

The girl next to us watches carefully. "My name is Leah," she says haughtily. "And I know where we're going."

"I do too," I respond defiantly.

"São Tomé." Leah brags.

I nod.

"Do you know what São Tomé *is*?" Leah asks, her face sharp, her cheeks bright red.

"An island?"

Leah laughs like a mad woman. "It's an island where giant lizards eat children!"

"No!"

"Yes," Leah smirks, pleased with her information. "We're all going to die - the lizards will have us for dinner."

Tama and I hold on to each other beneath the crazy cackles of Leah's laughter. I don't think I'll ever sleep again, but my eyes close, and . . .

I wake to the chanting of nuns and monks.

Glory be to the Father, and to the Son, and to the Holy Spirit;
As it was in the beginning, is now, and will be for ever. Amen.

My back aches from sleeping against the stone wall and supporting Tama. For a moment I forget where I am. I'm home again, waiting for Mama to wake me up, tell me my chores for the day, giggle with Marianna over the pretty purple flowers that she gathered yesterday in the fields, laugh while Catalina tickles me . . .

All-powerful God, help us to proclaim the power of the Lord's resurrection.

The words penetrate my thoughts. Present returns.

May we who accept the sign of the love of Christ come to share the eternal life he reveals.

In seconds, I remember what happened yesterday . . . Aldonça and Gonçallo trying to protect us; Gonçallo falling in the dust; Rafael shoving us beneath the straw; and Marianna holding me so tightly I could hardly breathe.

For he lives and reigns with you and the Holy Spirit, one God, for ever and ever.

I'm a Jew! I want to scream, as loud as I can. But Marianna has told me these are strange times and I have to be very careful. I don't understand . . . people hate *Conversos* so much that they took Mama and Papa from us. Now people hate Jews so much that they took me from Aldonça, Gonçallo, and Rafael who *are* Christians, and Marianna . . .

I shake my head.

I don't understand.

213

If the love of Christ is so powerful, why would people need to hurt me or Marianna, Mama or Papa? Why did God need to take Catalina from us? Why would any God let soldiers beat up gentle Aldonça and Gonçallo, maybe kill Rafael?

"*Novos Christãos,*" a monk says, thrusting bread into my hands. "Eat for your strength."

Our eyes meet. His are gentle, but glazed, as if his kindness is covered in ice. I take a deep breath and nibble on the bread. I'm not very hungry. I'm tired and hurt, and missing everyone very much.

I look next to me, but Leah is gone. I'm glad. All her talk about giant lizards eating us is too scary, and I want to make sure Tama is okay. Right now, Tama is sleeping fitfully, her tiny arms thrashing at the air. I split my bread in half and try to wake her very gently so she will eat. Instead, she starts screaming wildly, her eyes burning.

"Silence!" A nun orders.

"We'll beat her into quiet," a fat monk adds, "if we have to."

I remember the crazy girl with the brown hair who screamed the Hebrew prayer and how the monks beat her with their fists. I don't want that to happen to Tama. I pull her into my arms and hold her just like Marianna did to me in the straw next to the cow. I cradle her and cover her mouth so everyone thinks she's quiet. Tama trembles so badly it feels like she'll break into a thousand pieces. I softly sing one of Rafael's songs to settle her. It works. Finally, Tama is quiet. I feed her bread in tiny pieces like she's a baby. She doesn't eat very much.

"Can you talk now, Tama?"

Her big, sad green eyes widen in fear.

"It's okay; I'll talk for both of us. You're safe, Tama, I won't let anyone hurt you."

I follow Tama's eyes as she looks around the warehouse. Some girls are milling around, mumbling things under their breaths. Others are still, eating their bread and watching. Still others are frozen, their bodies lying like sacks filled with grain.

"Dead," I hear one of the nuns whisper.

"Get the boys," another says.

Suddenly a few older boys appear in the warehouse under the fiery eyes of a skinny, scowling monk. I know there are only supposed to be children between ages two and fourteen, but these boys look a lot older. There are a few girls carrying babies in their arms that look a lot older too.

"Bring them outside," the monk points to the motionless children.

One boy passes right in front of me, his eyes downcast. "They're dead," he hisses. "They're the lucky ones."

Like Catalina?

My heart pounds when the boy picks up a little dead girl not far from us.

Tama shivers and I think of the dead baby Isabelle, and dead Catalina, lying in the purple flowers.

"We're not going to die!" I cry loudly.

A nun hears me. She bends down to look at us, her habit flowing in dark directions.

"No, little one," she says sweetly. "You're now in the hands of our Lord, Jesus Christ. He won't let you die."

Her voice is so soft, I want to ask her to take me back to Marianna and Rafael. I want to tell her that I'm afraid to go to a strange island where lizards eat children. I want to tell her so many things . . .

She's gone before I can muster the courage to say one word.

"I won't let us die," I whisper to Tama, hoping, once again, that I'm not lying.

Tama's eyes flutter. I wonder if she hears or even understands what I'm saying.

When all the dead children are removed, the monks leave with the boys.

It's not long before the same priest, with the booming voice, stands before us. Next to him is a soldier with a fearsome helmet and a red cross on his chest, like the soldier who brought me here.

"*Novos Christãos*," the priest cries, "children of our Lord Jesus Christ, hear ye."

The soldier steps forward and removes his helmet. He's very ugly - with tiny brown eyes and a red scar that runs from the end of his right eye to his chin. Tama's mouth drops open.

"By Righteous Decree of His Most Catholic Majesty, King João II," the soldier roars, "all Jewish children, male and female, ten years of age and younger, are exiled and shall be transported to the Holy See of Africa. You have already received baptism, and are now the children of Our Lord, Jesus Christ. You will join the *degradados* under the

leadership of Alvaro de Caminha, *Donátario da Ilha de São Tomé,* to work and live in the colony of São Tomé."

São Tomé. The name stings like the bite of an ugly bumble bee. *Alvaro de Caminha.*

I shiver. We *are* going to the island where lizards eat children and our companions are *assassinos e ladrQ´es*, Portuguese murderers and thieves.

How will we survive?

"We'll make it," I whisper to Tama.

She's not listening.

They herd us like sheep from the warehouses to the wood docks at Lisboa port. The soldiers try to keep us calm, surrounding us as we enter the harbor plaza. The sky is clear, there are pigeons and gulls everywhere, but their noises are drowned out by the crazed, screaming crowds that stand at the dock. There is so much noise! Guards hover, holding back desperate parents struggling to reclaim their children. They attack anyone who breaks their lines, sending bodies bleeding and unconscious to the wooden ground. Arms reach out wildly for their children and soldiers cut them down like weeds in a field, immune to the blood and pain.

The children's yells pierce the air; they bawl really loud and fight to break away, arms reaching for their parents. Soldiers, monks, and nuns grab and twist their tiny bodies, shouting commands that fall on deaf ears. Parents toss travel bundles to their children, as soldiers raise their swords; children reach for them only to have their few possessions seized by their tormentors. Screams, blood, grasping arms . . . they're everywhere.

I close my eyes and try to block it out.

216

Think of purple flowers.
There's no one in that crowd for me.

We ran from Mama, Papa and the Inquisitors; Catalina died on the purple flowers; I faced soldiers at the border and later, black death in Lisboa. Now I've been stolen from my home with Aldonça and Gonçallo, wrenched from Marianna and Rafael, held captive by royal horsemen galloping across the countryside, and locked up in a dark, damp warehouse. My story flows like one of Rafael's songs, but never, until this moment, have I been so completely terrified.

What will happen to me?

A fat monk shoves me into the melee, and my eyes pop open. I hang on to Tama for dear life, although she seems numb and lifeless, not hearing anything. Across the dock, mamas throw themselves at soldier's boots, begging to be allowed to go with their children. Papas pray, their hands grasping at the air, begging God for help. The soldiers kick them aside like sacks of grain, laughing at their desperation.

Suddenly, everyone freezes. A mother breaks through the mob; she rushes to the children and scoops up her only child, a pretty, dark-eyed little boy. Embracing her son, she leaps into the water, drowning both of them beneath the hull of a caravel.

For a moment, there is stunned silence.

Her husband screams.

The cries return, louder and angrier - the shouts worse as the soldiers battle the unarmed parents, killing and wounding even more. A captain hollers over the din, roaring the same words we heard earlier:

By Righteous Decree of His Most Catholic Majesty, King João II, all Jewish children, male and female, ten years of age and younger, are exiled and shall be transported to the Holy See of Africa. You have already received baptism, and are now the children of Our Lord, Jesus Christ. Now you will join the degradados under the leadership of Alvaro de Caminha, to work and live in the colony of São Tomé.

A wail rises from the parents, but the soldiers form a deadly wall in front of them, weapons raised, killing anyone who breaks through. Some of the children cry out and they're slapped into silence by monks standing among us.

217

Suddenly, Tama stiffens. Her eyes are wide and her lips tremble. I follow her gaze to a woman, trapped behind two scary soldiers, her arms outstretched. Her wild, tangled red hair flies in all directions, her green eyes burn, and she's screaming something . . . a name . . . that I can't hear.

Tama's mama?

Cole

Cole loved Bryant Park. He had performed on streets and in parks, at train stations, and in small clubs throughout the city. Bryant was his favorite venue. It reminded him of a southwestern canyon surrounded by sprawling red rocks - the ground wild, untamed, bursting with life, yet trapped. Bryant Park was immersed in silver, blue, and mirrored rocks, screaming with city life, a splash of green in an asphalt world.

Cole couldn't believe his luck when he was selected for *ThursdaysAt5*. There were so many good musicians in the city; so many voices fighting to be heard. The summer gig was produced by *NewSong* - an independent music organization. Their goal was to identify and build what they called a "supportive community" of performers and songwriters. They brought "exceptional artists" to Bryant Park to introduce their work to a large public audience, referring to it as "where great artists are discovered." *NewSong* ran music series on weekdays throughout the summer. Thursdays was for "jazz, barbershop, piano, and more."

Cole clearly belonged to the "and more."

NewSong gave him promise of a future in music, chords away from street acts, into contracts, festivals, and tours. It was a different kind of hope for Cole, who, by nature, was a nomad, living in slow, steady movement. There was always this sense of something missing – something absent from his life. Maybe *ThursdaysAt5* was the missing link?

NewSong made a big deal about Cole's appearance. They described him as "having a unique voice that mixed past and present in sounds that compelled people to listen."

During his initial interview, he was stunned at their understanding of his music.

"You sing," he was told by Isaac, the *NewSong* representative, "with a new Spanish guitar and an old language that brings a different culture to the park."

"Arizona is a different culture?" Cole responded with a half-smile.

"No," Isaac responded, "you are."

Cole stared at the representative.

"Ladino," Isaac continued. "The Yiddish of the Sephardic Jews, before the expulsion. It spread throughout the world, picking up words from other countries, but still remained inherently Spanish."

Cole grinned. There was gentleness in his blue eyes, a message Cole couldn't quite read. "Are you Sephardic?" Cole asked.

Isaac shrugged. "Who knows after so many years?"

Cole sensed that Isaac wanted no more questions. After all, Cole *was* a different culture, here and in Arizona, a man of the southwest who often wandered alone for the sheer joy of company with cactus, sun, and sky. He had been many places in the world. Cole had eaten tapas in Spain and curry in Thailand. He bought his leather wallet in Morocco, and the iron circle pendant, that he wore every day, in Portugal. But it was his beloved mountain desert, beyond the bustle of Tucson, which brought him peace. The bitingly dry air and camouflaged-skin critters that slithered across the sandy earth were his favorite companions, along with the sweet Ladino melodies.

"There's nothing like a night in the Arizona desert," Cole added impulsively.

He thought of the black sky pocked with so many stars that it looked like an impossible background for someone's poorly designed video game. He touched the iron circle that hung on a leather thong around his neck.

Isaac nodded, as if he could read Cole's thoughts.

Cole stuck out his hand. "Done," he said to Isaac. "I would love to do *ThursdaysAt5.*"

Isaac took his hand. "My pleasure."

Isaac's handshake was firm.

"It's going to be a great gig," Isaac added.

Now Cole scanned the park - the performance of his life was about to begin. He waved at Isaac, dressed in a yellow t-shirt and blue jeans. Then Cole took a very deep breath.

Cole was a tall, slim man with dark hair, powerful shoulders, and a smile that no one could resist. He knew that, but used it wisely. Although he was in his late thirties, Cole appeared ageless.

He loved these moments before a performance. Tension and anticipation hung in the air, eyes watching every movement he made. Slowly, people were drawn to his space until a barely perceptible moment when they shifted from being a crowd to an audience. It was then that his music took on a life of its own; the words reverberated in time, and the energy of people, the echoes of the canyon, and the rhythm of his beloved guitar merged.

He watched as the people closed in, delicately separated by personal territories. New Yorkers never touched. They could race down a crowded street, be wedged in a suffocating subway, and still never touch one another. The best way to spot a tourist was to watch how he or she negotiated the streets. Tourists always bumped into people, looked in the wrong directions, and had no clue how to dodge a taxi and make it across the street before the light turned.

Although he wasn't a New Yorker, Cole understood the delicate balance between space and movement. Cole needed a lot of territory to play out his life; he had the heart of a rebel – a troubadour who donned masks and played roles wherever he went. Whether it was the streets of Manhattan, the beaches of Los Angeles, or the mountain deserts of his native Arizona, Cole blended by his own design, a mirror for the faces that adored him.

Cole grinned boyishly. He stood on the terrace, in front of the graceful French Classical fountain whose water was a perfect aural backdrop to his music. Beyond the fountain were the open white slats of the Summer Film Festival screen, a dramatic setting for his show. Past that, out of sight, was the lifeblood of Bryant Park - the Great Lawn, the tree-lined promenades, and the Upper Library Terrace, with concrete pots of flowers.

I'm ready.

When he wasn't performing at Bryant Park or in gigs throughout the city, Cole held the most iconic job in New York.

He was a hot dog vendor.

It began when Cole's cousin called him in Arizona.

"I need your help," Cuz said. "I just bought a new cart and I don't trust anyone to run it."

Cole wondered if Cuz really needed his help or it was a conspiracy between his mom and her nephew to give him direction. Cole wandered too much - a habit Mom hated. She wanted him fixed in place and time, kept safe in a world that was inherently dangerous.

"Can't you stay in one place?" She begged constantly, her large dark eyes edged with crow's feet, her lips paragraphed by permanent frown lines.

Cole would hug his mother and laugh, never answering her question. They both knew that no one could keep Cole in one place too long. His need to move and wander dominated everything and everyone. He was always searching for something he couldn't define; as if he were hunting for a missing piece of himself.

When the call came in from Cuz, he wasn't surprised. It sounded good and Cole was off on a new adventure.

Cole arrived in the city with his Spanish guitar, his iron circle hanging on a leather thong around his neck, a big smile, and charm that attracted everyone, from impatient grab-a-quick-lunchers to teenage girls. Cuz owned three street vending carts: two sold hot dogs and one sold hot, sweet nuts. In the world of New York City street vendors, Cuz was a rich man.

The city noise and energy assaulted Cole; the thoughts of millions of people invaded his space. He struggled to build a glass cocoon around himself. Thinking of *Kafka* and *Walter Mitty*, Cole knew the only way to survive was to go schizoid – split his world into two distinct parts. If it didn't work, it would be an interesting experiment that he could transport back to the mountain desert.

His lead role was hot dogs. His backup was street performer – a contemporary troubadour.

It fit.

As a hot dog vendor he was invisible, a fixture on the street. People saw through him - a means to an end. As a troubadour he was the end - the focus in a fragile moment of time, when life paused in the city.

222

New York street vendors were plagued by city rules and regulations, ridiculous fines, permits, storage costs - the list was endless. It was a tough way to earn a living. The city didn't issue permits anymore, so a vendor had to buy or rent from someone who already owned one. Back in the late nineties, a guy named Sean ran a food cart so he could work his way through school. He got a taste of the life and when he graduated Georgetown Law, started the Street Vendor Project for the 10,000 vendors in New York - part of the Urban Justice Center. *New York Magazine* dubbed Sean the César Chávez of hot dog stands.

When he sold hot dogs, Cole was one of many "immigrants." Most came from Third World countries like Sri Lanka, Viet Nam, Bangladesh, Columbia, and Brazil - places where people were hungry for food and work. It was a sidewalk United Nations, a turf where a drifter from Arizona didn't quite fit.

The words of a kabob vendor came to mind.

Most never see the vendor that yanks a kid about to run in front of a car, gives a homeless guy a few coins, or follows the vendor's etiquette as entrepreneurs.

Cole recalled how Cuz was nominated for the Vendy Award - the Grammy of street vending. Rolf won that year with his cart called *Hallo Berlin*. He was an East German who been on the streets since the 70's, selling bratwurst and other sausages. The guy spoke with a German accent and boasted specials called "Dictator" and "Democracy."

There was Hakim from Egypt, who lived in a two-bedroom walkup with his wife and four kids, right next to Yankee Stadium. They called him the kebab man of 42nd and 8th. Everyone loved Thiru, "Dosa Man" at Washington Square Park - the only vegan street vendor in the country. He made Indian food with a Sri Lanka edge. Juan, the fruit vendor from Sunnyside, Queens collected letters from customers when the police tried to get him kicked off his street corner. Nick was a 60-year old Greek-American who ran a Souvlaki cart in Astoria, while Veronica sold native Trinidadian/Jamaican jerk chicken and oxtail stew uptown.

Cole was one of them . . . and apart from them.

He was also the only street vendor who had singing gigs in his spare time.

Cole looked out at the crowd gathering on the fountain terrace for _ThursdaysAt5_. Many were sitting around the tiny green tables; others had pulled chairs in from different parts of the park. There was a tired-looking mom and dad, hanging on to the handle of a stroller stuffed with two sleeping kids. There was a sweaty lady, bathed in rolls of fat, uselessly fanning herself with a magazine. People wore sundresses and business suits, jeans and shorts. There was dark hair and thin hair, long hair and crew cuts, white skin, black skin, brown skin, and tattooed skin.

In front of him stretched a microcosm of the city. His touched the iron circle.

They were all waiting for him.

The fat lady in the crowd stopped fanning herself. Sweat poured down the sides of her face and over the huge mounds of flesh called her breasts. Cole could almost smell her from across the crowd.

Cole smiled at the crowd. The tension built as they waited for him to begin. Isaac stepped up to the mike.

"I want to introduce," he began, "one of the most unique performers ever to join us on _ThursdaysAt5_."

The crowd grew quiet; more people found chairs. Others started to drift in from the street and the Great Lawn.

"He calls himself Cole," Isaac continued, his blue eyes twinkling. "I'm sure most of you have never heard anyone quite like him."

A ripple of curiosity swept through the audience.

"This man is a real treat for all of us," Isaac grinned.

Cole glanced happily at Lev.

But something was very wrong.

Lev was Cole's helper. One day, without warning, Lev appeared from nowhere, during a performance in the gloom of Penn Station. Cole stood against the railing over the stairs to Long Island Railroad Tracks 20 and 21. On his right was the entrance to the 1-2-3 subway. Smells drifted over from the McDonald's on his left; skinny hamburgers, salty fries, and a lot of fat. Down the dim vaulted corridor were the lights and smells of stalls hawking stale popcorn, sugary waffle cones, oily pretzel twists, and freshly baked cookies. Next to him was *The Petal Pusher*, a cart offering bright colors and scents in fast-food flower bouquets that commuters brought home to apologize for being late, to make up for yesterday's argument, or as a last minute gift for an almost-forgotten birthday, anniversary, or holiday.

Only a few people were listening to Cole sing that day in Penn Station. It was right before rush hour, so Cole was gearing up, his guitar case open for tips.

Lev, gaunt in loose-fitting pants and a button-down shirt, just stared. Cole recognized the side locks shoved hastily behind his ears, black hat, and fringes dangling beneath his shirt. The boy was probably sneaking away from a *Yeshiva* to hang out in midtown.

Their eyes met.

"Ladino," Cole said softly. "I sing in Ladino."

"Yeah," the kid smiled shyly. "I know."

After a few songs, Cole stepped from the mike and held out his hand. Lev stared at the offering, but didn't move.

Cole went back to the mike. The rush hour crowd came and went, until the kid was the only one left.

Cole approached him again, his hand in offering. Lev thought carefully about what he was going to do. His eyelids closed, and his body swayed slightly. Finally, he opened his eyes and took Cole's hand.

The handshake was damp and timid.

"I'm Lev," the kid said.

Cole nodded.

It was the start of the oddest friendship in his life.

Lev showed up for all of Cole's gigs. He became a trusted helper; always there to lift, move, or pack. He never asked for money or attention. Cole had no idea where Lev lived or what he did when he wasn't with him on a gig. Many times, Cole wondered what Lev's parents would think about him helping a street performer/hot dog vendor from Arizona. But Lev never talked and Cole never asked.

Lev quickly picked up Cole's Ladino. He spoke several languages - English, Hebrew, and Yiddish, so Ladino was not difficult. Lev understood the rhythm of Ladino, as if he had heard it all his life. While he couldn't sing, Lev was able to say the words easily.

Ladino folk music was the heart of Cole's gig. The Ladino sounds mesmerized him – raised odd, smoldering emotions.

It makes me different - sets me apart from the rest.
It ties me to the past.

 Sometimes Cole wondered if it came from a role in another life. A leading actor in a medieval play? A turn-of-the-century song and dance man? Transmigration? There was no doubt he was a modern-day troubadour, an identity he carried with pride. As for the rest . . . Cole never found answers. He'd given in to his strange predilection and made Ladino folk songs his act. The Hispanics, Jews, folk music nuts, south westerners, and romantics loved the resonance - a strange, haunting blend of cultures mingling the sounds of Spain, the Ottoman Empire, northern Africa, Greece, and Hebrew.

So in some strange way, Lev fit - he belonged to the gig.

Now, Lev was scowling. What's wrong with him? Cole wondered. Was it that stupid superstition?

"He sings in a language few understand," Isaac boasted to the crowd. "It's called Ladino. The sounds bring us back into the 15th century . . . but don't worry, Cole will translate to help you really hear the music and words . . ."

Isaac turned to Cole.

"Your music connects us to each other, over time and origin, beyond our names, our properties, and our legacies," Isaac continued. "He brings us together, pairing the unlikely with the everyday."

Cole looked at Lev, expecting him to have his arms in the air.
Lev's eyes were smoldering.
Something was definitely wrong.
Why the hell was the kid holding his breath?

226

Lev was definitely out of tune. He was the kind of kid that couldn't hide it – discomfort showed in his face, his body language, and most of all, his eyes. Cole was confused. *ThursdaysAt5* was an incredible venue – a huge opportunity. Why was the kid frowning?

Isaac was smiling. Waiting.

Cole stepped up to the mike. He waited for a hush to spread across the crowd. Tension built.

What was wrong with Lev?

Zara

Tama comes alive, screaming, arms flailing, blindly fighting her way around a fat monk in smelly robes, holding the children away from their parents.

"Mama?" I ask Tama.

Tama nods, struggling fiercely against the monk who plucks her off the ground and holds her like a victory flag, taunting the red-headed woman.

The woman screams. I think I hear her voice above the others. The monk is plunging deeper into the crowd holding Tama and separating us.

I can't be separated from Tama.

I promised.

I wave my arms at Tama's mama. "I'll take care of her, I promise," I shout above the noise. For a moment, Tama's mother stops struggling. Our eyes meet. Her lips move.

Gracias. May the God of Israel protect you.

Then she disappears beneath the red cross on the rock-hard chest of a soldier.

The monk sets Tama down on the dock as I shove through bodies to stay with her. I grab her hand and green eyes thank me.

Suddenly a powerful, angry-looking man with a short, dark beard and stony face, blocks us. He stares down like an evil bronze statue, his dark eyes boring into us. He seems to rise from among the children, a dangerous creature not to be defied.

Alvaro de Caminha.

Donátario da Ilha de São Tomé.

For a moment our eyes meet. When he speaks his voice freezes my blood, a chunk of ice thrust inside.

Quiet, child.

The Captain of our ships and the Colonial Administrator of *São Tomé* throws wide his arms and pushes his way through the crowd, immune to the grief of everyone on the dock.

Tama trembles, but is silent.

For some reason, I follow him, dragging Tama with me, shoving through the bodies, tripping over feet, arms, and monks, desperately trying to hang on to her. I'm determined to stay close to the *Donátario*. There is little resistance; everyone is pushing in the opposite direction. There's no one on the dock for me, and now, there's no one for Tama. Whatever our future brings us, it lies in *São Tomé* with this strange, fierce man.

We reach the edge of the mob, and Alvaro de Caminha stares at the sight before him. There's a fleet of two-masted caravels bobbing on the water, ready to be boarded. They're beautiful. The ships rise high into the air, made of smooth wood, shiny and ready for the sea. They're bowl-shaped, with a high rear deck, a bowled middle, and a lower rising front deck. The masts loom into the air, covered with unfurled sails, ropes hanging everywhere. There are more ropes than I've ever seen in my life. Rope ladders lead to the highest point on each ship; a tiny platform they call the *crow's nest*. Men dressed in rough, homespun clothes are everywhere; they watch the scene on the quay - a fascinating show - revealing yellowed teeth in broad smiles, huge, pulsating muscles, and evil glints in their eyes.

I shudder.

Alvaro de Caminha glances down at me and laughs.

"That's your home now," he says in an oddly gentle voice. He looks back at the ships, his voice heavy with admiration. "It's thirteen hundred leagues to *São Tomé*. Do you know how long that is?"

"No sir," I whisper.

"What?" he barks at me.

"No sir," I say louder.

He nods his head in approval. "It means," he speaks slowly, savoring his words like a piece of stewed beef, "that we will be at sea for two months."

He smiles at the shock on my face.

"Many will die," he laughs, "and others, who don't behave, will be tossed overboard for the sea demons to eat them. It's not a pretty sight."

My eyes widen in fear; I can hardly breathe.

Alvaro de Caminha laughs at my fear, spraying spittle on my face. "Do you want to live, little one?"

I nod, unable to speak.

"Then," he bends slightly, as if telling me a secret, "you will listen to everything the monks tell you. You will eat your food, send your sickness overboard, and stay quiet and out of the way. Perhaps then, you will be kept from the sea demons and the *degradados* who eat little girls like you for dinner." He tilts his head and laughs at the sky. It's a coarse, scary sound. "Of course, pretty girls like you have to watch out for hungry sailors, too." The Colonial Administrator grins. "You might be a little girl," he tucks his fingers beneath my chin and raises my head to examine my face, "but for a hungry sailor with no woman, you can be *his* dinner too."

In my mind I see Rafael and Marianna. He's holding her, *touching her*, she's squirming, as if in pain, like the animals in the field . . .

"Marianna? Rafael?" I screamed. "What are you doing?"

"Nothing my love," Marianna's voice trembled. "We're trying to warm ourselves."

"Leave her alone!" I shouted at Rafael.

"I would never hurt her," Rafael said breathlessly. "I love you. I love your sister. I loved Catalina. I would never hurt either one of you."

I stared at Rafael. I love you. I love your sister. I loved Catalina. I would never hurt either one of you.

"We need water," Rafael said, "and food. We need to find . . . a place."

"Did he hurt you?" I asked Marianna.

"No," she smiled. "He was comforting me."

"You're breathing like . . . Catalina."

"I'm fine."

The Colonial Administrator seems to read my thoughts. He laughs again loudly, slapping his thigh with a thick, broad hand.

"Watch your back, pretty little one," he taunts me.

He stands up straight, surveys the sky, and then the crowd. He turns back to me with an evil glitter in his eyes.

"Remember," he wrinkles his face like a dog readying for a fight, "most people say that going to *Ilha de São Tomé* is a death sentence."

I gasp.

He throws his head back and roars, a sound that echoes with cruelty. Then he stalks away, his laughter drifting behind him like a plume of smoke.

This time, I don't follow. I look at Tama, and my whole body shakes. "We have to fear the sea demons and the *degradados*, the monks and the sailors. Is there anyone we can trust?"

Tama pulls at her tangled, wild red hair.

Once again, she has nothing to say.

I don't know how long we stand there, watching *Alvaro de Caminha*'s back and the caravels bobbing on the water. Suddenly the swarm of children shifts as the monks and sailors push us toward the boats. A wail rises from the crowd on the dock as they shove us up a gangplank and on to the second caravel. We're in the rear, with all the girls, little children, and babies. We huddle together. I find a spot on the edge, where Tama and I can see the docks, the other ships, and the Tagus River that flows into the ocean. The boys are separated from us by a low wood fence; we can see them but we're warned not to talk or have anything to do with them. The *degradados* are chained to each other in the bow; they look angry and hungry and I wonder if we need to fear them as much as the sea demons, the sailors, and the monks.

We will be on board for two months.

Alvaro de Caminha's words ring in my ears.

You will listen to everything the monks tell you. You will eat your food, send your sickness overboard, and stay quiet and out of way. Perhaps then you will be kept from the sea demons and the degradados *who eat little girls like you for dinner.*

I close my eyes and see Marianna's face in my mind. She's smiling and telling me to be brave; everything will work out. I take a deep breath. I have no choice . . . I have to be brave for Tama and for Marianna.

Tama pulls my arm and points. I open my eyes to see the gangplank being raised and hear the wail of the crowd grow louder and more desperate. The ropes that secure the ship to the dock are pulled away and slaves, on the banks, slowly move us through the water. The people on the dock shrink, the noise dims, small boats with oarsmen take the ropes and pull the ship to sea. Suddenly Alvaro de Caminha, standing high above us, lifts his arms.

"Raise the sails" he commands.

There's a hush from the people that cover every part of the ship, leaving little room to move or stretch. The babies are still, the little girls cry softly, and the boys and *degradados* are quiet.

Tama and I say nothing; there are no more tears. We hold hands tightly. Together we watch Lisboa disappear, until only smoke drifts above the hills and *Castelo de São Jorge* fades into the distance.

The days aboard the caravel pass slowly, falling into unfamiliar routines. We spend our time in the girl's section, sleeping outdoors on rough planks. When there's rain or a storm, they force us into the ship's hold and close the hatch, where we sleep next to the animal's stable, in complete darkness, drenched in smells of vomit, feces, sickness, and whatever else we can imagine.

Most days we're on deck, given biscuits, raisins, a lemon, sometimes dates, bad-smelling olives, and never enough water. For the first time in our lives we suffer from sunburn; our skins turn red, hurt, and then heal into an unfamiliar brown color. The monks constantly work on us, demanding we become good Christians. They make us sit on the splintery deck, forcing us to listen as they rant about how Hebrew is the language of Lucifer, and is banned from our minds and tongues forever. Sailors stand around and crack their whips over our heads, wearing evil smiles and hungry eyes. We're only allowed to speak Portuguese and the Latin used in Christian prayer. If the monks are unhappy with us, they threaten to "toss us" into the *degradado* section, and leave us to the ragged, hungry men chained to one another.

Sometimes we watch the sailors go through the *degradados* section,

232

using heavy axes to chop apart the chains of the dead ones. They pull the bodies from the others and then roll each corpse overboard as a monk recites a sharp, bitter prayer:

I commend your soul to the loving arms of our Merciful Savior, Jesus Christ.

I wonder how Jesus Christ . . . or any God, could love those pitiful creatures?

One day, without warning, it feels like we're in the middle of magic. The sun is high in the sky, the air cool, and the clouds hang like puffs of white wool. Tama points to the water and I scream.

Peixes gigantes.

Giant fish! They're beautiful, silver creatures with silky-smooth skin, and swim playfully around the ship. They dance and play gracefully as if in the middle of their own special game. Then one leaps into the air and I see the creature's smile.

Peixes gigantes.

I scream again, laughing.

One of the older boys, standing against the rail, laughs with me, his pale brown eyes sparkling.

"No," the boy shakes his head and smiles crookedly. "It's called a *golfinho.*" He lowers his voice. "In Spanish, it's called a *delfín.*" Dolphin.

Our eyes meet.

"*Delfín,*" I echo him.

"My name is Levi," he reaches his hand across the barrier between the boys and girls section. Our fingers barely touch.

"Levi," I say softly. "My name is Zara."

"I know," he grins. "I watch you with the little one."

"Tama?"

"Yes."

"*Delfín* - I like that name.*"

Tama grabs my arm and points. "*Delfín,*" she says sweetly.

It's the first word she's spoken since I met her, tossed across the soldier's saddle, at Aldonça and Gonçallo's hut.

"*Delfín,*" I cry.

233

"*Delfín*," Levi laughs as if he, too, knows it's Tama's first word.

Tama smiles, her green eyes sparkle. We look at each other with special understanding.

I will never forget the beautiful, silvery *delfín* and its grins as it leaps from the sea, telling me that everything will be all right. I will always remember the unfamiliar feeling of hope, in the middle of endless water, surrounded by *degradados* and hungry sailors, monks and their curses against Jews - so many ugly things.

Mama and Papa, Catalina, Marianna and Rafael are gone. Now, Tama is my family. I glance at Levi. A thought leaps into my mind.

Will Levi be my family, too?

Many more days pass, some with more sightings of the *delfín*. Then one morning, when the sun is hot, hanging high in the sky, I hear the call.

São Tomé ahead.

The sailor hangs from the crow's nest, his voice rough and excited, drunk with discovery.

We crowd the edge of the ship, eager to catch the first glimpse of what will be our new home, probably for the rest of our lives.

"We're here," Tama says softly.

Since the day we saw the *delfín*, Tama has been speaking. She has a sweet, babyish voice that makes me smile. She prefers to speak in Spanish, and often talks about the happy sea creatures that have spent many days with us, smiling, playing, and helping us pass long, dull hours.

The delfín lifts our hearts, I tell mama.

It makes us feel good again.

Levi spends time with us, too. Although he can't cross the barrier between the boys and girls, he stays as close as possible, sometimes passing extra bits of biscuits and raisins so we have more to eat. He's older than most of us, fourteen years, but was taken with the other children in the kidnapping. He, too, had come from Spain to Portugal, where his father was a shipping merchant. They had money, unlike us, but it wasn't enough to keep the soldiers from stealing him.

234

São Tomé ahead.

It's been two months at sea, just like Alvaro de Caminha promised. I have seen him often during this time; pacing the ship, staring hard at his officers, declaring punishments to sailors who get flogged for their misdeeds. He doesn't acknowledge me - perhaps doesn't even remember, but I can't forget his face, his eyes, and his threat:

You will listen to everything the monks tell you. You will eat your food, send your sickness overboard, and stay quiet and out of way. Perhaps then you will be kept from the sea demons and the degradados *who eat little girls like you for dinner.*

I shudder, although the sun is warm, Tama holds my hand, and Levi grins. So much has happened in these two months . . . corpses of *degradados* thrown overboard; little children dying, wrapped in coarse cloth, and rolled into the sea beneath the plaintive prayers of the monks chanting in Latin, a language I don't understand; and sailors brutally flogged for breaking rules. Sometimes I feel dizzy with all that I've learned and seen. The days with Mama and Papa seem like a world ago; I was a little girl then and now, at almost ten years old, I've grown up.

"Look," Levi points excitedly.

I follow his hand.

São Tomé ahead.

From this distance, São Tomé looks beautiful, an exotic island with pale brown beaches and strange plants they call *palmeiras*, palm trees. As we get closer to land, the sun gets hotter, the ocean winds die down, and birds squawk overhead as if announcing our arrival. The lone mountain rises like a stone church, surrounded by jungle so dense that I wonder how people or animals make it through.

"It looks beautiful," Levi says, "but the sailors say it's very dangerous."

"Dangerous?"

"A terrible fever lives here, and kills many people.

"I don't understand."

Levi shakes his head. "That's why Alvaro de Caminha was sent here. The *Donátario da Ilha de São Tomé* before him," Levi says bitterly, "was João de Pereira. He lasted only three years. Before him was João de Paiva. He lasted five years."

I am stunned into silence.

"Most of us will die," he adds mournfully.

Levi watches me carefully. His black, round eyes narrow, his thick, curly hair shudders in the breeze. His skin is so dark now that he looks like a Moor, thin, agile, the color of brown bread.

"But *we're* Jews," he says so quietly, I can barely hear his words. "God will protect us."

I nod. I want to scream, but I remain silent.

God didn't protect us before. He let the Christians steal us from our homes and then our families; He let them put us on this boat and watched when so many died, their bodies rolled over into the sea teaming with hungry monsters . . .

Levi's eyes burn, and although I'm only nine years old going on ten, I know better than to take *that* away from him.

As the caravel creeps closer to shore, it slows, as if avoiding contact. When the sails have caught the last gust, De Caminha orders that the anchor be lowered. We're in a small cove, shared with three other caravels that left Lisboa with cargoes of Jewish children and *degradados*. As we bob gently in the water, I look at the other children in the caravels. It's like a mirror, dark, burned faces, thin, starved bodies, hands grasping the rails looking toward our new home. Hundreds of seabirds fly above us, coloring the sky with their wings, squawking their welcome.

Levi reads my mind. "We'll be safe, Zara. You, me, and Tama. We'll stick together."

He reaches out to touch my fingertips, while Tama hangs on to my arm. For some strange, unknown reason, I believe him.

As the sailors lower small boats to go ashore, I examine my first taste of *São Tomé*.

A small wooden dock stretches over the brown sand - rickety and full of splinters. Dozens of people with skin darker than the Moors, so ebony they look like the color of black olives, stand and watch the boats. The men are barefoot and wear strange, rag-like skirts tied around their waists. Half-naked white men wearing woven palm leaf hats wait for us; their skin red from the sun, their bodies covered with sweat from the steamy heat, their chests heaving as if hard to breathe. The only buildings are sad-looking hovels, shabbier than Aldonça and Gonçallo's hut. A dirt trail leads from the beach into the jungle beyond - between the leaves I can see a few larger buildings the color of wet sand.

My heart sticks in my throat.

"São Tomé," the sailor calls joyfully from his perch above us.

The girls, the boys, and the *degradados* are strangely quiet. We have left too much behind. We all watch as the monks lead a quick prayer onboard and the sailors climb into small boats. De Caminha and his officers clamber into the boats as rowers pick up the paddles. They work their way to shore, their skin glistening with sweat.

De Caminha leaps out of the boat, followed by his men, into knee-deep water and wades ashore. He's greeted by a group of men and monks. I can't hear what they say, but they all kneel before a large, wooden cross that's stuck deep in the sand. It must be a prayer, because the monks onboard the ship are chanting something in Latin, as if echoing their brethren.

Levi shakes his head in disgust. "As if God brought them here," he mumbles, so only Tama and I can hear.

"Shhhhh, the monks will beat you," I warn him.

"They already have," he grins proudly. "And I'm still a Jew."

As we wait to see what happens next, I think about the new rules. De Caminha is very clear about who is allowed to join his new colony. Only the strong and healthy can go ashore. The sick and weak have a few weeks to regain their health. If they don't get better, they'll be tossed into the sea to die when the caravel returns to Portugal.

Many have already died, and now I fear for the two sisters who are thin and weak, and shiver every night. And for the little boy who has been ill for the entire voyage, his face pale from the sea sickness. I wonder what will happen to the three older girls who have been used each night by the sailors and returned, broken by their ordeal. It's said that one of them is pregnant, but she's too thin to see a belly.

We're fine, but Levi's friend, who was flogged by a sailor for stealing food, has open, festering wounds that aren't healing. Will he be left behind?

Nearly half of the *degradados,* chained to one another and constantly exposed to the sun, rain, and wind, have already died. Perhaps those are the lucky ones.

Levi and I are separated for the first time, as they load us into the small boats. Tama and I cling to one another.

Have we lost our little family?

Levi waves and mouthes the words. *I'll find you.*

We wave back as the sailors row us to shore.

São Tomé rises from the water like a beautiful creature, thick jungles, mountains, cliffs that hover over empty beaches. I squeeze Tama's hand, and she smiles bravely. Like De Caminha, we wade to the brown sand beach, through water that feels cool on our skin. The air is so hot! Hotter than I've ever experienced, like steam rising from a pot of boiling beef stew. The ebony-colored people seem comfortable in the heat; they're lean and smiling while the white men, many of them puffy and fat, drip rivers of sweat that make them smell like barn animals. The monks are waiting for us, ready to herd us like animals. But it's been too long for us; discovering land beneath our feet *feels* so good. Many children run and scatter. Levi arrives and immediately crosses between the groups of boys and girls. The monks don't notice - they're trying desperately to keep the kids in control. Levi doesn't say a word; he simply grabs Tama and me in his arms and hugs us. We hug him back . . . we're truly family now.

Suddenly, there's a scream. We break apart and see that the kids are racing toward a silky brown beach scattered with big black rocks. Everyone is yelling - the kids from

joy and a new sense of freedom, the monks trying to control us, the fat white men waving their arms, and the agile ebony men racing after the children. Levi and I look at one another.

"Let's go," I cry.

"No," Levi says, "there's something wrong."

238

"What can be wrong with a beach?"

"Look, the black men are trying to stop them."

"They just don't want us to have fun."

Tama starts to cry. "Let's go!"

Levi holds her back.

The fastest-running children reach the beach - a brother and sister named Rosalia and Joseph. They're racing so hard - having so much fun - that they never see what's coming.

"The rocks are moving," Levi says, panic rising in his voice.

Everyone freezes - the kids behind Rosalia and Joseph, the men on the beach, and the monks. The rocks suddenly come alive, transforming into horrible, scaly monsters with mouths the size of wood carts, evil sharp teeth springing in every direction. Rosalia and Joseph, racing one another, don't see.

They leap on to the brown sand and before they realize what's happening, the black rocks slither over and surround them.

"Crocodiles," Levi whispers, his voice thick with fear. "I heard about them from the sailors."

I hear Leah laugh like a mad woman, in the warehouse in Lisboa.

It's an island where giant lizards eat children!

We're all going to die - the lizards will have us for dinner.

I've seen men beaten and Black Death victims die, their faces covered with pus-filled wounds. I've seen bodies tossed to sea, grabbed underwater and eaten by monsters, leaving trails of blood behind them in the bubbles. I've seen sailors and *degradados* beaten until near death as the boat rocks jauntily in the ocean. None of it prepared me to see the two children, Rosalia and Joseph, torn apart by ravenous crocodiles on a brown, silky beach, beneath a cheerful, blazing sun.

There's no saving them - the other children turn, as if one body, and race *away* from the water. Monks grab the littlest ones, helping them move faster. The men push and pull the older children, dragging them off the beach. The air is filled with screams, pocked by the squawks of seabirds gathering overhead to see if there will be any remains for them, and the oddly soothing slap of waves against the sand.

De Caminha watches, not moving. An angry smile plays on his lips.

"They will learn now," he snarls, and turns away.

Rosalia and Joseph are only children!

I cover Tama's eyes, but it's too late. The crocodiles lunge, tearing off arms and legs, sending blood in a million different directions, tossing heads like balls of wool, in minutes making two children bloody heaps of flesh that they devour, fighting among themselves for the best tidbits.

My throat is thick; I taste bile as my stomach does its own nauseating dance.

Another family lost to time.

By now, all the children are back with us. They watch silently, with the ebony men and the white men, the monks, sailors, *degradados,* and Alvaro de Caminha.

"This is an evil place," Levi whispers.

The adults lead us from the beach and deposit us in a crowded compound, divided by a low fence. On one side are the girls and youngest children; on the other side are the boys. It's hot and humid, insects buzz constantly overhead. The air is so thick that it's hard to breathe, like gasping through a bucket of water. The children from all of the boats have been put together, and it's clear that many have died along the way. At first, many brothers, sisters, and cousins are united. Many are mourned. Sometimes, when the monks aren't looking, the older children say Hebrew prayers that they have committed to memory. We sit close, not remembering all the words, but recognizing the melodies, and moving our lips along with those who do. The little children cry from homesickness while the older ones, like me, try to comfort them. The monks come to teach us about their God, but they are slow-moving in their heavy robes, and sweat drips down their bodies until they smell awful. We never say anything about their body odor; we're too afraid of the beatings. They like to whack us with bamboo if we don't behave or we're caught whispering a word in Hebrew. They give us food, mostly fruit from the jungle, bits of stale bread, and never enough water.

Everyone is so hot, the sun beats down on us, the air is heavy like steam from Mama's cooking pot. The compound is surrounded by a rickety fence with a gate that's always open. No one tries to escape . . . we can see beyond the compound, past the hovels, to the dense, dark jungle. What would children do in the jungle? Tama believes that there must be horrible animals, like the crocodiles on the beach, waiting to eat us.

We're there for two days when the oldest and strongest boys are pulled out to work in the sugar cane fields. Levi is one of them, and I fear for his safety. If Tama is right . . . if there are monsters in the jungle, what will happen to him?

The older girls must gather fruit and food for the livestock, while others are assigned to clean the compound, help with the cooking, or deal with the sick, housed in a flimsy hovel they call the infirmary.

Each day, someone gets sick from the fever, and each day someone dies before they can be carted off to the infirmary. I don't know why Tama and I are spared the fever. Levi says that some people get it and never know it, others never get it at all. Perhaps De Caminha was right - *Ilha de São Tomé* is a death sentence.

Although we're not allowed to mix with the boys, Tama and I meet Levi every day. We talk about what's happening, what we have heard, and what we must do.

Then we plan.

"We have to get out of here," I whisper to Levi. "Each night, men come from the huts and take the oldest girls. . ." I shudder. "They use them and disgrace them. When they're finished, they return the girls to the compound, crying, bleeding, dishonored."

"They make them into whores," he snarls.

I nod. "Some are pregnant already. The others . . ."

"They won't even know the father of their child."

I shake my head.

Levi takes a deep breath. "Have they come for you . . . or Tama?"

"No. Tama is too little and I look younger than my age." My voice shakes. "It's only a matter of time, though. No one is spared."

241

Tama says nothing, her eyes flicking back and forth between us. I wonder how much she really understands.

"The gate is open," I add, "all we have to do is slip out at night. . ."

"Go where?"

"You go out each day, to the fields. What's there?"

Levi scratches his dark curls. "When we go to the sugar cane fields, we work hard - long hours, back breaking work . . ."

"What's past the fields?" I demand.

Levi clears his throat. "I don't know. The jungle is so thick, I don't know how anyone can get through it, but . . ."

"But what?"

"I've heard," he tilts his head conspiratorially, "that way up in the mountains, in the middle of the island, there's a fugitive camp."

"What's a fugitive camp?" Tama asks.

We both look at her.

"It's a place," Levi begins, "where people run to . . . hide . . . to get away from this."

"Who lives there?"

"I hear," he continues, "that there are escaped slaves, ebony men and their women."

". . . and mixed bloods and *degradados*," I finish.

"You heard about it?" Levi looks at me curiously.

I nod.

Levi takes a deep breath. "I don't know how safe. . ."

"If we stay here," my voice is high and shrill, "they will rape us." I look at Tama's tangled red hair. "Both of us. It's only a matter of time."

"I don't know. I don't know what we might be getting ourselves into. It could be worse than here."

"I don't want a filthy man to take me," I cry, "I don't want to have a baby."

Tama grabs my arm. "You'll be okay. I know it."

"No," I look at Levi. "I won't be okay. I pause. "I'm old enough to have a baby."

Levi knows exactly what I mean. "The blood?"

"Yes."

"It *can* happen," he lowers his head.

"What do you mean?" Tama demands.

I look her straight in the eyes. "You may not understand this now, but if one of the men comes for me in the night, I can have his baby."

"But you don't want his baby."

"It doesn't matter, Tama, if the men start doing to me the same thing they're doing to the older girls, I will have a baby."

"The baby will die," Tama says stiffly.

"Maybe," I agree.

"We can't wait here," Levi says suddenly. "Tomorrow night, when everyone is sleeping, we'll sneak out of the compound. We'll find our way."

"Thank you," I touch his hand.

Levi nods. "Gather and hide as much food as you can."

But the next day the rains begin.

We have to wait.

He first notices me when Tama and I are huddled under a canopy of leaves protecting us from the relentless downpour.

His small eyes are streaked with red and filled with a raw hunger. His white skin is charred brown, with large scars across his stubby hands and the side of his face. His voice stings - vermin looking for blood - when he finds a girl he clasps her to his swollen belly like a stolen pouch of gold.

The girls are terrified of him. He comes to the compound several days a week, swoops up his choice and disappears back into the maze of hovels they call town. Sometimes, the girls don't return for days; sometimes they don't return at all. I see his work in their eyes, glazed and defeated, and in their bodies, broken and beaten, with open sores.

He notices me and I cringe, flattening myself against the leaves. He bends over and examines me, touching my privates, grabbing my face, and licking my skin. But he already has a girl tucked under his arm - her name is Miriam and she's silent and limp.

He laughs. "Tonight," he whispers in my ear, "this one is mine." He shakes Miriam. "She's not pretty, but she'll do. Tomorrow . . ." he twists my arm, "is your turn. You're pretty and fresh, a sweet virgin." He roars so loud that his spittle stains my cheeks. I dare not wipe it away.

He moves back from me. "Today, I have her for dinner and tomorrow you'll be my desert."

He snarls, dragging Miriam along with him.

Tama is trembling so hard I can barely feel my own, pounding heart.

Tomorrow.

"Will he make a baby in you?" Tama asks, pulling at her hair.

For a moment I can't find an answer.

He can make a baby.

He can also kill me.

I am out of time.

Although the rains are so heavy, I can hardly see in front of me, I know that now is the time.

"Gather everything," I say to Tama, "we're leaving."

Tama quickly locates our food, hidden around the compound, and brings it back to me. I roll it, along with our few belongings, into the leaves - the way the girls in the compound have taught me. I take Tama's hand and plunge into the torrential rains, wading through mud toward the boy's compound.

We stand in the rain for a long time, calling Levi's name.

A small boy appears, not much older than Tama.

"He's sleeping," the boy says grumpily.

"What's your name?"

The boy has straight, blonde hair. His eyes narrow.

"Why do you want to know?"

He grabs at the rags that he's tied around his body, although they're hanging, saturated with water.

"Levi will be happy you got him. He'll reward you."

The little boy looks interested. "My name is Yaco," the boy says slowly.

"I'm Zara," I smile impatiently. "This is Tama. Now find Levi

244

and wake him up. Tell him we're here."

Yaco shrugs.

Tama and I wait as Yaco disappears in the rain.

"What if he can't find Levi?"

I can't answer Tama's question. I don't want to frighten her, but I know we have to leave now. If Yaco doesn't find Levi, if Levi doesn't show up soon, Tama and I will go by ourselves.

I don't know how long we wait, but the rain stops and a full moon breaks through the clouds. Light starts to filter into the compound. We flatten ourselves against the divider. I'm so tired, but I fight sleep.

"Zara! Zara!"

My eyes snap open. It's Levi. I stand up quickly, only to see that the sky is beginning to lighten.

"Levi. I'm here."

He reaches across the divider and grabs my hands. "I've been looking for you. Yaco said . . ."

I cut him off. "I think I fell asleep. Tama, too. Levi, we have to get out of here. *Now*. One of the men, the one that rapes and beats the girls for pleasure, is coming for me tonight. If I don't leave . . ."

Levi needs no more explanation. He thinks quickly and devises a plan. "We'll leave now, before the sun is up. We'll go into the jungle and hide until nightfall, and then walk inland, to the mountain, until we find the fugitive camp."

"I'm so tired," Tama says sleepily.

I put my arms around her. "We have to go."

"I'm going, too."

We follow the voice.

It's Yaco, who has heard everything.

"I'm going, too," he repeats stubbornly.

"You can't," Levi says gently. "We're going far, traveling much, and I don't know if there will be food. We might find wild animals . . ."

Yaco's eyes, which I now see are gray, widen. "No," he says stubbornly. "I don't care. I want to be with you."

245

Levi and I look at one another.

"Are you sure Yaco? We don't know what's going to happen - what's ahead of us."

"It can't be worse than here."

"Okay," Levi decides. "But you have to do everything I tell you."

Yaco nods, his gray eyes serious.

"We leave now," Levi says, and I nod in agreement. "The gate is open because they know there's no place to go. The guards are probably drunk and sleeping, but we'll still have to be very quiet."

I put my hand on the divider, Levi covers it with his, and Tama and Yaco join us.

Four Jewish children.

We're in this together.

The rain starts again, but now it's lighter and doesn't obstruct our vision. Gray clouds fill the dark sky. Levi and Yaco are on one side of the divider, we're on the other. Silently, we make our way to the compound gate, careful not to splash in any mud, slip on any bodies, or disturb the debris that lies throughout the compound. This is my only chance. If I don't make it out now . . .

Please Mama, watch over me.

Protect us.

I look straight ahead.

The gate is in front of us, dangerously close. Our feet are sucked into the mud; they make tiny noises that sound like grunts in the half darkness. My heart pounds so loudly it feels like it will break. Although I'm saturated by the rain, sweat pours down my face and my back.

Tama holds my hand so tightly, it hurts. I don't try to take it away. She's so small, yet so brave.

It's hard to stop from conjuring pictures in my mind, but I widen my eyes and force my head back into the compound. I have to be completely alert as we creep closer to the gate. We pause. There are two guards at the gate. They're lying on the ground, heads turned to the side, snoring loudly. Next to them are empty wineskins, once filled with the cheap, brownish stuff they make on the island. The guards are drunk, sleeping it off.

I glance at Levi. Our eyes meet. We don't have to say anything. The light is coming quickly now, and there's little time left. Beyond the gate is the dirt trail that leads into the jungle. The rains have made the jungle so dense, that the trail is almost gone. *Almost.* If we make it past the guards, we can run into the jungle and hide. It won't be hard, even if they're looking for us. With the morning field crews, and the rain, they might not even notice we're gone until *he* comes for me at night.

Levi touches my hand. He knows what I'm thinking.

One of the guards stirs, and I hold my breath. He flips over, revealing a pool of vomit that he slept in all night. Levi wrinkles his nose in disgust.

I freeze.

I think of everything that has happened since that awful night when the inquisitors came knocking at our door. I think of Mama and Papa, their eyes burning with purpose, their hands shaking as we slipped through the trap door. I remember the sound of the table dragged over our heads and Marianna's push to move on through the darkness. I think of beautiful Catalina who lost her breath the minute we left Mama, and the heartbreaking burial on the side of the road with the man Samuel, saying words that felt like a piece of my soul was left with her. I see Rafael and Marianna, holding each other in a way that scared me - a way that I saw many times after that, on the boat with the sailors and older girls, in the compound. I picture the long road to Lisboa and then Aldonça and Gonçallo's hut, the only peace I felt since leaving home. I see Tama and her mother reaching for one another on the dock in Lisboa.

I look at the little, red-headed girl who I have vowed to protect. Is that how Mama felt about us? Is that how Marianna felt about me? Is that why Papa and Rafael fought with their lives?

The guard's snoring is a roar, his lips bubble with each breath, saliva trickles down his chin. Levi watches me.

Now!

He shoves my shoulder - I yank Tama's arm. I take a deep breath and run. I have never run so hard in my life. The rain stings my face, the mud sucks at my feet. We slither between the guards like two jungle animals, racing for our lives. The guard lying in vomit doesn't stir. We're almost safe . . .

Suddenly, I feel fingers curl around my ankle. The second guard is awake. His bloodshot eyes pierce me, his smile jeers as he hangs on. I don't scream - I don't want to wake the other guard. He wrenches me down into the mud.

I'm trapped.

I struggle to pull my ankle free, but the guard is too big and too strong.

"Go," I hiss at Tama.

Tama refuses to move.

"You're not going anywhere," the guard cackles, pulling me slowly closer to him, dragging me face down through the mud, as I struggle to regain my footing. I claw at the ground, at his hand, but he easily overpowers me. Grabbing at a patch of hard ground, I flip myself over to meet his eyes.

It's him.

The man with the small eyes streaked with red and filled with an ugly hunger. With white skin charred brown, large scars across his stubby hands and the side of his face. His voice stings, like vermin looking for blood, and when he finds a girl he clasps her to his swollen belly like a stolen pouch of gold. As he pulls me through the mud towards him, his fingers wrapped around my ankle, I see the girl, Miriam, he took away hours earlier. She lies broken and bloody next to him.

His stubby hand draws me closer as he snarls with pleasure.

"I had one for dinner and now . . ." he shakes with delight, "I'll have one for breakfast."

"Run," I cry to Tama.

Tama flies into motion. She doesn't run, instead she turns on *him*, kicking and punching with all her strength. He laughs louder, and pushes her away like a mosquito.

"I have one for dinner . . ." he says again, pleased with his chant, "and now I'll have one for breakfast."

Tears fill my eyes.

Is this where it's going to end, Mama?

Out of nowhere, there's a whooshing sound. From the corner of my eye I see a blur of motion. He never saw it coming. It's a log, the width of a man's arm. It connects with his head; there's a sickening *thud* and he falls back. Levi drops the log and lunges for his throat; Tama and Yaco kick and punch his body. His fingers slip off my ankle; I wrench my leg free from his grasp, and scramble to my feet. Trickles of blood run from the corner of his mouth and his ears. I watch in horror and joy . . . they're doing this for *me*.

I join them - kicking and hitting him with all my strength.

This is for Mama and Papa.

This is for Catalina.

This is for Aldonça and Gonçallo.

This is for Marianna and Rafael.

Although the four of us are small, the anger and loss inside is huge; we spend it on this evil man. When we finally stop, he's dead.

I have killed a man.

"Let's go," Levi says, catching his breath. "Before the other wakes up."

We pause to survey our work. Who would have believed that not so long ago, tucked comfortably with our families and our God, four children would be capable of killing a man?

The dead man lies next to Miriam. I lean over his body.

"Come with us," I whisper.

The girl, whose face is swollen and purple with bruises, smiles weakly. "Leave me. I'm already dead," she whispers.

"Please," I insist. "There's hope."

She smiles and turns her head away.

"We have to go!" Levi demands. "*Now.*"

I take one last look at Miriam, but her eyes are already closed.

Is this what they call justice? Will I ever forget the joy of this moment; taking the life of a rapist and murderer, and the tragedy of yet another child whose soul was slaughtered?

"We have to go!" Levi repeats, his voice shaking. "*Now.*"

He doesn't have to say anything else. If they catch us, they'll kill us. We're now murderers.

I bury the vision in my mind. It will stay with me forever.

Silently, the four of us join hands. We *walk* into the jungle together.

It's dark and scary, but we're together.

Free.

Cole

"What's wrong?" Cole had asked Lev while they were setting up for *ThursdaysAt5*.

Lev's eyes were dark. "You wouldn't understand."

"Try me," Cole smiled, touching the iron circle on the thong around his neck.

Lev shook his head.

"C'mon," Cole insisted, "we've been waiting a long time for this day."

Lev pressed his lips together.

"It can't be *that* bad," Cole grumbled.

Lev took a deep breath. "It's the 9th of Av."

"The ninth of what?"

"Av," Lev said patiently. "The 9th of Av."

"What does the 9th of Av mean?"

Lev shook his head. "Bad luck."

"I don't get it," Cole said, a tinge of annoyance in his voice.

"*Tisha B'Av*," Lev said, his voice so low that Cole could hardly hear.

Cole stared at the kid. He had *almost* forgotten that Lev came from the black hat community. Lev had pushed his side locks behind his ears, taken off his black hat, and showed up in a white, button-down shirt and dark trousers.

"Bad things happen today," Lev continued. "I should be praying, fasting, mourning . . . not here."

"C'mon man," Cole put his arm around the kid. "That's just superstition."

Lev looked up at Cole. Lev's eyes were burning with an intensity that sent chills down Cole's spine. "It's not superstition," Lev hissed, "it's very real. It's when bad things happen, like the destruction of the first and second temples, the Jewish expulsion from Spain . . ."

"Be cool man," Cole cut him off. "This is the twenty-first century."

Lev's eyes turned to ice. "Something bad is going to happen; something that should have happened a long time ago."

251

Cole shrugged.

Something bad is going to happen.

Something that should have happened a long time ago.

Cole frowned. "Enough gloom and doom, dude, let's get to work."

After all, it was *ThursdaysAt5*.

Tisha B'Av, bad-luck days, and omens were old.

Cole tried to ignore Lev's warning.

He stood at the microphone. Isaac was grinning. Lev was smoldering.

Something bad is going to happen.

Something that should have happened a long time ago.

Cole couldn't get it out of his head. He turned on one of his most charming smiles and surveyed the audience. A woman with dark, smoldering eyes and a backpack caught his eye. She had a magnetism that drew him; when he spoke it was like a private conversation with *her*.

"Thank you, Isaac. And thank you, New York, for joining me today in this visit to the past."

There was polite applause.

"This is a love song," Cole said into the mike. "*Por una Ninya*, For a Girl."

Something flickered in her smoldering eyes.

"*Por una ninya tan fermoza*," Cole sang. "For such a beautiful girl:"

L'alma yo la vo a dar
Un kuchilyo de dos kortes
En el korason entro.

I will give my soul
a double-edged knife
pierced my heart.

No me mires ke'stó kantando
Es lyorar ke kero yo

252

Los mis males son muy grandes
No los puedo somportar.

Don't look at me; I am singing,
it is crying that I want,
my sorrows are so great
I can't bear them."

Cole paused.

On the other side of the crowd, an olive-skinned girl with four friends, found chairs. She was beautiful. Cole's gaze moved back and forth between her and the woman with dark, smoldering eyes.

They look familiar.

Frighteningly familiar.

Cole was shaken. He forced a smile and scanned the rest of the crowd. Then it happened.

The crowd became an audience.

Cole shivered and Lev's frown deepened.

It wasn't good to focus on only two faces, Cole reminded himself. He talked, played the guitar, and sang. He was determined not to let anyone see how the two faces rattled him.

Lev watched from the back, his eyes getting darker.

Cole tried to ignore him.

Something bad is going to happen.

Something that should have happened a long time ago.

When Cole was a little boy he loved puzzles. He and mama would sit at the rickety kitchen table and put together thousands of pieces to complete a puzzle that looked like a wall of guitars, an orchestra in full black tie, or an extravagant philharmonic performing on the red rocks. That's how they passed the time waiting for Father to sleep off his binge.

Father drank every weekend, stumbling home at night and passing out on the worn couch in their pitiful living room. They would listen to him snore, smell his stale cigarettes, and clean up his vomit that he left, like a Hansel and Gretel trail, on the front steps, through the door, and next to the couch. Father would sleep away Saturday and Sunday, missing Cole's life, from the soccer field to birthdays, as if they were packs of chips that he shoved into his vending machines. During the week, Father was so busy servicing his machines that he had no time and no words, for his tiny, lonely family.

Puzzles held mama and Cole together, snapped into a fantasy of music and illusion.

When the cocoa-colored skin woman joined the audience in Bryant Park, Cole knew, without words, that she completed his puzzle.

Cole stared, mesmerized.

There was the woman with dark smoldering eyes.

The olive-skinned girl.

The woman with cocoa-colored skin.

They all fit – the solution to a puzzle.

He could hear the snap of the final puzzle piece, as his mother put it into place on the rickety kitchen table to the background music of Father's snores and the lingering smell of vomit.

"It fits," mama would say softly.

They would take the puzzle and paint it with varnish until it was hard and permanently connected. Then they would add it to the stack, a pile of cardboard that grew each year, covered with dust, and forgotten.

Another puzzle solved.

Another puzzle to follow.

Cole took a deep breath, as if he were living a puzzle this time, the pieces drifting together by unseen hands.

The words came to Cole, on their own accord. He sang to the Bryant Park audience with his eyes closed, his voice drifting across the Great Lawn.

Where is the key that was in the drawer?
Onde sta la yave ke stava in kashon?

My forefathers brought it with great pain
From their house in Spain.

254

Mis nonus la trusheron kon grande dolor
De su kaza de Espanya.

We told our children this is the heart of our home.

Cole's back was to the fountain, and the white slatted film festival screen. He couldn't see the Great Lawn, stretching out behind him or the Upper Library Terrace where the dark man in cargo pants stood on the cobblestones, next to the old couple.

He couldn't see anything.

But Cole knew an old couple was singing along with him.

Zara

The jungle is dark, only a touch of the morning light penetrates the thick canopy above us. We feel our way down the trail, overgrown with dense plants, roots, and trees. Slowly, streaks of sunlight, like trickles of golden water, break through the canopy.

"This is the lowland jungle," Levi explains.

The compound, hovels, and buildings of the São Tomé colony have been gobbled up by the jungle, as if they no longer exist. As the light filters through around us, we seem to be wandering in a nether land, unlike anything I've ever seen before. Everything is painted in shades of green . . . more greens than I knew existed. Thin, lanky trees reach for the sky, flanked by larger, thick-trunked trees that twist as they battle for light in the canopy. Wherever I turn are sprawling ferns with huge, lace-like leaves that spread in all directions; greenery I've never seen before, and leaves and flowers in bursts of different colors and shapes. A constant chorus from birds fills our ears. Dangling from the ends of branches are the long, woven nests of giant, shiny black sunbirds; tiny black and white thrushes take short flights between the leaves, and golden brown grosbeaks fly overhead. A pair of lemon-yellow bellied birds pause to watch us, while a brightly-colored quail stares from its perch. The birds chirp, squawk, and sing to one another, dissolving my fear. Before I entered the jungle, I thought it was dangerous, full of death. Instead, it throbs with life, in all colors, shapes, and sounds.

Levi stops. He's the oldest and the leader.

"We have to hide," he says softly. "They'll be coming through soon, to work in the sugar cane fields. We can't let them find us."

We nod in agreement, although I'm now reluctant to leave the magic of the jungle.

"Are there monsters here, like the crocodiles?" Tama asks softly.

"No," Levi pats her red hair, "they only live on the shore."

Levi pushes a little further down the trail then turns off into jungle so dense it's nearly impossible to move. His arms are strong, and he beats away huge leaves, tangled bushes, and thick vines.

We don't have to go very far; the jungle is so thick that once off the trail we're easily concealed.

Levi points to a cluster of rocks. "We'll stay there for now," he says, "until it's safe to move on. If we can't see the trail, then they can't see us."

I wonder how Levi has learned these things, but I remain silent.

We scramble on the rocks and huddle together, beneath a sprawl of huge fern leaves. I tear off a few leaves, roll them, and make pillows for each of us.

"Sleep," Levi says, "I'll keep guard."

I help settle Tama and Yaco on the leaves. They curl up and fall asleep immediately. I look at Levi fighting sleep. Is this what Marianna felt when Rafael watched over us on the road to Lisboa?

"Watch out for snakes," Levi adds softly.

Snakes? Are they dangerous?

Levi read my thoughts. "There are snakes in the jungle, but if we're careful, they'll leave us alone. They're not like people who *love* to kill."

I shake my head but say nothing. Instead, I try to leap from my body and visualize what we look like . . . four children huddled on a rock, hiding from their captors. After all that's happened, are we children anymore? Perhaps in body, but in mind?

And then I think of him.

We killed a man today. How do you remain a child after you killed a man? How do you remain a child after losing everything and everyone you love - after surviving the horrors of human punishment, the sea voyage, and the constant smell of death?

Even Tama, still so young in years, is no longer a child.

My eyes snap open. Everyone is sleeping. Levi, sitting so stiffly on the edge of the rock, has drifted off. Good. He needs his rest.

I'm curled up on the rocks, with the fern leaf unrolled. I don't want to move and wake the others. Suddenly, something green moves across the fern leaf. It's a creature that looks like a fragile stem . . . long and thin, with transparent wings and delicate legs that move

257

silently across the leaf. I think they call it a mantis, but I'm not sure. I watch as the creature makes its way across the leaf and disappears beyond the rocks. That's when I notice the flowers. They're the most beautiful purple flowers I have ever seen in my life. Some are tiny, with flat petals and yellow-and-purple centers. Others drape down like purple cloth, held together with a green tip at the top. The prettiest are made up of uneven pale purple petals, with dabs of pink arranged in a delicate balance on a thin green stem.

Purple flowers, Mama.

I'm going to make it.

Beyond the purple flowers I hear a familiar sound - not the noisy clatter of the jungle. I stiffen. It echoes above whoosh of leaves, the songs of birds, and the chirps of unknown jungle creatures.

I look at Levi. He's awake now, too. Tama and Yaco are asleep, so he puts a finger to his lips to tell me to stay quiet. The sound begins low and then grows louder; I recognize the unmistakable thud of human feet on a dirt trail. There are voices, some harsh, some singing, filtering through the jungle. I think I hear the *Shema,* drifting lazily through the trees, like an ancient song, but I can't be sure.

Shema Yisrael Adonai Elohaenu Adonai Echad

Hear O Israel The Lord is God, The Lord is One.

I hold my breath. I can hear them, but not see them. If we're silent, they'll never know we're here. Levi grabs my hand and we wait.

Time stands still.

Butterflies, in the most amazing colors, flutter in front of my eyes. A tree frog, the color of green bark, pauses to stare at us with bulging orange eyes, and then leaps away. A huge, hairy spider saunters over the rock, his legs brushing against my ankle.

We watch, listen, and don't move.

I don't know how long it takes before the sounds begin to fade and my breathing returns to normal. My shoulders sag; I suddenly realize how rigid I am - how my whole body is frozen in place, on top of the rock, holding Levi's hand.

"We're fine for now," Levi says softly. "We'll wait until they come back, after their work, heading for the compound. Then we'll own the trail."

"Why not follow another trail?"

Levi shakes his head. "There's only one trail that I know about. It leads to the sugar cane field, not far from here. On the other side of the field the trail continues, but people don't go that far."

"Where does it lead?"

"Deeper inland, away from the shore. That's what the slaves told me. It climbs into the mountains . . ."

"To the fugitive camp?"

Levi shrugs. "I don't know anyone who ever took it that far. We have to go very deep, onto the mountain, to find the camp."

"If it exists?"

"Yes, if it exists."

I work to piece my thoughts together. "What if it's a story . . . that there really isn't a fugitive camp? What if we're all alone?"

Levi shrugs.

"How will we know we're going in the right direction?"

"We won't. If the fugitives are in the mountains, they'll find us long before we find them."

I shiver, but it's not from the cold.

We spend the day on the rocks, sleeping, telling stories, playing games with pebbles. Yaco and Tama complain that they want to leave, but Levi and I know better. We wait for the voices and the feet to pass, returning to the compound.

At one point, Levi scrambles off the rock and disappears into the jungle. He returns with a strange yellow fruit that grows in large bunches.

"What's that?" Tama asks.

"It's called a banana," Levi explains. He peels off the thick skin, and inside there's a soft, pale yellow meat with a very sweet smell. "Try it," Levi offers.

Tama and Yaco refuse. Tentatively, I take a small bite out of the soft flesh. It's the most delicious thing I've ever tasted - sweet, with an exotic flavor that I've never experienced, and a soft texture like a boiled egg yolk. I finish it quickly, and Levi laughs.

"Try it!" I encourage Tama and Yaco.

Levi hands them each a banana.

Tama hesitates, but Yaco bites into it, skin and all.

"Ugh," he cries and spits everything out.

Levi laughs harder. "You're not supposed to eat the skin." We all watch as he takes Yaco's banana and peels it. "Now try."

Reluctantly, Yaco takes a small bite. His smile says it all.

The four of us spend the rest of the day eating bananas, playing with banana skins, listening to the birds, and watching the butterflies. It's the first day we've felt happy since taken from our families in Portugal.

The sun is low in the sky and the jungle darkening when we crawl from beneath the ferns and leap off the rocks.

"We're safe for now," Levi says.

Tama and Yaco are very playful, stiff from sitting on the rocks all day, happy to stretch their legs. Levi grabs their arms.

"We have to be quiet," he says sternly. "Until we know that we're completely safe."

Tama and Yaco nod. No one wants to return to the compound.

"Where do we go now?" I ask.

"Back to the trail," Levi whispers. "We'll keep moving until we reach the fields, cross them, and continue on the other side. The sun sets late, and there are streams on that side where we can get water, bananas, and other fruits. We'll rest and then keep on moving down the trail."

I nod. "Do you know where. . ."

Levi shakes his head. "Don't ask that question. Just pray."

I take his hand. "This is better than being in the compound and catching the fever."

A picture of the man we murdered fills my mind. I shudder. Even if we did return to the compound, what would they do to murderers? There's no turning back. Levi watches my face and knows what I'm thinking. He doesn't say anything.

We find the trail and silently continue, our hearts pounding even though we know the workers are gone for the day. We reach the edge of the field as the sun is setting. In front of us are rows of leafy cane with long, thin stalks swaying gently in the wind. We pause, staring at the empty field, fenced only by dense jungle.

"Taste this," Levi says, and breaks off a stalk for each of us.

I'm hesitant, but Yaco and Tama chew on it eagerly. Their eyes light up.

"*Caña de azúcar,*" Yaco cries. Sugar cane.

Hesitantly, I follow suit.

The sugar cane is sweet like candy, raw, and chewy. Grinning, I join the others in our feast. Suddenly, we hear an eerie squeal, and there are thousands of creatures flying right above our heads, with angled wings and points, tiny black eyes, and spiky ears.

"Monsters!" Tama cries and tries to run away, but Levi catches her arm in one hand and Yaco's arm in another.

I'm frozen with horror. Are these people-eating monsters like the crocodiles?

Levi laughs. "It's a *bastao* - bat. They don't like us anymore than we like them. They won't hurt us."

He snares one to show us.

The bat is dirty brown, the color of rocks covered with loose soil. It has long, ugly wings and beady black eyes that stare right through me.

I shiver. Tama and Yaco examine it, fascinated.

After several minutes, Levi throws it skyward, so it can join the others.

"Are there other monsters here?" Tama asks, her voice unsure.

Levi shakes his head. "The only big animals are the ones that come over on the caravels with people. Everything . . . except the crocodiles . . . are small and either crawl, jump, fly, or creep along the jungle floor."

I'm not sure I believe him.

"No one is left in the field now," Levi adds, "let's cross it to the other side and pick up the trail. If we walk a little bit further, there's a stream with fresh water and we can stay there for the night. Tomorrow morning we continue on the trail, long before anyone gets to the field, so they'll never find us."

"Will they follow us?" I ask hesitantly.

Levi meets my eyes. "Who cares about a bunch of Jewish kids? No one would even bother."

We're murderers.

I want to say the words, remind him that they might want to take revenge for killing one of their own. I say nothing.

Levi leads us through the swaying stalks of sugar cane, and the buzzing insects that are everywhere. I'm glad when we reach the other side. The trail leads away from the field, and further away from the compound.

We follow the trail until we hear water. Levi breaks through the jungle plants and leads us to a stream with fresh, cold water. We're all very thirsty, so we drink for a long time. When we finish, Levi points to a cluster of rocks on the other side of the stream.

"That's where we'll spend the night," he announces.

The creature is small and hairy, with a long, rat-like tail. I watch as it crawls over the rocks, like a chain, with four babies hanging on by their tails. It's not like the rats I saw on the caravel; big, ugly gray rodents that live in the hold, feasting on garbage. Sometimes, the sailors caught one and cooked it for dinner . . .

I shudder.

Light is trickling in through the forest canopy, and once again, I'm the first to awake. My stomach grumbles; we've had nothing to eat but fruit, the "safe" greens that Levi recognizes, and chunks of sugar cane. I wonder if I'll ever taste bread or olives again; eat meat like Mama's Shabbat stew; or nibble on tiny brown chick peas.

"It's called a *shrew*," Levi whispers, giving the rat-like creature a name.

"It looks like a rat."

He laughs softly. "I hope we never see a rat again."

"I hope we never see a monk again."

"I hope we never see a *Portuguese* again."

262

"I hope we never see De Caminha again."

"I hope. . ." Levi laughs, "we never have to see any of them again."

We giggle.

Tama and Yaco stir. When they're fully awake, we climb off the rocks, leaving our leaf-beds behind us, and drink from the stream. We're all eager to get started, to move further away from the compound.

"Will we find the fugitive camp today?" Tama asks.

"I don't know," Levi replies. But he does know - we will have to go deeper into the island, climb higher up the mountain, and wait for them to find us.

We follow the trail for hours, silently trekking through the jungle, when the fog suddenly falls upon us, and everything is dripping with water. The trees reach higher in the canopy - taller and thinner than the ones we saw earlier. The fog makes it feel like

we're walking in a dream, covering everything in delicate mist, as if we're in a haze of our own imaginations.

We pause.

It's staggeringly beautiful.

"What is it?" I ask softly, afraid to speak too loud and break the vision.

"I've never been here," Levi whispers, "but one of the slaves told me about it. They call it the cloud forest. It means we're climbing higher."

Tama and Yaco stare upward, trying to catch handfuls of mist.

It's the most awe-inspiring place I've ever experienced. Surreal and otherworldly, I wonder if only God could create a place like this . . . the same God that allows evil men to kidnap children. The thoughts confuse me, so I push them from my mind, taking in the cloud forest like it's an illusion, a fairyland of peace.

Mama would have loved this.

Levi nudges us forward.

We continue walking up the trail, although it's very narrow and often hard to follow. Not many human feet have been here. Our mood shifts as we drift through the fog; Tama begins to hum a song. Yaco follows with a Spanish folksong, and we all join in, our voices muffled by the mist.

Somewhere in my mind I hear Rafael and his *trovador's* Ladino song, once crooned in the privacy of our home so no one would know we were *Conversos*.

Onde sta la yave ke stava in kashon?
Mis nonus la trusheron kon grande dolor
De su kaza.

We're all singing, our voices rise in the mist, and hope returns like a long lost friend. As we climb higher in the cloud forest, the air gets cooler and the trees get shorter. It feels good to breathe, and we're reluctant to stop as the sun dips in the sky. We find a group of rocks near a cold stream, with fruits growing everywhere. Tama, Yaco, and I prepare our leaf beds as Levi collects the fruit. All of us are sad to see this day end.

We drink the water, eat the fruits, and sleep, blanketed by the mist.

Again, I am the first to wake in the morning. I expect to see butterflies or shrews, hear birds or the whooshing of leaves. Instead, I see two black human eyes.

My heart pounds wildly; I throw out my arms ready to attack, and scream as loud as I can.

Levi leaps up; Tama and Yaco cower behind us.

The eyes retreat, disappearing into the mist.

Did I dream them? I blink my eyes, and peer through the mist. *Nothing.*

"What's wrong?" Levi demands.

"Did you see him?"

Levi searches the cloud forest with his eyes. "See who?"

"You?" I turn to Tama and Yaco.

They shake their heads.

"You must have been dreaming," Levi sighs. "If anyone was here, I would have seen him."

"You were sleeping."

"I would have heard him. No one can be *that* quiet."

I'm not sure, but I back down. "Let's get moving," I say lightly, hugging Tama. "I must have been dreaming."

The day passes as the one before; following the narrow trail, climbing through the mist; stopping to drink from the many fresh streams that flow downward - the direction from where we've come. We sing, eat fruits, and even stop to play. For a moment, we act like children. There are no people; the only animals we see are the birds overhead, small creatures like shrews and geckos, and the constant buzz of insects. After everyone falls asleep, I keep my eyes open, peering into the mist. Eventually fatigue overtakes me.

Something startles me. I open my eyes and it's very early, the sun is just starting to rise, piercing the canopy, and trickling down through the mist. I sit up and look around. Everything looks the same . . . except for a slight movement behind a cluster of large, sweeping leaves dripping water. I wait, not moving, not sure that I'm seeing anything.

The leaves move again.

It must be human.

Suddenly, a head peeks out. It's the same black eyes that I thought I saw in my sleep. The man has the darkest skin I've ever seen - darker than the ebony slaves back at the compound. He appears disembodied; only his head is visible. I want to scream, but something stops me.

He's as frightened as me.

We stare at each other for several minutes until he retreats back into the forest. Should I scream, should I wake the others?

I'm not sure, so I do nothing.

The day moves like the day before - we walk, we sing, we eat fruit, and we drink from the streams that we pass. No one is afraid anymore, so I don't tell them about the man. They would probably assume I was dreaming.

This continues for several days, and the trees get shorter and more stunted, the air cooler, and it's clear that we're climbing higher.

Each morning I see the man's face, and each morning he creeps closer, as if less afraid. One morning he steps from the brush and I see that he's entirely naked except for a ragged loin cloth tied around his middle, covering his privates. His body is thin but muscular, his skin so black I gasp. He sees my fear and slinks back into the forest.

I know now that he's following us.

"There's someone watching," I say to Levi.

Levi nods.

"You've seen him?"

"I think so. Very dark, slipping between the leaves."

"Who is he?"

Levi shrugs. "I don't know. Maybe he's one of the African slaves."

"A fugitive?"

"Maybe."

"From the fugitive camp?"

"He could be a guard or something. Watching us as we get closer." Levi scratches his head. "They have to be very careful."

I never thought about *that*. The fugitives have to be as careful and secretive as we are.

"We're kids. Why would he be afraid of us?"

"That's why he's just watching."

An icy chill runs down my spine. "Instead of . . ."

Levi stopped me before I said the words.

Instead of killing us.

"Should we do anything?"

"No, just wait and see what happens. Maybe he'll start to trust us."

In an instant, the cloud forest is not quite as beautiful. It's fraught with danger; not from people-eating monsters, but from *people*.

"Don't say anything to Tama and Yaco," Levi adds. "Let's not frighten them."

We continue on the trail, but Levi and I don't sing along with Tama and Yaco. We constantly look around us; although we don't *see* the man, we sense his presence. Mid-day, we settle on a pile of rocks near a stream. Levi and I stand guard while Tama plunges into the mud puddles next to the stream, laughing and splashing, as Yaco looks on.

"*A lura sosai!*" The man screams and leaps from the leaves, pulling Tama out of the water. We rush to help her, our cries mingle with fear and anger.

We freeze.

Tama wails, her voice sounds like Rosalia and Joseph, when the crocodiles were tearing them apart. I scream, Levi raises his fists, and Yaco looks wildly around, not knowing what to do.

Tama's ankles are covered with fat, evil worms, sucking out her life.

The black man is the only one who knows what to do. He scoops up Tama, balances her on his knees, and picks off the black worms, leaving trickles of blood behind. He tosses the worms back into the water, then pulls some leaves from a pouch on his waist. He wraps the leaves around Tama's legs, balances himself on the rocks, and then cradles her like a baby, singing in a strange language.

No one moves.

Tama stops crying as he sings softly. She nuzzles into his chest. Yaco stands behind Levi and me as we watch, not knowing what to do.

"Leeches," Levi mumbles.

After many minutes have passed, the three of us approach the man. Tama is very quiet, her eyes closed.

The ebony man looks at us. "*Suna na . . .*" he says slowly, "*Nweke.*"

We stare at him. None of us have ever heard his language.

"*Suna na . . .*" he repeats "*Nweke.*" He points to his chest.

Tama opens her eyes. She's not afraid of the black man. She smiles. He smiles back, his teeth look like a flash of light in his dark face. His eyes are gentle.

"*Suna na . . .*" he smiles at Tama. "*Nweke.*"

She understands him. "Tama," she says, and sits up in his lap.

He smiles so hard that it seems like the white teeth take over his face. "Tama," he says slowly, with a thick accent.

Tama slips off his lap. "Nweke," she grins.

267

Nweke peeks under the leaves he's wrapped around her ankles. "Eh," he nods, and takes them off, throwing them into the brush.

There's no blood.

He bows his head and turns to Levi. "Nweke," he points to his chest. His eyes have changed, they're not soft like they were for Tama, but firm, slightly wide to show respect.

"Levi," Levi responds.

Nweke nods and turns to me. I grin. I feel like I have known Nweke for several days. "Zara," I point to myself. "It's good to meet you, Nweke. And this is," I touch Yaco's shoulder, "Yaco."

Nweke nods. He says all our names slowly, struggling with the sounds. "*Livre*," he adds in Portuguese.

Free.

Nweke must be an ex-slave who ran away so he could be free.

"*Livre*," I point to all of us.

Nweke nods, his face serious. He says something in his language and I shake my head to show I don't understand. Nweke takes a deep breath and struggles with another Portuguese word.

Seguro. Safe.

We don't need any more words.

Nweke leads us off the trail, and out of the cloud forest. The air is cooler, the land more rugged, and the forest not as dense. We can see jagged peaks above the trees; we're now very high. I think of my first view - the mountain emerging from the water - and realize that we're now part of that mountain. The birds are still noisy and we often hear the *woo woo* of the Owls that live at this altitude. There are many cool streams, but we're very careful not to go near muddy puddles where leeches might live. Nweke shows us many things - fruits and greens we can eat, berries, and roots we can dig up and cook over a fire that he builds. Although we speak different languages, we're able to communicate many things to one another. I try to imagine what Nweke's life was like before the Portuguese made him a slave. I wonder if he lived in a tribe, if he was a chief, or the son-of-a-chief. Like us, he was wrenched from home and all he knew, chained, and forced to this island to work for the Portuguese.

We have much in common with Nweke. We feel very safe with him.

Tama has taken a real liking to him; often she holds his hand as we move through the forest. His eyes light up and a smile plays across his lips. Perhaps Nweke was a father when he lived in Africa; perhaps he had a daughter like Tama . . .

I wonder if we'll ever know.

After several days of walking, Nweke pauses in front of a clearing in the forest.

"*Livre*," he says in heavily accented Portuguese. "*Casa*."

There's a path of raised logs. We step on the logs and follow Nweke, wondering what we'll see next. As we walk down the path, people emerge from the forest: ebony-colored black men, bare-breasted black women, mixed bloods with skin the color of roasted almonds, and white men, ex-*degradados*, with scars from the chains that bound them together by their ankles, wrists, and necks. The people are silent as we pass them; they stare at us without smiles. At the end of the log path is a single, common hut with a thatched roof. We stop.

A crowd gathers around us.

Nweke says something in his language and their heads nod.

A *degradado*, with only one arm, and a wild, tangled beard steps forward. "Who are you?" He demands in Portuguese.

Levi speaks for all of us. "We're the Jewish children stolen from our families in Portugal, forced to colonize the island."

The *degradado* turns to the others and translates. "How did you get here?" He demands.

"We ran away," I whisper. "The Portuguese . . . the monks . . . were very cruel."

Suddenly a woman with dark hair and dark eyes emerges. "I know," she lowers her head. "The Portuguese brought me here to be a whore."

I gasp. We're silent for a moment, sharing the horrors that we were forced to endure.

"Is this the fugitive camp?" Tama asks.

269

The woman nods her head.

"Can we live here?" Yaco asks.

The *degradado* laughs and translates for the others. Nweke grins broadly.

"You're home," the *degradado* raises his arms in welcome.

The Old Couple

The old couple knows that time is running out. They hold hands, but their bodies are tense. Their eyes are hard. They sing to one another, but the words come out staccato and harsh.

Where is the key that was in the drawer?
Onde sta la yave ke stava in kashon?

My forefathers brought it with great pain
From their house in Spain.

Mis nonus la trusheron kon grande dolor
De su kaza de Espanya.

We told our children this is the heart of our home.

Taymullah

She lies on her back, in the middle of the Great Lawn.

The dark man in the cargo pants watches her, his heart pounding.

She's the third.

The third infidel.

He trembles with anticipation. His time has arrived.

Slowly, the black woman sits, stretches, and stands up. She has cocoa-colored skin, fawn-like eyes, and a tall, willowy body. She turns and stares straight into his eyes.

She's not afraid.

He shivers. She's the dangerous one, he reminds himself. He has to watch out for her.

She looks to her right, then her left, then back at him, as if daring him to do something. The dark man freezes.

It's almost time.

Almost.

The three must be together.

Then he can kill them.

Five: Rafael and Bryant Park

Rafael

There are no more Jews in Portugal. My adopted people are all *anusim* - Jews forced to convert to Christianity. Manuel broke them to his satisfaction, declaring that Jews no longer exist in Portugal. He's awarded his *Novo Christãos* a 30-year grace period, during which there will be no inquiries into their faith. To him, the problem is solved - he believes he has succeeded where Spain has failed. It's ironic that the Jews have been, once again, forced underground - partaking in a dance of deception that ridicules my own lineage of *limpieza de sangre*. You fool only yourself, Manuel. You're no different than Ferdinand or Isabella or any of the people that have tortured the Jews during their conflicted history.

Everyone around us believes I am one of them.

Although I never underwent conversion or circumcision, I feel as if I have fully adopted the faith of my beloved Marianna. In truth, I believe that God accepts all souls, whether you worship Jesus, follow the Laws of Moses, or pray to Allah. Heaven welcomes those who have lived a good life, based on what they do, not what they say. If a monk or a monarch tortures a man to force him to embrace another's belief, *he* is Satan, not the faith inside the victim. If murder is in your heart . . . and your hands . . . without cause or self-defense, then *you* are Satan as well. Evil comes dressed in many different doublets while God is draped in spirit, energy, and light.

These ideas are heresy to all faiths; I do not dare speak of my ideas. I hold them close, within my heart, and conduct my life based on these principles.

Perhaps that's why guilt drives me unmercifully; the *limpieza de sangre* within cries for repentance, like the monks that flagellate themselves until their flesh swells into purple welts and blood drips down their bodies in twisted crimson rivulets. The questions endlessly assault me: is God angry or forgiving? When I meet my God, whoever He is, will He understand *why?* Will He forgive the monster in *me* and

273

give me entrance to dwell in eternity with my beloved Marianna? I have done so much, committed so many grievous sins, that I doubt that God will ever accept my repentance.

I sigh and bury my face in the perfume of Marianna's hair. In this quiet before the sun rises and the day begins, I dwell on the evil that is *me*, the cowardly creature that savaged everything I loved.

I remain quiet and introverted. No one really knows who I am - even Marianna. People would think I am possessed and try to wrench Satan from *my* soul for such heresies. Marianna would never forgive me, however deep her love. My most evil sin is to remain silent, embrace my love while I deceive her, join her people, and do my best to protect them through the malevolent duplicity that thrives, like poisonous venom, wherever I go.

Perhaps that's not my sin, but my penitence?

I know now, after living with them, that Manuel does not have the ability to destroy the Portuguese Jews any more than Ferdinand and Isabella destroyed the Spanish Jews. I love my new people for their strength and resilience; for their ability to continue, in plain sight or hidden, what they so deeply believe; and for that elusive but omnipresent spirit that Marianna calls the Jewish Soul.

Os Estãos gave birth to transformation. The *Sephardim* or Iberian Jews in Portugal, dragged, cajoled, and forced into baptism in the church, are now all *Conversos*. I hear Marianna's words, whispered between clenched teeth, as we struggled to find our peace.

You can change our robes, but never our hearts.

I wish I were as strong and determined as Marianna. She has lost so much and yet she continues, unfailing, to assure that the seed of her family lives on through her. Everyone else is gone . . . her parents, her sisters, her home.

Marianna endures.

After *Os Estãos,* and the rape of the holy water, we took a new home in Lisboa, rather than return to the countryside to Aldonça and Gonçallo. The kind, old couple could never be our people. Marianna insisted we live among the *Conversos*. Home is now a narrow, winding alley, a tiny whitewashed structure with a red earth-colored tile roof, and walls that lean from centuries of inhabitants. Inside, an ancient wood ceiling sags with age, matching the rough-tiled floor that slopes into each corner of the room. We have one window that looks over the alley, letting in errant rays of sun that trickle between the buildings that surround us. On one side of our room we sleep on a straw-filled mattress; on the other we have a kitchen and a tiny oak table, scarred by years of use. It's a far cry from the luxury I shared with Father, but it's ours, and when we close the heavy green door that's so small I have to bend to enter, we shut out the world and leave the *Conversos, Novo Christãos,* monks, and soldiers outside.

I lay here, in our home, on our paltry, lumpy mattress, Marianna's head pressed against my chest, her breath steady as she sleeps. I think about what has happened since the moment I first saw Marianna to the instant I knew that the Inquisitors were headed for the Sorguetos family.

I was fourteen years old and very lonely. Father barely talked to me, or anyone, since the pox had taken Mama and my three younger brothers. In the six months following their deaths he had become a bitter, angry man. I was a constant reminder of what could have been; thin and delicate, more like my mother with a passion for music and beautiful things. I strummed on Mama's precious *vihuela de mano*, until Father banned me from earshot, saying he couldn't stand the sound since Mama was gone.

Mama's *vihuela* was a beautiful instrument, given to her from her mother and from her mother before. It was built many years ago when the lute had given birth to the modern sounds of six double-strings made from gut. Built from golden-colored wood, laid in thin sheets curved to form a bowl shape, the *vihuela* made magical sounds, soothing to the mind and ears. The neck was a solid piece of wood, glued to the body, and contoured to fit the fingers perfectly. The body had graceful waist cuts that gave it an elegant appearance, decorated with holes, ports, and pierced rosettes to assure a more perfect sound. It was small, fitting comfortably in my arms.

When I think of all the people and things I miss from my old life, Mama's *vihuela* is my deepest loss.

Mama had taught me how to play, recognizing that I was the most musical among her four sons. She helped me place my fingers correctly, feel the melody, and sing the many songs that she'd committed to memory. Father was not happy about his son playing a musical instrument *and* singing; he believed that it was for *trovadores*, men weak of heart, and not the son of a wealthy, highly-respected man who produced clothing for the royals, known throughout Spain for his fashionable, magnificently crafted doublets.

The royals and their nobles loved their doublets, cut from the most delicate silks, brocades, and linens, decorated with designs and laces that bespoke power and wealth. Father knew how to shape the garment perfectly, enhancing the male body with a tiny skirt and narrow waist that slimmed the hips, tight-fitting sleeves with upper padding that exaggerated broad shoulders, and a flat back with padded chest to enhance the popular inverted triangle shape. Father had become a rich man producing doublets customized to the tastes of the royals, nobles, and wealthy men. He used only the best textiles, purchased from Spain's acclaimed textile merchant, Lucas De Sorguetos.

One day, without much thought, Father decided to bring me along to view new textiles carried by De Sorguetos. I was wildly excited; Father normally paid no attention to my needs and I saw his request as the first sign of him recognizing that I was his only remaining son, perhaps his successor in business. I dreamed about Father teaching me his trade, joining his business, being respected by the men that he dealt with . . . my future, I believed, was finally changing.

That was my first mistake - to trust that Father, a bitter, angry man - could forgive me for surviving Mama and my three brothers.

The Sorguetos warehouse was a fantasy of colors and textures, as delicious to my eyes as the sounds from my *vihuela*. I felt very important, and struggled to conceal my excitement as I stared at the bolts of fabrics in red, blue, green, and gold. There was linen, silk, brocade, velvet, fine wools, fustian, and broadcloth. Sunlight bounced off the brilliant colors, the air heavy with the smell of textiles imported from many exotic lands. Lucas de Sorguetos bowed deeply to my father, addressing him with the respect given to a man of his importance. The textile merchant glanced at me, the edge of his mouth tilted upward in an almost-smile that I will never forget. I was bursting with pride and a sense of my own importance. Two other customers, the highly respected Andrés de Martinez and Jose de Lucero greeted Father. They gathered around him, eager to trade news and be seen with such a prominent man. Father was sharp; his tongue revealed little as he encouraged the others to speak. They talked about textiles, caravels, and foreign lands. My eyes wandered, drawn away. I could not stop *looking*.

Suddenly, between two bolts of crimson silk, I saw movement.

It was the barest of motion, but I caught two dark, intense eyes watching the men. The eyes turned to me.

I smiled, expecting her to run. Instead, she poked her head between the fabric, dark, curly hair cascading over the silk, and smiled.

I would never be the same.

She was just thirteen years old, a fact I would learn later. In that wild, mischievous moment, between bolts of crimson silk, gold brocades, and blue velvet, Marianna captured my heart.

Minutes passed before her eyes shifted back to the men talking with Father, silently ordering me to listen. I obeyed without hesitation.

The men were heatedly discussing the Jews.

"I've heard," Andrés de Martinez rubbed his huge, protruding belly. "That the Jews are the cause of the Black Death." He grinned, showing yellow, rotted teeth and expelling a blast of fetid breath that made Father wince.

The others were silent, waiting for him to continue.

Sorguetos looked away for a fraction of a second. Father shifted his gaze from Martinez to the textile merchant. A strange expression flashed in Father's eyes . . . perhaps a question? It passed so quickly I had no time to fully understand what I saw.

Martinez continued. "The Jews poison Christian wells, all part of a conspiracy to kill us. They make potions of spiders, frogs, vermin, and the flesh of Christians. They mix it all together with the flour of the sacred host. Then they wash it down with the blood of Christian children."

"Ahhhh," Jose Lucero shivered, "they *are* the children of Satan."

"In some towns," Martinez added gleefully, "they have thrown open the gates of the *Judería* and slaughtered the Christ-killers, burning their homes, raping their women, and slicing open their throats when finished."

"Ahhhh," Lucero grinned lasciviously, "brave men serve God when they destroy Christ-killers."

"I'm thrilled," Martinez lowered his voice, "that Torquemada and Queen Isabella plot to expel all Jews from our lands. They have to convince the king. God will bless us with wealth and prosperity when we live only among good Christians."

Father, Lucero, and Sorguetos nodded sagely.

"A good move," Lucero mumbled.

"They have made it very cheap to buy Jew businesses and homes," Father observed.

Martinez laughed conspiratorially. "I have bought some myself."

"Wise choice," Lucero smiled.

The men laughed.

Sorguetos had a strained look in his eyes, but voiced his agreement with the others.

The talk continued, discussing the values of abandoned Jew businesses and possessions. "Once the Jews are gone," Martinez boasted, "we'll all be wealthy men."

"Let the ships take them," Lucero waved his fist. "The sailors can take their women, toss their men overboard, and feed their children to the sea monsters."

"The Portuguese can have them for dessert," Father added.

"Yes," Sorguetos said softly. "For dessert."

I listened to the conversation and for a moment, thought I saw a shadow pass across Sorguetos' face. I looked at Father, but his eyes were veiled. I turned to the pretty girl hiding between the bolts of crimson silk, but she was gone.

Later, when we left the store, I impulsively asked Father the unthinkable. "Is he a Jew?"

"Who?"

"The textile merchant?"

Father stopped and in front of everyone who could see, slapped me so hard that my knees crumbled and I fell to the cobblestones. Tears stung my eyes as I rubbed my cheek which would bear the marks of Father's fingers for days.

"Never ask that question!" Father roared fire in his eyes.

In that moment, I knew that there was a piece missing in a very complicated puzzle. Father knew too. Perhaps he was afraid of losing his favorite textile merchant to the fires of the Inquisition? In some convoluted way, I like to believe that Father didn't want me to bear the burden of knowing *or* the responsibility of reporting that knowledge to the Inquisitors.

But Father was a bitter man, and I will never know for sure.

In that same moment, I also knew that I could not live my life without the dark-eyed girl next to me.

The weeks passed and I found reasons to go to the Sorguetos warehouse. I played my *vihuela* less and spent more time working with Father, searching for ways to be with the textile merchant. I placed orders for Father, picked them up, and dragged them over to our part of town. I made payments, never in full, so I could return many times in hopes of seeing the dark-eyed girl.

Lucas de Sorguetos began to like me. There was a twinkle in his eye when I entered the warehouse; a smile easily shared. Unlike Father, he was a good man, kind and gentle with young people and, at the same time, a crafty businessman. I was almost an adult, and he treated me with respect. I didn't see the dark-haired girl, but I looked forward to spending a few minutes talking to the textile merchant, listening to him tell the stories behind his fabrics, speaking of the exotic places where they were made.

One cool, sunny day I entered the warehouse and could see that something was very wrong.

I asked the textile merchant why he looked so troubled, but he smiled and shrugged off the answer. Several days later, I saw that there was no difference.

279

"Don Sorguetos," I asked gently, "What troubles you?"

The textile merchant was surprised at my question. I was even more surprised that he replied. "It's my child," he admitted, "she's very sick."

My heart started to pound. "The pox?" I whispered.

He shook his head. "No, she doesn't have the pox. She suffers from a malady since birth; she's very fragile and breathes very weakly." There was a faint, tragic light in his eyes.

A parent's grief.

I saw the same light in Mama's eyes after my brothers had caught the pox and before she was afflicted. She picked up the *vihuela* and played her best, fighting for a smile. How precious those smiles became.

"Will it make them better?" I had asked her.

She'd smiled sadly. "I don't think so, but it will make their passing sweeter."

When Mama caught the pox, I played the *vihuela* for her until *she* died, with a smile on her lips.

"I know what will help her!" I cried.

The textile merchant looked at me quizzically.

"I'll get it."

Without regard to the business that needed to be done, to Father's inevitable anger at me for playing the *vihuela* for the textile merchant's daughter, I raced home and retrieved my beloved instrument. I brought it back to the warehouse and told him the story of my mother.

Lucas de Sorguetos smiled for the first time. "Come with me," he said.

He led me through the labyrinth of alleys that connected his warehouse to his home.

"Don˜ a Sorguetos," the textile merchant pointed to a small, graceful woman, dressed in clean, brightly-colored robes that flowed around her. "This young man has come to help Catalina."

She looked at me with curiosity, but did not question the word of her husband. Silently, she led me to the bed of Catalina.

Their home was bigger in size than mine, but much simpler and cleaner in design. Carved wood ceilings lorded over whitewashed walls, spotless tile, and heavy, dark furniture. There were many crucifixes and religious statues; they stared at me from their prominent perches. I felt as if God and his angels were watching; relying on me to cure the textile merchant's daughter.

The girl named Catalina was painfully thin, her fawn-like eyes barely open, and her skin pale beneath its natural olive color. Her long, curly hair cascaded over the pillows; next to the bed was a pot filled with wild, alluring purple flowers. Her breathing was raspy, more like a wheeze that made her body shudder with the effort.

She looked at me blankly.

The textile merchant and his wife watched as I unwrapped my *vihuela* and began to play, singing the songs that Mama had taught me.

By the second song, Catalina's eyes were focused.

I came each day; and each day Catalina grew stronger. The physician said it was a miracle, that my music had coaxed her from a sure death. The Sorguetos could not do enough for me - offering me food and sweets, thanking me, telling me I could have anything I wanted. I made one request.

"Don't tell Father - or anyone - about what I'm doing."

They were surprised, but did not question my desire.

On the second day, Catalina's little sister, Zara, drifted into the room and sat on the edge of the bed, listening and watching. Zara had a lively look in her eyes, and we instantly liked one another. It wasn't until the third day that the dark-haired girl I saw between the bolts of fabric, appeared.

"My name is Marianna," she said, her eyes capturing me in a visual embrace.

I fell into their depths; in that moment I knew that our fates would be entwined forever.

I smiled and continued my music.

Catalina got better, and I became a part of the Sorguetos household. I played music for them, laughed with them, and took meals with them. They were the family I had lost. They called me their *trovodor* and treated me with something I had never experienced - respect and affection. Don˜ a Sorguetos and I formed a special attachment; she saw me as the man who saved her daughter's life. I felt happier and light-hearted, like the way I was before Mama and my brothers died. Father noticed the change but said nothing; I wanted to believe he was pleased that my life had taken a new turn. At first, I hid the *vihuela*. After a few weeks, I left it out for Father's eyes. He said nothing, pretending he didn't see it. Father was a very wise man - he knew something was happening, but he was content to observe the change, rather than to know or be part of my secret life.

Whenever I was with the Sorguetos, I would search for Marianna, hoping she would join the music, and celebration of Catalina's survival. In the beginning she was a shadow, mischievously hiding and appearing at will. Slowly, she emerged from her secret places, and joined the rest of us. No one knew I was wildly in love with her; the more I

saw her, the more I heard her voice, and the more time she spent near me, the more my passion grew. When I wasn't with Marianna or her family, I would dream about her dark eyes, curly hair, and quick smile, practicing how I would ask her father for her hand in marriage. At night, when I slept, I had more embarrassing dreams; I saw her in my bed, her body naked next to mine, touching her breasts. I would wake with my body fluids smeared around me, terrified that Father would discover my indiscretions. It became my covert life - making love to Marianna every night in the privacy of my dreams.

And yet there was something I couldn't quite touch, a mystery that lingered in their eyes and flashed briefly like a spot of sun on an overcast day. I sensed it, but couldn't put it into words. The Sorguetos were hiding something.

I didn't spend much time thinking about *their* secret. My own deception filled my thoughts, and controlled my days. I prayed that if I convinced Father, he would approve of the marriage. I would tell him of my love, win his approval and . . . I did nothing. I was too afraid of Father. I planned, in my mind, how to approach him, rehearsing every word and every gesture. I raised my voice and then modulated it; Father would respect control, not passion. I needed to be very business-like in my request. I created a dance in my mind, squaring my shoulders, placing my feet wide apart, puffing my chest out in one of Father's favorite doublets. Nothing seemed right. All I needed was Father's approval; then he could approach the textile merchant and negotiate a union. I had no fear that Father or Don Sorguetos would refuse.

It had to work.

Father wanted to be rid of me, and what family would not want to marry their daughter to my family's status?

A match unquestionably arranged in Heaven.

I waited for the right time.

It came, as such things do, after a sweet evening with the family, tasting Dona Sorgueto's savory beef stew, and everyone singing along with my *vihuela*. My heart was filled with joy as I made my way home. I knew I would summon the courage to request Father's blessing very soon.

Father was in a nasty mood when I entered our home.

"Where have you been?" He demanded.

Father had not asked my whereabouts since Mama and my brothers had died.

"Out," I said stubbornly, concealing my mixture of anger and disappointment. I tried to move past him, but he blocked my way.

"Where have you been," he grabbed my arm.

I pulled my arm from his grasp, realizing, for the first time, that I was physically stronger than him. "Out," I repeated, tasting the anger rising in the back of my throat.

"Where?" He roared, his voice thunder in my ears.

Pictures of Marianna flashed through my mind. The sound of my music and the voices of the Sorguetos filled my ears. For one fatal moment, I couldn't see anything but my own passion.

"I was with *them,*" I shouted. "The textile merchant and his family. They laugh, they sing, and they treat me with honor."

Father stepped back, his face pale, as if he had just been attacked. I relished my new-found power.

"There's something else," I stepped closer to him, into his face. "I'm in love with their daughter Marianna and she will be my wife."

I have never seen Father look like he did at that moment; even when Mama and my brothers died; even when we lay them to rest, beneath the chants of the priests, and he knew only two of us remained. In seconds, his face went from shock to grief to anger that froze his eyes like the coldest marble. His lips trembled, then curled back, a wild animal baring white, sharp teeth.

"Never," Father hissed.

That single word was a slap across my face, a knife in my heart, boiling oil poured down my throat. I trembled from the assault and stumbled backward.

"You will never marry the *Marrano*."

At first, I didn't understand what he was saying.

"*Marrano*," he shouted, his eyes filled with blood. "I will never approve of you marrying a *Marrano* - disgracing our family name - tainting our *limpieze de sangre*."

"*Marrano*?" I whispered numbly.

"Jewish swine," Father roared, spittle spraying from his lips. "*Heretics. Conversos. Judaizers. Christ-killers.*"

Father raised his arms, his fists clenched. "*Never*," he snarled, "will I allow you to dishonor this family . . . and the blessed memory of your mother."

I shook my head, thinking about the crucifixes that hung throughout the Sorguetos home, the religious statues, their rosaries, and the frequent mention of Jesus Christ. I didn't understand.

Impossible.

"Idiot," Father roared. "You've been with *Marranos*. You were too stupid to realize what you were doing." He rubbed his hands together. "If only your brothers had survived instead of you. My life would be so different . . ."

I listened to his words but didn't hear them. Perhaps there were *too many* crucifixes in the Sorguetos home. Often, I thought their show of Christianity exceeded others. They didn't eat pig. They *tried* to eat it, but when Dona Sorguetos served it for dinner I noticed that I was the only one who consumed it with relish. Everyone else seemed to ignore it, as if they weren't hungry.

There was the day I came to visit, a holiday in the Jewish quarter, when the house was strangely empty. So quiet. I wondered where they were . . .

And there was that mystery in their eyes.

The puzzle.

As the pieces began to fall together, Father continued his rant. "My son will never marry a filthy *Marrano.* He will never sow his seed with the Christ-killers, drink the blood of Christian children . . . shame our name and *limpieza de sangre.*"

When the words finally came, I was calm, strong, and resolute. Father had given up his right to tell me what to do. "I don't care," I said boldly, "I am marrying Marianna."

I left my Father speechless, went to my room, and climbed in my bed, fully clothed, to think through what I would do next. Father didn't pursue me; my words were left hanging, like a threat, between us. But there was too much to think about, too much to understand about the family I had come to love, and too much rage. I cried; I cried for my mama and three brothers, for the father I never had, and for Marianna. Eventually my tears stopped, my eyes closed, and I fell into a deep sleep.

I dreamed about blood and torture, exquisite pain, the Inquisitors seizing the Sorguetos, and my *vihuela* lying broken on the cobblestones.

Suddenly, voices awoke me from my nightmare. It was Father. He was talking to someone in the other side of the house. I strained to hear his words, but I was too far away. I climbed from my bed, mildly surprised to find myself fully clothed. In seconds, I recalled my words with Father. I listened to the voices. Could it be? Would Father go that far?

Careful not to make any sounds, I crept to the other side of the house until only a wall separated me from Father and his visitors.

"*Marranos,*" Father said. "I have seen it with my own eyes. The Sorguetos practice Jewish rituals, attend secret services in Jewish homes; they scoff at the Host and the body and blood of Christ, profaning the sacred rites of true Christians. I have seen them wear clean clothes on Saturday, use clean table cloths on Friday, cook kosher meat overnight on Friday, with fat and leg tendons removed, then eat it for the Jewish Sabbath meal on Saturday. I have seen all of this with my own eyes . . ."

I froze. Father was sending the Inquisitors after the Sorguetos and my beloved Marianna.

I had to warn them.

Or they would die.

For a single, fatal instant, I hesitated. Time ceased to exist. If I warned the Sorguetos, they would have to escape. I would lose Marianna. I would betray Father's trust. That meant forsaking Father, robbing him of his only surviving son. I would bring dishonor and tragedy on our family, forever staining our bloodline.

Without my seed, my family would cease to exist.

I prayed to God for help.

There was silence. The choice was mine.

Perhaps I could do both – warn the Sorguetos and return to Father?

I could not lose Marianna.

Knowing that I would bear Father's betrayal, forever in time, along with my betrayal to our bloodline, I made my decision.

I had to save Marianna.

With my heart pounding crazily in my chest, and my body swathed in icy sweat, I slunk to the front door. It was open. I stepped outside and faced a band of Inquisition soldiers, blocking my path.

I had to think fast.

"Father sent me to check our wares," I said, trying to conceal the terror in my voice. "He told me the *Marranos* are trying to steal everything."

The soldier grunted with approval.

"Burn Satan's Christ-killers," I shouted, perhaps a bit too loud.

I held my breath. They could believe me or go inside and ask Father.

The seconds passed like hours; spots danced in front of my eyes and I struggled to hide my terrified breathing.

"He's fine," one of the soldiers said finally. "Let him through."

The others were unsure. I waited for their decision. The night hung heavy around us; the darkness settling permanently in my soul.

It was my fault they were here.

It would be my fault if they got to the Sorguetos before I could warn them.

Still unsure, the Inquisition soldiers parted so I could pass between them. The last thing I saw was the red crosses on their chests.

I walked normally until the soldiers and my home were out of sight. Then I broke into a run, forcing my legs to move faster than I thought possible, cutting through every alley that would take me to the Sorguetos sooner. I had to be in time, I had to beat the soldiers. Wild thoughts raged through my mind as I concentrated on my race. What will happen if they get there first? What will happen to Marianna?

What will happen to me?

Like everyone else in Spain, I had attended *auto de feys,* watched the pageantry of the Church as they condemned their victims; heard their cries as the flames took them, and swallowed the sickening smell and taste of burning human flesh.

I had to warn the Sorguetos. Even if I never saw Marianna again.

I ran until my legs ached with the demand; my breath tore through my chest like daggers, and my heart beat so quickly I wondered if it might explode. I reached their street and paused, looking both ways.

All was quiet.

I pressed myself against the walls of houses and slinked down to the Sorguetos' home.

I banged on the door with all my strength.

There was no answer.

They have to be home.

I banged harder, until my fists were bloody. I heard footsteps on the other side, and an agonizing intake of breath as Don Sorguetos slowly opened the door. The textile merchant's eyes were filled with sadness.

"Run!" I roared. "They're coming for you. Run *now.*"

Bryant Park

It was time.

The audience was drifting away and Lev was signaling that it was time to cut out. Cole stood still, watching. The sweaty woman was gone, along with her makeshift fan. The family with their sleeping kids had wandered off onto 6th Avenue. The business casuals had cut across the terrace and down the 42nd Street Promenade, heading for Happy Hour at the B.P. Café. A few others lingered; two men went back to their checkers and several skinny teenagers headed for the chess tables. Even Isaac had left.

Only three people remained, standing far from each other, waiting for something to happen.

Lev busied himself with the equipment.

Cole stared from one face to the other - the woman with the smoldering eyes, the olive-skinned girl, and the cocoa-colored skin woman whose eyes penetrated everything.

The friends of the olive-skinned girl were trying to get her to move.

"It's over Ria," one said.

"Let's go," another insisted.

The olive-skinned girl refused to move.

"We'll leave without you," a third one threatened.

It was as if she didn't hear them.

She's not going anywhere, Cole thought.

Ria's friends were annoyed.

"The show's over Ria," Madison said.

"Let's go," Hawk demanded.

Ria refused to move.

"We'll leave without you," Jaime threatened.

Ethan tilted his head. "Let's go to the Café," he said slowly. "You'll catch up with us there?"

Ria looked at him gratefully.

"C'mon," Ethan said, struggling to hide the concern in his voice. "She'll catch up with us."

The others looked at him doubtfully.

Ria nodded, her eyes on the singer. "It's ok," she whispered. "Just give me a few minutes."

Ethan edged away.

"OK," Ria said again. "I'll be there in a minute."

Cole stared at them.

Shira, watching from the other side of the Fountain Terrace, followed the scene like it was a movie. As soon as the olive-skinned girl's friends headed down the 40th Street Promenade, Shira edged closer.

Ria glanced at the woman with dark smoldering eyes and returned her gaze to Cole. Cole looked away, to the middle of the terrace where the cocoa-colored skin woman was standing, frozen in place.

Shira felt the other woman's eyes on her. She struggled not to look in that direction.

What's going on?

Why is everything so weird?

Shira wanted to turn, leave the Fountain Terrace, escape Bryant Park, and hide out in her apartment. The day had unnerved her; it was too real for her writer's fantasy life, an assault on her skillfully plotted life.

What about the singer?

Shira shuddered. Sure, she could erase the women from her consciousness. She could forget about the park and the music. But the singer? He seemed to leap straight out of her romance novels, screaming to be heard.

Those eyes.

Shira shook her head. It was all too crazy.

But those eyes?

Shira had never been in love with anyone but her characters. Was this what it was like? She frowned and tried to think of Emma and Mason.

And the Ladino?

Maybe it was just the Ladino. Shira knew her Sephardic family history and carried it like a cover bio on her sleeve.

I'm proud of it.

Of course the Ladino would affect me.

She fingered the leather pouch in her pocket.

Was that the connection?

Shira knew instinctively that there was a lot more to this plot than a summer afternoon in the park.

"His voice is beautiful," the olive-skinned girl edged closer. She spoke breathlessly, playing with her necklace.

She's Hispanic. That's why she likes the music — it sounds familiar.

"Yes," Shira said stiffly. It was a simple explanation. Shira tried to brush away the questions that pounded at her.

"My name is Ria," the olive-skinned girl smiled. "I work around here." She pointed to a building on 40th Street.

Shira didn't look.

I don't care.

Ria looked at the singer as she spoke to Shira. "Do you work around here?"

Shira ignored the question.

"Do you work around here?" Ria repeated, an edge creeping into her voice.

"No," Shira said finally. "I mean, yes."

"What is it — yes you work here, or no you don't work here?"

"I work in the . . . park."

"With a laptop?"

Shira looked at Ria.

How does she know there's a laptop in my backpack?

"I'm a writer."

"No kidding."

"Why would I kid?"

"I'm kind of a writer, too. I do websites."

"That's not a writer," Shira corrected her. "It's a designer."

Ria shrugged. "Whatever."

290

"I write *books*."

"What kind of books?"

"Mystery romance novels."

Ria was silent. She hated romance novels.

Cole took a few steps toward the two women. Lev watched helplessly from behind. Cole played a few chords on his guitar.

Esta Montana
D'en frente
S'ensiende y va quemando

Shira caught her breath.

Ria gasped.

"Do you understand it?" Shira asked gruffly, looking at the ground.

"Yes."

"How?"

"I don't know . . . I just *do*." Ria tossed her dark hair over her shoulder.

Cole came closer. He spoke softly.

The mountain I see before me
Flames and smolders

Shira refused to respond. She fixed her eyes on the ground.

Get out. I'm crossing a line I've never even seen before.

Get out before it's too late.

Shira's heart raced and she was ready to bolt when the woman with cocoa-colored skin joined them.

"I'm Aliki," she said. Ria looked surprised.

"That's Cole," Aliki added, smiling at the singer who was standing a few feet away.

Cole grinned.

Aliki looked at all of them, one by one, as if in a secret ritual. "For some reason we're all *meant* to be here together, today."

Ria opened her mouth but no words emerged.

M'asento y vo yorando.

291

Cole continued.

And I sit here and weep.

Shira shuddered. She looked at the singer and *his* eyes were boring into her. Panicked, she backed off, terrified of the drama that was unfolding.

There was Jake the tuna-fish man and the suits. There was a little girl with tangled red hair and a priest that looked like he came from the Middle Ages. There were so many *others* that she recognized but didn't know, like the characters in her story, invading Emma's and Mason's life. There was even the dark fat man in cargo pants standing on the cobblestones of the Library Terrace and the old couple sitting beneath a green and white umbrella next to a concrete pot of purple flowers.

Stay.

Shira heard the word in her head.

It's time.

Although she couldn't see the old couple, Shira knew they spoke to her.

Cole dropped his hands from the guitar, letting the instrument dangle from the strap around his neck.

Aliki offered her hand to each of them, one by one.

No one smiled.

Shira's hand was jammed into her pocket, her fingers curled around the leather pouch. Reluctantly, she reached out to Aliki.

Their hands touched. Aliki felt herself plummeting into a dark, bottomless hole, her head spinning with nondescript images. It was a dizzying fall, with green, white, and

purple swirls passing through her mind's eye. On the edge was a vaguely familiar man; dark skin, fat face, and loose-fitting cargo pants.

Salaam aleikum.

Salaam aleikum.

Salaam aleikum.

A boy with a haunted face fringed with straight black hair, big, dark eyes, and scrawny arms and legs, floated on the periphery. A girl with tangled red hair watched desperately.

Aliki struggled to hang on.

Shira's fingertips brushed Aliki's peculiar iron ring, shaped like a cross with one bar cut off, slightly rusted, and worn smooth by time. Shira felt an electric shock jolt her into a strange, unwritten romantic novel with characters drawn from a different part of her mind. Faces, names, sounds buzzed through her head like a Pandora's box of images and voices. She yanked away her hand and buried it inside her pocket, clutching the leather pouch.

The women moved apart quickly.

"Have you heard him before?" Aliki asked, hiding her reaction to Shira's touch.

"No," Shira replied, her voice shaking. "But I know Ladino."

Cole was silent.

Aliki and Shira both briefly closed their eyes, watching the blurred images in their minds. It didn't frighten Aliki; she was used to strange, other-worldly experiences that jumbled time. Shira was shaken to her core; she needed to control her world, like the symbols in a novel, playing God to characters and plot. The glimpse into an inner chaos that she *owned*, showed her something that she never wanted to acknowledge.

"I'm a Sephardic Jew," Shira said suddenly, opening her eyes. She didn't know why she needed to tell that to the strangers.

Aliki acknowledged her with a quick nod.

"I'm a Catholic," Ria confessed.

"Do you *know* what a Sephardic Jew is?" Shira frowned.

Aliki shot her an odd, patronizing look.

"Sorry. . . I've heard Ladino music before," Shira stumbled on her words. "Although never with a singer this good."

"Thank you," Cole said softly.

Aliki thought of *Neuhaus* São Tomé chocolate compared to *Hershey's*.

"The only Ladino I've heard is on CDs," Shira continued. She had a strange need to fill the silence. "Even though I'm Sephardic, not many people speak the language anymore. It's like Yiddish – a victim of time."

Aliki smiled tightly.

"I love *Ladino*," Cole said suddenly. "It just works. I call myself a modern *trovador* or in English, troubadour – an educated poet-lyricist from the 15th century." He chuckled.

"You're not Jewish?" Shira asked.

"No," Cole replied flatly.

"Here," a new voice cut in. It was a kid who looked like he was trying to hide the fact that he was Hassidic - his side curls tucked securely behind his ears, his white button-down shirt replaced with a wrinkled t-shirt, tassels dangling. The kid was holding a CD. On the cover was a photo of Cole, holding his Spanish guitar, standing in front of a colorful Manhattan hot dog cart with a blue-and-yellow Sabrett's umbrella.

Shira stared at the CD.

"Put it away, Lev." Cole said. "We're not allowed to sell stuff in the park."

Lev turned away, going back to pack up the equipment.

Shira glanced at Aliki. Her eyes were fixed on Lev. There was an odd light, as if she recognized the kid.

Shira shrugged.

This is all so weird.

Shira glanced at Cole. Their eyes met in a visual embrace. It was as if she'd known him all her life; like plunging into one of her romance novels.

Hopelessly confused.

Distraught.

Dizzy.

Clichés tumbled through her mind. Shira searched for a comfortable word to label the sensation. For the first time in her life, she couldn't find the words.

Cole waited.

He expects something.

Shira's eyes widened in panic.

Why can't I find my words?

It was only a moment but it felt like eons, as if something old and long lost had suddenly been retrieved.

Shira wrenched herself back. "You . . . sing. . . beautifully," she stuttered.

Cole nodded. There was no smile or friendly tilt of his head.

This is crazy. Aliki. Ria. Cole. Maybe I'm losing it . . . writing too many novels. Maybe I'm merging fiction and nonfiction; reality and virtuality. . .

Shira clutched the leather pouch in her pocket like it was a lifeline to the present.

I need to go back to writing.

Street performers and hot dog vendors were unforgivable clichés. Shira forced herself to visualize her editor redlining it out of a manuscript.

"Street performers?" The editor would chuckle. "You know better than that."

The scenario pulled her away from Cole. Shira stepped back.

"You're magical," Ria said suddenly, staring at Cole like an adolescent groupie.

Cole glanced at Shira and then back to Ria. "Thank you," he said in a silky stage voice.

Aliki followed everything. The fear from Shira. The awe from Ria. The magnetic draw from Cole. What was it about? Why did Shira make sure everyone knew that she was a Sephardic Jew? Why did Ria confess to being Catholic? No one asked. There was no way that the strangers could have guessed Aliki's mixed lineage.

Where did the strange, haunted singer fit in?

Vague, diaphanous images flooded her mind. Aliki knew that whether it was the dark, malaria-ridden jungles of São Tomé or the gray, concrete streets of New York, it always meant the same thing.

Something in her life was about to change.

Rafael

Someone bangs loudly on our door.

I cradle Marianna, but she wakes to the sound. She looks up at me, a question in her eyes. I smile. I never saw Father or my *vihuela* again. I never learned the fate of the Sorguetos, either. I lost Catalina and Zara. I, alone, was responsible for the destruction of their family.

I saved Mariana for myself.

Sometimes, I'm repulsed by my selfishness - repulsed by my history - wracked by my guilt.

Then I look at her.

I wake each morning and feel her beside me, knowing, in some way, I made it possible for at least one Sorguetos to survive my betrayal.

"Who could be at our door?" Marianna whispers, her voice heavy with sleep.

Today is Saturday. We'll meet in the secret room and pray together. I'll don the garments of the Jews and struggle to follow their prayers, as one of them. Marianna will smile and stay with the women, also whispering prayers. We're all *Conversos* now.

The banging on my door persists.

I rise from our lumpy mattress and cover my nakedness. Marianna doesn't move. Slowly, I go to the door, feeling her eyes riveted to my back.

"Don't open it," she mumbles, so softly I can hardly hear.

Something moves me - compels me to open the door. There's an echo of a moment passed, when I was the one banging on the door, in the dark of night. Do I dare *not* answer the door? Is this the way Lucas Sorguetos felt when he heard me banging on his door, that fateful night? I shiver, reluctant to face what's on the other side, yet compelled to discover the source. Time is so strange; there's a compulsion to repeat until we make it right. Over and over, until all have paid for their trespasses. Perhaps my betrayal is a repeat from an earlier event; time's persistence to repair the damage I caused. The Jews have a word to describe that:

Gilgul.

Taking a deep breath, I open the door a crack.

"Rafael," a familiar face peers at me. It's Isaac de Torres, the leader of our *Converso* community in Lisboa. Like the others, Isaac received a Christian name after *Os Estãos*. He uses it in public and all business dealings. To me, he will always be Isaac.

"Ah, Isaac," I open the door wider, and speak warmly. "What can I do for you this morning?"

Isaac is a tall, thin man with dark penetrating eyes and brown hair that falls in neat layers over his ears and onto his shoulders. His beard is small and cropped, a compromise between faith and safety. He's a good man; proud and gentle at once, who takes joy in helping the people around him.

Isaac has been a friend since *Os Estãos*. He and his family were dragged together to the baptismal font. The Torres family was one of the luckier ones, they remained

together. Stronger than many, Isaac secretly gathered and organized the *Os Estãos* Jews, now Portugal's newest *Novos Christãos,* in a secret room beneath his home to pray and study the Laws of Moses. Marianna and I helped him and his family heal many broken Jews, offering solace in shared grief.

"Rafael," Isaac insists, "please open the door." His voice is strained, not the usual gentle tones that fill his speech.

Is something wrong?

I glance at Marianna. She dressed quickly, leaving only a question in her eyes. Her body is stiff, as if ready for a new round of bad news. While Marianna works hard to conceal it, I know she will never completely recover from the horror that invaded our lives. She nods.

I wonder if she, too, recalls the banging on her door that night so long ago.

My words echo in my own head, burning like the fires of the Inquisition.

Run! They're coming for you. Run now.

I open the door and smile stiffly at our friend.

He's not alone. Next to him stands a man I haven't seen since before the night I banged on the Sorguetos' door. Enrique's eyes are sharp and dark; his almost Moorish skin is pimpled with pox marks. Enrique was a childhood friend, always bullied, always disliked by the other children.

"Enrique," I say lightly, without thinking. "What are you doing in Lisboa?"

Enrique sneers at me, and I remember that I, like the other boys in my childhood, didn't like the awkward, secretive child. Enrique turns to Isaac, his mouth twisted into an angry smile.

"Yes, Don Torres, it's *him*. This man is *limpieza de sangre* - I grew up next to him and his family in Spain. His mother and three brothers died from the pox, and his Father, a wealthy producer of doublets for the rich, became a bitter man. There is not a drop of Jewish blood in this man . . . *he's* not one of us. He is no more Jewish than the King of Spain."

After the agony of *Os Estãos* and our forced baptism, we lived a good life. We were accepted into the newly-formed community of Portuguese *Conversos*, created from exiled Spanish Jews and the freshly-baptized Portuguese Jews. Before *Os Estãos,* the Jews lived openly in Portugal. Manual changed all of that.

They were good people; Marianna and I thrived in their camaraderie. We were childless, like so many *Conversos* who had lost their children to *Os Estãos*, São Tomé, and the Portuguese kidnapping of Jewish babies. The Jews shared a common bond, a mutual sorrow that stretched back thousands of years of Jewish persecution. The Laws of Moses became my guide - each night I secretly studied them, beneath the watchful eyes of Marianna, learning how to think and have faith like a Jew. I learned many Hebrew prayers, tasting the ancient words and melodies like sweet fruits on my tongue. Although scarred by our struggles; mourning our own losses; we became part of the community, connected to them, thriving in the drama of our daily lives. Marianna grew even more beautiful, and when she told me that she was carrying our child, I believed that God had forgiven me for betraying the Sorguetos.

How foolish I was.

298

I will never forget the look on Isaac de Torres face when Enrique cried out the words that forever tarnished our lives in Lisboa.

"*It's him.* This man is *limpieza de sangre* - I grew up next to him and his family. His mother and three brothers died from the pox, and his father, a wealthy producer of doublets for the rich, became a bitter man. There is not a drop of Jewish blood in this man . . . *he* is not one of us. He is no more Jewish than the King of Spain."

My first response is to defend.

Ah Enrique, we all know that the King of Spain has Jewish blood in his veins. And so does Torquemada, the Chief Inquisitor of Spain.

We all know that.

Instead, my blood becomes ice.

Marianna turns white. I lose my words.

A strange image leaps into my mind. It's Mama's *vihuela* and she's teaching me a popular ballad. Her voice is soft and her hand rests on my shoulder.

Ah Rafael, she sighs with pleasure, you are truly a gifted musician.

Where will it take you?

"Is it true?" Isaac demands, his face red. "Is it true you're not one of us?" His voice is confused, tinged with anger, sadness, and disappointment.

Why would anyone pretend to be Jewish?

I open my mouth, but there's no sound. How do I explain, my friend? How do I explain my love for Marianna; pretending the Sorguetos was my own family; confess why Father summoned the Inquisitors? How do I say that although I was born Christian, the child of many generations of Christians, my heart has become one with the Jews and the Laws of Moses? How do I tell my friend that I could never be Christian *again*, not after living the expulsion, watching the Inquisition in all its savagery, and celebrating the spirit of an incredibly courageous people?

How do I say that I betrayed Father and my own bloodline, for Marianna?

Marianna comes from behind, wrapping her fingers around my arm.

"He's my husband," she whispers. "He saved me from the Inquisition." Her voice is stiff and frightened.

"If he's not Jewish," Isaac says, "then you have broken our laws. You've married a man who has no covenant with Abraham; who has not learned our ways; who does not pray to our God. Why have you done this, Marianna? Why do you shame your family?"

Marianna's head snaps, as if she had been struck.

I wrap my arms around her protectively.

Enrique grins.

"And you, Enrique? Are a Jew? You came to church with us," I snap.

Enrique scratches his head. He's enjoying the scene, reveling in the disgrace that he brings upon us. "That was how we *appeared*. We were always *Conversos*."

I shake my head. If my neighbors were *Conversos* and the Sorguetos were *Conversos*, who were the *limpieza de sangre*?

Me.

"We left with the Jews," Enrique continues.

"So did I," I frown.

Isaac shakes his head. "If you want to be a Jew, you must convert."

"How can I convert?" I stare at him incredulously. "It's illegal to be an open, practicing Jew in Lisboa; punishable by slavery or death. Should I put myself or Marianna at such risk? Should I jeopardize the life or our unborn child?"

I touch Marianna's swollen belly.

Isaac sighs. "Most of us have lost babies to remain faithful to our God. What's one more when *you* have betrayed us?"

My head snaps, as if I've been hit in the face.

If only you knew, my good friend.

"Haven't I proven my loyalty to the Laws of Moses?" I persist.

"It's our law," Isaac says softly.

"Marianna," I gasp, "tell them."

Haven't I repented for my betrayal to Father?

She starts to speak, but Isaac stops her. "In the eyes of God, you have committed an egregious sin." He looks at her belly. "The

300

baby of a Jewish woman is always Jewish. Your child will be one of us - but not your husband."

Marianna covers her mouth in a silent scream.

"After all we have been through, after we have been beaten and robbed *as* Jews, you refuse me the right to be part of your community?"

Isaac lowers his head. "I'm sorry, my friend, but that is our law. You are no longer welcome to pray with us, sing with us, or celebrate holidays with us. You are not a Jew until you convert."

I want to hit him; threaten *him* with betrayal.

I can tell the Portuguese they are Conversos, just like Father told the Spanish.

My blood turns to ice. My thoughts raise my hackles; I taste bile in the back of my throat. I am horrified by my own, unbidden vengeance.

Isaac shakes his head sadly and turns from our door. Enrique grins malevolently. I hold Marianna tightly.

She pulls back and stares at me, wide-eyed, her face heavy with a mixture of horror and grief. How much more can she bear to lose?

Life in Lisboa changed after that morning. Our friends stare at us with mistrust and turn their eyes away when we meet them in the streets. I'm no longer allowed to attend the Sabbath with our *Converso* community; most turn their backs to our pleas. We're shunned in our new home - not one of them opens his heart to our plight.

Marianna cries every night as her belly grows bigger and her heart, already broken once, now shatters.

"What can I do my love?" I beg to no avail.

She shakes her head and turns away, her eyes red and defeated. "Why did I bring *you* into this?" she wails. "We're treated like lepers."

I think, over and over again.

I brought you here.

This is my doing.

Am I doomed . . . are my children doomed . . . along with the ones I love?

Occasionally, one of our old friends pulls me into a hidden crevice in an alley and tearfully explains what's happening. "We're all wounded;

301

we've lost our homes, our children, and our land, for our faith. For many, our God is all we have left. Now, we fear that the Portuguese will bring the Inquisition to our doorsteps, and life will be like it was in Spain . . . tortured and exposed. You have lived among us, worshipped among us, and betrayed us."

I want to argue. I wasn't born a Jew, but I have embraced the *spirit* of the faith. I practice the rituals, and celebrate the festivals. Although I haven't officially converted, I protect Marianna and my soon-to-be-family. My child will be raised as a *Converso*. Perhaps most significantly, I have suffered as a Jew.

Isn't that enough?

The answer comes unbidden, a picture with words, in my mind. Father, talking to the Inquisitors.

"Marranos," Father said. "I have seen it with my own eyes. They practice Jewish rituals, attend secret services in Jewish homes; they scoff at the Host and the body and blood of Christ, profaning the sacred rites of true Christians. I have seen them wear clean clothes on Saturday, use clean table cloths on Friday, cook kosher meat overnight on Friday, with fat and leg tendons removed, then eat it for the Jewish Sabbath meal on Saturday. I have seen all of this with my own eyes . . ."

My life is crumbling.

I deserve this punishment from the God of Moses. But what about Marianna and our unborn child? Is it their cross to bear as well?

I can't tell Marianna any of this without revealing the truth about who turned her family in to the Inquisition. Instead, I remain silent, bearing the pain of a pariah, shunned by the Jews, not one of the Portuguese. I lose weight, my heart pounds out of control, I sweat when it's not hot, and frightening thoughts invade my mind, all without provocation. Although we have food and a home, I worry, each day, how we will survive.

I beg forgiveness from the Sorguetos each night in my dreams. I see Mama Sorguetos with her purple flowers and Papa Sorguetos with his orange freckles and gentle, toad-like stature. I hear Zara singing to my music and see Catalina lying peacefully in her roadside grave. Marianna is like a breeze of fresh, warm air as she dances around me, her arms filled with my child. Then she, too, collapses into the filthy muck of our times. I awake sweating and agitated.

What have I done?

When Marianna verges on the edge of death after birthing our first child, I pray to the God of Moses, that I will make this right. Only one choice remains. I must leave. I must take my small family to a place where we can live in freedom, without fear. I will make sure that the seed of the Sorguetos family survives.

Please God, help me save my children.

Bryant Park

"Now what?" Cole asked.

They were silent.

"Something very strange is happening here," Aliki took over. "We all feel it; we all know it. I think we need to figure things out."

"I don't know what you're talking about," Shira protested.

"Yes you do," Ria frowned. "We all do."

Cole stared at the three women. It was as if they were engaged in an odd, metaphysical production with the Great Lawn as their stage. Soon, the characters would emerge, the plot thicken, and the drama replace the opening pains. Like a book with a slow start, it was definitely worth pursuing.

"Why don't we sit," Cole asked smoothly, "and talk? It's a strange day. Trees cry for rain, purple flowers shudder in the wind, and the sky is filled with thin, shape-shifting clouds."

Shira's eyes snapped to his face. "What did you say?"

Cole grinned. He'd captured her attention. "It's a strange day. Trees cry for rain, purple flowers shudder in the wind, and the sky is filled with thin, shape-shifting clouds."

Shira froze.

Didn't I just write that?

"Don't do it," Lev pounced on them. "Just turn around, leave, and pretend you've never met."

Cole glared at the kid. "Why don't you pack the equipment?"

Lev shook his head, his eyes wide. "I should be praying . . . it's Tisha B'Av. I sinned," he said softly, "because I knew I had to protect you."

"Tisha B'Av?" Ria asked.

"It's a Jewish bad-luck day," Shira explained. "You know, like Friday the 13th. Except the bad things only happen to Jews."

"Like the destruction of the temples and the 15th Century Spanish expulsion of the Jews," Aliki mumbled.

Shira looked at her oddly. "It's just superstition," she continued.

Lev's mouth dropped open.

"I guess I don't have to worry," Ria laughed, "I'm not Jewish."

"Leave," Lev insisted again.

Cole put his hand on the kid's shoulder. "Listen, if you're feeling so guilty about not praying today, why don't you go home and I'll take care of the equipment. Do your thing."

Lev silently stared at him.

"C'mon man," it's just a day."

Lev shook his head. *"Sholom Aleichem,"* he whispered. He turned to the stairs that led to 6th Avenue, waving slowly. Cole watched Lev go, and returned to the women.

"It's ok," he said to them.

Cole never saw Lev double around 42nd Street and return to the park, standing behind a London Plane tree where he could see everything and not be seen. Cole gathered his equipment and stacked everything on a rolling cart on the Great Lawn. The women watched, not saying anything and not looking at one another.

"Let's sit down," Cole suggested when he was finished. "See if we can figure this out."

Rafael

I stand here on the caravel that will take me and my small family to the new world. My young daughter sleeps happily in her Mama's arms, her chubby face rosy and at peace. She's too young for the knowledge that's preceded her; too young to understand the many losses she's already suffered. She will learn. I have promised myself and the memory of the Sorguetos family, that my daughter, and any children who follow, will know everything that happened. They will be raised as Jews and never know my secret of *limpieza de sangre*. No community or country will throw them out. I'll protect them until my death. If I live long enough, my grandchildren will receive the same legacy . . . as well as the promise, which went with the broken iron key that remains in Portugal, to remember who they are. I've failed the Sorguetos in almost everything *but* that.

I will not fail them again.

I stare at the *Castelo de São Jorge*, Lisboa's manly symbol of strength and pride, standing atop three of Lisboa's seven hills. Its ten towers, stone face, and fierce ramparts dominate and protect the city. Lisboa spills from its feet like insects on an ant mound; scattering down and across the hills on which it resides. The sky is filled with thin clouds that shape-shift above the castle – a bird cloud suddenly transforms into a handsome *trovador*; a child cloud drifts into a crouching man.

I wish I could have my *vihuela* with me; I wish my mama and Mama Sorguetos could see their granddaughter; but all that exists only in my mind - flashes of memory that will be my children's legacy. I feel no grief on leaving Lisboa. Portugal, like Spain, has been ruthless to me and the Jews. Marianna and I vow to seek another way.

Today we begin.

Marianna moves closer to me, leaning against my arm, and following my gaze. I touch my daughter's chubby cheeks and smile with all the hope of a man that's seeking a future.

"In the new world," I say softly. "We'll be safe to follow our hearts."

Marianna nods, but after all we've been through, she has lost hope.

"It's been eight years," she speaks gently, staring at the baby. "I don't trust anything. It's been eight years since Mama slammed the trap door over our heads. Eight years of agony. Eight years of torture and death. Eight years of discovering that my soul can and *will* survive."

I nod in silent agreement.

We don't speak; instead we stare at the shore that we'll never see again.

"Eight years has also given us this," I say finally, stroking my daughter's head.

We watch as the boat prepares to set sail. Last night - our final night in Portugal - I woke up screaming. Marianna tried to comfort me, tried to scatter the demons that fill my mind. Her sweet voice soothed me for the moment, but then the child started crying and Marianna had to leave our bed. I know I don't have the power to make us forget; our story is a trail of tears; the story of all Jews who have inhabited - or will inhabit - this hostile world. As I recall what has happened, as I pray for safety and freedom, I'm not sure I'll ever find it.

Mama and Papa Sorguetos are surely dead now, burned at the stake. Catalina lies in her roadside grave. I have no doubt that Zara died at sea, at the hands of *degradados,* in the jaws of man-eating monsters.

All because of me.

I destroyed the family I loved so much.

Father is alone now – without an heir. He will live in bitterness for the rest of his years, the victim of my betrayal. His family – his bloodline – is done.

Marianna, Zara and I entered Portugal on the same day the Jews were expelled from Spain. We had barely made the deadline. Some people whispered that it was an unlucky day – they called it the 9th of Av or the day both the first and second ancient temples in Jerusalem were destroyed, by the Babylonians in 586 B.C.E. and the Romans in the year 70. Others said that was why the explorer, Christopher

Columbus, didn't leave on his voyage until the next day. The Jews believe that Columbus is a *Converso*. He's a bold, arrogant braggart who depended on Jewish scholars and cartographers, like Don Abraham Zacuto, to plan his voyage. No one would support him but Ferdinand and Isabella, using money confiscated from the expelled Jews to pay for his voyage. There were many *Conversos* on board his ships, and some whispered that Columbus hoped to find the lost tribe of Israel.

Ironically, it's Columbus' work that has opened the way for us. We're headed for Recife, in the New World, to begin our lives.

There is no Inquisition in Recife.

Yet.

I think about the children Catalina and Zara will never have. I think about the grandchildren Mama and Papa Sorguetos will never see. And then I think about the children that died - the little ones sent to São Tomé with Zara; the sons and daughters wrestled from their parents on the first day of Passover; the youth, dragged screaming to the baptismal font at *Os Estãos*. They're gone now, hopefully at peace in God's heaven. The rest of us move on, dragging ourselves through the injustice of this world.

I take a deep breath. As the caravel edges away from the dock, Marianna and I clasp hands. We will try yet again in the new world.

Time is on our side.

The Old Couple

They sit beneath a green and white umbrella on the Upper Library Terrace in Bryant Park. It's a beautiful summer day. Their silver hair shimmers in the late afternoon sun. The old man reaches out to a concrete pot of purple flowers. He plucks a single flower and hands it to her. She smiles girlishly and pins the flower in her hair.

The Great Lawn sprawls before them. The old couple sees and hears everything. But they can only watch *gilgul* unfold.

They sing softly to one another.

Where is the key that was in the drawer?
Onde sta la yave ke stava in kashon?

My forefathers brought it with great pain
From their house in Spain.

Mis nonus la trusheron kon grande dolor
De su kaza de Espanya.

We told our children this is the heart of our home.

Taymullah

At the end of the Great Lawn, in direct view, the dark, fat man in cargo pants tenses on the Upper Library Terrace.

Allah.

It's time.

Convergence

They choose a table and four chairs on the Great Lawn. The table tilts, the chairs are scattered, waiting for someone to impose order. Cole rolls his equipment near them so everything is in one place.

They sit.

Shira, the writer with dark, smoldering eyes waits cautiously, ready to bolt at the first chance. She sits stiffly, one arm pressing her backpack to her chest, the other hand clutching the leather pouch in her pocket. Ria, the fragile web-designer with olive skin and fawn-like eyes watches, her eyes flickering with curiosity. Aliki, the cocoa-colored skin *chocolatier* who sees beneath everyone's skin, scrutinizes them, looking for clues. Cole, the street performer - troubadour - and charismatic hot dog vendor takes a deep breath. He carefully balances his guitar case against his leg.

No one speaks.

The Great Lawn is nearly empty; most of the people have joined Happy Hour at the BP Grill. Others sit along the promenades, nibbling on dinner and snacks, or drinking lattes and health waters. Some read the newspaper, get lost in their latest novel, or peer at evening business reports. There are a few mothers with strollers taking in the last moments of the day, old people reluctant to go home, and a smattering of students with laptops and iPods plugged into their ears. The dark man in the cargo pants lingers on the cobblestones on the Upper Library Terrace; the old couple watches him.

Shira follows a young woman in a cream-colored *hijab* leave the park. She's pushing a stroller and dragging a boy by the hand.

Isn't she hot in that thing?

Shira wonders if there's a place for a fundamentalist Muslim woman in her new book. She could be Emma's best friend or Mason Portsmith's next-door neighbor. She could preach about the immorality of Emma's affair or the cruelty of Mason's lifestyle. On the other hand, why would she want to put a *heroic* Arab in her book when they were so determined to destroy Israel and the entire west? Perhaps she could be the "other woman" in Mason's life, ripping off her *hijab* to have wild, kinky sex when Emma wasn't available? Unconsciously, Shira nods and makes a mental note, safe in her fictional world.

Cole watches Shira carefully. She's intriguing. There's no doubt that the other women at the table are more compelling. Ria is breath-taking – she could be a model. Aliki is elegant and exotic. Yet it's Shira that grabs his attention; a strange attraction that Cole can't quite define.

Ria scans face-to-face, wondering why she didn't go to Happy Hour with her friends. Everyone is probably mad at her. She hates to upset people; she shivers with the image of disapproval tossed her way. When? Tonight? Tomorrow morning? When exactly will she be able to pull herself away from these strangers? She catches her breath. There's a vague sense that nothing will ever be the same after this moment. It annoys her. Ria tries to push it from her mind but it lingers, like an unwanted icon on her desktop.

Aliki *feels* the small group, as if she's careening into a dark hole that's not quite unpleasant. Strange. All her senses tell her that there's a tenuous connection; a reason for being here at this time and place. She takes stock of them – the Jew, the lovely, olive-skinned Catholic, the Ladino street performer, and herself, the black woman. What forces are pulling them together?
Why?

Ria breaks the silence. "I love Bryant Park," she says emptily. "We come here year-round – you know, to see the ice skaters in the winter, the holiday Christmas shops, the fashion week tents . . ."

"Nice," Cole replies, his eyes fixed on Shira.

"I'm a web designer," Ria continues, unsure of herself. "I work in one of those buildings. 70 West." She adds weakly. "I . . ."

312

No one is listening.

"Well, you all know what I do," Cole says to Shira.

Their eyes meet.

"What *do* you do?" Shira asks accusingly.

Cole is taken aback. "What do you mean?"

"You don't spend your whole life singing at Bryant Park, do you?"

"No," Cole grins sheepishly.

"Then what do you do with the rest of your day?"

Cole tilts his head. "I'm an entrepreneur," he says quizzically.

"What does that mean?"

"I work my own . . . my cousin's . . . business."

"What kind of business?"

All eyes are on Cole.

How can I elevate selling hot dogs?

He arranges his most charming smile. "I'm a hot dog vendor."

"No!" Ria giggles.

Aliki watches him carefully.

Is he embarrassed? Is he proud? Is he stating a fact?

Shira stares. Cole believes she will lose interest.

Who cares about a hot dog vendor?

Shira's eyes suddenly sparkle with interest.

"Where's your spot?" Shira asks.

"Midtown," Cole answers quickly. "The garment center. I work with my cousin, who covers downtown."

"Does he sell hot dogs too?"

Cole nods. "Hot dogs, pretzels, sausages . . . the whole thing. He has a third cart that sells hot nuts as well."

"What color is your umbrella?"

"Yellow," Cole salutes, "and blue."

"*Sabrett's*," Shira grins. Her eyes soften. "You must have a million stories."

"You wouldn't believe half of them."

Everyone laughs nervously.

Cole grins at Shira.

She's not afraid to step outside her world.

313

It's odd. In a strange way, that is more significant than the olive-skinned girl's beauty and the black woman's exotic draw.

The tension between the web designer, hot dog vendor, romance novelist, and chocolatier dissolves. Shira gently lays her backpack on the ground. She loosens her grip on the leather pouch in her pocket, stroking it with her fingers like a *hamsa,* a charm that protects against the evil.

Aliki senses everything. Action without definition; movement without purpose.

It's as if we've known each other all our lives.

Aliki wonders about what's happening in this instant. It's as if she's waited patiently for this moment, this glitch in time. Whatever it is, Aliki knows it's inevitable; a part of something far greater than this hot summer day in Bryant Park.

"I'm an author," Shira offers impulsively. "I write romantic mysteries."

"What's that?" Aliki asks.

"You know trashy books that you find on the shelves in airports and supermarkets. The ones that merge reality shows, ghosts, and trash TV."

Everyone laughs but Aliki.

"It's an American thing," Cole explains.

Aliki shakes her head. "Are your books good?"

"Yes," Shira nods defensively. "I'm a good writer."

"Then why do you write trash?"

There's dead silence. They thought that Aliki didn't understand. *She's not American.*

How can she possibly understand why a good writer would create trash?

Aliki produces a fresh bar of *Godiva São Tomé dark chocolate with cocoa nibs.* "I'm a chocolatier," she explains haughtily. I only offer the best. I wouldn't sell *Milky Ways* if you paid me a million dollars." She glares at Shira.

The others exchange glances.

"Try this," Aliki continues sharply, without a smile. "This is the best chocolate on the market."

Ria nods, as if the cocoa-colored skin woman is referring to a tome of literature.

Aliki unwraps the bar and breaks off four pieces.

"It's superb," she explains, placing a chocolate square in her mouth, waiting for it to titillate her senses.

At the end of the Great Lawn, in direct view, the dark, fat man in cargo pants tenses.

Cole takes charge of the conversation.

"We all have stories, like the vendors," he speaks, his eyes boring into Shira. "I think we're meant to share them."

"What do the street vendors have to do with us?" Ria asks.

Aliki touches her hand. "We're just like them. Don't you see?"

Ria shakes her head impatiently.

"Stories," Shira mumbles. "I think we're here to tell our stories."

Aliki smiles. "I think you're getting it."

"What's your story?" Shira looks at Cole.

Cole winces, as if he has been hit. "I just told you."

"Not really . . . you just told us about the street vendors, not about *you*."

"You already know about me. I'm a hot dog vendor who sings Ladino songs in Bryant Park in my spare time. I come from Arizona and . . ."

"What?" Ria asks.

"I . . ."

"We have to say it all, to figure out why we're here today."

Cole glances at a dark man in cargo pants. Nearby, there's an old couple sitting beneath a green and white umbrella next to a concrete pot of purple flowers. They're watching him. He's used to people watching him, but somehow, this is different. They're oddly familiar, although he's never seen them before.

He turns back to the women. "Do you believe in coincidences?"

"No," Aliki replies quickly. "Everything is meant to be."

Shira is quiet, and Ria listens intently.

315

"I think," Cole begins, for the first time verbalizing how he arrived in New York, "that I was meant to be here. I love the west, but somehow, I drifted here, to help my cousin, to build my stage, and to meet . . . people."

Shira catches her breath.

He takes her hand and gently strokes her palm with his guitar-calloused fingertips. "I have this strange dream - of trees, and purple flowers, and clouds that shape-shift. . ."

"No!" Shira pulls her hand away. "You *can't* dream that, because I wrote it." She grabs the leather pouch in her pocket and holds it tightly. No one can see.

Cole stares at her.

"I have that dream too," Ria says softly. "The trees cry for rain. The purple flowers shudder. The sky is filled with thin clouds that shape-shift as they pass overhead. A bird cloud suddenly transforms into a handsome troubadour; a child cloud drifts into a crouching man. Suddenly there's a dull thud; a large cow with dark, soulful eyes faces me. I've seen this creature before; she's visited my dreams many times. She wears a broken iron key on a leather thong around her neck. I reach out to touch the key and the metal burns my fingers, the sky turns black, and the clouds scatter in terror."

"I scream, but no sound is heard," Aliki adds.

There's a pause, like a freeze frame in a thriller movie. No one moves, but the tension is palpable. Cole clears his throat. A few drops of sweat trickle, unseen, down the back of Shira's neck. Ria plays absently with her lucky pendant. Aliki takes a deep breath.

Is this really happening?

"We share the same dream," Shira says finally. "We can probably get one of those paperbacks at the checkout in every supermarket . . . you know, the one that says "interpret your dreams" and find the same story."

No one believes her.

"I never heard *that* dream before," Ria responds defiantly.

They're silent.

"I'm a Jew," Shira's voice is strained, as if it comes from

somewhere beyond Bryant Park. "My family . . . we're Sephardic Jews. After the Spanish expulsion, they fled Spain for Portugal. Eventually, they went to Recife, Brazil. The Portuguese soon followed, and they fled the inquisition for New Amsterdam in hopes of finding tolerance. Peter Stuyvesant, the Governor of New Amsterdam, wanted to kick them out. He didn't want any Jews - they were too much trouble. He wrote to the Dutch East India Company to request permission to oust them, but too many Jewish investors were part of the company. They received sanctuary. At least one line of the family has been in New York since then."

Shira's proud of her story and proud of her lineage. Her family has been New Yorkers from the very beginning.

Cole takes her hand.

"We're one of the oldest Jewish families in New York," Shira finishes softly. "That's why I carry *this*."

Shira slips the leather pouch from her pocket and lays it on the small green metal table.

Cole, Ria, and Aliki stare at it.

"What is it?" Ria asks softly.

Shira shakes her head. "It's been with my family for a long time. They brought it from Spain. My mother gave it to me and I use it like . . . a good luck charm," she finishes sheepishly. "I only know it's very old and precious."

Cole reaches for the pouch. He opens it tenderly, as if it holds something incredibly fragile. He slips out a piece of iron, in the shape of an "L" that's slightly rusted and worn smooth by time. They all stare at it.

Ria takes a shallow breath.

"I don't know *why* I wear this," she explains, unhooking a pendant from around her neck. "I just *do*."

Ria lays the L-shaped pendant on the table. It's also made from iron, slightly rusted and worn smooth by time.

Aliki is shaken. She removes the ring from her finger that looks like a cross with one bar removed, made from iron that's slightly rusted and worn smooth by time. "My grandmother gave me this."

317

Cole stares at the three pieces. He gently removes the circle pendant hanging on a leather thong on his neck. "I bought this in Portugal. I never understood why it called to me."

Then he sings softly, in an old, distant voice.

Where is the key that was in the drawer?
Onde sta la yave ke stava in kashon?

My forefathers brought it with great pain
From their house in Spain.

Mis nonus la trusheron kon grande dolor
De su kaza de Espanya.

We told our children this is the heart of our home.

Cole's fingers tremble as he lines up the four pieces: His circle pendant on top, Shira's piece next, Ria's pendant in the middle, and Aliki's ring at the bottom.

Together, the four pieces form a medieval iron key.

Shira gasps.

What does it mean?

"We're here for a reason," Aliki speaks, her voice light and featherlike, carried in the breeze that drifts through Bryant Park.

A cloud passes over the sun.

"I'm not a Sephardic Jew," Ria insists. "I'm a Catholic."

Cole stares at her. "Where are you from?"

"New Mexico."

"Did you play *pon y saca* when you were a kid?"

"Huh?"

"Did you light nine candles for Christmas, baked *pan de semita* at Easter or left tiny pebbles on relative's gravestone?"

"Of course. Everyone did."

"No," Cole says slowly. "It's been said that when the Converso Jews fled Spain for the New World, they still practiced in secret. The

318

Inquisition followed them everywhere. Many moved north . . . into what would eventually become the American southwest . . . Arizona, New Mexico, and California. They continued as Conversos, but slowly, the faith faded, and only a few rituals remained."

"Are you saying I'm Jewish?" Ria sits up straight. "We were taught that the Jews were Christ-killers. . ."

"We were too," Aliki whispers. "But even in tiny São Tomé I knew I was different."

"I always felt different," Ria admits. "That's why I came to New York."

There's a long, awkward pause. Ria scans the Great Lawn, seeing nothing. Shira lightly touches the iron pieces on the table. Aliki folds her hands tightly, as if trying to squeeze out an ancient truth.

"Does it mean," Aliki says softly, "that we might be *related?*"

"You're black," Shira says bluntly. "How can we be related?"

"I'm Catholic," Ria adds stubbornly. "Not Jewish."

"Impossible," Cole says thoughtfully. But as soon as he speaks, he knows it's not true.

"I'm from São Tomé," Aliki speaks as if drifting back through hazy centuries. "My skin color is different, though. Most São Toméans are darker. The lighter ones, like me, have Portuguese blood."

The story was vague and undefined; it fluttered in Aliki's mind like a piece of European lace, filled with graceful swirls that had more holes than substance . . . They could trace their history for hundreds of years, recalling pirates, slaves, slave traders, convicts, laborers, rebels and plantation warlords as characters in their personal dramas.

Aliki *knew* there was more to her history than the *Angolores* and the white-skinned Europeans that she wore on her skin every day. Now, she thinks about her ring, lying on the green table, a piece of a very old puzzle.

We pass this down to our daughters her mother explained when she gave Aliki the ring on her twenty-first birthday.

Why Mãe?

That's the way we've always done it in our family.

What does it mean?

319

Mãe shrugged. Some say it's the heart of our home.
Heart of our home?
Mãe frowned. I don't really understand. We've done it so long that the story has been lost, but the ring remains. My Mãe used to say that if it was ever lost, its magic would find its way back into the family, curled around the right fingers.

The others wait.

Aliki takes a deep breath.

"I was a teenager," she begins slowly, "before my mother, gave me the ring. She was on a committee that sponsored an International Conference in São Tomé. That's a big deal on such a tiny island. It was held to coincide with the 20th anniversary of the independence of São Tomé and Principe. The conference commemorated the Jewish children taken from their parents in the 15th century to settle the island."

Shira's eyes widens, her voice sticks in her throat.

"People came from the U.S., Israel, France, Holland, Portugal, and Spain."

Ria's breathing gets thin and raspy. The others turn to look at her. Ria reaches into her pocket and retrieves an inhaler.

"Asthma," she whispers.

Shira stands up and pushes away from the green table. She's terrified. She stares into Cole's eyes, drowning in a visual embrace that brings the moment to a standstill. There's a sudden, exquisite rush of time . . . she hears children laughing on the other side of the Great Lawn, smells hot dogs from a kiosk on 40th Street, sees Nweke's jewelry capturing the slowly diming rays of the late afternoon sun. She reaches out her hand.

Cole stands, next to her, and gently takes her hand.

Words that she knows, but never heard spoken, dance in her mind.

Make one promise before you leave.
Promise me that you'll stay together connected through time.
Meet once again beyond the horror of today.

Shira and Cole are assaulted by images never seen; colors speeding through their minds, voices crying, trees, shape-shifting clouds, purple flowers, and an overwhelming sense that they have waited for a very long time for this moment.

On the Upper Library Terrace, the dark, fat man in cargo pants stiffens, tightening his fingers around the Glock.

The old couple stands, purple flowers forgotten.

People pause in Bryant Park, vaguely aware that there's a change - a shift in the air that they don't quite understand.

A voice in the dark man's mind roars.

Where are your children, Jew?

He shakes his head violently.

Where are your children?

The dark, fat man in the cargo pants is enraged.

"I know where they are. God has saved my children.

The dark, fat man is wild.

Now!

Allah commands it.

Now!

Allah speaks loudly. The dark man's eyes blur with rage, his fat lips form a predator's smile. Spittle runs down his chin.

He hears the old woman whisper something.

Please God, save my children.

The old man lovingly takes her arm. "*Gilgul*," he whispers.

Ria and Aliki watch the singer and writer link, inseparably in time. They stand up and close the circle of four, their fates entwined.

The dark, fat man in cargo pants on the Upper Library Terrace pulls the Glock from his right pocket. He aims at the three women standing around a tiny green table with pieces of scrap iron.

I have enough bullets for all of them.

The old lady cries out.

Please God, save my children.

Cole hears. He turns. In an instant, he takes in everything. The old couple, the dark man with the gun, the purpose. Rafael emerges from deep within Cole.

He meets the dark man's eyes.

Rafael knows exactly what must be done.

He shoves Shira so hard that she stumbles against Ria and Aliki. They lose their balance. All three women fall to the ground, behind the green table and chairs. Aliki feels nothing but the inevitability of the moment. Ria cries out. Shira screams - a primeval keening from a place she never knew existed.

Rafael throws his arms in the air and uses his body to shield the girls.

The dark man in the cargo pants gets off three shots before the old couple tackles him with surprising strength.

People scream, bodies hit the lawn as if it's a horror show. Clouds race across the sky as agonizing cries of fear fill the air, turning everything red and orange and black. It's a battlefield in the middle of New York.

Rafael sighs. A smile flickers on his lips. His eyes fill with peace. *Now it's right.*

Rafael is peppered with three bullets as he hits the ground.

Epilogue

Shira, Ria, and Aliki stand on cobblestones, in front of a stone building in Spain. It's in the heart of a preserved medieval town, where the twisting streets bear names like *St. Llorenç* – the street of the synagogue. Nearby, a red sign marks *Call Jueu* – the Jewish quarter.

They have traveled thousands of miles and years – through books, old records, and in the air, to get here. They have spoken many times to *Casa Shalom* in Israel, the heart of Sephardic research. They have worked together, and planned together.

Now they are back to the heart of their home.

"The key," Shira says softly.

Cole, the keeper of the four iron pieces, worn smooth by time, and now forged together into a medieval key, puts it in Shira's hand.

Cole touches Shira's back. She sighs deeply. They are together, once again.

Unseen, Rafael watches everything with The Old Couple. Purple flowers scatter by their feet. Soon, they will be gone.

Shira, Ria, and Aliki step forward. Shira slowly slips the key into the old lock.

It's a perfect fit.

About the Author

Dr. Jeri Fink is an author, Family Therapist, and journalist, with over 19 books and hundreds of articles to her name. She writes adult and children's fiction and nonfiction, and has appeared on television, radio, book events, seminars, workshops, and the internet. Dr. Fink's work has been praised by community leaders, educators, reviewers, and critics around the country.

Also available from Dailey Swan Publishing

Mystery/Suspense